Copyright © 2024 by Ryan Marie

No part of this publication may be reproduced, distributed, or transmitted in any form or by any means, including photocopying, recording, or other electronic or mechanical methods, without the prior written permission of the publisher, except as permitted by U.S. copyright law. For permission requests, contact Ryan Marie at authorryanmarie@gmail.com.

The story, all names, characters, and incidents portrayed in this production are fictitious. No identification with actual persons (living or deceased), places, buildings, and products is intended or should be inferred.

Cover artwork by Renee Reynolds

Magnolia Publishing

❄ Created with Vellum

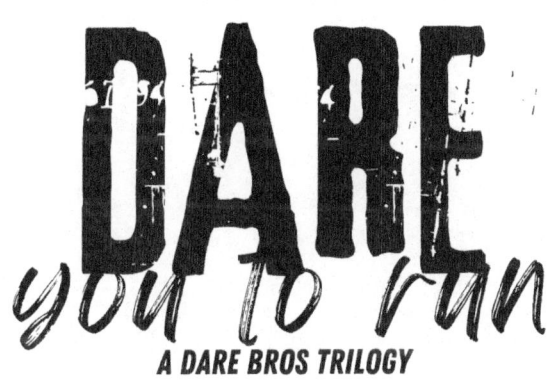

DARE you to run

A DARE BROS TRILOGY

RYAN MARIE

To the ladies who dream of being hunted by the Big Bad Wolf.
He's here....
You're welcome.

You're either a Lana girl or you're not.
IYKYK

A NOTE TO READERS

The book you are about to read contains themes related to dominance, death of a parent (off page), sexual assault (off page), pregnancy, loss of pregnancy, age gap, degradation, primal play, and explicit sexual encounters. If you find these topics emotionally triggering, please practice mindfulness and do not continue.

The characters in this story are of many different ethnicities and backgrounds. You will encounter characters of Indian, Italian, Black, Latino, Caucasian and Mixed-race. Their skin tones are a variation of colors, as are humans. While I may not make constant reference to a specific race or color, please note that this book will contain people who are from all walks of life and it is their character that matters most.

DAGEN'S PLAYLIST

- *"I'm Tired"* - Labrinth & Zendaya
- *"Blue Jeans"* - Lana Del Rey
- *"Freak"* - Lana Del Rey
- *"Guess"* - Charlie xcx & Billie Eilish
- *"Muse"* - Isabel LaRosa
- *"Diet Mountain Dew"* - Lana Del Rey
- *"Bad Idea Right?"* - Olivia Rodrigo
- *"All The Good Girls Go To Hell"* - Billie Eilish
- *"Wow"* - Kylie Minogue
- *"Gods & Monsters"* - Lana Del Rey
- *"Wicked Game"* - Chris Isaak
- *"Angels"* - The xx
- *"Can I Call You Tonight?"* - Dayglow
- *"Love Is Complicated (The Angels Sing)"* - Labrinth
- *"Summer Song"* - Remy Bond
- *"Apocalypse"* - Cigarettes After Sex
- *"You, Always"* - Angelo Shinohara
- *"Radio"* - Lana Del Rey
- *"The Night We Met"* - Lord Huron
- *"Heavenly"* - Cigarettes After Sex

HENDRIX'S PLAYLIST

- *"Tear You Apart"* - She Wants Revenge
- *"Lake of Fire"* - Nirvana
- *"Sex Type Thing"* - Stone Temple Pilots
- *"Wicked Garden"* - Stone Temple Pilots
- *"Need You Tonight"* - INXS
- *"Gorgeous Nightmare"* - Escape the Fate
- *"Adrenaline"* - Shinedown
- *"Bleeding Me"* - Metallica
- *"Welcome to the Jungle"* - Guns N' Roses
- *"Closer"* - Nine Inch Nails
- *"House of Cards"* - Radiohead
- *"Parabol"* - TOOL
- *"Heavenly"* - Cigarettes After Sex
- *"Stinkfist"* - TOOL
- *"Be Yourself"* - Audioslave
- *"Nothing's Gonna Hurt You Baby"* - Cigarettes After Sex
- *"Fade To Black"* - Metallica
- *"Last Resort"* - Papa Roach
- *"So Far Away"* - Staind

- *"Sober"* - TOOL
- *"Lonely Day"* - System Of A Down
- *"Running Blind"* - Godsmack

CONTENTS

Prologue	1
One	11
Two	25
Three	35
Four	41
Five	47
Six	57
Seven	65
Eight	75
Nine	89
Ten	97
Eleven	105
Twelve	115
Thirteen	123
Fourteen	133
Fifteen	143
Sixteen	151
Seventeen	163
Eighteen	171
Nineteen	177
Twenty	187
Twenty-One	201
Twenty-Two	215
Twenty-Three	221
Twenty-Four	227
Twenty-Five	235
Twenty-Six	249
Twenty-Seven	259
Twenty-Eight	265
Twenty-Nine	275
Thirty	285
Thirty-One	295
Thirty-Two	303
Thirty-Three	311
Thirty-Four	319
Thirty-Five	325

Thirty-Six	331
Thirty-Seven	339
Thirty-Eight	351
Thirty-Nine	357
Forty	369
Forty-One	375
Forty-Two	385
Forty-Three	389
Forty-Four	397
Forty-Five	409
Epilogue	416
Acknowledgments	423
Also by Ryan Marie	427
About the Author	429

PROLOGUE

DAGEN - 8 YEARS OLD

MOM'S CHEST rises and falls and she makes this wheezing sound like she can't breathe. Her lips are really chapped and grandma said she would rub an ice cube over them. I don't know what an ice cube will do. Mom and Dad always make me put on chapstick when my lips are chapped.

Daddy is sitting in the chair in the corner of the room while the nurse checks on cords and the machine that is hooked to mommy. The nurse said the tubes send medicine straight into her to help with the pain.

Mommy has cancer and they told me it's painful, like a bad cut but on the inside. Daddy said she needs special medicine to kill the cancerous cells but the other day, mommy gave me bad news. She told me the medicine they gave her didn't take the bad cells away and that there is no more that the doctors can do to fix her. She said she's going to go to Heaven. I cried a lot when she told me.

I really don't want her to go to Heaven. If she's with God, then who will be here to take care of me? Daddy said he will

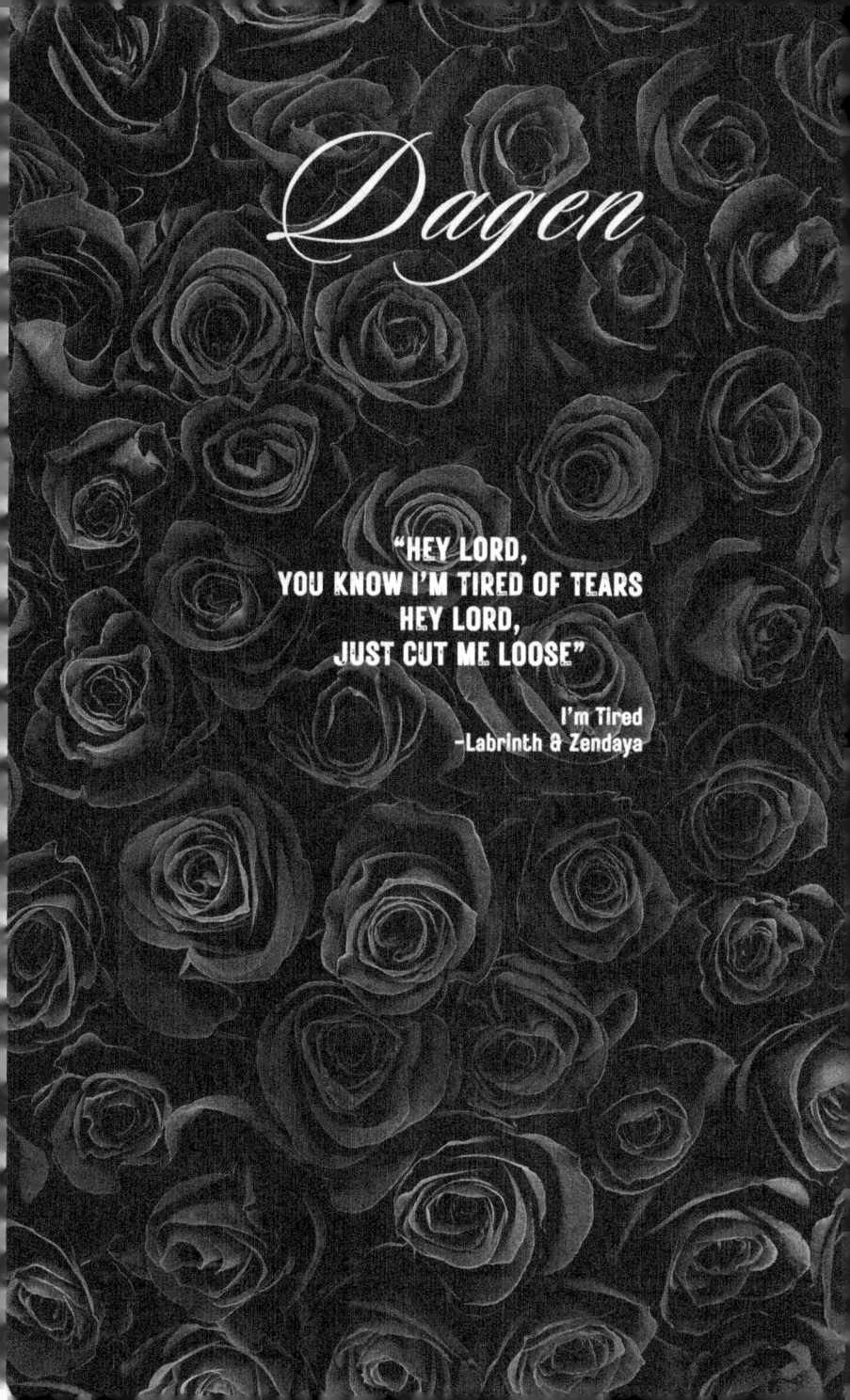

ONE

13 YEARS LATER

MY STOMACH GROWLS with anger as I push on into the fifth hour of my drive. I'm so close to where I need to be that I just can't stop now. That cup of coffee and bagel from the hotel buffet didn't quite fill me up. And the five fitful hours of sleep I got after driving for six hours into the middle of the night is really starting to wreak havoc on my clarity.

It was close to midnight when I stopped at the twenty-four hour super gas station that is more of like a mini Wal-Mart with a restaurant and bakery that, oh yeah, sells gas. My body was aching from having my butt in a seat and my foot on the peddle after hauling ass away from home.

It was all just too much. I had to get out of there. My chest felt like it was caving in when I overheard my parents talking, and I just had to leave.

"Are you kidding me? They said that? God Vaughan. I am so tired of their shit. I know they're her grandparents but they're disgusting human beings who protected a rapist." Mom's voice was laced with anger and sorrow and I couldn't understand what she was talking about.

I crept closer still, eavesdropping on their conversation.

My Mom –stepmom, actually– and Dad sat close and looked worried as I peeked through the slit in the door.

"They said that if I didn't convince her to take the internship at Derek's firm they would tell her that I was divorcing Steph because I was cheating on her." Dad said to her, and I realized they were talking about my grandfather and my late mother, Stephanie.

"Lemme guess. Was I the person you were supposedly cheating with?" I watched Dad nod his head from where I continued to watch. *"I fucking hate them. I can't even sugar coat it. I hate them with a passion. How dare they threaten you with such lies. And the internship is up to Day. She's not even studying pre-law. Why in the hell would they think that a marketing major would want to work at a law firm? Did you tell them CeCe already has an internship set up for her with the Wranglers?"*

I was shocked to hear that Aunt CeCe had gotten me an internship with the Wranglers because it was the first I had heard about. I was excited as hell, but in that moment there was something that was stealing my joy.

Mom continued on. *"I know this is a moot point and I am not in any way placing any blame on you, but I wish you would've reported Steph. Even if it didn't result in anything, at least what she did to you would be documented. That would give us some leverage against them."*

I grew more and more confused with every word that spilled from mom's mouth and even more so when dad spoke.

"I know, Cam. I can't tell you how many times I wished I could go back in time and stand up to Derek. I was so afraid that they'd take Day away from me that I couldn't bring myself to tell the police what she did. Even if it did result in people not believing me, at least I would've been free of Steph and her parents."

Dad sat in a chair with mom in his lap, her fingers combing through his hair, trying to ease the tension on his face. *"I hate that you're stuck with them in yours and Dagen's life. They're horrible people. They are the parents of a rapist and complicit in her activities. They knew what she did, they protected her, and they sentenced you to a life of misery. I hate having to hold my tongue when they call. The only thing that I am grateful for is that our sweet girl doesn't know any of this. I don't want to shatter her memories of Steph, even if I do think that woman doesn't deserve the amazing young lady she birthed."*

It was those final words from mom that had me pushing through their door. *"What are you talking about?"* I asked them.

They both scrambled to explain and ask what I had just heard. *"Sweetheart. How long...how much of our conversation did you hear?"* Mom asked me with pure panic in her voice.

"Enough to want to know why you're calling Steph a rapist and claiming my grandparents are threatening you." My words had mom practically passing out, but dad caught her before she could hit the ground.

They tried telling me I didn't hear what I thought, but when I screeched, demanding they tell me the truth, the story they told me knocked the breath out of me.

"Day, I'm going to preface this by saying you are my greatest gift. Our gift." Dad approached me like I was a cornered animal. *"I can't imagine my life without you, so please remember that when you hear what I'm about to tell you. So, when I moved to Florida for school, Cam and I had been together for almost four years and we decided we would work through a long distance relationship. It was very difficult for me because while mom was here with Aunt Cat, Uncle Bish, Aunt CeCe and Aunt Viv, I was basically all alone. I befriended a girl who I thought understood that I was committed to Cami. But I guess my words weren't what she wanted to hear and one night..."*

I grow sick thinking of my dad being drugged by a woman he thought was a friend, then essentially raped because she knew he would never leave Cami. Mom...my step-mom. What sent me over the edge was knowing that for eight years, dad lived with the woman who violated him and had me as a result. He was so afraid of losing me that he chose to tolerate a life of misery with her rather than live without me.

The perfect image of my mother I've held on to for thirteen years was shattered in a matter of minutes. The mother I sat next to, watching her take her last breath, was a lie. My memories of her were all tainted as was I.

I'm the product of an assault, and the evil that was Stephanie lives in me.

I grew dizzy and nauseous, and I just wanted it all to stop. *"Stop. Please. Just...stop."*

Mom sat down next to me and took my hand in hers, squeezing it three times to let me know she was there. *"Honey, we never wanted you to find out about this. Dad made a decision many years ago to be there for you, and together we decided that the manner in which you were created was not something we felt we needed to share with you. The fact that you are here with us is all that matters. We love you with all our hearts and I'm sure your mom did, too."*

How could she say that? Of course it mattered.

"Dad! She drugged you and took advantage of your unconscious state. If she was a man, she'd be behind bars. And you-you never reported her? Why? I don't..."

My heart was pounding in my ears and I needed air. I could feel my lungs tightening, and then something even worse crossed my mind.

"Did you even want me, Dad? I mean...how could you?"

He looked at me with unshed tears and his voice shook when he said, *"Dagen. Of course I did. I figured...I figured that mo-Cami and I would get back together and we would work to raise you as best we could with Steph. But things didn't happen that way and there was no way that I could live without you. No way."*

Tears began rushing over my lids and I just wanted to scream. *"You should've told me. I had the right to know! All these years you let me believe that Steph was a loving mother."*

"She was, Day. She loved you. Believe me. That is the one thing I know for sure." How could he defend her? After everything she did to him, he still tried to convince me she loved me.

"No, people with a conscience and good heart don't ra–don't do that. She was sick. And now that sickness lives in me." I finally reached my breaking point as I tugged at my hair. *"I need to get outta here."*

I sprinted from their bedroom, my feet barely touching the steps as I ran down them, all while Mom and Dad shouted my name behind me. I ran into the garage and grabbed the first set of keys my hand touched and clicked the fob. The lights to Mom's BMW flashed, and I jumped in without a second thought. The tires screeched as I slammed my foot on the gas in reverse, and it fishtailed over the gravel when I threw it into drive and sped off.

I looked in the rearview to see Dad running after me. But the faster I drove, the smaller he grew until he was out of sight completely. I had no idea where I was going, only that I had to get as far away as I could. If I could have jumped out of myself and left me behind, I would have run to the moon to escape.

Now it's midday twenty-four hours later and I'm so close to the home of the people I once called grandparents. But they are no grandparents of mine. In my eyes, they're barely human. They're monsters who bred an evil disease and I am an extension of that evil.

I let every call that came in go straight to my voicemail for the first two hours until it was full. Mom and Dad called more times than I could count. In between those calls, a barrage of texts from Mara, Sami, Jenelle and Lizzie had my phone pinging so much, I had to turn it on silent.

Yes, I left my friends without a word. One minute we're enjoying a day at my parent's house, and the next I'm driving off to somewhere unknown. But I couldn't deal with them while I battled the thoughts in my head.

When they seemed to be failing at getting through to me, they called in reinforcements. First to call was Aunt Viv. I guess they thought that her fiery attitude and persistence would have me breaking. But when that didn't happen, her call was followed by Uncle Nix. Nice try, but he was a softie and he'd probably ask if I needed any money or a plane to get me where I was going.

After that, it was like they just went down the list. Aunt Cat, Aunt CeCe, Gran and Pops, Zio Luca and Uncle Hayes. They even stooped so low as to have Abuelo Juan and Mamita Alma call me. What almost had me breaking was when Forrest and Emily's name popped up on the screen. They weren't related to me in any way but because they loved Cami so much, they became a fixture in my life, too.

Forrest and Emily are the parents of Mom's first husband, Robbie, who died many years ago. It was his death that had Mom coming back home to her family and friends, and eventually me and dad. Mom told me that Robbie was Forrest and Emily's only child and they felt like they were losing a daughter when they lost him. But here heart is so big that she could never shut them out as if they didn't exist. Everyone welcomed them as part of the motley crew of a family that had only grown over the years.

Hence the reason for so many phone calls from people who weren't really blood related, but family all the same.

I finally caved when Uncle Bishop's name and picture of him and I from his wedding lit up my screen. I closed my eyes and gripped the steering wheel tighter, and let the phone ring until the last second.

I tapped the phone icon on the steering wheel and took a deep breath.

"Hello?" My voice shook and if they could see me, they'd see sweat dripping down my face.

"Dagen Rayne. Where are you?" Uncle Bishop's deep voice boomed through the speaker.

"I, uh, I'm just taking a drive," I told him.

"And where are you taking this drive?"

I bit the inside of my cheek and said, *"I'm just in Houston. At that park you used to take me to."*

"You know your mom and dad have GPS and can see where you are, don't you?"

I whispered *"shit"* having forgotten about that. Then I asked him, *"Well if y'all know where I am, why are you calling me?"*

"Just because we know where you are doesn't mean we know where you're going." I stayed quiet, the wheels in my head spinning. *"So. Where are you going, Day?"*

"Would you believe me if I said I didn't know?" I asked him.

"Yeah," he replied. *"Although, deep down, I think you know exactly where you're going."*

He was right. If I could just admit it to myself, I'd be brave enough to answer the phone when Mom and Dad called. But I wasn't ready to face the truth.

"Give me the phone," I heard in the background and knew I was in for a talking to.

I looked at a sign on the side of the highway and saw that there was a rest stop up ahead. I switched lanes and decided to make a small detour.

"Day. What are you doing?" Anais, a woman who was my aunt but really more like a sister, was now taking over guilt trip duties.

Anais was only six years older than me and married to Uncle Bishop...who's twelve years older than her. And she's also the niece of his and Dad's best friend, Uncle Phoenix, AKA Nix. AKA, Aunt Viv's husband. AKA, ex-MLB pitcher and one of the best to ever play the game.

When Uncle Nix found out Uncle Bishop and Anais were together, it was almost the end of our family. It was months that I went without seeing Uncle Bish and it was pure torture, for me and my parents. Mom and Dad cried a lot during that time, but they also felt stuck in the middle of their friends who had chosen sides. It hurt like hell to have a piece of our family missing.

Uncle Nix and Uncle Bishop eventually made up as did he and Aunt Viv and Anais, but it took a bit before everything was back to the way it should have always been. Now, you'd never know there was a huge rift that almost tore the Mag Creek crew apart.

"*I really don't know, Ana,*" I answered, truthfully. "*I'm so pissed at them. How could they hide that from me?*"

The tears began to fall again but this time they were hot and angry.

"*Day. Be serious. Do you really think your mom and dad would burden you with something that heavy when you were so young?*"

"*Well what's their excuse for not telling me once I was old enough to understand?*"

"*I can't say exactly, but I do know a parent will do anything to protect their child. Your parents love you so much, Dagen. I have no doubt that they did what they thought was best.*"

I pulled into the rest stop and parked under a bright lamp. "*When did you find out?*"

"*Well I knew your mom had died when you were young and that your dad's relationship with her wasn't a good one. But it was probably the end of my freshman year at Rice when your mom, Camille, told me the truth about—*"

"*About how I'm the product of a rape?*"

Her sigh was amplified in my quiet car.

"*But now you are a product of pure love. You know what Cami once told me? She said that she despises the woman who brought you into this world for what she did to your dad. But then she said that as crazy as it sounds, she was also grateful. She said that it didn't take knowing you for very long to realize that you were always meant to be her daughter.*" I felt a lump in my throat clog the sob that so desperately wanted to break free. "*You are so loved, Dagen. Your story may have started as a tragedy, but it has been filled with nothing but love and laughter ever since. You have to understand that your family did what they thought was right to protect you. Be angry. Yell, scream, kick something. But when you're done and you remember what a selfless, loving family you have, be an adult and get your ass back home and apologize to your parents for making them worry."*

It was a tough pill to swallow, but she was right. From the first memory I can recall, I have never felt anything but love. Dad, Steph, Mom, all my grandparents, aunts and uncles. Even to this very day with all the cousins who look up to me like I'm some great superstar and treat me like one, there has never been a moment where I doubted their affection. But is it all overkill because they know how I came to be? Are they simply making up for the fact that I now carry an evil that I wish would have died with Stephanie?

My stomach roils and I swallow down the bitter bile that rises in my throat. My eyes begin to grow weary and my heart hurts like never before. Not when Steph died, not when I thought Mom and Dad broke up, not even when Dad was in his horrible accident. This right here, knowing who my birth mom really is, is a pain like no other.

I make a left turn onto a quiet street, one you'd find in anytown, USA, and pull to a stop in front of the cream and coral colored house with palm trees in the front yard. Its manicured lawn is envious with its tropical flowers and hedges, and the large entryway gives that awe effect.

I turn off the engine and slowly slide out of the driver's seat, then inch my way to the front door. Taking a deep breath, I press the doorbell. I can hear the chime echo in the house and I wait for the blurry image to appear behind the obscured glass door.

The locks click and the door swings open, and a gray haired woman with a large smile stands at the threshold.

"Oh Dagen. What a surprise. Oh my goodness, I can hardly believe my eyes. Derek! Your grand-daughter is here."

She reaches out to hug me and I step back, holding my hand in front of me.

"Don't touch me," I hiss and her face scrunches in confusion. "You make me sick. How could you?"

"Dagen?" a deep voice calls as Derek walks up behind Susan. "Don't talk to your grandmother that way."

"She's no grandmother of mine. And you're no grandfather. You're sick, twisted people who raised a vile human being."

"Now you stop it, young lady. I will not have you coming to my home and speaking to us that way." His voice grows stern with warning as if I'd be afraid of him.

My hands ball into fists and I feel the rage begin to work its way up my body. "You raised a rapist and helped cover up her disgusting behavior and sentenced my Dad to misery. You two should be in jail and if Stephanie were alive, I'd help throw her in there too."

"That's it!" Derek yells as Susan begins to cry. "What lies have they fed you? That horrible woman who your—"

"That my Dad cheated with? Yeah. Nice try but I know that's a lie. And they have fed me no lies. In fact, it wasn't until I overheard them talking about how you were going to tell me Dad cheated on Stephanie with Mom unless they convinced me to come down here for the summer that I finally learned the truth. They've done everything to protect me. To protect *her*, and all you've done is lie to me. My entire life."

"That is absolutely false. I knew that man would try to brainwash you against your mother. He did that their entire marriage. And I told Stephanie she should leave him, but he wouldn't go," Derek tries to defend.

I scoff. "Really? So then who was that man that mom would always take me to see? The one that we had to keep our little secret. The one that came to see her on the day she died?" Their mouths work to find a lie, but I guess they've run all out of shit to spew. "I hate you. I will never forgive you for what you did, and I'm glad she's dead because if she wasn't, I'd want to choke her myself just to watch the life drain out of her evil eyes."

A hand collides with my face in a loud thwack and it burns. I look at Susan who gasps and holds her hand over mouth.

"I'm sorry. I shouldn't have done that," she says, her voice shaking.

I take two more steps back and glare at them. "That is the last time you will ever touch me. And this is the last time you will ever see me. I never want to hear from you again. You are both dead to me. When you die, I hope you rot in hell like your horrible daughter."

My feet move quicker to get me away from them.

Derek shouts my name and I spin, running to my car. The second time in as many days that I find myself running from my problems. I jump in the driver's seat and stab at the ignition button like it's done me wrong. There's a pounding on my windows and I look over to see Susan standing there with tears rushing over her lids and her lips trembling.

I roll it down and she pleads, "Dagen Rayne. Please just come inside so we can talk. I don't want you to leave like this."

I shake my head slowly and explain, "The time to talk was twenty-one years ago when you found out what your daughter had done. The time to talk was twenty-one years ago when a nineteen year old boy was scared out of his mind that he'd lose the child he never wanted with a woman he hated. There's nothing left to say except goodbye. Don't ever call me again. You'll never see or hear from me, and I don't ever want to hear from you. Try repenting in this life so that maybe you have a chance to go to a better place when your time's up on earth. I can assure you that your daughter won't be there to greet you, but maybe you can gain some forgiveness from God because you'll never have mine."

I roll the window up and watch her grab at her chest as she continues to cry. I look back once more at the grandparents I thought I knew, then bury their memory deep, never to be mourned or thought of again.

TWO

I DIDN'T THINK I had anymore tears left to cry after yesterday and this morning, but it seems I was wrong.

After leaving the people formerly known as my grandparents, I decided I needed to put some actual food in my stomach before making the long drive back home. I never wanted to set foot in Florida again, but if I didn't eat I'd end up stuck in the hospital from either getting in an accident or exhaustion.

I pulled up to my favorite local restaurant, ordered my favorite meal for probably the last time, and then sat in my car eating, working up the strength and courage to call my parents. When I had enough food that I felt like I could steady my hand long enough to tap the screen, I made the call that I've dreaded for almost twenty-four hours.

It rang twice before Dad answered. *"Are you okay, baby bird?"* is what he asked me instead of yelling which, honestly, is what I deserved.

But I should've known better. Dad isn't a yeller. He's a listener and a thinker and I can count the number of times he's raised his voice to me on one hand. I can tell you I only need one finger for the number of times he raised his voice to

Mom. He's never tried that again and I can guarantee he never will.

"Yeah. I'm okay. I'm sorry, Dad." The tears began immediately upon hearing his tender voice.

"You don't have to apologize, sweetheart—"

"We're sorry," Mom chimed in, her voice thick with emotion. "We should have talked to you and stood up to your grandparents. This could have been avoided."

"They are not my grandparents and I told them as much when I saw them this morning." I waited for some type of shocked response but got none.

"I'm sure you did what you thought you had to." Dad was very matter of fact, leaving it at that.

"Will you come home now?" Mom asked, her voice full of plea.

"Yeah. I'm eating and then I'm going to come straight home."

"Do you think you should just stop for the night and rest? Head out tomorrow after a good sleep?"

"No, Dad. I want to get out of this state and into my own bed as soon as possible." I needed to hug my parents and siblings tonight now that the worst was over. "I'm fine. I promise."

"Okay, sweetheart. As long as you're sure you're okay. Just drive carefully and call us if anything happens." Mom said about a dozen *I love you*'s after that, as did Dad, and I hung up feeling a little better now that I knew they weren't mad.

I finished my food and decided to stroll past a park Dad used to take me to for our daddy-daughter days, which were quite a lot now that I think of it. I can remember very few times where I wasn't with him. If I wasn't at school, then I was with Dad at dance practice or horse riding lessons or doing some type of craft that was always super girly but he never complained. The more I thought about it, the more I realized that I didn't spend as much time with Stephanie as I did with Dad. Of course I remember our manicures and when we played salon or dolls, but she spent many nights out while I had movie nights with Dad.

I was quite young when we lived in Florida, but I feel like the trauma I experienced was enough to seer some memories into my mind. Like the memory I have of Dad not really having any friends. I remember he would always kiss me goodnight and be there to wish me good morning when I clambered out of bed. On the many mornings Stephanie wasn't home, Dad would say she went to the gym or to run an errand. Looking back now, I know that wasn't the truth.

Dad always helped me preserve the good memories I had of her, and I realize now that was to help erase the bad ones that I didn't understand were bad at the time. I know Dad isn't perfect, but compared to Stephanie he's a freaking saint.

Which is why I'm praying he's a forgiving man once I call him and tell him about my current predicament.

The sun beats down on me as I stand beside my car, looking at the crushed back end as dust still settles around it. I decided to make a detour off of I-10 and pass through Gulfport, Mississippi, a place where my family has spent many spring breaks. Everything was going great until I tried to get back to I-10. I thought that all I had to do was reach the end of Highway 90 and take a right, then it would lead me back to my original route.

I really should have used my GPS sooner because when I realized I was lost and had no idea where I was going, I tried yelling at the car to help me get back on track. But the damn thing wasn't understanding me, so I grabbed my phone, typed in Magnolia Creek, Texas and hit search.

Well…I attempted to do those things. I got as far as typing Magnolia C when I took my eyes off the screen and put them back on the road. I was a bit too late and had to make a hard jerk of the wheel to the left, causing me to fishtail on the sand and gravel shoulder. Remembering that I needed to steer into the skid, I did just that. However I forgot the most important thing; not to hit the brakes. I also did that, which made my back end to smack straight into a light pole

"Dammit," I curse, and kick the tire like it's the car's fault and not mine for not paying attention to the road.

I huff out a breath and drop my hands from my hips and sag my head. Guess it's time to face the music and call Dad, then figure out what to do with the car.

I pull out my phone and decide to call Mom this time. The phone starts ringing before I remember that I'm driving her car and she won't be too happy about this.

"Hi sweetheart," she answers with a chipper voice. "How's the drive going?"

I squint my eyes at the glaring sun. "Um, well, it was going okay but I…I kinda had a little accident."

"Oh my gosh. Are you okay? Day, where are you? Do you need the police? An ambulance? Oh dear grief."

"Mom. Mom, slow down. I'm okay. I just spun out. I wasn't paying attention and hit some gravel and hit a light pole."

"Dagen! Did you hurt yourself? Vaughan! Day was in an accident," she shouts.

"Mom. No. I–" I sigh and lean against the car.

"Day? What happened?" Dad's voice joins in.

"Okay, listen. Please." I explain how I wanted to drive along the coast and see the small beach town we like to visit, and how I got lost trying to get back to the interstate

"And I just fishtailed, and I tried to–"

"Steer into the spin," Dad reminds me.

"I know, Dad. And I did do that, but I hit the brakes and that sent me drifting straight into a light pole."

I hear him blow out a heavy breath, and my fingers find their way into my mouth and I begin chewing on my nails.

"How bad is it?" he finally asks.

I turn around and stare at the point where the right back end is crunched against the pole.

"Well, the back end has a pretty good dent in it. And the passenger side back tire is sitting pretty weird." I move on from chewing on my nails and start chewing on the inside of my cheek.

"Cars can be fixed. The most important thing is you're okay. I'll call the insurance and see what it's going to cost to tow the car home and then I'll find the closest airport and get you a flight back home. You may have to stay a night in… where are you?" Dad wonders, and I wonder the same.

"I'm not sure. Hold on a sec," I tell him and pull up my map to find my exact location. "Cattywump Bay? What the hell kind of name is that?"

"Cattywump Bay? Are you making that up?" Mom asks me.

"According to the map, that's exactly where I am. I'm close to Diamond Head but still on the South side of I-10."

"I don't want you sitting there alone, so is there any way you can–"

"Hey there. Are you okay, darlin'?" A sweet voice with a thick southern twang cuts into Dad's words.

I turn around and see a woman staring out the window of her faded blue pick-up truck.

"Give me a minute, Dad." I pull the phone from my ear but don't hang up, and walk closer to her. "Hey. Yeah. I need to find a tow. Would you know of a place?"

"Seems you got into a little bit of a disagreement with that light pole. Unfortunately darlin', I think you lost," she tells me and I let out a small laugh and a shrug. "There's only one place in this little town that can tow ya otherwise, you'll have to call the big city and have one of them big wrecker places get ya. And they charge more than Carter's got little pills."

What in the high heavens did that girl say?

"Dad. Someone has stopped to help, and she says she knows who to call for a tow. I'm going to talk with her then call you once I know where I'm going."

"No, I'll just stay on the phone. Who knows what that woman may do." Concern laces his voice.

"Dad. This woman looks to be about the size of Aunt Viv, and as harmless as Mom. I'll be fine," I assure him.

"You keep your location on and I want to know the name, number and address of the place once you get there. Understand?"

I roll my eyes and smile. "I understand. I promise to use my hunting skills if I feel like this five foot nothing woman is going to harm me."

"Smart ass. Love you, baby bird."

"I learned from the best...Uncle Hayes. Love you too, Daddy-o." I hang up and turn around to face the friendly face once more.

"I'm five-four, thank you very much," she says.

"Huh?"

"You said I was five foot nothin', but I'm five foot and four inches. Don't rob me of them four inches. Every little bit is needed."

I laugh and she turns off her truck and hops out. Or rather down.

"How in the heck do you drive that giant thing?" I ask her as she rounds her big blue beast.

She comes to stand in front of me, and looks over her shoulder as if only realizing how big her truck is. "I learned how to drive on ole blue. It's just normal for me."

"I'm Dagen," I say and hold out my hand to shake.

She takes it and says, "I'm McKinsley, but you can call me Kinsley. Or Kins. The Mc is not necessary. Makes me sound like a shake or somethin' at McDonalds." I laugh and then have to agree.

"Yeah. I could see myself ordering a Big Mac and a large McKinsley."

She begins to laugh and we chuckle together. "Lawd, I

told my momma she cursed me with that name. But she just had to be 'original'."

"Hey. My name is Dagen Rayne McCallan. Talk about original. You ever meet another Dagen?"

She scrunches her face and looks up as if she's thinking real hard. "Can't say I have. But I tell you what, with that twang I hear wantin' to make an appearance, the Texas license plate, and the name, I'd say we're cornbread sisters."

I snort and ask, "What's a cornbread sister?"

"You know. We come from the same batch. We're alike despite being a little different. Still amazing, but with our own little twist. Southern cornbread."

"I've never heard it, but I like it."

"Welp. It looks like you ain't drivin' that shiny car any time soon, so I called on my friend to get ya outta there. He should be here soon."

I sigh in relief. "Oh thank you. I just wasn't paying attention and hit a patch of gravel and spun out."

"Well hell. That don't sound like any fun. Especially with that fancy car of yours."

I close one eye and scrunch up my face. "Yeah, it's my Mom's."

"Oooowee, someone's getting their birth certificate canceled when they get home." I laugh yet again, because this girl's euphemisms are better than anything I've ever heard. "Come sit in ole blue. It's hotter'n a goat's butt in a pepper patch."

She waves me over and opens the door for me to slide in. The door shuts behind me and that little thing makes her way to the driver's side. On the radio plays *Cowboy Break My Heart*, a song I've had the misfortune of knowing something about.

"So what're you doin' in Cattywump Bay, Mississippi?" Kinsley asks when she settles into the driver's seat.

"I don't think you want to know. It's a whole story spanning twenty-one years."

She rubs her hands together and her eyes light up. "Hell, girlie. That sounds like my kinda story. Spill the beans. All my friends are guys and I never get to hear good girl gossip."

I shrug and say, "Okay. You asked for it," then proceed to give the abbreviated version of my fucked up life.

"Damn girl. That story's like a soap opera. All it's missin' is someone coming back from the dead and a long lost sibling." She shakes her head in disbelief.

"I told you it was a whole story. Ever met anyone with a crazier life?" I ask.

She squints her eyes and twists up her lips in deep thought. "I mean, I guess I have a pretty whacked out story. My mama did marry her daddy's best friend who was twenty years older than her."

"Oo. I have an aunt –who's more like a sister really because she's only six years older than me– and she's married to my uncle who happens to be my other uncle's best friend. And he's twelve years older than her."

Kinsley blinks and says, "I'm sorry. What'd you say? That was all sorts of confusing."

I chuckle and explain. "So my Uncle Bishop is my Mom and Dad's best friend from high school. He's not my real uncle but you know how southerners are. Well Uncle Bishop's best friend is Phoenix whom he met in college when they played baseball together. Uncle Phoenix was an MLB pitcher and he married my Aunt Viv who is Mom's best friend from when they were little girls." I take a deep breath then go on. "So Uncle Phoenix has a niece, Anais, who just happened to move to Texas for school and fell in love with Uncle Bishop. Their relationship almost tore everyone apart, but luckily it all worked out and now we have one big family with more aunts and uncles and plenty of little cousins."

"Soap opera," she says, shaking her head. "But I'm

digging all the aunts and uncles that ain't really aunts and uncles. I only have one aunt and uncle and two cousins who are much older than me. We don't really see them, so it's just me, mama and daddy."

I open my mouth to continue comparing our crazy lives, but a loud engine interrupts our little girl's chat.

"Oh look. Henny's here."

"Who's here?" I ask.

"Henny. His name is actually Hendrix, but all his friends call him Henny. Now if he comes off a bit grumpy, don't let that scare ya. It's all an act. He's really got a heart of gold. He just doesn't know it yet."

A large tow truck pulls up beside Kinsley. It's black and the words *DARE Towing* in neon blue are right along the side of it. The windows are tinted and I can't see inside, but I assume he's some backwoods feller with a few teeth missing and a beer belly.

I climb out of the truck and turn around to greet Hendrix and immediately have my mind blown. Ever hear that saying, assumption is the mother of all mistakes? Well mistaken I most certainly am.

Hendrix is the farthest thing from backwoods as one can get. Not to mention he has all of his teeth and I have no doubt that underneath that white t-shirt lies a perfectly chiseled body.

No, this man is definitely not your average small-town tow truck driver. He's the kind of man your daddy greets with a shotgun.

I know my dad would.

HENDRIX

"ESCAPE WAS JUST A NOD AND A CASUAL WAVE
OBSESS ABOUT IT HEAVY FOR THE NEXT TWO DAYS
IT'S ONLY JUST A CRUSH, IT'LL GO AWAY
IT'S JUST LIKE ALL THE OTHERS
IT'LL GO AWAY"

Tear You Apart
-She Wants Revenge

THREE

I PULL up to where Kinsley's old blue truck sits on the side of the road and notice someone in the cab with her. I also notice the shiny silver BMW kissing a light pole. The truck door opens and Kinsley hops down with a giant smile on her face. Typical Kins.

I bring my truck to a stop and climb out, dust clouds rising from where my boots touch down, and swagger around the front. The passenger door opens and long brown hair swirls when a gust of wind blows by. The sun shines in my eyes and I lose track of her. I shield my hand over my eyes and watch as the spots clear and my vision returns. And when it does, I almost wish I could be blinded by the light again.

Bright green eyes meet mine and I watch the black shrink, the green saturating her wide orbs. Lips, plump and pink, slowly part and stretch into a shy smile. A small bead of sweat drips down from her collarbone to the valley between her breasts and I gulp and quickly move my eyes back to meet hers. The ones that slowly peruse my body from head to toe.

"That yours?" I ask her.

She blinks and replies, "Huh?"

"The car. Is that yours?" I jut my chin towards the sleek car and her head slowly follows.

I see her face scrunch in torment then turn back to face me. "Yes. Well, my mom's, but I'm driving it."

I give her one quick nod and walk over to where it sits. The right rear fender is caved in from where the pole stopped it and the wheel sits a little askew. The tail light is cracked, but it's an easy fix and I can get a replacement piece from the dealer in the next town. The most concerning problem is the possible damaged rear frame rails and any electrical issues that will be a result.

I stand up from my squatted position and wipe my hands on my jeans. "Let me get this hooked up. My shop isn't far and Kins can drive you there. You got a place you're staying at?"

She squints in the bright sun and kicks at the dirt. "Um, well no. I was on my way home so this was just a pass through."

I look at her neatly manicured nails and the rings that adorn her fingers. On her wrist sits a pricey watch and gold bracelet with inset diamonds right next to it. I know that the two of those items alone could buy her a pretty nice car. It's obvious this girl comes from money and this spoiled brat just wrecked her mom's ninety thousand dollar luxury car, and they'll probably just turn around and buy another like they're replacing the sheets on their fucking bed.

"Well you may want to call mommy and daddy and tell them to send the private jet, because this is going to take at least two weeks."

"Excuse me," she whines and crosses her arms over her chest. "Private jet? What's that supposed to mean?"

I shrug. "It means that if your britches are too big for this little town, you might want to have your parents send the butler to pick you up. We'll ship the car home when it's done."

"You don't know me. Don't make assumptions about things you don't know. I called you to tow my car, not to be judged by a guy who looks like he bathes in a bucket of dirt and worms." Her arms fall to her side and her hands ball into fists.

She takes a couple steps closer to me and I can see her nostrils flare and those beautiful bright eyes grow dark. Kinsley winces just over her shoulder and I'm sure she's thinking if this girl only knew who she was talking to.

"You should take your own advice. Don't make assumptions sweetheart." I stride past her, bumping her on the shoulder as I go, and hop back into my truck.

The loud diesel engine still runs so all I see is the pretty young thing griping to Kins, no doubt about me and my surly attitude. I don't make excuses as to why I'm so pissed at the world, obviously people around here know, but I won't apologize to this little brat.

I maneuver my truck around the back end of the car, working it until I get the right angle. I lower the boom and position the brackets to slide under the tires. Sweat drips down my back and I can feel the girls watching me as I work.

It's only March, but in the south, the weather runs a little differently. What is categorized as spring in other parts of the country is early summer here in Mississippi. Then, when the rest of the country is enjoying nineties at the peak of summer, we're sitting on hell's front porch. So a little sweat elsewhere is a sopping mess here which means I'm going to have to change my shirt at the very least.

It takes me a good thirty minutes to get everything hooked up and ready for me to winch it in. I stand up and wipe the sweat from my forehead with my forearm and turn to where the ladies stand. The eyes of the girl whose name I failed to get, focus on the spot where my t-shirt has ridden up and exposes my stomach that is covered with tattoos. Most of me is covered with tattoos. At this point only about ten percent of my body is untouched by ink.

Her eyes trail up my body and meet mine, and her cheeks stain pink with embarrassment over being caught. I can't help but smirk. She quickly looks away and I finish cranking the car up. The two of them talk to one another but the sound the crank drowns out what they are saying.

With everything hooked up, I decide I should use the small amount of manners that I picked up along the way of my haphazard upbringing and introduce myself properly.

Wiping my hands on my jeans, I extend one to her. "I'm Hendrix Dare, by the way."

She stares at my hand as if I'm offering her a venomous snake and after a moment of hesitation, places her hand in mine.

"I'm Dagen McCallan." Her skin is soft and the closer I stand, the better I can smell her sweet scent.

"Dagen, huh? That's an unusual name," I just have to add.

"It's a family name. What kind of name is Dare?" she challenges back.

I clench my jaw and give her the same smirk I gave her when I caught those eyes wandering over my body. "It's a family name."

She yanks her hand free from mine and says, "I have a couple of things I need to get from my car before you leave."

"What? You afraid I'm going to steal something from you, princess?"

Her eyes turn to little slits as she glares at me. "What is your problem? Did you wake up with your dick in a grinder? I'm sorry if you did, but that's no reason for you to take it out on me. I'm a paying customer and I am more than happy to call someone else if you can't handle the job."

I stare at her silently, fuming that she spoke to me like

that. I'm also kind of turned on that this spoiled brat doesn't back down to a good word spar. I can't even really say why I'm acting like I am. It's not like me to be so rude, especially to women. But something about her has my blood boiling.

Without a word, I walk over to her car and pull open the front door as it is easiest to get to. I look at her and hold out my hand, indicating that she should get what she needs before I change my mind and slam the damn door on her face.

She stomps her way to me, keeping her eyes locked on mine the entire time, and I watch as the sun shines off of them, lighting up a prism of greens. She rises up on her toes and reaches inside. Not gonna lie, I take a good long look at her tight ass in those tiny shorts. It's so round and perfect and I imagine what it would look like bare and laid over my knee.

A throat clears and I see Kins watching me with an arched brow and arms crossed over her chest. I curl my lip and snarl, but it does nothing to scare her. I don't know that McKinsley Sawyer is afraid of anything.

"Got it. Thanks," Dagen says, and quickly struts away.

"We'll see ya at the shop," Kins shouts out, and I give her a thumbs up.

"What the hell is that guy's problem?" I hear Dagen ask Kinsley.

"Oh, he's just sour because I told him he needs to smile more and quit lookin' like he just smelled a fart."

Dagen snorts out a laugh and I do everything I can to hide my smirk. Kins is always good for a chuckle.

I watch them climb into that old blue clunker and before they drive off, Dagen looks out the window at me and her face softens. I try to turn away, pretend I'm not staring, but it's useless. The girl with the hypnotic eyes is going to be my downfall. I just know it.

Dagen

"LEATHER BLACK AND EYES OF BLUE
SUN REFLECTIINIG IN YOUR EYES
LIKE AN EASY RIDER"

Freak
-Lana Del Rey

FOUR

KINSLEY'S TRUCK pulls up to a black building with the words *DARE Bros Mechanics* in the same neon blue as the truck on the front. There's no contrasting trim color. The only color on the building aside from the bright blue letters are the four silver chrome garage doors, two of which are rolled up. Inside the bays are vehicles being worked on by a few guys, and loud music is spilling out.

The engine stops and I can suddenly hear again. Between the loud diesel engine and Kinsley's country music, we spent the drive yelling at one another just to hear what was being said. We arrive before the tow truck so I sit inside the cab.

"Come on, silly goose. You don't wanna wait here. Let's go inside. Henny always has cold soda and snacks in the back room. And before you say anything, no I am not allowed in the back room, but go anyhow."

I shake my head with a smile. If this girl lived near me, I'd have the best set of abs in Magnolia Creek from the workout they'd get with all of the laughter she would induce.

"Does he have a vending machine in there? I could use a chocolate bar."

"He does, but I know where he keeps the free stuff." She

hooks her arm with mine and struts her brown boots across the pavement.

The door chimes when we walk in and I'm greeted with a sight that is not what I expected of a garage. The inside is white with sleek chrome halfway up the walls. A reception desk wrapped in that same chrome and topped with black granite counters. The motorcycle logo on the outside of the building sits on the front of the reception desk.

Tires of various sizes with various rims are on the wall, along with pictures of cars and trucks. The most impressive wall is the one behind the reception desk. It's covered in a large vinyl poster with three motorcycles. They aren't Harley's like my dad's and uncles', they're sports bikes. Otherwise referred to as crotch rockets.

To the left of the reception area are some low black leather chairs and a chrome table with magazines displayed. With a few plants and a coffee bar, it's fair to say that I had a very preconceived view of what the inside was supposed to look like.

"Pretty impressive, right?" Kinsley says over my shoulder.

"Yeah. I was expecting stained floors, yellow walls, and a sad lonely vending machine with expired snacks." She laughs and pulls my arm further into the shop.

"Hey Miss Shirley. How's it goin'?" We pass the reception desk with a woman who looks to be in her sixties, sitting there, pounding away on her keyboard.

"Hey darlin'. It's going. You know how it is with those boys." She presses her lips into a tight smile and shakes her head. "Who's your pretty friend?"

"Hello. I'm Dagen, ma'am. Nice to meet you." I walk closer to her and hold out my hand to shake it.

"Ma'am? Oh boy. What southern state do you come from?" She takes my hand in her warm and soft one and shakes it.

"She's from Texas. Manners and all. She's my new cornbread sister, so give her the red carpet treatment." Kinsley throws her arm over my shoulder, popping up on tiptoes to reach, and hugs me to her.

"Well, it's nice to meet you, Dagen. I'm Miss Shirley. Just stick with Kinsley and she'll show you all you need to know. And be aware that those boys are all bark and no bite." She winks and I would laugh if I didn't already have my 'friendly' encounter with Hendrix. "You new to town?"

"Oh, no ma'am. My car had a little...what'd you call it, Kinsley?"

"A disagreement with a light pole. Henny should be pulling up soon with her car." She points over her shoulder and I turn my head to look out the large picture window and see his shiny black truck pulling up with my poor car in tow.

"Looks like he's here. I better get the intake papers ready. You girls go grab some cookies and I'll call you when I need to get your information, Dagen." Miss Shirley opens a drawer and pulls out a carbon notebook.

"C'mon sister. Let's see what they got today." I follow Kinsley to a chrome wrapped door as she pushes through.

We enter another open room much like the lobby, but less sleek and organized. A long, white counter with black cabinets line the far wall. A refrigerator sits at the end, and the counter is littered with a plethora of snacks that looks like a pack of hungry teenage boys is scattered about.

Kinsley makes a beeline for the large black table placed right in the middle and lifts the plastic wrap that covers a half empty dish. A small stack of cookies remains, and she quickly snatches one away. She chomps about half in one bite, and closes her eyes with a moan.

"Oh my gosh. These are so good," she says with mouth full and bits of cookies flying out. "Ya gotta try one. Do you like kitchen sink cookies?"

I walk over to where she stands, assaulting that poor cookie, and ask, "What's a kitchen sink cookie?"

Her mouth stops chewing and her eyes fly open. She swallows and quietly walks to the fridge, pulling out a carton of milk and pouring it into a glass that she got from the open shelves.

She chugs it down and when she's done, she looks at me and scolds, "Girl, did you grow up repressed? A kitchen sink cookie means it's got everything. Chocolate chips, pecans, salty pretzel bits, and toffee chips. It's the mama of all cookies."

My nose scrunches up, not quite sure if those ingredients encourage the kind of moan Kinsley made, but I pick one up anyhow. Taking a smaller bite than the one Kinsley did, I immediately regret my questioning of her food IQ.

I do the same closed eye moan, but maybe slightly more obscene.

"Oh shit. It's so good."

"Been a while since you got some action?" The deep voice that filters in from behind me quickly wipes away my happy mood.

With narrowed eyes, I turn to him and say, "Did someone kill your cat when you were a kid? What is wrong with you, and why do I offend you so much?"

"Well for one, you're in an employees only area and two, you're eating my fucking cookies."

I pop the last bite of cookie into my mouth and lean back against the table, pressing my palms onto the cool surface.

"Mmm. Best thing I've ever had in mouth," I moan, squeezing my legs together.

When my eyes open I see him watching closely, his Adam's apple bobbing in his tattooed throat as he swallows. I slowly lick my lips, then slide my finger into my mouth and suck it clean. My mouth makes a popping sound when I pull it free and I challenge him with a smirk.

His nostrils flare as he watches me silently. When he finally opens his mouth, he says, "If that's the best thing you've ever had, well then, you're not putting the right things in that mouth of yours." Now I'm the one swallowing down my embarrassment. "Miss Shirley needs you. When you're done shoving *my* cookies in your mouth, go fill out the paperwork."

He stomps out of the door, his boots echoing harshly as he goes.

"Oowee! If that wasn't some thick 'I wanna kiss you' tension then…" Kinsley looks at me with wide eyes, shaking her head slowly from side to side.

I scrunch my brows and ask her, "What are you talking about? That jerk has it out for me, and I can't figure out why. I'm a paying customer just trying to get my car fixed and he's acting like I'm robbing him blind."

I throw my arms up then let them flop down to my sides, completely exasperated and confused.

A sly smirk works its way across her face. "Girl. That ain't Henny having it out for you. That's Henny having a *thing* for you."

"Good grief, you have got to be out of your mind."

"Nuh uh. No ma'am. I have known that man for many years and I can tell you right now, he's still like a middle school boy. When he likes someone, he's a meanie. You know, pulling pigtails, sticking gum on your seat so you get it all over your butt. Only since he's an adult, he's picking on you. But I see it. That boy's got a fire in his eyes and in his pants for you."

I exhale with an exaggerated roll of my eyes. "Is everyone around here crazy or is that proprietary to you?"

She skips over to me and bumps my hip with hers. "It's in the water so be careful, because it's contagious. C'mon. Miss Shirley is waiting."

HENDRIX

"WHERE DO BAD FOLKS GO WHEN THEY DIE?
THEY DON'T GO TO HEAVEN WHERE THE ANGELS FLY
THEY GO TO A LAKE OF FIRE AND FRY
SEE 'EM AGAIN 'TIL THE FOURTH OF JULY"

Lake of Fire
-Nirvana

FIVE

MY EYES TRACK every move she makes as she shuffles from foot to foot while talking on the phone to her daddy dearest.

"Dad, I know. I'll email my professors and tell them there's been a family emergency. It'll be two weeks and I'm doing great in everything. I can do remote classes. I promise it will be okay." She grows quiet and chews on her bottom lip. "I don't know. I can...I don't know. I have no solution for how I will get a computer. Maybe I'll go buy an iPad. I gotta go find a place to get some clothes, anyhow. I have the outfit I'm wearing and the one I wore on the drive out. I don't think a short denim skirt and cowboy boots are going to cut it for everyday wear."

I hear a little noise –the kind that tells you someone wants your attention and you try your best to ignore it, but just can't– and look over to see Kinsley standing next to Miss Shirley, the two of them watching me with judging eyes. I know exactly what they are trying to infer and I'll be damned if they guilt trip me into it.

"Do you think the beach condo is available?" She asks and plops down into a comfy chair. "Well, when you find out, please let me know right away. I may just take an Uber to a strip mall and get some necessities. If it isn't available, I'll just look for a hotel." She shakes her head, listening to the other end and I can only imagine her daddy is sending her the number to his black card to take care of everything. "Love you too, Dad. Give Sloaney and A.J. a big kiss from me. Bye."

She presses end, puffs out a defeated breath and stares at the phone in her hands, looking sad and deflated. I look over to the ladies again, they're non-verbal gestures intensifying. Kinsley glares at me, and Miss Shirley raises her eyebrows and widens her eyes. Those are universal symbols for *'you better say something before I do'*. My hands ball into fists and internally I'm screaming. At Kinsley and Miss Shirley, at this woman for being so devastatingly beautiful, and at myself for what I'm about to do. I clear my throat and take a couple steps closer to her.

"Dagen." She lifts her head and looks at me, nervously. "If you're planning to stay here while we work on your vehicle, I...I have a loft that is private from the rest of my house. You're welcome to stay there if you'd like."

A loud, audible gulp falls from her mouth and her eyes flit to where Kinsley and Miss Shirley stand with wide smiles.

"Um. I-I don't know if–"

"Oh honey, don't worry about Henny. He's not a creep or anything, Just an asshole." Kinsley bats her hand in the air like she's swatting away the crazy notion that I may take advantage of her.

"And I live very close by and will make sure he is a perfect and *gracious* host." Miss Shirley adds.

I sigh and don't understand what I did in my life to deserve these two. Wasn't my upbringing enough punishment to escape ladies like the ones that seem to want to run my life?

"I mean, if you're sure. I don't want to impose. My parents

are contacting the people we've rented a beach house from in previous years, so it's possible I may be able to use that."

"And if it's not available?" I ask her.

She twists her mouth and says quietly, "I was just going to find a hotel."

"For two weeks? Do you know how much that will cost in addition to the repairs? Are you ready to foot a bill that big?" She opens her mouth to speak and I interject. "Wait. I forgot. Daddy's paying for it so I guess it doesn't matter. We don't have a Ritz-Carlton, so you may have to be okay with the local motel."

She slams her hands on the arms of the chair and jumps to her feet. "I am so sick and tired of you being a top tier jerk to me. I am not a spoiled brat like you are implying. Yes, my father will be paying for the repairs, but don't think that means it's just another day. I'll have to make it up by shoveling horse shit out of the stalls. They'll put me in charge of feeding the animals and checking on the cabins. Not to mention I'll probably be the one busting my ass every weekend, leading horseback riding lessons and teaching kids how to shoot an arrow. Do you know what it feels like to get tagged by a rubber arrow? You'd think it doesn't hurt, but that rubber is a hard tip and when it comes flying at your head, you can only hope and pray that you're left with a bruise and not down one eye. Don't get it twisted and think I'm on a free ride thanks to mommy and daddy. Nothing is free in my home."

Her green eyes glow with anger, but damn are they beautiful. Maybe I am being a little too harsh on her. She's done nothing but be a mesmerizing woman who is slowly draining me of my ability to reason and form sentences. I can't fault her for being gorgeous.

"I apologize. I have no excuse and I'm sorry for how I've spoken to you."

"What?" the three women say in shock.

"Don't make me say it again. You'll get blood from me before a second apology." She works hard to hide her smile, pressing her full lips into a tight line. "You can let your family know you found a place to stay. If it makes you more comfortable, I will stay somewhere else."

"I'll be sure to pop in to check on ya. My work is pretty lenient and I can set my own hours." Kins walks out from behind Miss Shirley's desk.

"Your work is lenient because your boss is your dad," I tell her and she replies with a tongue out.

"Dagen, why don't I take you to get whatever things you are needing and then we can go by grumpy's house to drop it off." She turns to me, holding out her hand, and says, "Keys, please."

I scowl, but she only wiggles her fingers at me. With an exasperated sigh, I pull out my keys and hand it over.

"There's an alarm so let me write down the code fo–"

"I already know it."

"What? How the fuck do you know my alarm code?"

With a roll of her eyes she tells me, "Malik gave it to me once when he needed me to stea–I mean borrow something. The code just stuck."

I make a note to call Malik later and possibly bust his head. "Well, don't take anything this time, okay."

"Yeah, yeah. Sure. Let's go, Dagen. Time to put a dent in daddy's credit card." Kinsley grabs her hand and begins tugging her towards the parking lot.

"Um, thank you," Dagen says, skidding to a stop in front of me. "This is very kind of you and I appreciate it. I gave Miss Shirley my parent's phone numbers so you can give them updates. My dad, Vaughan, is the one you'll most likely want to talk to."

I dip my chin and watch as she follows Kins out the door. I can't help it when my eyes trail up and down her body, tracing the way her ass moves in those barely there shorts.

She wears a cropped sweatshirt that shows a small hint of her flat stomach, and the thoughts that run through my mind would definitely be rated R.

"Eh um." A clearing of a throat breaks the movie reel playing in my head with Dagen as the star. "You keep eyein' that girl like that and it'll earn you a right smack in that big head."

My face pales remembering those smacks she administered to the guys and me. I'm pretty sure I have a dead spot on my head as a result.

"Yes ma'am. Sorry." I walk over to where she sits at the desk and lean on the top. "You have all of her information?"

"Of course. This is ain't my first rodeo, boy." She scribbles some information down on a paper and hands it over. "Here's her cell phone number. You're going to need it to contact her."

I shake my head. "I'll just speak with her dad. Seems like he's the one who will know what's going on and footing the bill."

"I know that. But you may want hers, because it'll be mighty hard to ask her father for a date. Unless you're trying to be a decent human being. I've never known you to be a traditional type boy."

"What in the world are you talking about? I have no desire to ask that girl out. And I am *not* a boy. I stopped being a boy around the age of fifteen when I–"

"Aah you hush," she scolds and holds her hands over her ears. "I do not want to know that about my boy. You just keep that to yourself. Tell Malik and Danté the same thing. In my eyes, you boys are still just that; boys. Now are you going to take this number or do I have to program it in your phone myself?"

My eyes narrow, giving her an irritated look, but by now she's immune to it. I snatch the paper from between her fingers and it gets me a satisfied grin. This woman, I tell ya.

"I've ordered the parts and those should be here by Wednesday so at the latest, the car will go into the shop on Thursday." I give Dagen's dad, Vaughan, the breakdown of what the repairs are going to look like and how quickly we can get it all done.

I've decided to move this up on our priority list so that I can have that girl out of my home as quickly as possible. The sooner she is gone the better for my sanity.

"Okay, that sounds great. Thank you Hendrix. Feel free to text me with any updates. I know you can speak with Dagen regarding all of this, but she has a lot on her mind right now in addition to remote classes, so I'd like to take this one thing off her plate."

He sounds like a very caring father. The kind I would've liked to have growing up. Vaughan has been quite understanding of it all and asked me if it seemed that his daughter was okay. He acted like the car could be totaled and he wouldn't give a damn as long as Dagen is safe. I assured him she looked and seemed fine, but I have no prior knowledge of her so it's really a blind observation.

"One other thing I want to mention. I'm not sure if Dagen spoke to you about this or not, but I have offered her the use of my private loft while she is waiting for repairs. She said that she was hoping to find somewhere closeby, and I have a separate and safe place she is welcome to use," I stand from where I sit looking at my computer screen, and begin to pace the small office. "I have a friend, Kinsley Sawyer, who actually helped Dagen after her accident and has taken her to get some items she will need. Kinsley has offered to stay there with her, and I will stay at a friend's house myself to make it more comfortable for the two of you."

The line is eerily quiet and now I'm wondering if I have an angry father on his way to put a bullet between my eyes.

"How old are you, Hendrix?" He finally asks.

"I, uh, I'm twenty-nine sir."

"Have you ever been arrested or convicted of a crime? Please keep in mind that I am friends with some very important people who could get me every answer I need in a blink of an eye. But I'm hoping you are a trustworthy man and will give it to me straight."

I feel a cold sweat spread across my lip. I don't know if what he says is true, but I would rather not find out and end up with problems that I really don't have time or headspace for.

With the clearing of my throat I tell him, "Yes, sir, I have been arrested. However, it was when I was seventeen years old. I was arrested for drag racing which is a misdemeanor in the state of Mississippi. Because I was a minor and a ward of the state, I served community service and my record was expunged."

"Hmm," is the only response I get.

I scrub my hand over my face, irritated that I am having to explain myself to a man I don't know because I have offered a place for his daughter, a girl I don't really know or plan to, to stay while I repair her vehicle that she crashed. The day started so great. No emergency calls from the shop, no annoying texts from Malik, and no complaints from Danté about the bar. Miss Shirley brought in my favorite cookies and I was looking forward to an easy night at home, watching whatever the hell I want.

Then Kinsley had to go and call me out for a young girl who needed help. Dagen is no young girl and the moment I saw that, I knew my day was shot to hell.

"Should I be worried about your ability to keep your

hands to yourself? The same friends that I have also have friends who would be fine teaching you a lesson if you are not able to refrain yourself."

Okay, now I'm just getting pissed off. This guy thinks his daughter is a fucking block of rare gold and I'm going to steal her away the moment he turns his head.

"Sir, I can guarantee you that I will have absolutely no problems with keeping away from your daughter. I don't mean to be rude or disrespectful, but your daughter is not someone who interests me. No offense, sir. She's just quite young and in addition to that, I don't date clients...in any capacity."

"That is exactly what I like to hear. And you said your friend, Kinley-"

"Kinsley, sir."

"Right. Kinsley. Is she a good person?" This man is going to worry himself to an ulcer.

"The best. She and Dagen have already made fast friends. I promise you, you will have nothing to worry about."

With a big sigh he says, "Thank you. I know this seems a little extreme, but it's a parents job to worry about their children. It's just how it is."

I wouldn't know, because aside from Malik and Danté and Miss Shirley later in my teen years, I've never had anyone who gives two shits about me.

"I understand, sir. And this is the number you can reach me at any time. For anything. I assure you that your car and most importantly, your daughter, are safe."

I can't guarantee my safety, because if he somehow manages to climb into my head and see the thoughts about his daughter running rampant in there, I'll be a dead man. And a man like me wouldn't got to Heaven. I'd burn in the pits of hell.

Dagen

"YOU WANNA GUESS THE COLOR OF MY UNDERWEAR
YOU WANNA KNOW WHAT I GOT GOIN' ON DOWN THERE
IS IT PRETTY IN PINK OR ALL SEE THROUGH?"

Guess
—Charli xcx & Billie Eilish

SIX

WE MOVE UP a long driveway lined with palm trees and oleander bushes, in full bloom and bright pink. The sun is starting to set, lighting up the sky with pinks and oranges and light purples. As we draw closer, a large modern style home greets us.

It has straight lines and is made of a light colored stucco and some type of stone in the same neutral colors. Large windows line the outside and landscape lighting turns on, illuminating the lush foliage.

On the left side of the house sits a four car garage with doors that look more like frosted window panes than any garage door I've seen. And the driveway isn't a regular slab of concrete or gravel. Bright green grass peeks between slabs in a neat and precise pattern, making it look more like a gameboard than a driveway.

"Holy shit, Kinsley. Your home is gorgeous," I exclaim, my eyes still taking in all of the details.

"Oh honey, this isn't my place. This is Henny's house." I'm sure the shock on my face says more than my words could. "See, I shouldn't really say this, but since we're best friends now, I can tell you. Henny and his brothers –adopted, not birth– developed this protective gear for bike riders that can send a signal to EMS if an accident occurs. It monitors heart rate and breathing. Those boys are damn smart and spent years creating it. Each one lending a skill to come up with a million dollar product. Well, it was more like a twenty million dollar project."

"Shut the fuck up," I tell her.

"I will not. It's the God honest truth. They sold forty-nine percent of their company to a speed bike company and control the majority. They invested in a bunch of different stuff here in Cattywump Bay. They all co-own the garage and the bar, and also invested in a few restaurants. But they mostly stay silent on those. They also donated money to a charity that helps troubled youth in foster care. Not a lot of people know about it because they like to keep up the façade that they're asshole deviants." My jaw drops and I stare at her as the truck comes to a stop, and she shifts it into park. "Oh yeah. Don't let that surly attitude fool you. Hendrix and Malik and Danté grew up in foster care and created their own family. Now those boys have more money than they know what to do with."

My face grows hot and my teeth clench. "And that asshole had the nerve to call me a spoiled daddy's girl? Meanwhile he's sitting on a throne of gold amongst his millions of dollars. Does he have a room with rubies and diamonds?"

I push the door open and jump down from the truck. Reaching behind the seat I grab some of my bags from today's shopping trip, and Kinsley grabs the others.

"No, no. Nothing like that. His secret room holds gold bars." I freeze and look at her from the other side of the truck, the door still gripped in my hand. "I'm kidding. He splurges on his bikes, and that's about it. All three of them do. That big ole bike sittin' behind Miss Shirley at the shop? That's

Henny's pride and joy. I'm sure it's covered by a velvet cloth in that garage."

She slams her truck door closed and I do the same and follow her towards the garage. It's then that I notice a small breezeway between the house and the garage that was hidden behind large oleander bushes with bright pink buds.

A loud turr of an engine pulls my attention away from following Kinsley, and I turn around to see a bright blue and green bike speeding up the driveway. I assume it's Hendrix on the bike as it's the exact bike that is on the wall in his shop and the one Kinsley mentioned as being his pride and joy.

I watch him draw nearer, the setting sun shining off of his black helmet and his body clad in a black jacket with bright green piping and the letters DBI on the chest, outlined in the same green. The jeans he wore earlier, the ones I noticed fit his ass so beautifully, are still on as well as his black boots. I watch his hands work to downshift as he slows down, quieting the engine.

He comes to a full stop in front of his garage doors and flips the kickstand before turning his bike off. Instead of getting off he simply sits there, pulling his gloves off one finger at a time. He places them on the bike when they're off and then leans forward, helmet and jacket still in place.

I swallow and look back at Kinsley who catches my eye and simply shrugs. It seems as if he's trying to intimidate me in some way, so I turn to face him completely and cross my arms over my chest. Well, I try to cross my arms but I have bags hanging from my wrists so I don't do it very successfully.

Neither of us budge as we stand in this silent stare-off, waiting for the other to break. And why are we even doing this? Shouldn't he be welcoming me to his home? Inviting me in for a tour? But instead, he just sits there with a chip on his shoulder and an arrogant look on his face. I assume it's arrogant because that's the way he looked when his helmet was off, so I can only guess it's the same with his helmet on.

I exhale and decide to be the bigger person and greet him.

"Hello Hendrix. Thank you for letting me stay here with you while you fix my vehicle. I promise to stay out of your way, as I plan to work on school stuff and simply wait until you are finished." I let my hands drop to my side with the bag still hanging from my wrists and hands.

His head moves up and down the length of my body, from my sneaker covered feet to my ponytail that sways on my head. He slowly pulls the helmet from his head and as much as I want to punch his stupid face –because yes, the look is that of arrogance– I also want to kiss the damn thing.

His eyes are piercing blue and his lips are full and pink. Sweat beads along his hairline, and he pushes back the short, blonde strands. His eyes narrow and focus in on my bags then on my face.

"Are you moving in? Seems like a lot of bags for just a week or two?"

My peace offering gratitude is wiped clean out with his, once again, sour attitude.

"I'm here for two weeks. I can't very well wear the same clothes the entire time. Plus, unless you plan to provide me with everything I need for my day to day life, I thought it would be a good idea to buy toothpaste and soap to clean myself. I don't know about you, but I like to bathe often." I arch a challenging brow at him, waiting to see what kind of comment I'll be met with next.

He kicks his leg over his bike, his boot clad foot stomping on the concrete and smashing the poor grass, and languidly walks over to me. I'm an average size girl standing at five six, but Hendrix towers over me. He's almost as tall as Uncle Bishop and much more menacing as he looks down at me. But I'll be damned if he sees me cower. I look back at him with the same intense stare and clenched jaw.

His nostrils flare and I hear rather than see the gnashing of his teeth. I wish to God I knew what I ever did, aside from breathing, to make this guy hate me so much.

"D'you eat?" Is all he says.

I screw up my face, completely confused by this man, and nod my head.

"Yessir. I took her to the Rusty Bucket for crawfish and all the fixin's," Kinsley says from close behind me.

She throws her arm over my shoulders and tugs me close. She's a little thing, but her fierce attitude is six feet tall.

"I'll show you around," he mumbles and pushes past me.

Stepping up to the garage, he flips open a keypad on the side and presses his thumb to it. A beep sounds followed by the soft whir of the garage door opening. I watch as it rolls up to reveal a glossy floor that looks like it should be in a showroom and not a home. A set of wheels comes into view followed by a car that knocks my socks off.

Now I don't consider myself some kind of car expert, but having a mother and a father who have a love for classic muscle cars means I know a lot about vehicles of a certain era.

The green metallic shines under the fluorescent lights and the black tires are slick, like not even a speck of dirt has touched them. The rims are polished chrome and my fingers itch to feel the smooth, cold surface.

My feet have a mind of their own and begin moving before I can think better of it. My eyes are glowing with envy for this beautiful green machine and if Mom were here right now, she'd be jumping through the window and speeding off like it was the General Lee.

"Sixty-nine, seventy?" I ask him, my eyes still glued to the shiny metallic surface.

"Sixty-eight," he replies, moving closer to where I stand, my fingers ghosting over the curves. "You know something about cars?"

My head pops up, meeting his face with question. "Can a *girl* not have an appreciation for cars?"

"I didn't say that. I just asked if you know about classic cars." His arms cross over his chest and his brows furrow.

"Oh," I swallow, feeling a little embarrassed by my reaction. "My parents really love classic cars. My mom has a sixty-seven Camaro SS. It's gorgeous but this is...wow."

I peek inside the window and see all the original interior, shined up to look new. I close my eyes and imagine what the leather smells like, a familiar scent I know very well. The garage is silent, or at least I think it is. I'm so lost in the car that all I can hear is my internal thoughts saying *I wonder if he'll let me take it for a drive.*

While lost in thought, I manage to not notice where Hendrix stands and I end up slamming into him when I round the back end. His hands catch me and I let my eyes roam from his fingers that grip my forearms, tattooed and strong, to his haunting blue eyes. His features soften and I feel his warm breath lick my skin. As quickly as the moment comes on, it ends. He takes two giant steps back and clears his throat.

"Let me show you the place," he says quickly, and walks off.

I shake off the goosebumps that roll over my body and turn to follow him. When I do, the face of a snarky Kinsley meets me, a sparkle in her eye and a sassy comment sitting on the tip of her tongue.

The corner of her lip pulls up in a lopsided grin. "Well well well," she coos. "Someone is grinning like a possum."

"What are you talking about?" I take a step and feel her right on my heels.

"What I'm talking about is you and Henny having the hots for one another."

"The hots? Who in the hell says that?" I whisper, making sure Hendrix doesn't hear us.

"Oh hush. It don't matter none who says it. All that matters is it's a fact." She arches a brow and smirks before growing quiet and skipping up the stairs.

To put it in Kinsley terms, that girl is as nutty as a squirrel's turd.

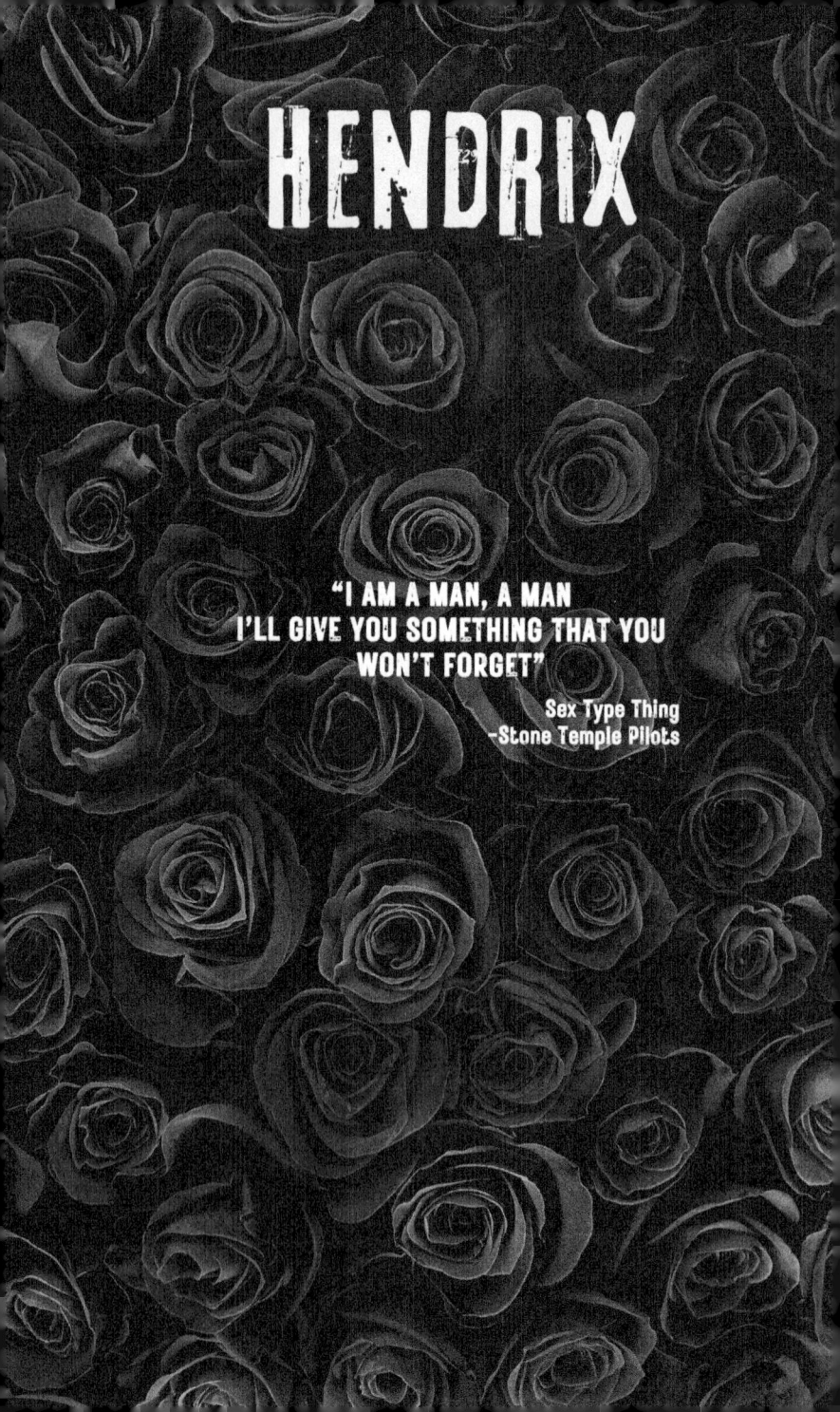

SEVEN

"SO YOU'RE TELLING me that you have a virtual stranger living in your house for the next two weeks while you work on her car? Oh, and this stranger is a girl who, according to Kins, is as gorgeous as a summer sunset." I can hear Malik's smarmy grin on the other end of the phone and if I could, I'd reach out and smack him Miss Shirley style.

"She's a kid, Mal. I'm just helping her out. She was trying to find a place to stay when I offered. Rather, Kins and Miss Shirley forced me to offer up my place. I'll probably never see her. She has homework and classes. You know, kid stuff." It's a lie I tell myself, because more than anything, I wish I could see her as just a kid.

The line is quiet for a moment longer before Malik says, "I gotta see this for myself. Danté and I will be there in fifteen."

"No, Malik. Don't do–" my words are cut off when his side of the call goes dead. "That." I sigh and hang my head, shoulders slumped as my elbows rest on my knees. "I don't have time for this shit."

I toss my phone on the couch and stare out into the vast living room. Kinsley left thirty minutes ago saying she needed to get pajamas for their sleepover at *my* house. I begged her not to come back, but that girl is as persistent as a fly on dog shit. Of all the people for her to find stranded on the side of the road, it had to be Dagen. I'd have rather it been a scared kitten. That at least I can handle. Dagen...she has my head all sorts of fucked.

How can one person spark a fire with just a look? Add in the smartass mouth and a body that I'd like to roadmap with my tongue and she's an instant bad idea. I should be thankful that Kinsley will be here to keep her occupied and out of my hair. Instead, I'm pissed that I won't have her all to myself. Even a hundred feet away, I can still smell her sweet scent.

When she bumped into me in the garage as she made heart eyes at my car, her perfume invaded my senses. I smelled her, which led to pictures flashing behind my eyes that made me want things.

I wander to the kitchen and yank the fridge door open, diving in and retrieving a cold beer from the back. I flip off the cap and toss it on the counter, not caring where it lands, and take a long pull. It doesn't satisfy my thirst like it normally does, and I can only attribute it to the woman who will be sleeping between my sheets and bathing in my tub, her naked body wet and slick.

I gulp down the entire bottle and slam it down when I'm finished, letting out a deep belch so loud I'm worried she'll hear it and think less of me. *What the fuck am I talking about?* She can't think any less of me than she does already. I've treated her like absolute shit for no reason. I'd be surprised if she didn't want to smother me in my sleep.

Now I'm thinking about burying my head between her full tits and it only takes minutes for me to have to adjust myself when my dick grows hard thinking of her nipples in my mouth.

The doorbell rings and I groan. Dealing with Malik and Danté are not on my list of things I want to do right now. In fact, at the moment they rank below cutting my toenails with a belt sander.

Stomping to the door, I let my sour mood grow until it's seeping from my pores. My hand grips the black handle of the door, and I tear it open like there's a fire.

"Fuck my life right now," I growl and come face to face with a pale faced Dagen.

"Oh, I-I'm sorry. I didn't mean to–I'll go back to my room." She spins to retreat and my guilt hits with a pummeling wave.

"No. Dagen, I'm sorry." I reach out and take hold of her arm, pulling her back. "I thought you were someone else. I didn't mean that for you."

She gives me a wide eyed stare with a bite of her lip and there goes that damn dick again, imagining her lips wrapped around it.

"I don't mean to bother you. I was just wondering if–" A loud shrilling pierces her words as Danté and Mal come speeding up my driveway.

"Fuck." I roll my eyes and drop my hand from her arm.

Dagen looks over her shoulder to watch the two men clad in all black turn off their bikes and climb off. Malik, despite his happy and friendly demeanor, is always dressed head to toe in pitch black. Not even a stitch on his jacket is a different color. Sit him on top of his black Aprilia RSV4 bike and he's like the grim reaper flying through the night. Danté wears black with streaks of fire red, the kind suited for the devil himself. Most people call him Satan so it fits quite well.

Helmets get pulled off and a menacing grin covers both of their ugly mugs. Neither takes off their gloves or jackets, and they swagger across my lawn, not caring one bit that there's a perfectly good sidewalk they could use.

Under her breath I hear Dagen whisper, "Holy shit."

It has me clenching my jaw with anger and my hands balling into fists. The two of them look like sin and sin's more devious and insane brother, walking side by side. Malik's deep olive skin and eyes that look like amber gemstones, and Danté with his short cropped black hair and eyes of the same color.

"Well who do we have here?" Danté hisses, slithering up to stand right in front of her. "Hello gorgeous."

He holds out his hand and Dagen places her smaller one in his. Instead of shaking it, he brings it to his lips and leaves a kiss on the back. My eyes narrow at his as they lift to meet mine, a gleam in them.

"H-hi," she stutters, her voice a breathy rasp. "I'm Dagen."

He drops her hand as his gaze travels up and down her spandex covered curves.

"Danté Dare. It is truly *my* pleasure." He smiles and his white teeth shine like diamonds amongst black coal.

Danté's skin is covered with tattoos, more than me, from his ears down to his damn feet, and his nose and ears are pierced, shiny diamonds and silver hoops adorning him. The guy decided he wanted to be anything but who he was growing up, so he remade himself into a dark force that founded a new family of misfit men who no one wanted, and became something that people fear and desire.

Malik steps in and elbows Danté out of the way, and with a huge grin on his face, introduces himself.

"Hello beautiful. I'm Malik Dare. The most handsome of the three brothers. You don't have to say it with your words, but I can see it in your eyes that you agree."

Dagen giggles at Malik, and he leans in to kiss her cheek. When he pulls back I can see her face flush and a shy smile that she tries to hide.

"Are you coming on a ride with us, Dagen?" Danté asks Dagen the question but looks at me as he does.

"Who said we were going on a ride?" I ask them.

"We did. Now get your gear. Dagen can ride with me."

Danté grabs her hand and starts to pull her towards where their bikes are parked.

"Oh. I don't think I can. Kinsley is—"

"On her way over. She heard we were going for a ride and said she and old blue would be right over." Malik smiles, proud of himself for thinking of reasons Dagen may protest and covering his bases.

"I don't think I'm dressed appropriately. I mean…" She looks down at her body —leggings, sports bra and sneakers— and we all do the same.

"You look pretty damn good to me." Danté licks his lips then bites down as he rubs his hands together.

I smack his shoulder and he glares at me.

"Don't be scared. We'll show you what to do. Just hold on tight and we'll do the rest."

"I know what to do," she tells Malik. "My dad and uncles all ride. They ride Harley's, but I imagine it's the same. Right?"

Her eyes flit between the three of us, a smirk plastered on all of our faces.

"Not the way we ride, little mouse. The Dare brothers ride hard, fast, and dangerous," I tell her, the nickname rolling off my tongue like it was just waiting for the right time to pop out.

She purses her lips and rolls her eyes in response. "I think I can handle it. And if Kinsley is going, then so am I."

When her arms cross, they push up her perky tits and I just can't stop my eyes from soaking in the round mounds that sit perched high on her chest.

"Then you ride with me. No more discussion. I made a promise to your father that you would be safe while under my watch."

"Your *watch*? You act like you're on babysitting duty. I'm not a child."

"You sure about that? Daddy dearest seems to think you

are. I'm surprised he didn't ask me to set up a nanny cam so he can keep an eye on you."

A comeback sits on her tongue, but she doesn't get the chance to spear it at me because just then, Kinsley comes rolling up, the loud rumble of her truck drowning out everything. We all turn to watch her park and jump out of her beast on four wheels. With a wide smile, she comes bouncing over to where we stand, still on my front porch.

"Hey y'all. We ridin' or what?" Her arms rest on her hips and she looks from one person to the next.

"Hell yeah we are. Are you riding with me, sweet thing?" Malik winks in the way that only he can, making Kins blush.

"Of course. I wouldn't ride with anyone else, King." Kinsley winks back, using the nickname that women in Cattywump Bay have monikered him with.

Kins hops back to her truck, and climbs into the passenger side to retrieve her helmet and jacket that we insisted she purchase if she was going to ride with us. And by purchase I mean we gave her a custom DareBros Inc. gear, because we can't have her wearing a competitor's subpar gear.

"Okay. Then let's go." Malik grabs Kinsley's hand and pulls her over to his bike while Danté stares at Dagen and I.

"She's riding with me, D." My eyes shoot fire at him, letting him know to back the fuck off.

I love my brothers and would slit a man's throat for them. But I'm not afraid to throw down if need be. And this is one of those times that I'll go toe to toe with him because I gave Dagen's father my word.

I quit my stare down with Danté and take Dagen by her wrist and start pulling her to the garage.

"I have stuff you can wear. Your shoes are fine."

I stab at the keypad and the whir of the opener sounds. The lights flick on when we step in and I continue to lead her to where my bikes sit, now covered and guarded against a spec of dust.

Letting go of Dagen's wrist, I pull the cover off one of them, revealing it like a magician would, and smile when I see her all shiny and waiting for me to ride her.

She's a Ducati Superleggera V4 and my ultimate pride and joy. Even above my company. I used to dream of the day I could afford a bike like this and vowed to myself that I'd make it happen, one way or another.

I leave Dagen to stare at my beauty while I walk over to the storage closet and grab my stuff along with a jacket and helmet that I think will fit her. I toe off my sneakers and step into my riding boots, then swagger over to where she stands, ghosting her fingers over my bike much like she did my car.

As if it weren't enough for this woman to be a fucking siren, she just has to have a love of cars and now it seems bikes. It's like God decided to throw me a big middle finger and drop this perfect girl in my lap, knowing I can't have her.

"Here," I tell her, sticking out my hand with the jacket and helmet. "Zip up the jacket to the neck and snap the collar."

She cautiously takes it from me and slides her arms through it. My eyes follow the zipper, watching each tooth catch one by one. Her delicate fingers snap the button snuggly on her throat and I wish it were my hand wrapped around it.

She tugs at the hem of the jacket, adjusting it and making sure it's in place, then lifts her head to look at me. The moment grows quiet and intense as our eyes stay locked, and I take another step closer to her. Slowly, I raise my hands and slip the helmet over her head, and I'm disappointed when I lose the ability to see her beautiful greens.

I tug on it until I see it's secure, then fasten the chin strap. The carbon helmet is in a fierce shade of crimson red and has a red iridescent visor. It's a sexy helmet and it's perfect for her. The black jacket with red accents matches perfectly, and hugs her full breasts.

I flip open the visor and her pupils shrink from the intrusion of the light. "Feel okay?" I ask her.

"Yeah." Her breath is sultry and breathy and it sends a tingle down my spine.

I nudge my head in the direction of my bike and she follows as I pull my balaclava and helmet on.

I push it out of the garage then set it on the kickstand once more. I steady the bike and throw my leg over, sitting comfortably. Once I'm situated, I look over my shoulder and hold my hand out to help her. She pushes my hand out of the way and climbs on like an expert, using the pegs to steady herself.

Flipping my own visor, I tell her, "This is going to be different than riding on a Harley. You're going to use your core and your legs to stabilize yourself while sitting back on the seat. Can't have you giving me a crushed crotch or a concussion when we knock helmets every time I brake."

She smiles and sits back just a bit, wiggling around to find a comfortable position.

"Bear hugs do nothing but make it difficult to ride, so you can either hold on to my shoulders or my waist. You want to basically mimic my moves on the turns. Just don't try to control them."

"I know. I got it." She rests her hands on my shoulders, but must not feel secure because she lowers her hands to my waist and tightens her grip.

I feel my dick twitch and say a silent prayer, thankful she can't see it. I exhale and lean back.

"You good?" I ask and she nods. "Okay. Hold on tight. I'll try not to go too fast."

"Give it all you got, Hendrix Dare. Don't hold back on account of me." Her eyes hold mine before she flips her visor down.

I'd love to give you all I got, Dagen McCallan. But I don't think this little mouse could handle a snake like me.

Dagen

"BABY, TELL ME THAT YOU WANT ME
YEAH, I'M THINKIN' 'BOUT IT ALL THE TIME
PUT YOUR HANDS ALL OVER MY BODY
YEAH, WE BOTH KNOW OUR EYES DON'T LIE"

Muse
-Isabel La Rosa

EIGHT

HENDRIX WALKS his bike with us on top slowly to meet the others. I see Kinsley already suited up and on Malik's bike, her visor up and a big smile on her face. My nerves begin to grow but not because I'm afraid of the machine I sit on. I'm nervous because of the man on the machine and how badly I want to strangle then kiss the living tar out of him.

My hands were shaking when I walked up to his front door. I'm sure I could've just walked down the long corridor that leads to the interior stairs, but I was too chicken shit to walk into a virtual strangers living room and ask for a cup of sugar. Well it wasn't sugar, but wanting to know if he had some popcorn was basically the same thing.

When that door flew open and I saw his bright blue eyes blazing with anger, my ass crawled into my stomach trying to get away from him. He was definitely apologetic over mistaking me for what I assume are his friends, but it didn't make me want to punch him in the face any less. And if anything, his apology followed by his hand touching my heated skin made me want to climb up his fit body and rub my scent all over him.

And now I sit gripping on to his waist and my legs practically wrapped around him. We pull up right next to Danté and Malik who, might I just say look delicious and terrifying in their own right. When Danté kissed my hand I felt my vagina swoon and faint. I can only imagine the things that man can do with that wicked tongue. Malik's sweet demeanor relaxed me, but I have a feeling he is anything but sweet. To be honest, all three of them look dangerous and like the things that go bump in the night that your parents warn you about.

The engines of the three bikes scream when they start up and I jump, my fingers digging into the thick material of Hendrix's jacket. I take two calming breaths and feel the hot air as it traps in my helmet. I look over at Kinsley and the smile she gives me says that I am in for quite a ride. She winks, gives me a thumbs up, then slams her visor down before gripping Malik's shoulders. His bike jumps as he peels off with Danté close on his heels. My body tenses as I anticipate Hendrix to move next and he lives up to his promise to ride hard and fast.

I jerk back when he punches the gas and we fly down the driveway. I have to restrain myself from leaning in and wrapping my arms tight around his body. My teeth gnash together when he shifts and we leap forward, falling in behind Danté and Malik.

Even with the helmet, the wind whistles as we weave in and out of traffic. I'm not positive but I'm pretty sure lane splitting is illegal in most states. At least, in Texas it is.

The lights flash as we speed down the street and soon we're entering the highway. Now the jitters set in as we go faster and faster and the night turns pitch black, only lit by the lights of the city.

"You doing okay?" a voice asks inside my helmet and I jolt in my seat.

"Um, Hendrix?" I'm so unsure of the voice filtering through and how it's happening.

"Yeah. Bluetooth," he explains.

"Oh. Yeah. I'm good." I shout into my confined space.

"Then hold on tight," is the warning he gives me before switching gears and rushing past the guys to lead the trio.

I let out a yelp and this time, I do lean forward and circle my arms around him, my hands splaying across his chest. My helmeted head rests on his back and I close my eyes, breathing deep. When I feel my heart settle back into my chest instead of my throat, I push back slightly, returning to where I was seated before and tighten my grip.

Hendrix's gloved hands move and I can feel his leg tense as he switches gears. Everything from my eyelash to my toenail polish begins to quake, knowing that once he opens the throttle we're going to fly at lightning speed. It only takes a quick moment when his hand grips the handles again and the scream that comes from my mouth is pulled out from my lungs.

I don't even care anymore. I feel like I may fall off and the last thing I want is for my dad to yell at me as my body gets scraped off the pavement. Especially since I have first hand knowledge of what a motorcycle accident looks like. Clinging to Hendrix, I let my arms snake around his waist and slide closer. The cars come fewer between and I start to grow more comfortable with less vehicles around to slam into. The bike moves around a few, weaving left and right, and I let my body follow Hendrix's lead. My chest to his back and my legs bracketing his, we look like one person zipping down the highway.

"Don't let go. I'm going to do something and I need you to stay calm and keep your hold on me. Okay?" His amplified voice asks.

"Okay. Just be careful, please. I'd like to make it home in one piece." His hand reaches back and pats my thigh, reassuring me he won't let anything happen.

Hendrix squeezes the break, abruptly slowing us down,

and I feel the back tire lift. We ride for just a short distance on the front wheel then we're back on two. Just when I think the tricks are done with, he lets off the clutch and we rise up on the back tire.

"Oh my gah," I yell, but it's filled with excitement.

My heart races and my adrenaline pumps through my veins. A smile stays plastered to my face as we continue to ride through the night until we make it back to his house, luckily in one piece.

All three bikes slow as we crawl up Hendrix's driveway and come to stop in front of his garage. My body is shaking from the thrill of the ride and it's difficult for me to flip my leg over and climb off. Hendrix sees my struggle and grabs hold of me like I'm a two pound doll and lifts me off the bike and sets me down on solid ground.

He unbuckles my helmet and carefully pulls it off. My hair falls in a staticky mess and I just know my face is flushed red.

"That was fucking amazing," I tell him, out of breath.

He gives me a crooked grin and the arch of one eyebrow and it's the sexiest damn thing I've ever seen a man do. I let my eyes greedily take him in, cataloging every inch. Tattoos down his throat that disappear under his jacket and that I know stain his fingers that are covered by his gloves. His close cropped hair and the gleam in his blue eyes. Full pink lips that he likes to lick right before he speaks. And these are just things I've observed in the few hours since I met him.

"Wooowee! That was one helluva ride. Wouldn't you say, Dagen?" Malik pushes back his short, ebony strands and wipes the sweat that beads at his forehead.

Danté swaggers towards us, peeling out of his gear like the devil coming to snatch my soul, a devilish gleam in his eyes. Most would assume this is a persona that he turns on for certain people, but I have a feeling this is just him. No act to put on.

"So. What'dya think? Have fun?" Kinsley bumps my hip

with hers, her helmet still in place and just her face shows with squished cheeks and a wide smile.

"Um, amazing. I was a little scared at first when he was weaving in and out of traffic, but the tricks," I shake my head with wide eyes and a flutter swirls in my belly. "I loved it. It was a definite adrenaline rush."

Malik throws his arm over my shoulders and looks down at me. "I think we got ourselves a crotch convert."

"What?" My head jerks back and my eyes scan the faces of everyone around us.

"Fuck, Mal. Don't say that. It's fucking creepy." Hendrix walks over and takes it upon himself to start unzipping me from my jacket.

My eyes follow his fingers, trying to make out the tattoos that cover them, until he reaches the bottom.

"Crotch rocket," Malik interrupts. "You know. It's what people call our bikes."

I chuckle and Hendrix continues to help me pull my arms free until he holds the black jacket in his hands. Our eyes lock and my chest feels tight, like one of those crotch rockets is parked on it and making it difficult to breathe.

A throat clears and I turn my head to see Malik, Kinsley and Danté watching us, each with a different look of curiosity on their faces. Kinsley looks like she's admiring fireworks burst in the sky while Malik resembles someone holding in a juicy secret. The most threatening of them is Danté. A dark cloud swirls in his black eyes and I can't tell if I should be afraid or turned on. My body seems to think it's the latter.

I squeeze my thighs when images of these three men looming over me, ready to consume every last morsel of their captured prey, flash behind my eyes.

A stuttered breath fills my lungs and I curl my toes in my sneakers. "Thank you for the ride. I really enjoyed it," I tell him and draw snickers from Malik.

Rolling my eyes, I smile and grab Kinsley's hand now that

she's peeled herself from her gear. "Yeah. She *really* enjoyed herself, Henny. Now be a gracious host and grab us some snacks. We forgot to pick some up at the store and we've got a movie to watch."

"Sweet. What're we watching?" Malik bounces on his toes and rubs his hands together.

"*We* ain't watching nothing. Dagen and I are having a girls night. So be gone with you stinky boys. Y'all need a shower. C'mon cornbread sis. Time to gossip." Kinsley drags me to her truck and retrieves her overnight bag.

We shuffle across the driveway and bound up the sleek metal stairs that lead to a balcony overlooking the luscious backyard, complete with swimming pool, and through the sliding doors.

She drops to her back with a thud, then turns to me and says, "I thought y'all were gonna start a forest fire with how hot you're burning for each other."

I knit my brows at her and shake my head. "You're crazy. He's an asshole. A very generous one, but an ass nonetheless."

She purses her lips, holding back a smirk and says, "Hm. But you gotta admit. That boy, despite being a prickly thorn on your hiney, is delicious. And you, my new bestie, looked like you were ready to gobble him up with a side of barbeque sauce."

I laugh awkwardly because I'd rather drink him down like ice cold water on a scorching day. He could definitely quench all my cravings.

A choking like snort pulls me from an uncomfortable

sleep. Kinsley is passed out on her side of the bed, arms spread like a starfish and half hanging off the bed. The sound that pours out from that tiny mouth of hers is ungodly.

I climb out of bed and stretch my arms high above my head, working the kinks out of my spine and shoulders. Kinsley and I stayed up talking until our eyes slammed shut. She spilled more information about Hendrix, Malik and Danté than an overturned semi full of eggs. Apparently the three of them have quite the reputation amongst the women in Cattywump Bay, and likely beyond the borders. It was a reminder that I should stay far away from a man like Hendrix Dare.

But as exhausted as I was having an extremely eventful last three days, my mind was full of worry. Worry over my classes, my parents, feeling guilty for the trouble I've caused, and it kept me tossing and turning.

I tiptoe to the chair sitting in the corner of the room and grab the sweatshirt that I threw over it last night, and pull it over my cherry pajama set. Kinsley dons the matching ones because what else do new besties do but buy matching pj's for a sleepover.

Quietly I walk out of the room and slide the back door open, stepping out onto the patio. The air is chilled and I pull the sweatshirt tighter around my body. I spot a beautiful deck with teak wood and black metal chairs sitting at the edge of the pool, and descend the stairs until the cool grass tickles between my toes.

It's crisp with a cool breeze, but the sky is ablaze in orange as the sun rises, making it look like the clouds are on fire. I sit on the lounger and pull my legs up, cuddling into myself. Laying my head back, I close my eyes to soak in the warm rays. It's peaceful and the soft sound of the water fountain's trickling water has me dozing off within moments.

I jolt when I hear the shutting of a door and my eyes fly open, my heart in my throat. I stay silent waiting to see who or what will come into view. The padam padam of my heart beats loud in my ears and sweat beads on my hairline. I watch a shadow grow larger as it comes closer and I hold my breath.

Hendrix walks by, not seeing me sitting on the chair, and stands at the edge of the pool, a coffee cup in his hand. But the cup isn't what has me picking my jaw off the chair. It's the gorgeous, shirtless man, covered in ink. He wears only a pair of black shorts, exposing all the beautiful art and my eyes gobble up every inch. From his neck to his ankles, roses and snakes, skulls and knives twist and turn over his sculpted muscles.

His hand lifts slowly, bringing the coffee cup to his mouth, and sips. He swallows and exhales deeply and props a hand on his hip.

"Fuck. What am I doing?" I watch the way his Adam's apple bobs when his head falls back.

I give him a quiet moment before interrupting his peace and putting a stop to eavesdropping on anything else he may say.

"Eh em." I clear my throat and he startles. "Sorry. I, um, woke up early and needed some fresh air. I'll leave you to your morning."

I push up off the chair, placing my feet on the cool tile that surrounds the pool, and stand.

"No. You don't have to do that. Sit," he insists, stepping closer to me. "Would you like some coffee, or tea? I have both."

His tone is less harsh than it was yesterday when we first met. It takes me by surprise and I watch cautiously for any sudden change, ready to defend myself. When he doesn't throw out a criticizing follow up comment, I release the tension in my muscles.

"Uh, sure. Coffee would be great." He gives me a short

and quick nod then motions for me to follow him into the house.

I walk behind him and study the intricate details of his tattoos. There's so much going on, it's difficult for me to focus on one thing. So difficult that I run smack into his back when he stops to open the back door.

My cheek sticks to his warm skin and I reach my hands up to steady myself. They end up splayed over his trim waist and I feel the way his muscles flex when I do.

"Oomph." The garbled sound slips from my mouth.

Hendrix hisses and I jump back, seeing that his coffee has spilled over his hand. He switches the mug into the other hand and shakes out the one with the hot coffee dripping off of it.

"Oh shit. I'm so sorry." I rip off my sweatshirt and begin soaking up the coffee.

"It's okay. Really. You don't have to..." His words stop and he turns as stiff as a marble statue.

My hand slows having wiped it all clean, and I remove my sweatshirt then look to find him staring up at the morning sky.

"Your, uh, top has fallen," he tells me, refusing to look at me.

My eyes immediately drop to my chest to see that in my haste to remove my sweatshirt and help Hendrix, I failed to notice that one of my boobs had fallen free from its cherry printed confines. My nipple is pebbled from the cool air as it sits exposed.

I yelp and tug my top up, shoving that bitch back under wraps where she should stay. I'm mortified and I can feel my face burn bright red.

"I am...so embarrassed. I think I will just go back to my room and stay there until you are finished with the car."

I spin on my heels and try to sprint as far away as I can get

–preferably to. the next state– but I'm stopped when a large hand grabs onto my arm.

"No. Don't do that. Come inside and get your coffee. Besides, I barely saw anything."

I look over my shoulder and see his face red and his lips rolled between his teeth as he works to stop the laugh that is wanting to explode.

My mouth presses into a flat line and I smack his bare and hard chest. "Hey," he objects.

I would love to leave my hand right where it is, but I'm afraid that I'd end up on my knees, begging him to make me his concubine. And I can't let that happen.

I pull my hand away like it's been scorched by fire and stick it behind my back with the other. I stop myself from reaching out and rubbing my hand across the smooth plains of his body.

"You're a horrible liar." His face softens and he gives me a boyish grin and shrugs. "Now you owe me coffee and a muffin."

"Settle for a kitchen sink cookie from Miss Shirley?" The door is pulled open and he steps aside to let me pass in front of him, probably to avoid me spilling anymore of his coffee on him.

"I'd trade my car for a dozen of those cookies." My mouth waters just thinking about the way those sweet morsels melted on my tongue.

My bare feet pad across the wood-like tile and admire the beautiful living room, complete with a cozy reading chair and sophisticated artwork. Add in a gourmet kitchen and this is not the house that I imagined a guy like him living in.

"And you gave me shit for having money," I grumble under my breath, not thinking he could hear me.

But of course, that's not my luck. It seems like I don't have any these days.

"The difference is I *earned* every penny I have. Mommy

and Daddy didn't hand it over on a silver spoon." Spinning around, I watch him lean against the kitchen counter and cross his arms over his chest.

I pretend to look at a watch on my wrist and tell him, "Wow. Almost a full eight hours without an insult. Was that difficult for you?"

Hard lines and furrowed brows wipe away any existence of the softer Hendrix that showed himself just a few moments ago. His chest expands and contracts with deep breaths, and I watch the way his nostrils flare. I'm sure if I stood closer to him, I'd hear the clicking of his clenched jaw.

His pink tongue swipes across his bottom lip just before his teeth sink into it. His tight muscles relax when he drops his arms and his gravelly voice asks, "Do you want regular coffee or espresso?"

"Just...a coffee. Thanks." This man is so aggravating and confusing.

He's so hot and cold –but mostly cold– and I wonder if he's like this with every stranger he meets or if it's just me that gets to be the lucky recipient of his foul mood.

With his back to me, he grabs a white, nondescript mug from the open shelf and places it on the sleek gray countertops. He picks up a pot that I realize is actually a french press and pours it into the mug. He pushes the full mug towards me, along a jar with sugar cubes and a pair of small silver tongs.

"There's creamer or half and half in the fridge. Help yourself." He refills his mug, adding one cube of sugar, then walks into his living room where he sits on a modern brown leather chair and acts like I don't even exist.

I add a cube of sugar to my coffee and find hazelnut creamer in his fridge. Once I've prepared my cup o' joe, I stand in his kitchen not saying a word and just sipping my drink.

Hendrix sets his mug down on a side table then picks up

his phone and begins scrolling. I didn't have the foresight to bring mine so I end up just being awkward. My eyes continue to wander around his home, taking in all the details.

"Dagen," my name is called, pulling my attention away from admiring the light fixtures hanging in the kitchen.

"Hm?"

"Come sit please. You're making me anxious and I really don't like feeling that this early in the morning." His eyes are stormy blue and they stare right at me.

"Okay. Thank you." I pick up my mug and carefully walk to his creamy colored couch and gingerly sit down.

The silence that existed while I stood in the kitchen resumes, and now we sit closer to one another, still silent and still awkward. Hendrix continues to scroll through his phone, and I continue to sneak peeks at him, admiring his tattoos and perhaps his face and the body beneath the ink. I decide to break this weird tension and clear my throat.

"Kinsley told me that you and your friends invented some safety gear. Is that what I was wearing last night?"

"Brothers," he replies, his tone cold yet flat.

"Huh? I thought your company was called Dare."

"You said Malik and Danté are my friends, but they're my brothers." He rests his phone on his lap and gives me his full attention. "And yes. The jacket and helmet you wore are Dare Inc. I wouldn't have anyone on my bike wearing anything else."

"Oh. Cool." It's a brilliant response, I know, but it's the only one I got.

He picks up his phone again and I decide it's time for me to go. A person can only handle being ignored for so long, and I've met my limit.

I drink down the rest of my coffee in three big gulps, and burn my damn throat in the process. I stand from his dreamy couch and return to the kitchen where I rinse out my mug and place it in the sink.

"Thank you for the coffee. In addition to all of the other things. I really appreciate it." I pass him a small smile and make for the back door.

"Why don't you and Kins come back down in about thirty minutes for breakfast. You should eat and I was just about to fix myself something before I leave for work." My face must contort into something awful because he adds, "I know there isn't anything, but candy and sodas up in the loft apartment. Just come eat."

"Oh-kay. Thanks." I run the time it will take to shower and brush my teeth and come back looking human.

My hand grabs the cool metal handle and just as I pull the door open, Hendrix calls out, "Oh and Dagen." I look over my shoulder at him. "I lied. I saw everything."

My heart drops to my stomach and the jerk has the nerve to just smile and wink. He licks his bottom lip and now I'm rushing to the shower to cool the heat building between my legs.

Damn that gorgeous jerk.

HENDRIX

"I WANNA DRINK FROM YOUR NAKED FOUNTAIN
I CAN DROWN YOUR SORROWS
I'M GONNA BURN, BURN YOU TO LIFE NOW
OUT OF THE CHAINS THAT BIND YOU"

Wicked Garden
-Stone Temple Pilots

NINE

I SCRUB my face like the soap and hot water are going to wash away what happened with Dagen this morning.

From finding her all cuddled up on my deck chair, her green eyes glowing from the morning sun, to watching her tit fall out of her top, her brown nipple pebbled and looking like it wanted to be trapped between my teeth has my head swirling. Cap it all off with me inviting her back for breakfast and I was totally fucked. Sharing a meal with that girl, watching the way her lips wrapped around a fork and the way her tongue licked the drop of syrup that stuck to it, was the worst kind of torture. At one point, I choked on my fucking bacon, little bits flying out everywhere, when she moaned and closed her eyes upon taking a bite of her pancake. It wasn't even anything fancy. Just some box mix with a little buttermilk, but she acted as if it were heaven in her mouth.

She was fresh faced with wet hair, obviously showered for the day, and clad in denim shorts and a simple white t-shirt. But the outline of her nipples poked right through the flimsy material of her bra and t-shirt. Was she even wearing a bra? *Fuck.*

Meanwhile, Kinsley looked like she'd been tumble dried in a tornado. Her hair was everywhere and she still wore her pajamas which were the same ones that Dagen had been wearing earlier. Let's not forget the eyeliner that was smeared across her eyes, and you had a contrast between the two that was wider than the Mississippi River.

Her voice rings loud in my head, her tone breathy when she said, *"I wish there was a way I could repay your hospitality. But other than what my Dad pays for the repairs to the car, there isn't much I can offer."* I wanted to tell her there were plenty of ways to repay me. Starting with her on her knees, those big green eyes zeroed in on me as I fucked her from behind.

Kinsley snorted when she said those words and I didn't even have to look at her face to see she was holding in a laugh, her blue eyes bulging and cheeks red. It's a face that we all are very familiar with. She's become an unofficial little sister and as much as she drives me nuts, we love her.

Which is why I can't be too mad at her for bringing Dagen into my life. Yesterday I was ready to strangle her when she and Miss Shirley offered my loft to Dagen. Or rather, forced me to offer it to her. Then the bike ride that I know she was in cahoots with Malik and Danté, had me ready to blow her hair back. But the moment I felt Dagen's hands wrap around my torso and her head lay on my back when I popped my front tire, I let all of that aggravation go.

Riding with her on the back of my bike last night was a struggle, because all I wanted to do was throw her down on my bed and ravage her. Each time her fingers dug into my sides, every laugh, every hoot, only made me want her more. The last fifteen minutes of our ride I had to talk myself out of throwing her over my shoulder and locking her in my room once we were home.

I don't know how I'm going to keep my sanity in check for the next thirteen days. I can only hope the guys at the shop can move her repairs to the front of the line.

I press my hands flat against the shower wall and drop my head, letting the water pelt my neck and shoulders. When my eyes close, the sight of Dagen with her tits on full display waiting for me to feast on is vivid and far too real.

I fist my hardening cock and tug it, feeling it grow harder in my hand with each stroke. I think about her body, wet and slick as she coats herself in soap. I can picture her soft hands running up and down her body, caressing all the places I wish I could be. The places I want my dick to be, sliding in out of her wet pussy.

I squeeze and tug once more on my thick shaft and I'm shooting off, cum hitting the tiled shower wall and sliding down the slick tiles. My chest heaves and I see stars and I wait for my breathing to recover. But I don't think any amount of recovery time is going to help because this is a feeling that Dagen can incite by simply smiling.

I am so fucked.

The sound of the torque wrench and air compressor is like a riot for most people. But for me it's a soothing sound, almost like a white noise one would play at night to help them fall asleep. It calms me, and right now it's also helping drown out the thoughts of Dagen that are running unrestrained in my mind.

I stare blankly at a spreadsheet, my eyes trying to make sense of the numbers while my brain has completely checked out, when my door is thrown open.

"If you don't get on that girl then Danté will." Malik comes walking into my office dressed in chinos and a pressed button up shirt.

It's so opposite of who I know Malik to really be. But this isn't Malik Dare, or King as many ladies call him. The man that stands in front of me is Mr. Dare, beloved kindergarten teacher.

"What the fuck are you talking about?" I push away from my desk, leaning back in my black leather chair with the word DARE etched in blue, and cross my arms over my chest.

"Dagen. D said if you aren't going to make your move that he's planning to. And from what I can sense, I don't think you want that to happen."

I screw up my face at him and let my eyes scan him up and down. "Are you a clairvoyant or something? How can you 'sense' that I don't want D to make a move on her?"

With a cocky smirk, he crosses his arms and leans against the door frame. "Henny…you act like I haven't known you for practically my whole life. I know what you look like when you want something. You, Mr. Dare, *want* Dagen. And the fact that she's under your roof and you haven't made a move tells me you aren't just thinking of her for a quick fuck. That would've happened before she had a chance to step foot out of this shop if that's all you wanted."

"Get the fuck out of here with that shit." I grip the edge of my desk and tug my chair along.

I'm pissed and it's only because he's right. If all I wanted was to fuck Dagen and move on, I would've had her feet in the air before I even towed her car. Usually the lip bite has women dropping to their knees, but my attitude towards her was a deterrent. It was the only way to keep me from falling to my knees.

"She's a kid, Mal. Not my type."

He walks in and plops down on my chair and kicks his feet up on my desk. "She don't look like no fucking kid. That girl is all woman and fucking christ, she's dolly."

My fingers pound on the keyboard and steam billows from my nose. He's right and he knows he is, that prick. But that doesn't mean I'm about to do anything about it. She'll be gone in two weeks and until then, I'll keep my distance. She can spend time with Kins and I'll stay busy with the guys. Maybe even find someone else to feed the hunger. But not Dagen.

"So you're just going to let D take a shot?"

My jaw clenches and I hear a ringing in my ears. Thinking of Danté touching her, kissing her, fucking her makes me sick. Not because he's a slimeball, but because I don't want anyone else touching her. It's irrational, I know, but it doesn't make it any less true.

"I don't know what you want me to do about it. If he wants to ask her out, then it's up to her." He snorts and I look up from my keyboard. "What?"

"Well if you don't care, I'll go ahead and give him the green light. I think he wants to ask her to go to Truth and Dare Inc tonight." That has me lifting my eyes to meet his.

Truth and Dare Inc is the bar that we all co-own, however Danté runs more of the day to day operations just as I do this shop and Malik does with our finances and legal shit. He's the number guy. Obviously D and I are more of the hands-on dirty kind of guys.

"Wanna go?" He asks me and I feel like I may jump out of my skin.

I play it off with a shrug then go back to pretending to work. "Yeah. Sure. She'll probably ask Kins to go with her, so we might as well, so that she doesn't feel like a third wheel."

"Right. That's the reason we're going." Malik's feet thud on the floor when he drops them from my desk and stands from his seat. "I better get back to class. I told my assistant that I had an appointment off campus and needed an extra thirty minutes for lunch today."

He smooths down his shirt and pants and leaves through the door. As he goes, he yells out, "If Danté gets his way, don't worry about her going back to your place tonight."

I ball my hands into fists and hear my knuckles crack. It's going to be a long night and I worry that my teeth may end up dust by the time it's all over.

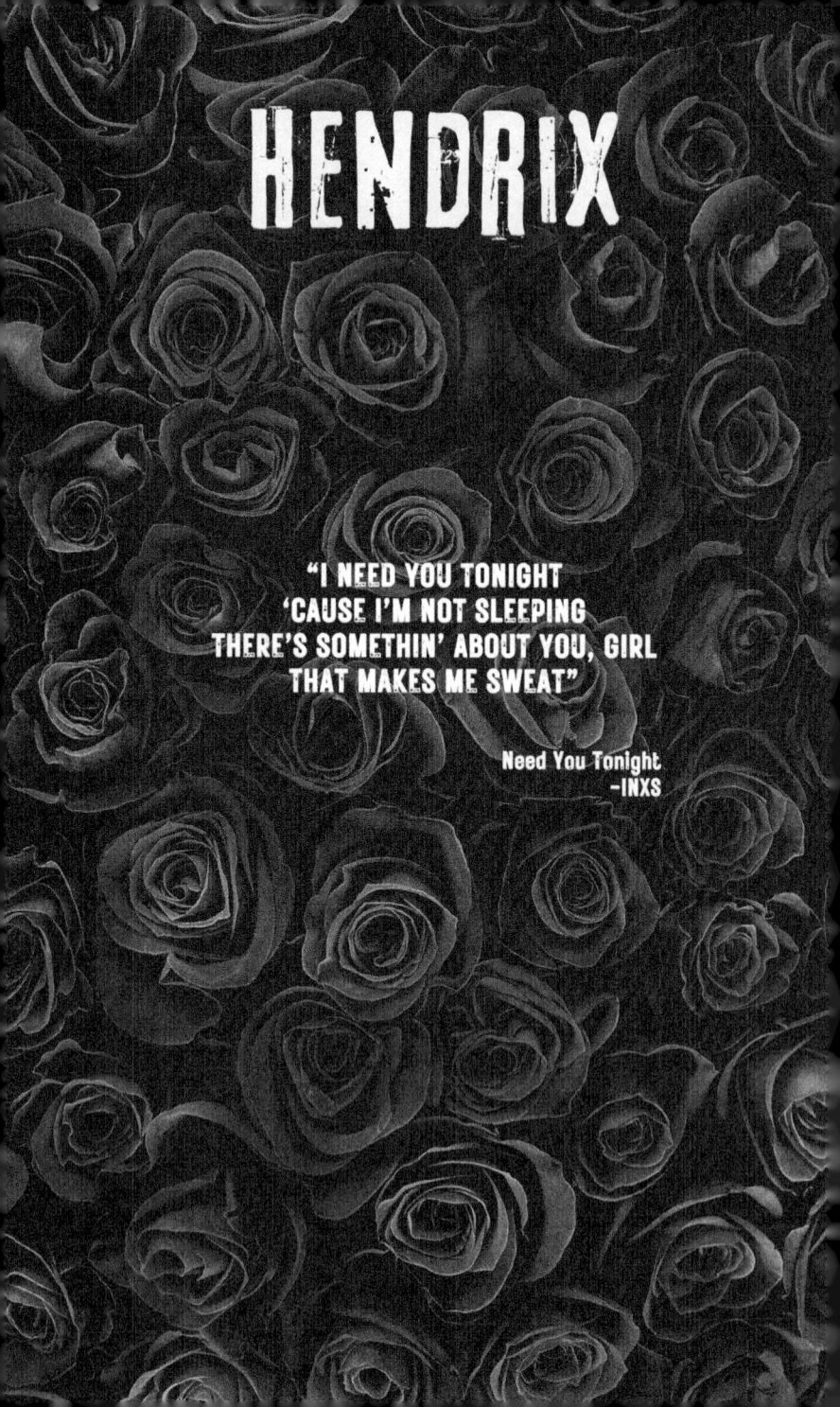

TEN

I STAND LOOKING out of my front window, waiting for the moment I see Danté driving up. I ignored all of his calls and texts today because I couldn't guarantee that I wouldn't tell him to fuck off after hearing from Kinsley that he did, in fact, ask Dagen out. Kins sent me a text that read *'Boy, you better have one helluva good reason for letting D ask Dagen out before you. See you later.'* I didn't bother replying to her either. I simply continued to read the conversation between Danté and Mal with all of the details and ending with them meeting here at my house.

I can hear a distant laughter from where Kins and Dagen get ready in the loft, and I have to close my eyes and count backwards from ten just to keep from punching through this window. My nails dig into my palms the tighter I clench my fists and my ring pinches the thin skin between my fingers.

The rumble of an engine blasts through my irritated mood and I see bright lights grow closer. It seems Danté decided to forego his bike tonight and drove his sleek black McLaren Spider. A two-seater that will only allow for he and Dagen to ride in.

Bastard.

I hear the soft click of heels and look over my shoulder to see Kinsley and Dagen walking down the main staircase and I fucking die.

Kins leads the way, a sly smile on her face, with Dagen right behind her. She wears figure hugging jeans that show off her drool inducing curves. In her right hand she holds a black leather jacket that I hope she never puts on because then I won't be able to stare at her luscious tits that are covered by a black bra that can be seen through a sheer black, long sleeved shirt or bodysuit or whatever the fuck. It's sexy as hell and I want to rip it to shreds.

Instead of heels that I would expect a girl to wear when going out to a bar, she wears black boots that lace up and to be honest, they're sexier than a pair of heels.

Kins comes to stand right in front of me and looks up. "Well?" she asks, her twang thick and sweet.

"Well what, McKinsley?"

Her lips flatten into a thin line and her eyes narrow. "How do we look?"

I look at her up and down exaggeratedly then turn my attention to Dagen, doing the same and pretending I didn't just think about whether or not she's wearing panties to match that bra.

"You ladies look nice," I tell them, then walk away to answer the door and give myself a breather.

The door swings wide before I have a chance to open it, and Danté stomps in wearing his usual all black outfit.

Actually, it's the same outfit that we all usually wear. Black pants, black shirt, black shoes. I strayed from that tonight wearing a white DARE t-shirt with my black jeans and black boots.

Danté lets out a loud whistle and steps closer to Dagen.

"Damn, girl. You're fitting to burn down the house with how hot you look." He takes her hand and spins her around, letting his eyes eat up every inch of her body.

She smiles and blushes then looks over at me. Our eyes lock and she has me spellbound. The world could come crumbling down around us right now and it wouldn't matter because all I see is this mesmerizing woman.

"You ready?" He asks and both she and Kinsley reply with a yes.

"We're waiting for King," I tell D, a little gruffer than I meant for it to sound.

"King is here." Malik walks in through the still open front door with a cheery grin as always, and his arms spread wide like he is truly the king gracing us with his presence.

"Who's ridin' with who?" Kinsley asks.

"Dagen's with me and the rest of you are on your own." Danté takes Dagen's hand and pulls her to the door.

"Oh," she says, looking from where his car sits to him. "I thought we would be on your bike."

"No, baby girl. I need to see that pretty face and I can't do that when it's covered by a helmet."

Her face falls and I see my chance to turn this around in my favor.

"I was planning to drive my bike, if you want to come with me," I tell her.

"Um, well..." Dagen's bottom lip is trapped between her teeth and she looks at one of us and then the other.

"Actually I think I'll drive my car. Kins and Mal, you guys can come with me if you want." I say the words that seem to be magic, because Dagen's eyes light up like a Vegas billboard.

"You're going to drive your Challenger?" Her voice and eyes are full of wonder, like a kid on Christmas.

I nod my head nonchalantly and tuck my hands into my pockets. "Yeah. I don't feel like taking my bikes or my other car, and it's probably best to take minimal cars so we aren't all out on the roads."

Her face freezes and I can see a thought come over her.

"Who's on DD duty tonight?" She asks us.

I lift my hand. "I am. I don't take chances with my green beauty."

She turns her attention to Danté, her eyes questioning. "I mean, I wasn't planning on a sober night."

"Sorry. That's my number one rule. I will not ride with anyone who drinks. I'd rather walk."

"I won't drink, then, if it bothers you. Now c'mon. Can we go already?" Danté grabs her hand again before she can protest and pulls her out to his car.

I nod my head for Malik and Kins to follow me and we pile into my car. "Don't get anything dirty or you will be walking," I warn, and we speed off after Dagen and the guy who may soon no longer be my brother.

Dagen slams back another shot along with Kins, and they wobble in their seats. Danté hangs his arm over her shoulders and watches her tongue when she swipes away the remnants of a drink called Deep Throat.

Malik ordered them for the girls, then gave me and Danté a look like the sneaky bastard he is. All night long he's been doing little things to bait me. It's apparent he knows I'm not really okay with Danté and how hard he's pursuing Dagen. He's been pouring it on thick all night and basically said everything but *come fuck me in my office*.

A little drop of whipped cream sits on the corner of Dagen's lip and Danté leans over and licks it off. It startles Dagen and she jumps back right as his snake-like tongue darts out to wipe it away.

I toss the last ice cube that sits in my glass in my mouth and bite down on it.

"Be back," I grumble, and slam my fist on the table as I slide out of the booth.

I push my way through the crowd, bypassing those who call my name, and step behind the bar.

"Do you need something, boss?" Lainey, our head bartender, asks just as she passes a drink to a customer.

"Nah, I'm good, Lainey. Just filling up my water." She nods her chin and goes back to taking orders.

I pack my glass with ice and throw the scoop back into the bin. For about five seconds I think about filling my glass with vodka instead of water, but think better of it and grab the water spray.

"What's wrong with you?" A terse voice asks from beside me.

I look to my right and see Danté standing there with a hazy fire in his eyes. Despite saying he wasn't going to drink, he's been filling that glass with more than just soda.

"Getting water. Something you should have been drinking all night instead of the jack and coke you've kept in your glass."

I shoulder past him and he clamps his hand on my bicep. "I asked you a question, Henny."

Shrugging him off of me, I take one step back, just far enough that I won't be able to throw a punch and connect. "Nothing is wrong with me except Dagen clearly said she wasn't going to get in a car with someone who's been drinking. Did you even think that maybe there's a reason why she said that? Yet here you are, throwing back drinks like alcohol is going to be banned tomorrow."

"You had your chance with her and you let it pass. Don't sit here and pout now that I have her." His words are slurred and his eyes are glossy and unfocussed.

"You don't *have* her, D. She came here with you. And

when the night is over, she'll be sleeping at my house. Think about that."

I leave him standing there, fuming over my words, and return to the table where the others still sit, laughing and not missing either of us.

"Wait, wait, wait. Let me wrap my head around this. So your uncle is Phoenix West, and your other uncle is Bishop Michaels. And your *other* uncle owns The Wranglers. Did I get that right?" Malik rests his elbows on the table and holds his head like it can't possibly hold another morsel of information.

"Correct."

"How the fuck did your family get so lucky?"

She lets out a soft chuckle. "Well, maybe they aren't family by blood. Like you and Hendrix and Danté, they formed their own family. Bishop and my dad have been friends since they were kids, and Phoenix and Bishop played baseball together in college. Phoenix married my Aunt Vivian who was a sports journalist, and she's my mom's best friend along with my Aunt CeCe who is married to the italian billionaire, Luca Amato, who owns The Wranglers."

I watch Malik shake his head slowly from side to side as he tries to comprehend all of the information she just threw at him. She stays smiling, waiting for him to catch up. And when he does he says, "So can you get me tickets to a Wranglers game?"

I smack his chest and he holds his hand to it like I stabbed him.

"Sure, King. I can get you tickets. I'll do you one better. I'll ask my uncle to give us the owner's suite. We can all go, and I'll block off the cabins at my parents ranch for everyone to stay in. See a game, ride the horses, and shoot some skeet."

"You better not leave here and forget about your promise. I'm gonna show up and you better have a room for me." He tries to lean over the table and hug her, but slips when his hand lands on some liquid.

I move quickly to catch him before he face plants, but end up spilling my water and it splashes on Dagen. She yelps and I abandon Malik for her when she jumps back.

"Shit. I'm sorry." I scoop up the few napkins that litter the table and hand them to her.

"Déjavu," she says and my hands stop moving.

"At least it's not scalding coffee," I add.

A flirty smile crosses her face. "I'm waiting for the nip slip."

I finish dabbing her wet shirt and feel the weight of her stare. "It was more than a nip slip, little mouse."

Her chest expands and I hear her stuttered breaths. The smell of Kahlúa fills my nostrils and I so badly want to taste it straight from her tongue.

"Maybe later, huh?" Her question surprises me and I find myself within an inch of her face, our noses practically touching and our eyes heated as they focus on each other.

"Let's play some darts, beautiful." Danté walks over and grabs Dagen's hand, dragging her out of the booth.

She stumbles on her feet and follows behind him, but her eyes stay locked on me. I keep watching as they disappear in the crowd knowing where they're headed.

"You better get after her before the devil steals her from right under your nose." Kins whispers right into my ear and the words *'steals her'* ring on repeat.

Despite my best efforts to leave her alone, I just can't do it knowing that Danté might get the first taste.

Without speaking a word, I stand up and hear Kins and Mal whoop behind me. I'm pretty sure Kins says something about putting the devil in his place, but I'm too laser focused on Dagen and convincing her I'm not the jerk I've pretended to be.

You lasted a whole twenty-four hours, Hendrix. Chump.

Dagen

"YOU'RE NO GOOD FOR ME
BABY, YOU'RE NO GOOD FOR ME
YOU'RE NO GOOD FOR ME
BUT BABY I WANT YOU, I WANT"

Diet Mountain Dew
-Lana Del Rey

ELEVEN

DANTÉ SQUEEZES my hand and he pulls me to the back of the bar where pool tables and dart boards are stationed. He's a nice guy and ridiculously good looking, but he's also incredibly full of himself.

The entire way here, he talked about nothing but himself and his accomplishments. I admit, it's very impressive. Going from foster care having never stayed in one place too long, to a millionaire before he was twenty-five is a hell of a rags to riches story. But it would've been nice to get a word in or even ask a question about something other than his money and the things it allows him to buy.

We step up to a board and Danté grabs the darts and holds out the blue ones for me.

"Red's my lucky color," he tells me with a wicked grin.

The black of his hair shines like an oil slick and matches his eyes…and his clothes…and his shoes…and basically everything about him including his personality.

He's so opposite of Hendrix. While Hendrix looks dangerous tonight, like a bad choice on a school night, Danté looks like alcohol poisoning at a ditch party. Neither is a good idea, but at least one can lead to some fun whereas the other just lands you in the hospital.

"Mind if I watch?" Hendrix slowly saunters up to the high top table we stand at and rests his elbow on it.

My eyes drink him in like they do every time he's near. Each time, I find something new to focus on. Right now, it's the way the rings of blue fade from azure blue to a dusty gray.

"Maybe you should play," I tell him and hold out my hand. "I'm not very good at darts. Pool, horseshoes, poker, I got those in the bag. But I've never been much of a dart thrower."

"You mean little miss pioneer girl can't throw a dart?" Hendrix asks as he pulls the darts from my grip.

Our hands touch only for a moment, but it sends a tremor of need through my body that I didn't realize it was missing. The look in his eyes is suddenly hungry and I get the feeling that he wants to feast on me. My brain screams to stay back, but my body is already thinking of how quickly it can wiggle out of these jeans.

"Shooting a gun or arrow is not the same as throwing a teeny ass dart at a board and hoping it sticks. The target is usually a tad bit bigger."

"Like what?" Danté asks. "You shooting animals?"

His tone is mocking and it unnerves me. Much like when Hendrix doubted my knowledge on classic cars.

"Sure do. I bagged a two hundred pound Scimitar Horned Oryx last fall on my family's ranch. Bow and arrow. No guns on that beauty. I've got him mounted in the main cabin. Ever shoot a thirty-one inch arrow at a moving target sixty yards away?"

"Sixty yards? Is that all?" Dante's arrogant tone irks me.

"Yes, considering the average distance a bow can pierce through the skin of an animal accurately and lethally is forty yards."

Hendrix snorts and we both look at him as he covers his mouth. Fingers inked with knives and letters hide his full lips that are spread into a smile. Danté looks like he wants to punch him in his face and it amuses me that I was able to not only make Hendrix laugh, but let Danté know I'm not some little woman who can only bake and hold her tongue until she's spoken to.

Fuck that shit. I'll kill the cow and cook you steak when I'm done. I can do it all.

"Let's play, D. What's on the table?" Danté's eyes turn from troubled black sea, to dark but calm waters. "Do we play for money or bikes?"

My shock must fall from my lips because they both turn to look at me.

Danté's lips curl and he says, "Nah. I think we should play for something better. Winner gets a kiss…from Dagen."

My heart skids to a stop and says *excuse me*. These two are betting with my chips and I'm not much of a fan.

"Um, shouldn't I be the one offering that? And since I'm not playing, maybe you should bet with your own money. Or in this case, your own kisses."

"C'mon sweetheart. It's just for fun. A quick kiss on the lips for the winner. No tongue. Nothing more." Danté's brows move up and down and Hendrix keeps his eyes focused on the darts in his hand.

It's a silly kiss, I know, but I'm worried that if Danté wins, he'll want more than I'm willing to give. And if Hendrix wins, I'm worried I'll want to give him more than he wants. My mind battles my will. My eyes move between the two and I chew on the inside of my cheek.

"What's goin' on over here?" Kinsley and Malik finally join us and it gives me a little more courage to have another woman by my side.

"Henny and I are going to throw darts, and we're trying to get sweet Dagen to kiss the winner."

"*You* are trying to get Dagen to give the winner a kiss," Hendrix corrects.

Kinsley looks at me with a sparkle in her eyes. "Aw shucks. A little kiss. You can do that Dagen. I'll make sure these boys keep their hands to themselves."

She winks at me then rolls her eyes in Hendrix's direction like she's trying to tell me something, but I haven't known her long enough and I'm in the early stages of learning to speak Kinsley.

An arm is thrown over my shoulders and I see Malik's tattooed hand. "You mongrels are scaring our new friend away. Back off," he tells them.

I jokingly punch his stomach and tell him, "You're just saying that because you want suite tickets to the Wranglers game."

He beams with a wide mouth and bright teeth and shrugs. "Can't blame a guy for trying."

The four of them stand around, all looking at me and waiting for my answer. Danté looks devious, Malik is far too jovial, Kinsley looks playful, and Hendrix has what looks like a hint of hope in his eyes.

"Fine," I finally concede. "A small, no tongue kiss for the winner."

Danté, Malik and Kinsley all cheer in their own way, and Hendrix stays looking at me, emotionless. I don't really know what to take from that, but I guess we'll see.

The guys are in game four of five and each has one dart left to throw. Danté won the first game with Hendrix winning games two and three. Now Danté leads and I anticipate this going one more round.

We've been laughing and hollering with each point, and it's drawn more attention. Now what was a game between five people is a spectator sport with at least ten others watching.

Danté steps up to the line and closes one eye, trying to focus on the bullseye. He aims and releases. The dart zips through the air and lands with a thunk on the triple ring in the ten spot.

"That's thirty, chump. I don't think you'll beat that. Dagen, sweetheart, I think you better get your chapstick ready." Danté picks up a shot glass that was placed on the table and throws it back.

I definitely won't be riding in the car with him driving.

Hendrix's fingers swipe the corners of his mouth as he stares at the board. He rolls his last dart in his hand and moves silently to the exact spot where Danté just stood. His head dips and he looks at his feet, one angled behind the other, then brings his eyes and his hand to face the board.

He blinks a couple of times then inhales deeply. A large gush of air expels from his mouth and he throws the small dart. I watch as it spirals its way to the board and sticks perfectly in the bullseye.

People around us shout and Kinsley jumps up, giving Hendrix a high five.

"That's fifty, D. Looks like I beat you." He walks over to where I sit at the table and comes to a stop. "Time for me to collect my prize."

He places his hands on my thighs and instantly I'm wet. Swallowing down what feels like a boulder coated in sand, I nod my head and lick my lips. Carefully and somewhat guarded, I lean in, my eyes wide with the nerves that wrack my body. Gradually I move closer and closer until I feel his warm breath mingle with mine.

"Don't be afraid, little mouse. I won't bite," Hendrix whispers for only me to hear.

With every bit of courage, I press my lips to his and immediately know it was a bad idea.

His lips are soft and pillowy and I would love to open my mouth and taste his tongue. Without my permission, a moan works its way out causing Hendrix to lick my lip, breaking the rule of a small kiss only set by me, nonetheless.

Fuck the rules.

I part my lips and invite him in. He wastes no time and quickly wraps his tongue with mine. I feel his hand come to rest on the back of my head and hold me tight to him. I spread my legs allowing him to stand between them, then hang my hands on his shoulders.

We're so lost in the kiss that I forget that we are not only in a public place, but that others are probably standing around watching us. I quickly pull back and gasp, my chest heaving and eyes wide. Hendrix's chest does the same but instead of shock from what just happened, a sexy smirk is splayed across his handsome face.

I look around and see Danté stomping off towards the bar with Malik on his heels and Kinsley watching with a shit grin and flushed cheeks. We make eye contact and she quickly spins on her heels and speeds off to the bar with the others.

Clearing my throat I turn to Hendrix. "I'm sorry. I guess I got carried away. Excuse me." I try to push my way off the chair but he stops me.

"I'm not sorry. Not one bit, little mouse." The noise in the bar is suddenly drown out by the pounding in my chest. "Do you want to go back to my place?"

"Well I am staying there, so yeah." I use my sarcasm to help lighten the tense mood.

He shakes his head slowly. "Not to the room you're staying in. To *my* room."

Oh boy. Here's where the tough part comes into play. I'm

not a virgin, but I have little experience. I'm afraid that Hendrix would do things to me that I've only ever heard Aunt Viv talk about...unfortunately. Lord, I wish I could bleach my brain because I will never be able to unhear the atrocities she spoke of.

"What about Malik and Kinsley? You drove them here. And Danté is far too drunk to drive. I think it would be irresponsible of us to leave them to their own devices."

"I'll take care of it. Don't worry about them."

My brain tries to find other means in which to delay. "I thought you hated me."

"No, little mouse. I don't hate you. It was a front to keep me from devouring you like the way I've wanted to since you hopped out of Kinsley's old blue truck. Now, are you going to walk out of here with me, or do I have to throw you over my shoulder and carry you out?"

Now I'm hot under the collar because how dare he act like I'm just going to run into his bed and throw myself down for him to have his way with me.

"What makes you think I even want to go home with you? You've been nothing but an ass to me and now you want me to just roll over...*literally*."

He stands tall causing me to crane my neck to look up at him. His blues turn dark with a hint of danger that seems to be permanent in Danté's.

"Oh, little mouse. I can smell how much you want me. And if that kiss was any further indication, I'd say you're about ready to lay across that pool table for me."

My jaw drops at his audacity. So what if he's right. I'm not about to let him know that. Instead of arguing with me, he takes my face in his hands and lays another kiss on me. I fall pliant in his hands.

Damn these hormones and his stupid, gorgeous face.

He releases me with a pop and asks, "Are you ready?"

His gravelly voice sends a tingle through my body and

I'm completely helpless. I nod and he helps me off the tall chair and grabs my hand.

We work our way from the back of the bar to the front and run into Danté, Malik and Kinsley.

"We're leaving," Hendrix tells them.

"Alrighty then. Let me just finish thi–"

"No. You misunderstood me," he interrupts Kinsely. "Dagen and I are leaving. I'll ask Lainey to get one of the guys to take you back to my place."

Kinsley mouths "oh" and it's the last I see of her face before I'm tugged straight out of the bar and right into his car.

"Hold on tight, little mouse. You're in for one helluva ride," Hendrix says once we're both inside and buckled.

I'm afraid to ask if he's talking about his car or…

Himself.

HENDRIX

"IS IT THE WAY YOU TALK THAT'S CAUSING ME TO FREAK?
IS IT THE WAY YOU LAUGH THAT'S MAKIN' MY HEART BEAT?
IS IT THE WAY YOU KISS?
IT'S GOTTA BE THE WAY
YOU TASTE, YOU TASTE, YOU TASTE, YOU TASTE
YOU'RE SUCH A GORGEOUS NIGHTMARE"

Gorgeous Nightmare
-Escape the Fate

TWELVE

"I-I," Dagen stutters as we pull into the garage after having been silent the entire drive back to my house. "I think I should just go to sleep. I have some classes I need to check in with early in the morning."

I bring my car to a stop, turn off the engine, and face Dagen. "If you want to go to your room, you absolutely can. I won't force you to do anything you don't feel comfortable with. But I have a feeling that you *do* want to come up to my room. So what's holding you up?"

Her lips roll between her white teeth as she contemplates how to answer me.

"I've known you for a whole twenty-four hours."

"So?" I ask and she freezes once again.

After a long moment she continues, "And I don't sleep with guys I barely know. Especially those who have been big jerks to me."

"I already apologized for that. What else?" She chews on her bottom lip like it's a piece of Juicy Fruit and I reach over, freeing it from her teeth. "It's okay. Why don't we just go inside and talk."

Her chest deflates with a whoosh of breath she was holding.

"It's not…it's not that I don't want to, I just, I don't know. I hope you don't take offense to this but I'm not the type of girl who has one night stands and you, well you seem like that's all you have." She winces and I want to say ouch, but she's absolutely correct.

I shrug and tell her, "I won't apologize for who I am."

"Oh no. I wouldn't expect you to. I'm," she scrunches her face up in thought then continues. "Would it be okay to maybe get to know one another? I mean, I'll be your roommate until my car is done, so it'd be nice to know more about you straight from the source."

"Yeah, sure. And just so you know, I don't really *talk* with women. Kinsley and Miss Shirley are the exception because they're family. I just said that in hopes of convincing you to sleep with me."

Her jaw drops and turns into a smile when she smacks my arm. "You jerk."

"Like Malik said, can't blame a guy for trying." She works hard to hide her smile and I open my door, climbing out and leaning on the roof in Dagen's direction.

When she gets out she faces me and asks, "Can I drive your car?"

"Fuck no. Nice try."

She raises her shoulder and replies with a snarky, "Can't blame a girl for trying."

Her door makes a loud clunk when she closes and I watch her walk towards my house. I won't let her drive my car, but I will let her fuck me in it. Eventually.

When Dagen and I entered my house, I could tell she was still very nervous. Instead of doing any talking, I kissed her cheek and said good night. It was already awkward having made out at the bar in front of half the town of Cattywump Bay, but now she had just turned me down and I really didn't think I could make it through surface conversation without thinking about her tits in my mouth.

She was a bit surprised but gave me a small smile and walked off to the loft. I threw myself on my bed and resisted the strong urge to burst into her room and run my hands over curves. Instead, I jacked off in the shower again to visions of her standing in front of me.

If I keep it up, I'm going to be the cleanest motherfucker in town.

I woke early because I just couldn't face her this morning. I need to give myself some time to decompress and get her out of my mind. So I left a note on her door to help herself to anything she wanted. I ignored the barrage of texts from Malik and Kinsley. Malik wanted to know if she was as wild as he imagined her to be, and Kins asked if we named our future babies. Not surprisingly I didn't hear a peep from Danté.

He doesn't like losing, and he saw Dagen as the grand prize. I'm sure he'll ignore me for a few days then show up like nothing happened. It's what he does. The only emotion that man shows is rage and locks up everything else, so it's best he stays away.

I sat in my office all morning almost completely unbothered except for the additional texts from Kins, and Miss Shirley buzzing me every hour to let me know she was on the phone. I finally decided to spend the rest of the day in the shop and did what I could to speed the repairs on Dagen's car along.

More thoughts of last night bombarded me and how it could've ended. And like a big neon sign, her age flashed and

I heard her dad's voice saying, *"I also have friends who would be fine teaching you a lesson if you are not able to refrain yourself."*

There was only one way that I knew of to rid her from my mind, if only for a night. And that's how I find myself driving to my house with a woman whose face is familiar but whose name I can't remember. She's been in the bar plenty of times, hitting on Danté, Malik and myself, but no one has ever taken her up on her offer. Tonight, when she laid it on the table, I took it.

She's dragging on about her job as…I don't even remember because honestly, her voice is a bit nasally and I kind of shut her out the minute she laughed and it reminded me of Janice from *FRIENDS*.

"Woah. This is your house?" She asks, practically gluing her face to the window as we pull up. I press the button for the third bay in the garage where I usually park my Maserati GranTurismo.

The Challenger is reserved for those who can appreciate it. People like Danté and Malik and Kinsley and…Dagen.

I park in the usual spot, exit the car, and walk over to help –fuck, what is her name– out. She holds onto my arm as we move from the garage to the breezeway that connects it to the house and into the mudroom. Every room we walk into gets commentary from her and it grates on my already thin nerves.

When we step into the den I tell her to take a seat and offer her a glass of water. She makes herself comfortable on my couch and when I return, the very short wrap dress she wore hangs open, revealing the fact that she isn't wearing a bra. She stands up, still wearing her sky high heels, and struts over to me.

With her hand pressed to my chest, she pushes me back until I drop to my chair, then straddles me.

"Let's not waste any time. Okay?" She tells me, lowering

to sit in my lap. "I like it rough so don't be afraid to really hurt me."

Her tongue flicks my earlobe and I close my eyes. She's not the beautiful brunette with green eyes, but it doesn't really matter what she looks like. I just need her to fuck Dagen out of my mind.

I let my hand glide down her back and squeeze her ass, digging my fingertips into her flesh. My dick begins to twitch, impatient and wanting to dive into her already. Her lips work their way down my throat and she grinds her already wet pussy down on me.

Just as she slides her hands under my shirt, I hear a high pitched yelp. My eyes fly open and I find Dagen standing at the bottom of the stairs and her hand over her eyes.

"Oh my gosh. I'm sorry. I was just—" she spins on her heel and smacks into the iron rail and stumbles.

The woman still seated in my lap, her hands now cupping her bare breasts, simply watches Dagen but doesn't budge an inch.

"Dagen, hold on. Can you," I wiggle underneath her and try to slide out. "Get up please."

She places one foot then the other on the tiled floor just as Dagen rushes up the stairs.

"Does your little sister live here too?" She asks me.

"Dagen is not my sister. She's, you know what, just wait here." I run up the stairs taking them two at a time, but don't catch Dagen before she runs into the loft and locks the door.

I step up to the closed door and knock. I don't know why I have to fucking knock on a door in my home, but I do.

On the other side I hear a muffled, "I'm so sorry, Hendrix. I didn't mean to barge in on you. I was just coming down to get some water."

I rap my knuckles on the door once more. "Dagen. It's okay. Don't apologize. I told you to make yourself at home. I'm the one who should've been more considerate."

I wait for a silent moment then hear the lock click. She pulls the door open slowly and I get a better look at her. She wears different pajamas than the ones she wore the other night. Instead of cherries, she wears plaid boxer style shorts and a matching t-shirt that looks like the bottom half was chopped off, exposing her belly button. My eyes eat up every inch of her smooth skin, from her perfect toes to her shapely legs, and ending on her vibrant eyes.

"Do you want to come back down?" I ask her.

"No thank you. I'll pass. Why don't you go back to your guest." She braces her arm against the door frame and her giant bun flops to one side.

I lick my lips and push a tendril of hair off of her face. "Why don't I get rid of my guest and you can come back downstairs."

Her face twists up and her lip curls. "Are you serious right now?" I nod my head and she bats my hand away. "You want me to go downstairs and take the place of that bimbo that was on your lap? You're a pig. Thank god I didn't sleep with you last night. I would've hated myself for it today."

She steps back then slams the door in my face. *My* door.

Maybe I was a little out of line with that comment, but it didn't stop me from sending my guest home in an Uber and an apology. After she left I took another fucking shower because I can't help myself. And if I can't have Dagen, I at least have my imagination.

Dagen

> "NOW I'M GETTIN' IN THE CAR,
> WRECKIN' ALL MY PLANS
> I KNOW I SHOULD STOP, BUT I CAN'T
> AND I TOLD MY FRIENDS I WAS ASLEEP
> BUT I NEVER SAID WHERE OR IN
> WHOSE SHEETS"
>
> Bad Idea Right?
> -Olivia Rodrigo

THIRTEEN

"HE SAID THAT?" Kinsley asks, a mouthful of potato salad and little bits flying out of her mouth.

After my encounter with Hendrix last night when I walked in on him and his friend, I texted Kinsley a summarized version of what happened, but she said that she needed every last detail. She showed up with lunch and a box of wine, and said we are sitting out by his pool until every drop of wine is drunk and every ounce of tea is spilled.

"Yup. And he was one hundred percent serious. I took one step back and slammed the door in his face. I can't even believe he thought I would thank my lucky stars for giving me a chance to fill a previously occupied spot on his lap. What a pig."

I take a bite of the chicken salad sandwich and watch her shake her head in shock.

"That son of a billy goat. I can't believe he thought you would go for that. He's so dumb he could throw himself on the floor and miss. I swear."

I smirk at yet another Kinsley-ism that I'll have to stick in my back pocket for just the right time.

"So...d'you think you'll still hook up with him?"

I freeze and tug on my ear, trying to figure out if I heard what I think I did.

"Kinsley. Did you not hear what I said? You think I want to sleep with him after that?"

She takes a swig of her glass of wine and nods her head. When she pulls it away from her lips she says, "Yes, I most certainly think you want Henny to grind your corn. I say you go for it."

"Grind my cor—you know what, just no. The last thing I will ever do is have sex with Hendrix Dare. He's a pig and I had temporary amnesia the other night, but he quickly reminded me what an asshole he is."

I pop a chip into my mouth to punctuate my statement, making the point to both her and I. Because, I'm not going to lie, I did think about taking him up on his offer. If my brain hadn't started working again, I would have followed him right back downstairs and helped him kick that woman out on her ass.

My phone begins to ring and I wipe my hands off on the napkin and flip it over to see Dad's face on the screen.

"Hold up," Kinsley says, and stops me from swiping my screen and answering the call. "Is that Daddy McCallan? Good gravy. You wouldn't by any chance be open to a stepmama only slightly older than you, would ya?"

I tug my hand away from her. "Gross. Stay away from my Dad. My mom will gut you if you lay a finger on him." She shrugs as if to say *I tried*, and I finally answer the call. "Hi Daddy."

"Hey baby bird. How are you doing today?" His voice is welcoming and the equivalent of a warm hug.

"I'm good. The same as when I texted you this morning… and last night…and yesterday afternoon." Much like his voice, my tone is currently that of an eye roll.

"I just worry about you. Is that man feeding you? Has he been any sort of inappropriate with you?" If I was hooked up to a lie detector, the needle would be going off the charts with as much as I'm about to lie right now.

"Hendrix has been very accommodating. He's quite nice and has been gracious enough to let me use basically his entire home. He even invited me to join him and a group of his friends for dinner the other night."

"Well that was nice of him. But you didn't answer my other question. Has he been inappropriate with you? I need to know if I should get Luca on the phone and have him employ some of his shadier family."

"Oh my god Dad, no. Stop that. Hendrix has been nothing but a gentleman with me. You have nothing to worry about." Visions of my Dad and Zio Luca, along with some Italian gangsters, filing off a private jet and ready to dump Hendrix in the Mississippi Bay fill my head.

Kinsley does a comedic level spit take when Hendrix's name is followed by the word gentleman. I shush her and she covers her mouth, tears of laughter rolling down her cheeks. My Dad is already suspicious about everything. I don't need him catching Kinsley cackling in the background sending up his hackles even more.

"Well that makes me feel a helluva lot better knowing I can trust that man to keep an eye on you. I can't have my baby bird alone and scared and so far away." His voice softens like he's speaking to my three year old sister, Autumn Jade.

"Dad. In case you've forgotten, I live three hours away most of the year. It's not like this is the first time I'm away from home."

With a sigh he tells me, "Yes, but even at school you're still in the state of Texas. This has given me a glimpse at what it would feel like to have you living so far away and I don't like it."

I forget sometimes that before Mom and Sloane and AJ came along, it was just him and I. We were not only father and daughter, but best friends too. When mo-Stephanie died, he was all I had. We only stayed in Florida a few months after she passed away, and even though Grams and Pops and Uncle Hayes were waiting for us, our little family was now Vaughan and Dagen. So the fact that the thought of him and I being separated by more than a few hours is unbearable, isn't totally ridiculous.

He cried more than Mom did when they dropped me off at college. Mom got all of her crying out early which I'm fully convinced sent her into labor on my graduation day. But by the time move-in day was upon us, Mom was calm while Dad was bawling his eyes out like I was heading off to war.

"Well rest assured Dad, I am just fine and will be home before you know it."

"Possibly sooner than later," he tells me.

"Oh?" My stomach drops, not sure what he means by that.

"Yeah. Hendrix called me this morning and said he was doing what he could to get the few parts needed sooner so that he can get you back on the road to home. He said he's made our car a priority."

"That's, uh, that's really nice of him." Silly as it may seem, my feelings are hurt knowing that he wants me gone as soon as possible.

I can only guess it has to do with me turning him down not once, but twice. I suppose he thought he'd get a little bit more than monetary payment out of this deal and now that he knows he won't, he wants me out of his house asap. I'm sure my interruption last night was a major kink in his plans.

"It is. I've already told him that I would love to shake his hand in person one day. You know, look the man who took care of my baby bird in the eye and thank him personally."

"Yeah, that would be something Dad." In the background I hear Uncle Hayes yell out.

"Uncle Hayes says hello but that he needs me in the barn. Make sure to call Mom later. She's missing her best gal pal."

"You two have serious problems," I joke but in all honesty, I miss them too.

The last few days have been more than a rollercoaster, and I could really use a hug from Mom, then crawl into her lap while she combs her fingers through my hair. It's those small comforts that mean so much more when they seem so far out of reach.

"I'll call Mom when Sloane and AJ are home so I can talk to everyone at once. Love you Dad."

"I love you too, Dagen Rayne." I can hear the smile in his voice and it causes a lump to form in my throat.

I press end and see Kinsley watching me, her spilled wine and tears now dry.

"How did you manage to keep a straight face when you told your daddy Hendrix has been a gentleman?"

"Hush your face." I tuck my phone in my pocket, then take a seat at the edge of the pool and dip my feet in. "Technically he is a gentleman in the original sense of the word. He aided a woman in her time of need. That is most definitely gentlemanly."

With an arch of her brow she asks, "Oh yeah? Was it gentlemanly when he wanted you to ride his pogo pony?"

"You know, you should really meet my Aunt Vivian. You two would really get along." Every euphemism, every off-collar comment makes me think the two of them are long lost siblings.

"If she's anything like me then I assume she is fabulous." She purses her lips and flips her sunglasses down over her eyes.

I may not be home with my family and friends, but Kinsley has definitely made me feel like a piece of them are here with me.

I'm sitting on the bed, clicking through page after page of my online textbook not really seeing anything, when a knock comes at the door. I assume that since Kinsley is at a family dinner –which she invited me to but I told her I had homework– that it is Hendrix standing on the other side.

I pad over to the door, my bare feet cushioned by the plush rugs, and slowly open the door. Hendrix stands on the other side, his arm braced on the door frame, and it's an instant kryptonite.

"Hey," he says, giving off all kinds of smolder.

I don't think it's intentional, it's just him. Most men have to work at exuding sexiness, but I think it was programmed into Hendrix at birth.

"Hello," I respond, somewhat curt and robotic.

Hold strong Dagen. Don't let him break you with those ocean blue eyes.

"I was wondering if you'd be interested in going to dinner with me?" I watch him with consternation, just waiting for him to add something crass.

When he doesn't, I quickly try to think of an excuse as to why I can't.

"Oh, thanks for the offer but I just ate," I lie, but my stomach betrays me like a little bitch and growls ungodly loud.

Hendrix's eyes fall to my stomach and he smirks.

"Well apparently it wasn't enough if that sound is any indication." My face burns red with embarrassment. "C'mon. It's just dinner and I owe you an apology after my behavior last night."

I narrow my eyes, skeptical of his words. "Why are you

being nice to me? This seems like some type of ruse to get me to do...*things*. Like, oh I bought you dinner now you owe me dessert."

He chuckles and I freaking want to melt. Why did the Lord make him so beautiful? And why did the devil practically drop me at his front door? Did I somewhere, somehow, make a wish to be put through an emotional wringer only to be tortured by the sexiest man I have ever seen?

"There's no ruse, Dagen. I know that Kinsley is out for the evening and you don't have a vehicle. I may be a jerk, but I certainly do not want to see you starving to death."

I inhale a deep breath and it was the goddamn wrong thing to do because now my lungs are filled with his scent. Cedar and Bergamot and a hint of motor oil mix to form the perfect aphrodisiac. A man like him knows what the smell of woodsy and hard working man does to women. It's like a call for horny women everywhere that a man is on the hunt.

I think for a moment knowing he's right because I am starving and I should've planned more efficiently and conserved some lunch or at least asked Kinsley to take me to the store to grab some chips and bananas to get me through the night.

Don't judge. It's called girl dinner.

"Fine. I guess I could use more than a piece of gum to settle my stomach."

"Why didn't you just go down to the kitchen and get yourself something? I told you to please help yourself." The look of concern is quite unexpected.

"I didn't want to interrupt you if you happened to be entertaining this evening." His face grows hard and I see a sort of wall go up, but it quickly crumbles.

"That was horrible on my part. I'm just used to being alone so I've never had to worry about privacy before. I was a little out of my mind last night, so I wasn't thinking clearly."

Studying him, I decide he seems genuinely apologetic and

just let it go. What's the big deal, anyhow? I don't know him from a hill of beans –thanks a lot, Kinsley– so it shouldn't irk me so much that he had a woman here that he was definitely going to do the dirty with right in his living room.

"Let me grab my shoes and my wallet," I tell him and turn toward the nightstand where my wallet sits and my shoes at the edge of the bed.

"You won't need your wallet unless you plan on drinking."

I freeze with my foot halfway into my sneaker and look up at him. "I can't let you do that. You paid for the bar the other night and have allowed me to roam your house while at work."

"Sorry little mouse. No woman, mine or not, will pay for a meal when I'm around. We can argue about this all night, but I know you're hungry so let's just go." He winks at me and my core yells at me to just sleep with him already.

Down bitch. It's been four days.

I finish getting my shoes and tuck my wallet into the back pocket of my shorts. I flash a look in the mirror as I pass to ensure that I don't look like trash on garbage day in the summer.

"You look fine. Trust me." His voice turns low and I shiver from my ears to my toes.

I walk past him and he shuts the door behind me. I may put a teensy bit of extra sway into my hips, but it's purely unintentional. I'm simply trying to free a wedgie.

Or so I tell myself.

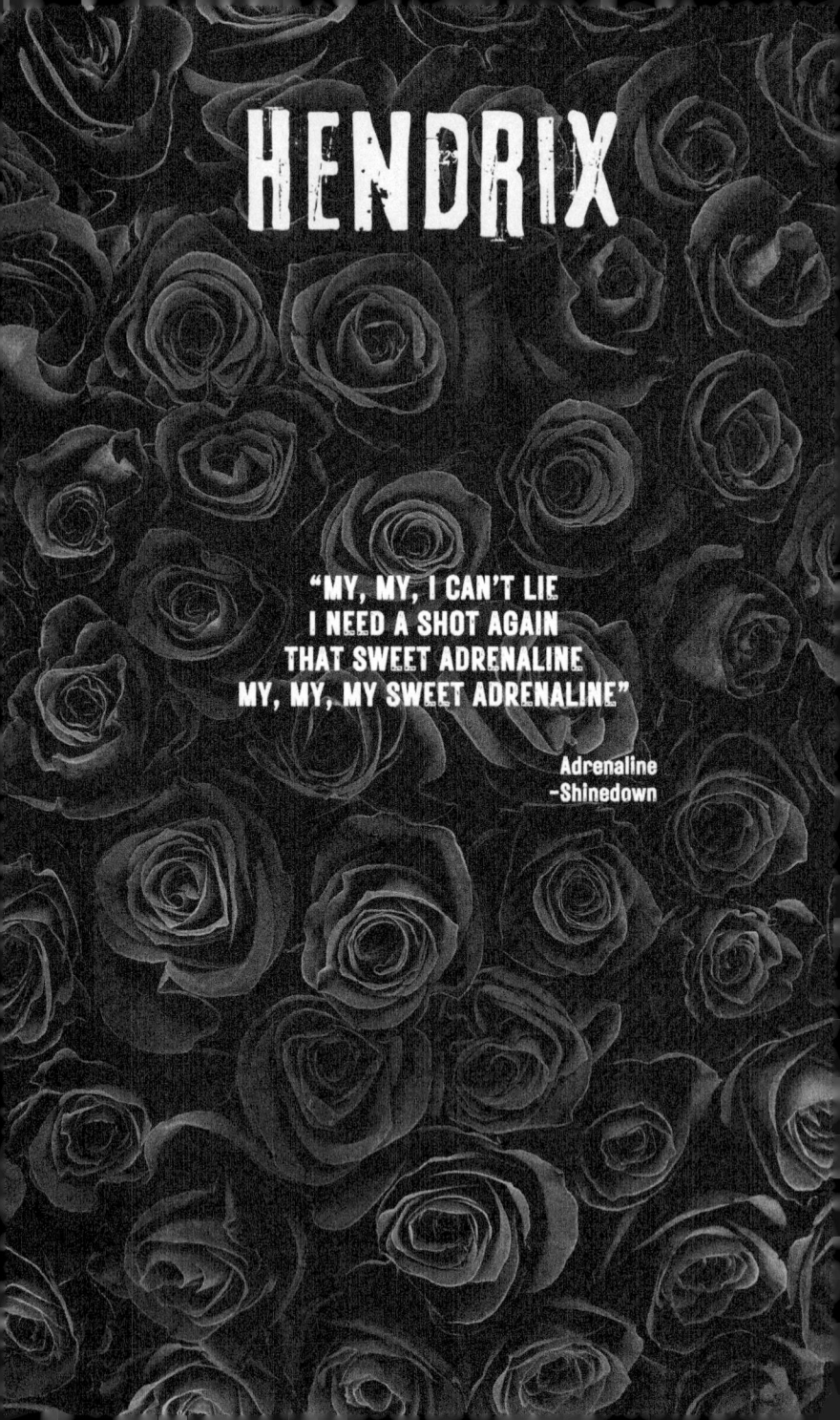

FOURTEEN

SPEAKING with Dagen's dad today made the guilt I already felt for the way I acted last night just fester for the rest of the afternoon.

"I really appreciate you looking after Dagen in addition to the repairs. There are a lot of creeps out there and man to man, I'm relieved to know you're one of the good ones." Sure, if one of the good ones means imagining your daughter riding me and screaming my name then I am the best you'll ever meet.

I also got yet another lecture from Kinsley letting me know I was acting like a tool and if I ever wanted to make cute babies with Dagen, I needed to quit being a jerk and make her smile instead of frown. No one said I wanted to make babies with Dagen. I wouldn't mind making the beast with two backs, but babies are just a far fetched fantasy.

Dagen seemed to perk up a bit when I asked her if she'd like to ride my bike again and now we sit at Wok This Way, waiting for the massive amount of food I ordered.

"I really am sorry for being so horrible to you."

"Why were you?" The small paper lantern on our table flickers and lights up the green in her eyes like sparkling jewels.

With a sigh I ask, "Truth?" She nods her head because it was highly unlikely that she'd want to be fed a bullshit story. "You're gorgeous and it was my defense mechanism."

Her face does this thing where it pales, but her cheeks heat to a bright red. It's clear that I have shocked her, but it really shouldn't be that much of a shock. I mean, I did try to sleep with her just hours after we met. That was pretty much a dead giveaway.

"How did you come to be in Cattywump Bay?" I ask her, trying to change the subject and salvage the rest of the night.

However I don't think I really accomplished that. In fact, I may have made it worse if the look of nausea on her face is any indication.

"It's okay. You don't have to tell."

"No, it's fine. It's just…" Her fingers twist the napkin she holds and I can sense her hesitation. "It's a long story with a lot of fucked up stuff, but I'll try to edit it as best as I can for you."

She takes a deep breath before starting, and the words that follow leave me completely speechless.

"I recently found out that the woman who birthed me actually conceived me after slipping my Dad some drugs and taking advantage of him while he was unconscious. Basically she raped him, then said she'd take me away from him unless he stayed with her."

"Holy fucking shit." My stomach drops and if possible, I feel even worse for lying to her father about not having ulterior motives to allowing her to stay with me.

"Yup. Fucking shit is right. When I found out that not only had my Mom and Dad kept it from me, but that my grandparents –the rapist's parents– knew all about it and threatened to take me away from my Dad, I kind of lost my mind. So I did the only logical thing I could think of, and took off in my Mom's car –technically my step-mom but she's more than that– and drove all the way to Florida to confront them and tell them to go to hell where their daughter surely is."

I'm trying really hard right now to say something other than *I'm sorry* because that would just be an idiotic thing to say. But how does one respond to a story like that?

"I was abandoned by my drug addicted mother after she decided that I was in the way of her lifestyle when I was four." Welp, I guess that is clearly the answer I could come up with.

"Looks like we're two fucked up peas in a pod," she jokes, a placating chuckle on her lips.

"I'd say so. But the good news is that you have parents that very obviously care for you. I went fourteen years without anyone wanting to adopt me."

She swallows and almost looks guilty for the fact that she had people that wanted her so badly that they were willing to do anything to be in her life. Including marrying someone who violated them in the worst way.

"Not to be disrespectful or anything, but why didn't your dad press charges?"

She shrugs with a sigh. "From what I understand, he didn't think anyone would believe him. A nineteen year old boy accusing a woman of raping him. He was drunk and on drugs –unbeknownst to him– so she could've easily turned the story around. Who would have you believed?"

"Damn. You're right."

We sit in silence for a moment longer before our food is placed on the table. We fill our plates and take the first few bites before we speak again.

"So," she starts. "You met Malik and Danté while you were at a foster home together?"

Nodding, I tell her our story. "We all ended up in a group home for boys when we were fourteen. Miss Shirley was the director there, which is why the three of us take such good care of her now. We put her through hell."

Dagen chuckles softly and says, "I have no doubt about that."

I fling a soybean at her and she dodges just before it hits her on her forehead. "D and Mal and I didn't really care for one another at first, but all it took was one night of underage drinking and idiotic dares to bring us together."

"And the rest is history?"

"Exactly. When we aged out of foster care, we decided that we'd make our own family. The three of us legally changed our last names to Dare and that's how we became brothers."

"Was this before or after the millions of dollars came? Which, by the way, you are a huge hypocrite."

I don't like talking about money. Growing up with none and suddenly having more than you can spend in a lifetime is a huge life shake up. Some people roll with it and show off their money, searching for the status and approval that they didn't have before. Example: Danté. Then there's me. Yes, I buy nice things. But my home is the only one I own and probably the only one I'll ever own because I designed it how I wanted and I don't want to have to go through that process again.

Everyone in town knows our story. Those who abandoned us came running with their hands out. There were very few who actually realized we were boys in need of guidance and love. Those people –Miss Shirley, Officer Ulrich and his wife, and our high school principal Mrs. Kirkland– we made sure to thank them in whichever way we could.

But even with all of that, I still like to keep to myself and fade into the background. I let Danté be the star that he's always wanted to be. I'm just the cranky rich asshole who doesn't like people that is either hiding in his home or riding bikes with his brothers.

Dagen still stares at me, waiting for me to say something. "How about we not talk about shitty moms or money?"

"I like that idea." She smiles and it instantly brightens the dim restaurant.

Kind of how it brightens my dark mood, and I'm not sure if I like it.

We spent another hour eating and talking and I did something I haven't done in years with someone other than my brothers. I laughed. Not one of those courteous laughs you give to strangers, but an actual feel it in my belly laugh.

"Did you want me to go ahead and drive?" She asks as we gear up for the ride home.

Another laugh expels from my mouth along with a smirk. "Nice try, little mouse, but that won't be happening on my watch."

"Why not? I've driven my Dad's Harley before?" She tugs her helmet on and flips the visor open.

"A Harley is a lot different than a Superleggera V4." I tug my gloves on, wiggling my fingers to ensure they're snug.

"I doubt that. A motorcycle is a motorcycle. Two wheels, two handles. Same."

A mischievous idea blooms. "Okay, little mouse. You let me take you on a real ride meaning I get to really open it up. If after our ride you still feel like you can handle a machine like this between your legs, I'll teach you to ride."

She smiles and flips her visor down and I swear I hear her mumble, "Maybe you can show me how to ride a different kind of machine."

"Huh?" I ask.

"Oh nothing," she says quickly and climbs on back.

She may not be ready to admit it, but I know what she

said. And though she may think she knows what she wants, I'm willing to show her what she needs.

I throw my leg over my prized possession and get situated. This baby isn't a mass produced bike and it's the one item I would've happily spent my fortune on. Who cares that it was made to race on a track. I wanted it in my hands and I was going to have it no matter what anyone said. So the thought of anyone driving it but me makes me want to crawl out of my skin. The fact that Dagen is riding with me is a feat. No one rides this bike but me.

I tap a button on my helmet then turn around and do the same to Dagen's helmet to connect the bluetooth speakers. Once they're paired up I tell her, "The other night, I took it slow. This bike is much more powerful than I let on. I took it easy on the ride over, but I won't hold back now. Engage your core muscles and if at any point you get scared, grip tight and just tell me to stop. Got it?"

"I got it but don't worry. I won't tell you to stop. I want all that you got."

My body tingles with her words, wanting them to mean more than just a fast ride.

"Be careful what you wish for, little mouse." I turn my back to her and when she places her hands on my shoulders, I move them to my waist.

I put my gear into neutral and turn the fuel tap on. Moving the choke, I press the electric start and listen to my bike roar to life. The vibration that it sends through my body is an adrenaline rush. I've never felt happier than when I'm on my bike. Tonight the rush is amplified with Dagen on the back.

My Superleggera V4 has a free-rev engine and it loves to talk. Once I get the motor spinning at ten thousand rpm's, Dagen is really going to wish she hadn't told me to give her everything.

The sound is ear piercing and I feel her hands grip me tighter.

"Ready?" I ask her.

"Um, yes?" Her confident voice only minutes ago sounds like she's already regretting her words.

"The torque has a big kick," I shout over the motor. "We're going to take off fast." I reach around and give her thigh a squeeze, assuring her that I got her.

One second we're standing still on my beast, and the next we're flying down the street at eighty miles an hour. Her voice squeaks and her hands wrap around my waist as she grips on for dear life.

I split between slow moving cars until I get on the highway. It's quiet tonight so I decide to take her down to the gulf, taking the long way from one highway to the next.

It isn't long before she's relaxing and falling into my sway like the other night, despite the speed I'm going. I can feel the rapid rise and fall of her chest and I realize mine moves to the same beat. Our gear makes it difficult to really feel everything, but I feel her fingers splay over my stomach. They creep their way to the hem of my jacket and work under the snug fit. She doesn't wear gloves like I do and the soft skin of her fingers ghost over my heated flesh. My muscles flex and my hands grip tighter on the handles as we speed faster down the highway. The tension in her body leaves and we fall into a comfortable silence.

Twenty minutes pass by when we cross the Bay St. Louis Bridge and roll up straight to Henderson Point Beach. I pull my bike off the highway and into the small parking lot that sits along the sand. I turn off the engine and throw my kickstand down.

When we're met with silence, I look over my shoulder and see Dagen pull off her helmet and her long brown hair tumbles over her shoulders. Sweat coats her forehead and I pull my hands free from the gloves and reach over to wipe it away. Her eyes glisten under the moonlight and I want to drown in them.

Climbing off, I turn around and sit back down facing her and leaning back against the gas tank. My helmet gets pulled off and I start to undo the zipper on my jacket. Dagen's eyes watch every tooth as it pulls apart from the other. It's a slow tease and she's a captive audience.

When my jacket is open, giving me a little more room to breathe, I do the same to hers.

"So what do you think? Still wanna learn to ride?"

Her eyes grow wide and she gulps with a nod. "Yes. More than ever."

Smirking, I tell her, "That's not what was supposed to happen."

"What was supposed to happen? Were you expecting me to run scared?"

"Well, yeah."

She leans forward, bracing her hands on the seat and whispers, "I think you've found a side of me that was waiting for the right person to unlock it. And now I want more."

This little mouse may have bitten off more than she can chew.

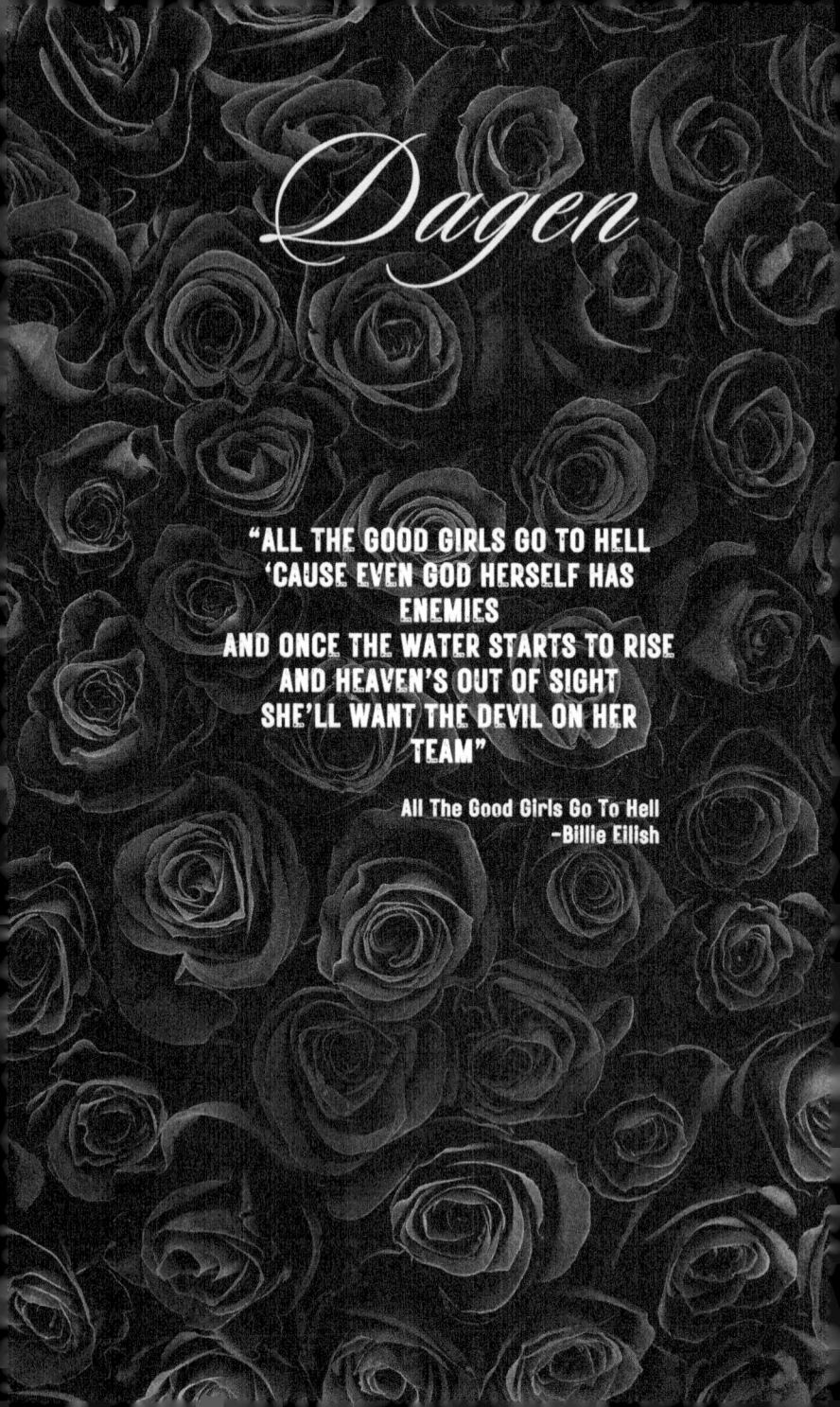

FIFTEEN

A DEVILISH SMIRK dances across his handsome face and I lock my lips to his. The cool breeze from the gulf brushes my hair against my cheek and Hendrix smooths it back and cups the back of my head. He holds me to him tightly and dives into our kiss. He draws out a moan and I find myself scooting closer to him until my legs wrap around his and he's leaning me back on the seat.

My hips roll and through the thick denim of his jeans, Hendrix's dick hardens and pushes up against my thin leggings. Our jackets are still on and we work to free ourselves from the constricting leather that holds us back from letting our hands explore.

When our jackets sit on the asphalt, Hendrix's hands dig into my ass and he massages each globe, his fingers pinching my flesh. He must tire of the fabric separating us because he slides his hands down the back of my pants, working to feel my skin against his.

"Is this the more you were wanting, little mouse?" he mumbles, our lips still pressed together.

"No. More, Hendrix. I want even more."

He groans and rips his mouth from mine. "Fuck, Dagen. We are at least fifteen minutes away from my house."

"Then you better drive fast, Mr. Big Bad Wolf."

With a crooked grin he asks, "Big Bad Wolf?"

I nod and explain. "Yes, because I have a feeling you're going to eat me alive."

"Oh little mouse. You have no idea."

He grips on to my waist and adjusts me on the seat. His legs are thrown over the side of his bike and he grabs at the clothing we just discarded.

"Hurry. Put these on." He holds the jacket open for me and I slide my arms in.

He hurriedly zips me up before placing the helmet on my head and securing it, then rushes to slip into his jacket and gloves and helmet.

"Hang on," he growls and I wrap my hands around him.

He fires up his bike and the loud turr of the engine breaks over the sound of the crashing waves. A hand reaches back and splays over my ass, pulling me closer to him until I'm practically glued to his back.

"Just like I thought. Perfect backpack," his gruff voice says through the bluetooth speaker.

My head jerks as he tears off and I count down the miles until we get to his house.

The garage door opens at the slowest pace and Hendrix revs the motor anxiously. Once there's enough room, he whips us inside and comes to a screeching halt.

Our helmets meet the concrete floor with a crash and I gasp.

"You're going to scratch them."

"I can buy a thousand goddamn helmets, but I'll only be able fuck you for the first time, once."

We jump off his bike and he grabs my hand, pulling me through the garage and across the breezeway into the house. He doesn't stop, dragging me through the living room and down a hallway that leads to what I assume is his bedroom.

The door flies open and I see the outline of furniture under the dim moonlight that filters in from the windows. He doesn't bother with the lights nor closing the door. I guess since we're the only ones here, why worry about things like privacy.

I'm dazed when he lifts me up over his shoulder and yanks my shoes off.

I screech and remind him, "I can do that. I'm not a child."

"You can't do it fast enough, and I need you now." My shoes are thrown across the room and he works my leggings over my ass.

A sharp pain has me yelping when he digs his teeth into it. Now I'm worried that his more may be too much.

He sets me on my feet, pushes my back against the windows, and drops to his knees to rip off my leggings and panties. A maniacal laugh rumbles from his chest and I grow embarrassed, thinking something is wrong. I don't have time to ponder on it though, because he clamps his mouth to my soaked pussy and begins drinking me down.

My head hits the glass with a thud and I squeeze my eyes shut. The feel of his tongue licking and his mouth gorging is blissful. The tingle that starts at my toes radiates up to my breasts as my nipples harden.

I grip the hem of my t-shirt and whisk it rapidly over my head. My bra is more of a struggle as I wear a sports bra. It's the most difficult act I've performed on a normal basis. But with Hendrix not easing up, it's a feat near impossible. But once I'm free, I breathe a sigh of relief that he didn't falter.

He looks up at me and all I see is the bright blue ocean in his eyes staring up at me.

"Are those real?" He pants.

"Are what real?"

"Your tits." I nod, my brow furrowed as to why he asks. "*Fuck.* Juicy lips, a sweet pussy *and* plump tits? Dagen McCallan, you are every bit my dream girl come to life."

I swoon at his words and feel the way they cause my belly to flutter. It could also be the way he feasts on me like a man who's never tasted food.

He throws my leg over his shoulder and I feel his fingers prod at my entrance. He slides them between my wet lips, spreading me wide and teasing when he pushes them in the slightest bit. I whine when he pulls them back and the vibration from his sinister laugh pushes me towards a path that will lead to my orgasm.

He repeats the tease a few more times before plunging two fingers deep inside of me. I hiss when he stretches me and it makes him lick with more voracity. The pounding of my heart echoes in my ears, muffling the wanton moans that spill from my mouth.

I rise up on my tiptoes with my orgasm sitting just out of reach. With his mouth still consuming me, and his fingers delving deeper, Hendrix glides his free hand over my stomach and reaches out for my breast. He palms one tight in his hand and massages it, rolling his thumb over my sensitive nipple.

Harder, faster, rougher he continues until I finally grasp euphoria. I don't know if Hendrix stops his efforts because the only thing I feel is the sensation of floating through air. Like my body is being thrown into space, I'm weightless. The breath in my lungs refuses to leave, giving me a high like no other. My ascent stops and like a roller coaster plummeting from great heights, I fall with a whoosh.

My fingers dig into Hendrix's short hair, my legs feeling

like Jell-O and my body limp. He catches me when I can no longer hold myself up and I wrap around him like a leaf clinging to its tree in a storm.

He kisses me, invading my mouth, and I taste the saltiness on his tongue. My body presses against the glass with one of his arms still holding me up, while the other busies itself with undoing his pants. I hear the zipper descend and feel it when he pushes them over his trim hips.

Breaking our kiss, he brings his fingers to my mouth and says, "Suck. Get them nice and wet." I open my mouth wide and suction my lips around them. "Good girl."

He plunges them in and out as if it's his dick fucking my mouth, and that itch to come again begins to buzz.

With a pop, he removes his fingers and reaches down to stroke his cock. I gulp and slowly my eyes fall to see his hand wrap around his thick shaft.

"Oh Jesus help me," I whisper.

The two guys I've slept with hardly compare to Hendrix and I grow uneasy thinking about the pain that will follow when he's inside of me.

"What's wrong, little mouse?" I contain the truth from slipping out and shake my head. "Tell me Dagen."

Gulping down my nerves, I answer, "You're...bigger than the other guys I've been with and I'm just a little scared it will hurt."

"I'll make it hurt so good. You'll be begging for more." He grips my jaw with his hand and kisses me. "I promise."

Nodding, I stare into his eyes and he mine. Languidly, he breeches my opening and nudges at it. Still gripping the base, he runs the engorged head up and down my seam. I brace for impact, then remember something quite important.

"Condom," I pant.

"Shit," he groans in response. "Do you really need me to wear one?"

I don't leave any room for persuasion and tell him, "Put

one on or let me go back to the room where I can finish this by myself."

He hefts me up, one arm anchoring me to him by my waist and the other positioned under my ass like I'm sitting on a strong branch.

"Not a fucking chance." He shuffles us away from the windows, his pants and underwear around his ankles constricting his movements.

We reach his long dresser and he sits me right on top, then begins rifling through a drawer. He curses under his breath, pushing various items out of the way.

"Are you telling me you don't have one?" I ask.

"I do. I just can't remember where I put–got it." He slams the drawer and it shakes the wood dresser.

Without hesitation, he rips the wrapper open and slides the condom down his length in record time. He takes a moment to tear off his clothes and I melt into a puddle. This man is perfection carved by a genius creator. Tattoos swirl down his torso and arms, and a few that wash over his strong thighs.

I'm spun around and flung on his bed, bouncing when I land on the soft mattress. Like a predator who knows he's caught his prey, the look of hunger is in his eyes. My legs are spread wider by his large hands and he lines himself up with my opening. I inhale a deep breath and when he finally sinks into me, a cry pours out.

I feel him so deep as he begins to move, rolling his hips and awakening my body. He draws back slowly then slides back in. Over and over he repeats this sweet torture, almost reaching the spot yet still so far away.

Hendrix drops his mouth and takes my breast, his tongue working me over, flicking my nipple then biting it. I'm wound up like a live wire and I need just a little bit more to release.

The deliberate movements turn desperate and he moves

faster. Pressing down on my lower abdomen with his hand, he grunts, "Fuck. You feel so good. Like your pussy was made for me."

He thrusts harder and I tether myself to him to keep from flying right off the bed. I lift my hips and it's like dousing a fireball with kerosene. I go up in flames, my body burning when another orgasm rocks me. I think I hear a piercing wail, but my mind is so foggy I couldn't say if I make the sound or if it's simply rolling around on my tongue.

My eyes snap open when a hand lightly wraps around my throat. I witness Hendrix's blue eyes turn black and feel his cock swell. He pulls out of me so fast it stings and I see him rip off the condom and throw it to the floor.

"Give me your hand," he demands and I lift one, weakly.

He takes it and with his, helps me wrap it around his steel-like shaft and moves it back and forth. I watch completely enraptured as he comes, spilling the milky white liquid all over my belly. Spurt after spurt turns into long ropes that seem endless. His head is thrown back and his Adam's apple works up and down in his strong throat. When he's done, his chest heaves as he looks into my eyes then down to where his hot cum puddles.

With a swipe of his fingers, he lifts it to my mouth and tells me, "Open up and swallow it down, little mouse. This is what a man tastes like."

Holy shit. His dirty mouth and sexy body are enough to make me beg for more.

He lays his cum on my tongue and the taste already has me signing up for seconds.

And thirds.

And fourths.

SIXTEEN

I LAY on my back with Dagen's head on my chest, her chestnut brown hair tangled from my fingers twisting and pulling at it when I fucked her from behind the second time. Her short fingernails tickle me and she runs them up and down my taut abs. I'm not big and bulky like many gym-heads, but my muscles are defined and I know they make many women drop to their knees in praise.

She's been inspecting my tattoos for the last several minutes and suddenly stops short of diving beneath the sheet to grab my dick, and I so badly wish she would.

"Is that..." she pauses and pushes up on her elbow, lowering her head closer to my growing erection. "Is that a woman *spitting* on your–"

"Dick? Yes. Not the wisest decision I've ever made." She laughs and relaxes back into my arms. "If you think that's bad you should see the ones Malik and Danté chose. Mine looks tame."

"Um, no thanks. I'll take your word for it."

Silence falls over us and I stare up at the ceiling fan that whirs. I replay the look in her eyes when she orgasmed the first time I fucked her. I saw the way her pupils enlarged when she watched my cum pour out all over her stomach. It was a beautiful sight to see and I want to witness it over and over again until I've had my fill. Or until she has to leave, which may come first.

She sighs and runs her hand along the snake that coils around my torso. "I guess I better get back to my room. It's getting really late and you probably want to get some sleep."

My arms clamp around her tightly when she tries to roll off of me. "What makes you think you're getting out of this bed? No no, little mouse. I'm far from done with you."

"I didn't think you were the kind of guy who let women sleep over.'

"What kind of guy do you think I am?" I ask her, my curiosity piqued.

"I assumed you were the fuck 'em and chuck 'em type."

I swiftly roll us over and flatten her to the mattress as I hover above her. "Fuck 'em and chuck'em? Give me some credit. I at least feed them a snack before sending them on their way."

Her mouth falls agape and a little squeak rolls out. "You jerk," she gasps.

I laugh and silence her with a kiss, stealing the breath from her lungs. She becomes pliant in my hands almost immediately and my body yearns to have her again. I run my fingers all along her rib cage, smoothing over her curves and feeling goosebumps roll across her body.

I release her and nuzzle into her neck. "Daddy Vaughan sure isn't going to like how I violated his baby girl."

She scrapes her fingernails across my scalp and down my neck and back. "What daddy doesn't know won't hurt him. Are you about to tell him you fucked his daughter against your windows?"

"Nope. Because I fucked you on my bed. I ate your pussy against the windows." I tap the tip of her pert nose and she smiles back.

I bet if I could see her face more clearly her cheeks would be tinged with red.

"Po-tay-to, po-tah-to. Same difference."

"Stay here, with me, tonight," I tell her.

The thin ring of green around her black pupil is electric and it hypnotizes me. So quickly this woman has me under her spell and I know I'm in trouble.

"Okay." Her whispered words are music to my ears and I want to show her the ways we 'dance' so perfectly together.

"You're late," Miss Shirley barks as I walk into the office.

I look at my watch, already knowing I'm late, but seeing just how far past starting time I am. I haven't bothered to look at a clock today, because I was too busy being wrapped up with Dagen. When I see the time flip to eleven twenty-three, I cringe.

"Yeah. Sorry. I had some things to take care of this morning."

"Mhmm," she mumbles, eying me skeptically.

I hang my head like I've just been scolded by my mother, and beeline for my office where I promptly close the door and sit at my desk.

Before I can even fire up my laptop, my phone begins buzzing in my pocket. With a sigh, I lift up from my chair slightly and retrieve it from my back pocket. My sigh turns deeper when I see Malik's name on the caller id.

"What's up, Mal?" I answer.

"Hey loverboy." His voice is drawn out and lyrical like he's singing a song. "How's married life?"

"What the fuck are you talking about."

"You and Dagen. Are you like two birds sitting in a tree, KI-SS-ING?"

I roll my eyes and I wonder what I was thinking when I agreed to be this man's brother. "You're an idiot. The girl needed a place to stay. I wasn't going to leave her out on the streets. That's all."

He laughs sarcastically. "A pillow to rest her head on is one thing. But offering her rides on your dick like it's a carousel is another thing completely."

"Shit," I curse under my breath because how the hell did this fucker find out.

"In case you're wondering, Kinsley told me after she went by your place this morning to take Dagen to breakfast. When she wasn't in the room, she let herself into the main house and heard you two...*talking*."

I groan and flop my head back against my chair. If ever someone wants to announce something to the entire town of Cattywump Bay and surrounding cities, all you have to do is tell McKinsley Sawyer. Forget hiring a billboard sign. She'll be in people's ears with business that isn't hers to tell quicker than a jackrabbit during mating season.

"So. Are there wedding bells in your future?" He sounds like one of the obnoxious kids he teaches.

"No, there aren't wedding bells. She's just...someone to pass the time with. Why are you even asking me that?" I pound my password into the keyboard, irritated and ready to rush back home and lock myself in and the world out.

"Oh Henny. I don't think she's someone to pass time with. That kiss you two shared at T and D the other night wasn't a simple peck on the cheek that I suspect Danté would have received if he had won. I'm sure he would've tried, but I don't think she'd take the bait. But you...you had her hooked like a goddamn mudcat. She watched every twitch of your muscle. It was so obvious she wanted you. Then I hear you took her out last night."

"How do you know that?" I jump up from my seat and grip my phone tighter.

With a huff he replies, "I have my ways."

I begin pacing around my office, feeling like the walls are caving in on me. If Kins knows and is talking to Dagen the way Malik is speaking with me, then maybe she's starting to form ideas in that pretty head of hers. What if she thinks we're a couple after sleeping together. I don't know if she's a clinger.

"Mal, I gotta go. I'll talk to you later."

"Wait. Wha–" I abruptly end the call and don't bother to hear what he was about to say.

I quickly stab at the numbers on my phone, copying the same ones on the paper that still sits on my desk, and bring the phone to my ear. It rings three times before she answers.

"Hello?"

"Hey. Dagen?"

"This is. And who may I ask is calling?" Her voice is proper and stiff like I'm some fucking solicitor trying to sell her new phone service.

"It's Hendrix." I bark out, slightly harsher than I mean to be.

"Oh. Hi. Um, is everything okay? You just left like, thirty minutes ago." I hear water running in the background and I wonder if she's washing dishes.

"Yeah. I just want to check to make sure we're on the same page about–are you washing dishes, or something?" I finally ask when the loud splash breaks my focus.

"No. I was just about to get in the shower. I had one foot in when you rang, so I jumped out really quick, not thinking to turn it off. Sorry."

My gut tightens, feeling like I was just kicked in the balls. I picture her gorgeous body wet and slick and all reason flies out the window.

"Get in that shower and don't get out until I'm there," I

growl, already slamming my laptop shut and digging into my pocket for my car keys.

"Wh-why?"

"Just stay there. Okay? Please?" My voice is desperate as I am.

"Okay. I'll stay."

I breathe out a quick goodbye and rush out from my office, slamming the door behind me and hauling ass through the break room. I stomp out into the lobby and Miss Shirley's eyes pop with surprise.

"Be back. Something came up." I practically run past her and straight to my car.

My tires screech as I peel out of the parking lot and fishtail when I spin out on the road. I watch my rearview for cops because I'm doing seventy in a thirty-five and I don't plan on slowing down until I have her in my arms.

My engine rumbles as I fly past vehicle after vehicle, weaving in and out of lanes. I speed closer to home and blow through the last light when I notice there isn't any oncoming traffic. When I finally reach my street and up my driveway, I stop just short of plowing through my garage door.

My seatbelt gets thrown off and I jump out of the car like it's a ticking time bomb about to strike zero. The front door slams against the wall and I don't worry about closing or locking it, and hurdle over furniture like I'm in the Olympics. Taking the stairs two at a time and burst through the loft door after racing down the hallway.

The shower is still running and I fling open the door to see Dagen standing under the spray. She yelps in that squeaky voice when the bang pulls her from the comfort of the warm water. I walk towards her, stumbling as I try to kick off my sneakers and pull my shirt off at the same time.

"Did you really just leave work to come here?" She shouts over the splashing of the water on the tiles.

"Yes, so you better fucking be ready for me, because it was

hell driving with a hard-on." I yank my feet free from my jeans and step into the shower, nearly shattering the glass with the force I jerk the door closed with.

Words and greetings are tossed to the side when I scoop her up in my arms and press her to the cold wall. Her back arches and her legs wrap around me, bringing her glorious pussy right where I need it.

I attack her mouth and grip her tightly as the remaining soap washes away. Her fingers claw at my scalp and she moans into my mouth, gyrating her hips and begging for purchase.

"I don't have a condom but I'll pull out. I promise," I mumble against her wet lips.

She pulls away and looks into my eyes. "I only worry that you're—you know. Are you?"

"I am. I wouldn't lie about that." Her greens search my blues and I wait for her to tell me yes or no.

She runs a hand over my jaw and whispers, "Okay. I trust you."

Without waiting another moment, I grip the base of my dick and slide into her, so wet and so warm. Her cries set me off and I begin to plunge into her deeper and deeper. The feeling that comes over me is like heat on your bones when you've spent a lifetime in the cold.

Her head smacks the tile when her head falls back and a moan floats off her tongue.

"Are you okay," I grunt out between thrusts.

"Yes. Don't stop." She scratches my back, trying to hold on and I fuck her harder.

Our bodies suction together, the water sluicing between us and causing us to slide. I need more. I must have more.

I pull out of her –probably a bit too harshly– and drop her to her feet. Her hands flatten to the wall but I spin her around, gripping those luscious hips and dragging them towards me.

When she starts to step her entire body to me, I lay my hand on her head and tell her, "No baby. Bend over and put your hands on the wall. Stick that beautiful ass out and let me watch the way it shakes as I tear you up."

I push on her head while pulling her hips, and she braces her arms and bends over. Her spine curves when she sticks her ass out more. I can't resist smacking it hard and stare at the spot that reddens with my handprint. I spread her full globes wide with my thumbs and see the way she opens up for me.

My mouth salivates for her taste and I hunch over to sample her. I let my tongue run from her sweet pussy to her puckered hole that I tease, circling a forbidden place. A breathy sigh of pleasure can barely be heard when it leaves her lips. I promise myself to return to eating my treat later tonight, but right now I need to be back inside of her.

Standing again, I slam into her, pulling a sexy mewl from that beautiful mouth. I pump in and out, loving the way my dick looks shoved in and out of her tight hole. She sucks me in and I feed her every last inch.

"Hen-drix." My name sounds like a plea when she speaks. "I'm so close."

My hand snakes around her waist, my fingers heading straight for her clit. "Let's get you all the way there, little mouse."

I begin to rub and roll her swollen clit between my calloused fingers and she cries louder, the melody echoing all around.

"Fuck. You feel so good. Do you know how perfect your sweet pussy is?" She shakes her head as best as she can with her cheek mashed to the wall. "It's perfect for me. I want to wear it out."

I pinch her nub hard and a piercing scream follows. Her body convulses and she begs God to never let it stop. Dagen's fingers scrape the tile, trying to anchor herself to it, but it's no use as I continue to slam harder and harder.

She sags and her arms can barely keep her stable from slumping to the floor. My balls start to tingle and my toes grip the wet tiles. I feel the first drop of cum and strangle the base of my dick, withdrawing it from the comfort of her tight walls.

"Get on your fucking knees little mouse and open wide." I'm holding on to my cock and my sanity for dear life. "Now Dagen," I bark and she scrambles to obey.

My hands guide her to face me and she sits on her knees. I squeeze her jaw, causing her mouth to fall open. It's a beautiful sight. Dagen on her knees before me, her pouty lips pried open and those gorgeous eyes looking wild.

My hand jacks my dick, pumping back and forth. The orgasm I was holding back I chase once again. It builds and my bulging head throbs until it finally explodes. I coat Dagen's mouth and chin with cum and it drips down, droplets falling to her breasts.

My teeth gnash painfully and my body goes rigid with my release. When my dick softens, I open my eyes and see Dagen with a mouthful of me. I gather the cum still leaking from the corners and shove my fingers into her mouth, returning every trickle where it belongs.

"Swallow it. Don't you dare waste it, little mouse." She struggles to swallow with my hand still holding her mouth wide, so I let it slide out and slam it shut.

I watch her throat work as it washes down. Her pink tongue licks her coated lips, doing just as I told her and not wasting an ounce. Her chest heaves when she's finished and a smile radiates across my usually hardened face.

"You look so goddamn good on your knees for me, little mouse. Maybe I'll keep you there." Her body shakes as the water turns cold and I quickly lift her into my arms and cleanse her of our dirty deed.

When I'm done, her head rests on my shoulder and I reach for a towel to dry us off. Carrying our damp bodies to the bed, I lay down with Dagen tucked into me.

My head is a mess with thoughts of her being here.

We fall asleep and when I open my eyes again, I don't know what time it is or where I am for a moment. When I realize I'm wrapped up in Dagen, I fall back into the comfort of knowing she's still with me. I quickly fade into the reality of a cold and empty life that will exist when she's gone. It's one that I know so well and probably will for the rest of my days.

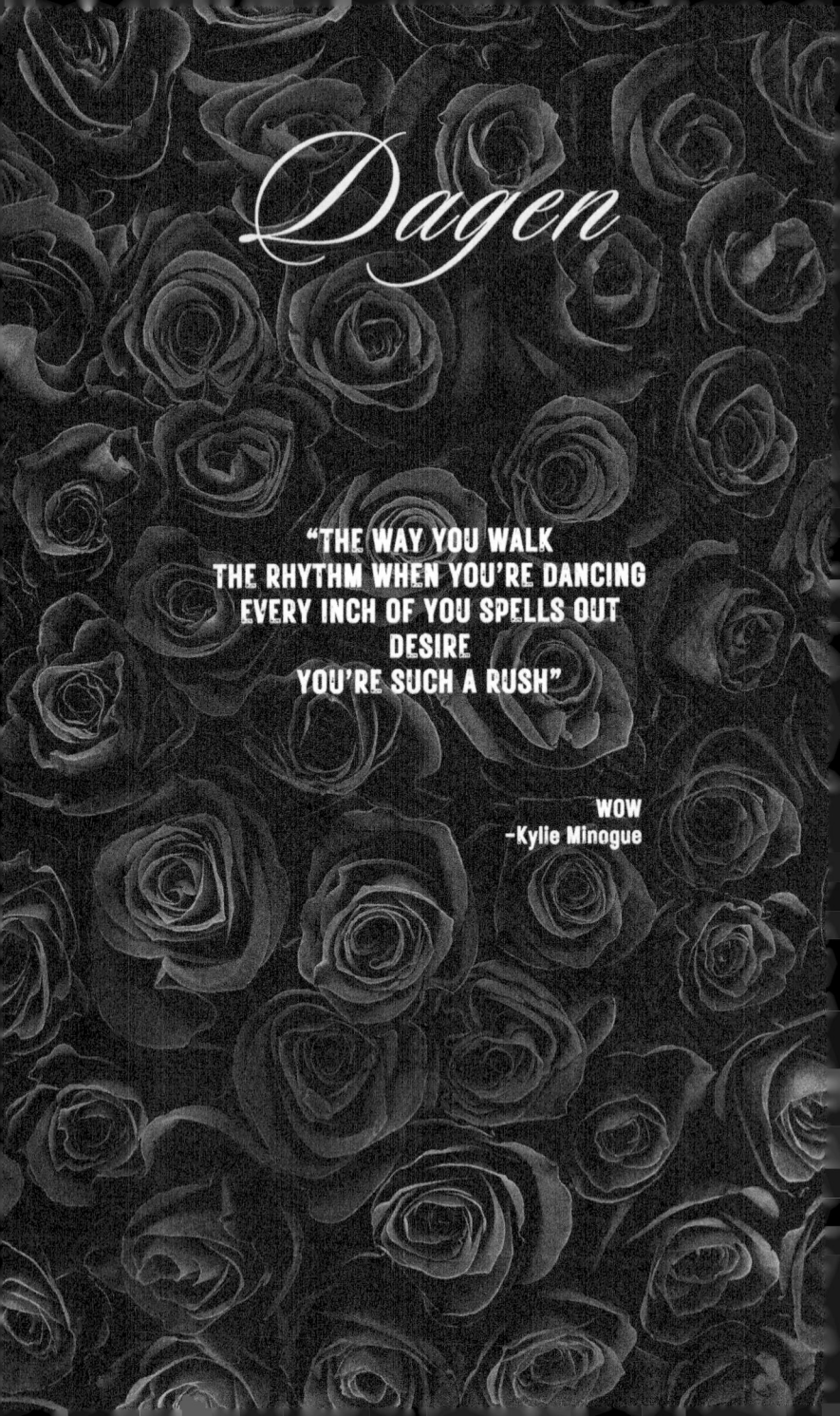

SEVENTEEN

THE PHONE RINGS and I anxiously wait for mom to pick up. It's been days since I've seen AJ and Sloane and even though I don't see them often when I'm away at school, I at least FaceTime with them a couple times a week. They catch me up on their week at school and on the ranch, and just hearing their little voices makes a gray day blue.

The ringing stops and the screen comes to life with two faces I miss so much smiling big and bright.

"Day!" Sloane shouts while AJ claps her little hands and cheers.

"Hi Sloaney. Hi AJ. How are my bestest friends?"

"Day, momma said you're in Missipissi. Where's that?" Sloane trips over his words, too many S's and P's for his tiny mouth.

"Mississippi, Sloaney. I'm in Mississippi, and it's only two states away. I'm close and I'll be home soon. I promise."

"Sissy. I go to abuelita's for a sweepover." AJ has the sweetest voice and her vocabulary grows every day.

"You did, AJ? Wow, did you have so much fun?" She nods her head enthusiastically, her tiny pigtails bopping around. "What else did y'all do while I've been gone?"

The two of them rattle loudly, trying to one up the other with their stories. I only understand about half of what AJ says, but Sloane is fluent in Autumn Jade speech so he translates much of it for me. AJ is animated, using her hands to talk and explain details, and Sloane is much more serious and concise with his words. They are very much like mom and dad. AJ has so much of dad in her –looks and attitude– and Sloaney is mom one hundred percent.

They start to argue, getting rowdy over discrepancies in an activity, and mom has to step in.

"Okay. That's enough, you two. Why don't you say goodbye to your sister, then Dad will help you get your teeth brushed." They both whine but quickly quiet when mom gives them 'the look'.

"Bye Day," Sloane says, his voice gloomy and sad.

"I yuv you, sissy." AJ puckers up and blows a little kiss to me.

I tell them I'll call again in a couple of days and say goodnight. They scurry off to Dad who stands behind them. He bends, his arms open wide, and they jump at him. I smile, remembering the days when Dad would sing songs as I got ready for bed, making the one thing I didn't want to do fun.

Mom waves to them then turns back to face me. "Hi my sweet girl. How are you?"

"I'm good, Mom. How's everything with you all? From what Sloaney and AJ said, it seems you guys had a busy week."

Mom sighs and nods. "Yes we did. It was very busy. Autumn is getting so big which means she wants to know everything about everything. And Sloane is all too anxious to fill her little heart with all the information she needs. According to him."

We chuckle and her face grows a bit serious, her brows scrunching and her eyes squinting.

"Dagen Rayne. What's that?" She waggles her finger side

to side, pointing at something I obviously can't see. "On your neck. There's like a red line or…I don't know what that is."

My stomach drops when I remember how Hendrix wrapped his hand around my throat last night when we were having sex. Then my cheeks flush remembering just how much I liked it.

I touch the picture of myself in the corner of the screen to enlarge it, and examine the marks that mom has pointed out. Looking closer I see it's actually a small line from where the helmet rubbed my neck.

"Oh. Um, Hendrix took me for a ride on his bike and I guess the helmet irritated my neck a little," I explain, running my fingers over it.

"His bike? Like bicycle or like Harley?"

"More like Ducati."

"Dagen!" Her eyes pop open and she gasps. "Why would you get on one of those things? Do you know how dangerous they are?"

"Not anymore than a Harley. Don't worry, okay. I wore a helmet and a jacket and Hendrix was very careful. We went with a few of his friends and it was a lot of fun."

She chews on her lip nervously, and I see doubt in her eyes. "Please be safe, honey. You know how skittish I am about motorcycles."

"Not enough for you to stay off of them." She gives me a narrowed look and I go on. "I understand and I promise–"

"Hey little mouse. Wanna go for a ride with Mal…"

The door flies open and Hendrix steps in wearing a black t-shirt and jeans that make him look like a wet dream on a stick. Tattoos peek out from his collar and the ones on his arms are beautifully displayed.

"I'm sorry. I didn't mean to interrupt. I'll wait downstairs." He lifts his hand to the screen and backs out, yanking the door shut.

I stare at the empty spot where he stood then slowly roll my head back to look at Mom.

"And who was that?"

"That's Hendrix. The homeowner and guy who's fixing your car." I bite down on my tongue and wait for some type of blow back.

Instead she nods languidly and thinks about her words as she so wisely does. I lick my lips and swallow as my mouth suddenly grows very dry.

"Does he just barge into your room unannounced often?"

"To be fair, this is his home. I'm sure he was just coming to ask if I'd like to have dinner. He's been really great about including me in his plans with his friends."

"Well that's...*nice*, I guess." She looks like she wants to say more but something is holding her back.

"Spill it. What do you want to say?"

I ready myself to hear some long, drawn out speech about trusting strangers and all the things a young woman would hear in a situation like the one I currently find myself in.

She clears her throat then says, "He's really handsome, Day."

"Mom!" I shout, shocked that she would say that.

"What? I'm married –happily– but I'm not blind. That man is incredibly good looking and I am just going to put this out there, and you can take it how you wish. You're young and beautiful and I have no doubt that man has two working eyes and can see all of that. But he is a man, so just be wise about *stuff*."

I gulp and choke on my own breath. "Mom. There's nothing to worry about. He–"

"I am not stupid nor that old to recognize when things are more than the story being told. Just be careful and make good decisions. Okay?"

My chest feels tight thinking about how careless I was in the shower this morning, but nod anyway.

"Okay, Mom." My cheeks flush bright red with embarrassment knowing that she's keen to everything going on. "So you think he's cute?"

"Daughter...he's not cute. That word is reserved for awkward high school boys. That man is hot."

I snort and start laughing then pale when dad comes strolling in right behind her.

"Who's hot? Tell me his name so I can go kick his ass." Dad wraps his hands around Mom's waist and pulls her close, kissing her cheek and smiling.

"Boston Christiansen. That new defensive lineman for the Houston Drillers football team." Mom says, quickly recovering.

Dad rests his chin on her shoulders, stars in his eyes for only her. "Well I don't think I can beat him up. The guy is a fucking train."

Mom reaches up and pats his face. "Don't worry, babe. I'm not old enough to be a cougar, so you're good."

I think about all of the love they have for one another, and a tinge of anger rises thinking about Stephanie ruining so many years for them. Maybe Cami would have been my *real* mom if Stephanie never got her claws into dad. Then again, maybe I wouldn't be here at all.

"Okay. Before you two start kissing and groping in front of your daughter, I'm going to go. I haven't eaten dinner yet and I'm starting to get hungry."

"I'll call you tomorrow, baby bird," Dad tells me and Mom rolls her eyes.

"We'll text you tomorrow, and *you* call if you need anything," she adds.

We said a thousand *I love you's* before hanging up and I gave myself a moment to collect my whits. I'm warring with being the good girl my parents expect me to be, and the woman that a man like Hendrix needs me to be. I don't know if it's possible to be both, so it's a good thing this...whatever it is with him will be short lived.

I stick my phone in my jeans and walk down the connecting hallway to the main part of the house and down the stairs where Hendrix sits at his kitchen counter, spinning what looks to be a quarter around and around.

"Hey," I greet as I descend.

"I'm sorry for interrupting you like that. I should have knocked." He spins on the stool, putting his back to the counter and facing me.

"You don't have to apologize. This is your house. Besides, it was just my Mom."

As I step closer to him, Hendrix reaches out and takes me by my wrist and tugs me to stand between his legs. His arms immediately wrap around me, his large hands resting on my butt.

"Was she instantly worried for your safety? Are they sending the scary uncles your dad threatened me with to take you away?"

"My Dad did what?" I lay my arms on his shoulders and scrape my nails through his hair.

With a smile and nod he says, "He told me if I was unable to keep my hands to myself, he had friends that would be happy to teach me a lesson."

My jaw drops, utterly surprised that my Dad would say such a thing. "I can't believe he actually said that."

"He's smart to warn me. Otherwise, I was planning to lock you in my basement and make you my sex slave."

"You can't enslave the willing." I've come to learn very quickly that he likes my sassy comebacks and word sparring.

His fingers dig into my ass when he squeezes it hard. "I'll remember that." He lifts one brow, waggling it, then kisses me with fervor.

He tastes of cool mint and it tingles my tongue. Just like his touch does to my entire body. The way he touched me last night and this morning –rough with a touch of tenderness– flipped a switch in me and I just want to contain that feeling in a jar and visit it every chance I get.

We separate and I keep my eyes closed for a moment longer, adding this feeling to my jar.

"Are you hungry?" he asks and I nod, eyes still shut tight. "Do you want to take the Duc?"

My eyes fly open when he mentions taking his bike. "You're what?"

He smiles wide and says, "My Ducati. Bikers call it a Duc."

"Yes. Let's take the Duc."

He doesn't need anything else from me. Hendrix stands, still holding on to me, and walks us to the garage where his prized possession sits. But the way he treats me, zipping me up into a jacket, strapping me snuggly into a helmet, makes me feel like I'm the prized one.

Just another reason why Hendrix Dare is a dangerous man.

HENDRIX

"IF YOU WANT YOU'RE GONNA BLEED
BUT IT'S THE PRICE TO PAY
AND YOU'RE A VERY SPECIAL GIRL,
AND VERY HARD TO PLEASE
YOU CAN TASTE THE BRIGHT LIGHTS BUT
YOU WON'T GET THERE FOR FREE"

Welcome To The Jungle
-Guns N' Roses

EIGHTEEN

WITH DAGEN on the back on my bike and Malik right beside us, we speed out of the parking lot of the restaurant we took her to. Danté is still in a sour mood and has yet to reach out to me. I don't plan on making the first move because I have nothing to be apologetic for. He wanted Dagen, and Dagen wanted me. Simple as that.

It was a fun time with just the three of us. Malik is a goof, so he had Dagen laughing most of the time. She talked a little more about her life back home, and it sounded like she was really missing her family. I told myself I needed to rush along the repairs on her car but also…I don't want to.

We pull up to a stoplight and a car with its windows down stops right next to us. Their music is loud and the girls are giggling. Malik starts dancing while still seated and the girls start to whistle. He looks over and holds his hand out to Dagen who grabs it and snakes her arms. Malik picks up where she left off, then they both start cutting up to the music. I hear her laughter in the speakers and I want to be the reason for that glorious sound.

The light turns green and the girls in the car wiggle their fingers and drive off. Malik sits back down and Dagen places her hands on my shoulders. For me, that just won't do anymore. I take her hands and move them to wrap around my waist. Then I snake my arm around her and place my hand on her ass, pulling her close so that not even air can pass between us.

"This is where you stay," I tell her through the speaker and she places her head on my back before I speed off.

We reach a stretch of I-10 that's quiet and just like the first night, I tell her to hold tight while Malik and I fuck around, doing things we definitely should not be with traffic around. Mal more than me since Dagen is with me. At one point he is standing on his seat while his front tire is lifted completely in the air.

Dagen shouts through her helmet speaker. "I want to do that."

"No way, little mouse. That takes a lot of years of practice," I tell her.

"Teach me to ride, Hendrix." Her hands skate up and down my chest before falling dangerously close to my aching cock.

"One day." *One day may never come.*

Malik parted ways with us and headed home, leaving Dagen and all of her attention to only me. I'm a selfish son of a bitch already, less than a week into her stay, and I want all of her, all of the time.

Once we've put away the gear, we get cozy on my couch, Dagen sitting with her feet tucked under her. She's talking animatedly about school after I asked her about it, and all I can think is how much I want to fuck that beautiful mouth.

"Apparently I have an internship with the Wranglers that I–"

"Dagen," I interrupt. "Have you ever played truth or dare?"

She scoffs and rolls her eyes. "Of course I have. Everyone has played truth or dare."

I lean in closer, my arm draped on the back of the couch, and I lower my voice. "Not the way I play it. Do you wanna have a little fun?"

Her bright smile slowly fades as her eyes grow wide. She makes an audible gulp and nods her head. "S-sure."

With a wolf-like smile I tell her, "We'll start slow. Truth or Dare?"

"Um, truth I guess."

"How badly do you want to fuck me right now, little mouse?"

I can see her pulse throbbing her neck as her chest rises and falls. "Very," she whispers.

Standing up I hold out my hand to hers and she takes it. I guide her back into the garage and straight towards the closet where I keep all of my gear.

"Time for a dare." I open the door and pull out two helmets.

Placing mine on, I secure it in place then do the same to hers. I open the visor on both of the helmets and her eyes look like that of a frightened critter.

"You know the woods just off to the left of the house?" Her head moves up and down sluggishly. "I'm going to give you a thirty second head start."

"Head start? To do what?"

"Run, little mouse. I dare you to run." I trail my finger from her collarbone up her neck and stopping where the helmet starts.

"Why would I run from you?" Her voice trembles.

"Because I like to play with my food before I eat it." The

color drains from her face, her rosy cheeks turning pale, and my body buzzes with need. "Are you ready?"

"Wait. What about wild animals? There could be dangerous creatures out there."

"Baby, I'm the only dangerous creature who will be hunting you." I pull her towards the edge of the garage right in front of the door. "As soon as this door opens up, you'll have thirty seconds to run. And then...I'm coming for you."

I slam her visor shut then mine, and press the button on the remote for the garage door that I grabbed off of the hook.

Her hand shakes in mine and I give her a little squeeze to calm the nerves. Dagen's head flies to meet mine, and though I can't see her face under the dark shield, I can tell she's surprised by the act.

The sound of the motor stops and I wait for her to make her move. When she continues to stare at me, I lower my voice and say, "Run run run, little mouse. The big bad wolf is coming for you."

Her body goes rigid and then I hear her gasp for air. In the blink of an eye, she's pulling away from me and sprinting down my driveway towards the dark woods. I watch her white shoes move farther and farther away until they disappear. I give her a few more seconds and then I bolt after her.

Dagen should have known better than to walk with danger. I'm bound to dim her bright light. But the dark side of me doesn't give a fuck. Because even if I never see her again after she goes back, there will always be a part of me inside of her. One that I awakened and will always belong to me.

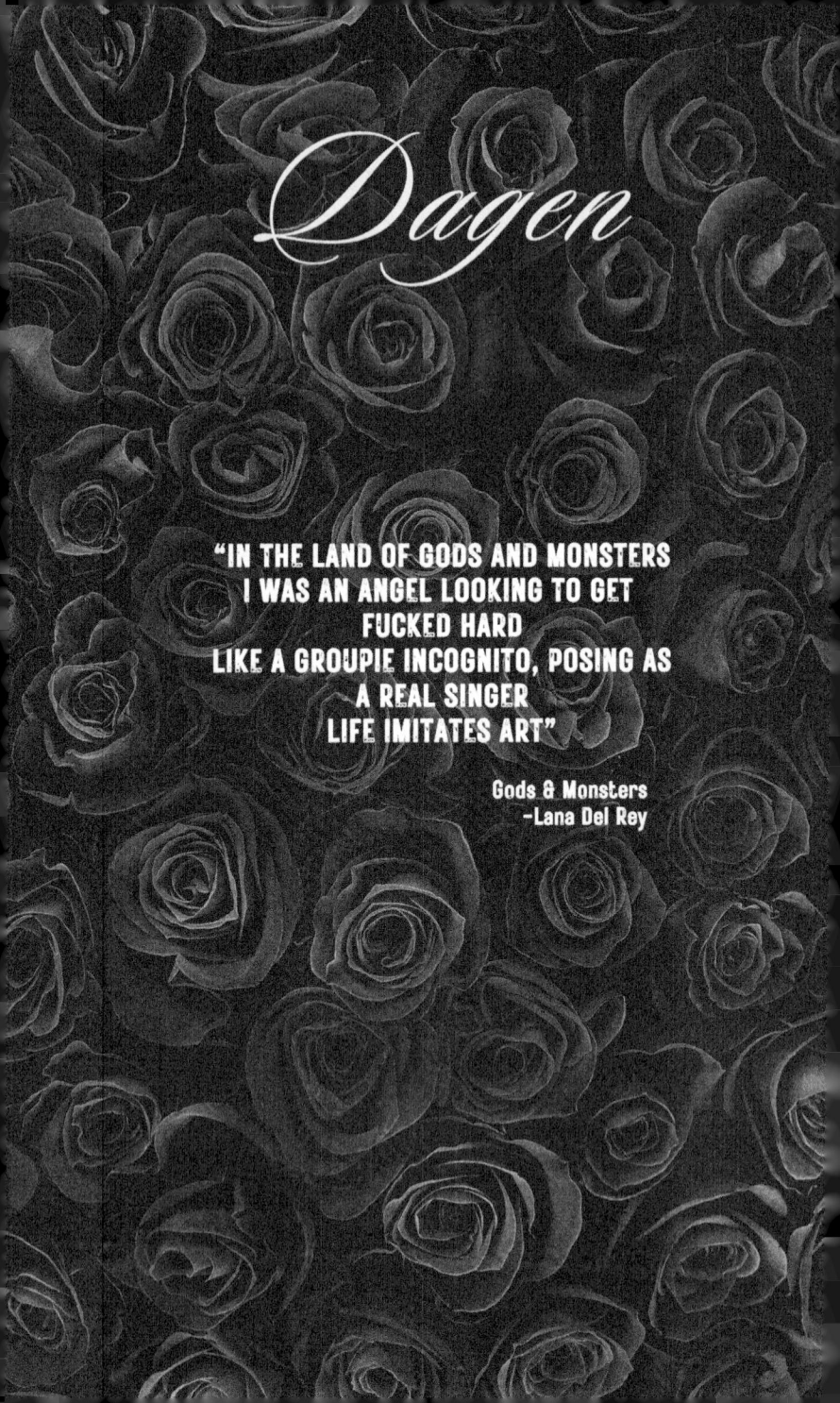

NINETEEN

"RUN RUN RUN, little mouse. The big bad wolf is coming for you."

Hendrix's deep smoky voice sends a rumble down to my core that has me frozen in place. Like the firing of a shotgun, my brain says to run and I take off. The landscape lights that surround his home shine across the yard and I use it to guide me to the edge of the woods that line his property.

The visor makes it difficult to see well, and I slow down as soon as I enter the dark shroud. There's a slight chill in the air and goosebumps pebble my exposed skin. I wear only a thin white t-shirt and leggings as the jacket Hendrix has me wear when we ride is thick and makes me sweat.

I push branches out of the way from smaller pine trees and trudge through dead grass and shrubs. My chest heaves and the inside of the helmet grows thick and warm. I spin around in a circle, trying to figure out which direction to go, but the moon and stars are hidden by the tall trees. I don't even know where I started. I'm totally thrown off and panic begins to build inside of me.

Just then I hear, "Little mouse, little mouse. Where are you?"

I choose to turn right and start running again. My steps are slow and labored as I stumble when my foot gets caught on something. Sounds from the creatures about –crickets and frogs and birds that prey at night– echo all around. It's like an ominous soundtrack of a horror film, and I'm the dumb girl who doesn't run fast enough from the serial killer.

My mind begins to swirl of what Hendrix plans to do when he catches me. Fear turns in my belly but so does a touch of curiosity. He's opening my eyes to a whole new world that I've only heard women speak about. Domination, rough sex, the hand on the throat. All things I told myself I would never like. But now I find myself craving those and more.

"When I catch you little mouse, I'm going to eat you alive. Mmm. I can already taste you on my tongue." His voice is that of a predator and it sends my pulse racing and my body humming with desire.

I continue to fight my way through the brush, narrowly missing running face first into several trees. I cut left and think I know which way is which when a large hand clamps on to my arm. I screech, but don't fight off my "attacker". This is one I will surrender to.

"I caught you." My back is pushed up against a tree and the bark digs at my back. "You're mine now, little mouse."

I raise a hand and lift my visor. "What are you going to do with me?" My breaths are heavy with each inhale and exhale.

His devious laugh is muffled by his helmet, but I hear it loud and clear. "I'm going to make you my meal. I'm going to eat every last morsel of you, leaving nothing for scavengers. I will be the only one to taste your blood on my tongue. No one else will know what your flesh feels like between their teeth."

His hand runs down the side of my body then moves to slide down the front of my leggings. I feel his fingers trial over my thin, and now soaked, panties. They dance along my covered mound and run up and down the damp fabric that separates us.

"Does this excite you, little mouse?"

"I-I think it does. You excite me, Hendrix." My hands hold onto the tree behind me, but I itch to touch him.

His visor remains shut and I move to lift it up, but he grips my hand and lowers it back down to my side then proceeds to pull my helmet from my head. I blink my eyes, working to bring the world back into focus and he sets the helmet down carefully at our feet.

The touch of his rough fingers on my stomach makes me tense as he rolls my t-shirt up over my breasts and then my face. It floats to the ground like a ghost in the night. My bra falls loose when he unclasps it, and a primal growl rumbles in his chest that I respond to with a wanton mewl.

Hendrix works to rid him of his shirt and struggles to pull it over his helmet, but I dare not tell him to remove it. He finally gets it off and tosses it carelessly. I hear the zipper of his jeans sliding down like a warning that he's about to strike. He takes my hand and guides me to where his cock stands thick and already dripping. I wrap my fingers around his thick shaft and slide up and down the velvet steel.

Unlike how he removed my shirt and bra with tenderness, he rips my leggings and panties down my legs, trapping my ankles. He drops to his knees and I hear the click of his visor raising. Through the sound of the woods' creatures, I hear him inhale my scent.

In the deep dark woods, I stand here ripped free from my clothing with a hungry man at my feet. I wait for him to take the first bite with nerves coursing through my veins.

His hand skates down my leg and he begins working my shoe off then my bottoms. He doesn't let my bare foot touch the cool Earth, but rather holds it in his hand when he stands. I drape my leg on his waist and he grabs the other, placing it on the other side. The bark that I thought was painful before now feels like searing hot pokers. It hurts, but not enough for me to stop Hendrix from what he's about to do.

The engorged head of his bulging cock slides between my drenched pussy lips before plunging deep and hard.

"Oh god," I cry out, digging my nails into his bare shoulders, adding a mark of my own to mingle with his tattoos.

He moves in and out of me, grunting and groaning with each thrust. His helmeted head presses against mine and I grab at it, trying to rip it off.

"I need to kiss you," I plead with him, but he ignores me and continues to sink into my swollen pussy. "Please Hendrix."

He pulls his head back and gives me a short nod. My fingers scramble to pull it off, but I don't drop it. Instead, I grip it tight with one hand and hold onto him with the other. My mouth anchors itself to his and our tongues begin a sensual dance.

The smell of Hendrix's cologne -musky and manly- mixes with the smell of pines and dry brush surrounding us. It's an aphrodisiac that will stay with me always.

"Your pussy feels like heaven wrapped around me." He murmurs against my lips and I swallow every word. "I think my little mouse liked being captured. You like the chase, don't you. The thrill and the fear turns you on."

I nod with a breathy "yes" as the adrenaline rushes through me. My feet taking me through the dark woods, the fear that I didn't know which corner he was lurking behind had me craving that flutter in my belly that whispered *he's coming*. I was definitely the girl in the horror film, but I wanted to be caught. I needed to be in the clutches of danger and feel how the darkness consumed me.

"Drop that fucking helmet and beg me. Beg me, Dagen. Beg for what you need."

My eyes are sealed shut as I let myself feel the pain, the pleasure, and the thrill of terror. I can't speak when bliss blooms inside of me, so I claw at his hand and show him. I place it around my throat and let him figure out the rest of himself.

"You want to touch the other side? Then open your eyes, little mouse. Stare at the evil that will take you there."

He squeezes my throat and my eyelids fly up like a broken shade. I can't see anything. Not even the man that is only inches away. He fucks me harder and harder, roaring into the ebony sky. I breathe, but the air I suck in is thin and barely reaches my lungs.

My hands scratch at his arms and back and anything I can muster the strength to touch. I blink, his face only coming into focus for only a moment before my head lols back when I feel the intoxication of my orgasm explode.

My mind is foggy as it tries to fight between the gluttony of wanting more and dragging me back into the luster of life.

My arms fall heavy and weak and I feel them crash against the harsh tree that I'm pinned to. Just when I think I may never experience the warmth of the sun, I heave for a scrap of air when he releases me.

"Welcome to my slice of hell, little mouse," he chokes out before pouring himself inside of me.

His cum floods me like a barren river thirsting for water, and my damn greedy pussy drinks it all in. I feel pain sear my flesh and realize he's clamped onto my shoulder and bitten through my skin. Just like he told me, he tastes my blood and I'm shaken by the whole thing.

Is this some satan-like sacrifice I'm making? Have I danced a little too closely with the devil?

When he draws back, I think he sees the panic in my eyes, because he says, "I'm sorry. I didn't mean to do that. I got carried away. It just felt so good."

I shake from the lack of oxygen and lack of reassurance I feel, despite what he said. Still holding me tight, he pushes my sweat drenched hair from my face and kisses my lips. "It won't happen again. I promise. Please don't be afraid of me."

I gulp, my throat dry and scratchy. "I thought...I thought you wanted me to be."

"Not like that," he confesses, shaking his head. "Not actually. It was just a game, little mouse and I took it too far."

I languidly hoist my arms up over his shoulders and search his eyes for truth. It's there, strong and sure. I know the weight of Hendrix's cock buried deep inside of me more than I know his true emotions. But I recognize what truth and genuine remorse looks like, and it swims turbulently in his blue ocean.

"Okay. I believe you," I admit softly and clamp onto his neck tightly.

"Why don't we go back. I think we need to wash off." I nod and he bends to scoop up all of our stuff.

"Put me down and I'll get my things. I need to put my clothes on." I wiggle in his arms but he only holds me tighter.

"No fucking way."

"Hendrix! I'm naked," I screech.

"I know. It's why I'm holding you and not letting you walk barefoot through these woods. Hang on and I'll carry you back."

"But I'm naked," I say again, this time whispering in his ear.

While he tries to balance everything in his arms, including me, I help tuck him back into his pants and zip them up. It's quite difficult, but we manage it.

He hands me one helmet and then the other as he gathers my shoes, then carries me out of the dark and into the comfort of his home. More specifically to the comfort of his bed and his arms.

I'm working on some assignments I received today out by Hendrix's pool, soaking up the warm sun and nursing my wounds. My back is a mess of angry red scratches after last night's little hunt through the woods. Hendrix carried me all the way back to his house and straight into his shower where he tenderly cleaned my cuts and rubbed ointment on them after.

He was very apologetic seeing the aftermath of his handiwork, but despite the pain, I reminded him that I wanted it just as much as he did.

So far Hendrix seems to be quite an enigma. He's cranky and rude and really doesn't like people. He told me he'd rather stay locked up in his home than have to interact with anyone other than his brothers and Miss Shirley. And according to Malik, he's not much of a smiler. I guess that has earned him the title of Cattywump Bay's most unfriendly resident.

But then there's the other side to his coin. With me –once we got past the initial asshole phase– he's somewhat sweet and thoughtful. The way he watches me with a look of yearning and a touch of darkness sets a fire in my belly. His touches are soft and supple, but in the next moment he's punishing and imperious. It's like the two sides of him are at war and sometimes they meet in the middle.

"What in the literal fuck happened to your back?" I jolt at the screeching voice and find Kinsley standing at the edge of the patio staring straight at me.

I was so lost in thoughts of Hendrix that I failed to hear the back door open and close.

"I-it's nothing. Don't worry." I quickly move to roll over

but hiss when my tender skin makes contact with the hard surface.

"Sure sister. That's nothing. It doesn't look at all like a cat in heat used your back for a scratching post." She props her hands on her hips and cocks her brow at me.

With a sigh I give her the details of my night. Well…not *all* the details. I left out a majority of it and summarized by saying we had a little fun in the woods and got carried away.

"I'd say. I knew Henny was kinky as shit, but I wouldn't have guessed you were."

"How do you know that?" I ask, jumping to my feet.

"Not personally, so don't get your girdle in a bunch. The women in this little town like to compare stories trying to one up the other about who's done what with which brother. Sorry. Just a fact."

I shrug and act like it doesn't phase me. "It's whatever. I assumed that was his story. Besides, I'm sure I'll never hear from him again once I go back to Texas."

"Well you sure as hell are going to hear from me. You're my new best gal and I will need daily updates on your life. Don't think you're going to be able to get away from me. I'm like a skidmark on your underwear. You can try to wash it away, but it's there. It's always there, just lingering around making your ass itch."

I snort with a burst of laughter. I really need to start writing these down and write a book. They're genius really.

"Don't worry, Kins. I'll never wash you away. You're my favorite skidmark."

She pops up on her toes and throws her arm over my shoulder. "Aww. Thank you, honey. That makes me feel so special. Now. Let's go get some better medicine for your back, because I'm damn near positive Henny only has a small tube of expired ointment and a few bottles of KY Jelly. And that ain't gonna do shit to heal your back."

We link arms and smile our way through the rest of the

day. I really am going to miss her when I go back home. It gives me a small ache in my heart.

I won't let myself believe that it's because one day, Hendrix's face will start to fade from my memory and he'll be nothing more than the boy who could've had all of me.

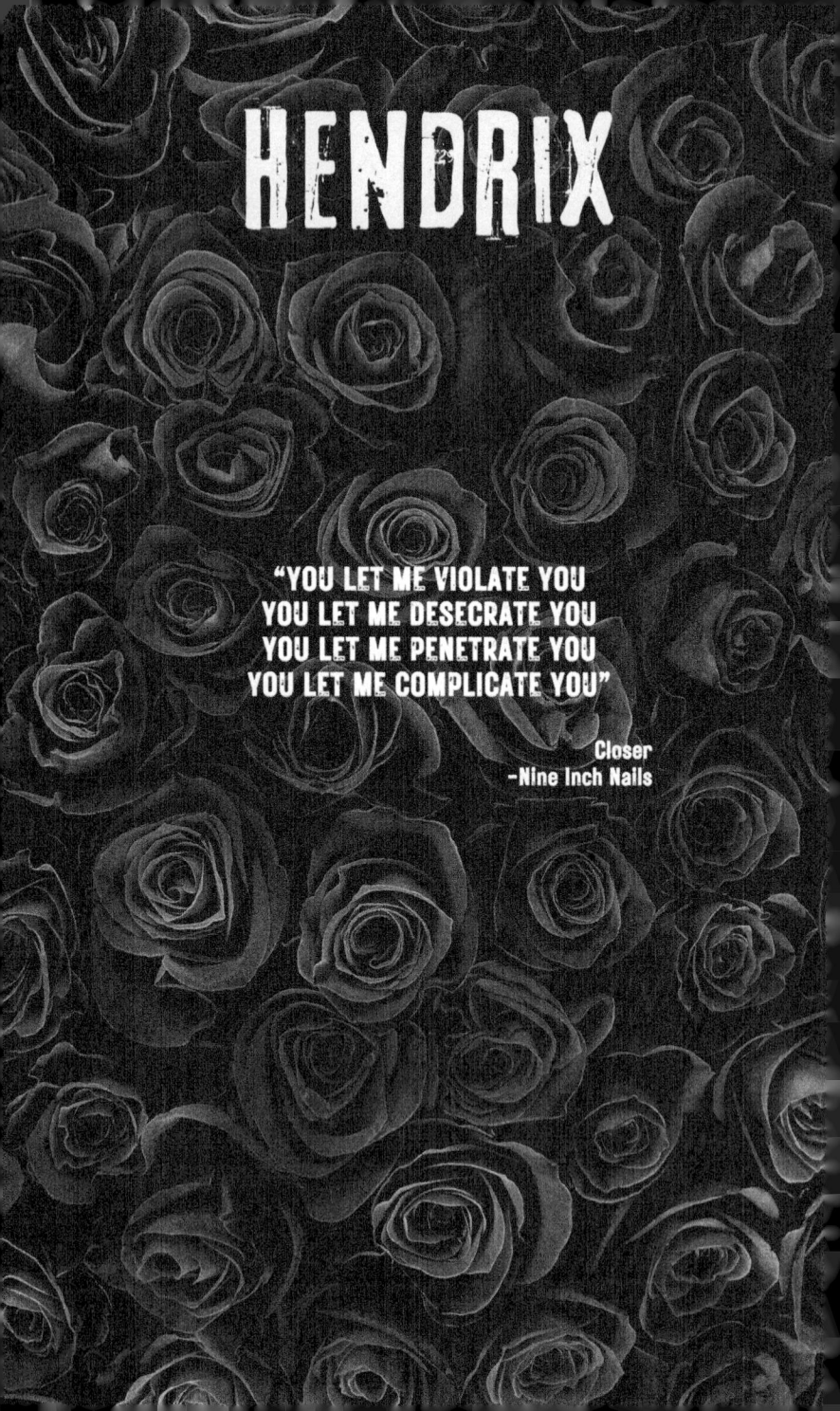

TWENTY

MY PHONE RINGS and I'm startled to see Danté's name on the caller id. He's not the kind of guy to pick up a phone to have an actual conversation. We barely get incomplete sentences via text. So I worry that it could be something bad and answer it.

"Hey D. Is everything okay?"

He clears his throat and grumbles, "Yeah. Nothing's wrong. I, uh, am just calling to say sorry for being a prick."

A small cocky grin pops up on my face. I knew eventually he'd quit nursing his wounds and come around. I didn't really expect him to apologize, because that's not his style. He usually just pops back up like there was never any conflict to speak of.

Come to think of it, that is one thing that Danté and I are very similar on. Neither of us likes the way the words *I'm sorry* taste in our mouths. It's easier to just never say it. Dagen, however, seems to be able to eat crow. The sorry's just keep rolling off my tongue. And to tell you the truth, the taste isn't all that horrible as I expected it to be.

"Yeah, man. Don't worry about it. It's fine." This is the only thing I can think of to say, because I refuse to lay any ground for another dispute, which it could very well turn into.

He breathes deep then goes on. "So are you and Dagen together or what's the deal?"

I turn up my face, thinking of the best way to answer. "I mean, for now I guess. We're just fucking around since she's only here for another week. After that, she'll go back to her life and I'll go back to mine."

Danté goes eerily quiet, the sound of my heart pounding in my ears as I wait to hear his response.

"Cool. So do you want to come by the bar tonight? I know you're usually tired after work, but Mal is coming by and a few of the guys."

When Danté says "the guys" he means the assholes we ride with from time to time. Some I like, a few I tolerate, and the rest I loathe. I usually stay silent when we're all together, ignoring most and chatting with the few who want to talk bikes and cars. I don't ask personal questions, I don't know anything about them beyond what they ride, and I like it that way.

D and Malik talk more with them, Mal just being a nice guy and Danté wanting others to envy and fear him. I just don't give a fuck.

But he's extending an olive branch and I'd be the asshole to push him away.

"Yeah, sure. I'll call Dagen and see if she'd like to join us, if that's alright with you."

"I already talked to Mal and he texted Kins. She said they'll meet us there after dinner. So just head straight over when you're done at the shop." My possible last way out is derailed with his quick thinking.

"Okay. I'll see you later."

"See ya." We both hang up and I set about wasting every last minute of the work day, thinking about Dagen about the return to my life once she leaves.

A return to the dark and dank life I seem to find myself in every day of my miserable life.

I pull up to our bar and park my bike right in front, next to Mal's. I see Danté's car parked in his usual spot, and spot Kins' big ole blue taking up two spaces in the back. I pull off my helmet and tuck it under my arm, walking into the bar and greeting our bouncers with my usual head nod.

The bar is busy with guys and girls crowding it for drinks, and our two bartender's busting ass to meet the orders. I search the rest of the faces for Dagen's, not even thinking twice about the guys who are here.

I spot her standing with Kinsley near a booth and she throws her head back in laughter. Her lips are spread wide and her face is full of youth and light. The contrast between the two of us is yet again so easy to see.

I make a quick detour to the office where I sit my helmet on the couch and toss my gloves inside of it. My jacket gets hung on the stand and I give myself a quick check in the small mirror before walking out. I don't usually care what I look or smell like when I'm grabbing a drink after work, but I've never really cared to impress anyone before.

I step out into the mass again and beeline for the booth where a group is gathered. The laughter grows louder as I near, but so does my rage when I see the men gathered around her.

Paolo sits at the edge of the booth with his hand resting on Dagen's hip. I feel a buzzing in my head and my vision blurs, only Danté's smarmy grin outshining everything around.

"You want to take your fucking hand off of her, Paolo?" I growl and Dagen spins her head to meet me.

"Hey! You're here." She lunges for me and throws her arms around my neck, the smell of alcohol wafting off her breath.

"Wassup, Henny? I was just talking with our new friend, Dagen." Paolo smiles at me with the fakest one I've seen yet.

"She's not your anything Paolo, so it'll behoove you to remember that and keep your hands to yourself. Got it?"

Out of the corner or my eye, I see Danté raise his glass to his mouth, covering up the smirk that he just can't seem to let go.

Paolo holds his hands up in defense. "Woah, Henny. Chill out man. We were just talking."

"Yeah, Henny," Danté chimes in. "They're just talking. Why are you getting so upset? It's not like she's your girl or anything. You're just fucking, right?"

My blood boils, bubbling over the lid and billowing out of my ears. My teeth grind painfully as I stare him down. The urge to wrap my hands around Danté's neck and watch his eyes bulge with fear intensifies.

Dagen releases me and takes a step away from my reach. She's probably processing the words that came from Danté. The very same ones I told him when I didn't want to divulge that I was looking at Dagen as more than just another fuck buddy who I'd forget in a few months.

"What the fuck is wrong with you, D? Do you have a problem because from where I stand, it sure as fuck seems like it." I step up to him as he stays seated at the table with an arm thrown over the back of the leather upholstered bench.

He looks relaxed, like he just got a deep throat from some chick in the back room and nothing can bother him.

"Nah. I was just clarifying for Paolo. You and Dagen are just fucking around. She'll be gone next week. Right?" He chuckles, challenging me.

"You prick. Are you still pissed that she wanted me and not you? Get over it. You can't always get what you want." Paolo lays a hand on my arm and I throw him off of me. "Take your goddamn hand off of me."

"Henny. It's alright. Just chill, brother." Malik sits at the juncture of the two sides with a girl I've never seen before on one side and another rider, Frank, on the other.

"Don't tell me to chill. I want to know what crawled up this fuckers ass and died. Dagen never wanted you Danté and you knew it just like I did. Quit playing a fucking game, because I'm not biting."

Paolo stands from the booth and catches me off-guard. Thinking he's going to throw a punch or push me away like a little bitch, I strike first, landing my fist right into his left cheek. There's a high-pitched screech and he crashes back against the table. Glasses fall over and shatter, sending water and whatever other drinks spilling across and off the edge.

"Woah, woah." Malik panics and jumps up and over the table to get to me. "What the fuck, Henny? Stop."

Paolo rises to his feet, having caught his balance, and takes a swing at me and catches Malik in the middle of it.

"Fuck," he shouts and ducks out.

I wrap up Paolo's arms and knee him in the gut. He folds over but recovers quickly and catches me with a weak ass uppercut. It still rings my bell, but I would have knocked him out landing a punch like that.

The bouncers separate us, holding our arms back and away from the other.

"You're a bitch, Henny."

"Yeah, come over here and say that so I can bust your fucking ugly face." I spit at him and it falls to the floor, bloodied.

"Knock it off, Henny. Go outside and get your mind right. Maybe just go home," one of the bouncers says and walks me to the door. He doesn't kick me out, because it's my goodman bar, but he pushes me out and blocks the doors, stopping me from reentering.

I swipe the blood from the corner of my mouth and see Dagen walking with Kins towards her truck.

"Dagen. Wait!" She halts in her steps and I jog over to her.

"You have some nerve, Hendrix Dare." Kinsley steps between Dagen and I, pointing her finger right in my face. "That was lower than a snake's belly in a wagon rut. I oughta knock you into the middle of next week looking both ways for Sunday for behavin' like that."

"Kins, can you chew my ass out another time? I'd like to speak to Dagen." She narrows her eyes at me and crosses her arm.

Her eyes travel to meet Dagen's and she gives Kins a short nod.

"I'mma watch you, boy, like a fly waitin' for shit to rot."

"I don't know what that means, but okay." She uses two fingers to point from her eyes to mine, then stomps off to her truck.

I turn my attention back to Dagen and see her looking down at her foot that's kicking a rock, her arms crossed over her shoulders.

"I apologize for that. The guy just really pissed me off. Maybe it's stupid because, I know you're not *my* girl, but I didn't like his hands on you."

Still concentrating on the ground she says, "Did you really say that to Danté? We're just fucking?"

I swallow down my guilt, but knowing it was just something I said to get him off my back. "I did but listen," I spit out when she raises her head with unshed tears in her eyes. "Danté hasn't talked to me since that first night after darts. He was pissed that I 'won' you. He doesn't like losing anything, and he saw that kiss you and I shared as a loss for him. He definitely wanted a quick hookup with you, but Dagen…you have to know that I didn't feel that way. I *don't* feel that way. And I think he sees that. He's trying anything to get under my skin. Clearly it worked."

She pushes away a single tear that falls from the corner of her eye and a little bit of my black heart starts to warm.

"I'm ashamed to admit that I have used women for only one thing over many years. You already know that my asshole demeanor is my norm, but with you it was extreme. But only because there was this immediate kickstart to my mind and body. It pissed me the fuck off, to be honest. Why after all of these years did a stranger stuck in a ditch have to make me feel something I didn't recognize?"

"It wasn't a ditch," she mumbles.

"What was that?"

With a sigh she downplays a smirk and repeats, "It wasn't a ditch. Just the side of the road."

I reach out and grab her hand, pulling her close to me and wrapping my arms tightly around her as she does the same with me. "Smartass. The point is I'm not a guy who wants a girl for more than one night. I'm sure as shit not a guy who sees stars when a spoiled girl with green eyes smiles at me. But here I am, exactly where I never thought I would be."

She smacks my back and giggles. "Says the millionaire. And I'm not spoiled, just loved."

I stare at her, completely captivated by her beauty, and draw her in for a kiss. She melts into my arms, my body coming alive from her touch. My hunger is intense and I need to feed.

"Let's go. I need this mouth on other places." She lets out a soft mewl and nods. "Shit. I rode my bike and I don't have any extra gear."

"I'll just have Kinsley drop me off. No problem," she shrugs.

"It is a fucking problem. You should be riding backpack."

"Sorry, big bad wolf. Looks like you'll be practicing the art of patience." She smacks my ass then withdraws her arms from mine. "Race ya." She winks then tears off for Kinsley's truck with a laugh. "Start the truck McKinsley. We got a race to win."

Kins lets out a whoop then cranks her engine. I wait a moment longer then run back into the bar to get my things. I don't bother to pass anyone a second look, especially not Danté, and quickly tug on my jacket, gloves and helmet.

I'm back on my bike and zipping out of the parking lot in minutes. I know the girls won't beat me, so I plan a little surprise for Dagen. It might not be one that she's wanting... yet

I park my bike in the garage and hustle out to slide behind a large shrub just near the breezeway away from any light. My black clothing allows me to completely disappear in the darkness and it's exactly what I want. I raise my visor to help me see better and then just wait.

Within a few minutes, I hear the wheezing of Kins' truck dragging up. The door opens and a country song blasts from the speakers.

"I don't think he's here. I think we beat him," she tells Kins.

"Well that'll be a first. I'll check in on you in the mornin'. It's Saturday, so that means no classwork and beach time."

They exchange good-byes and the door slams shut with a bang. The sound of the engine fades as her truck pulls away and I wait to hear the side gate open and shut. When I know she's closed and locked the gate, I quietly step out as she passes and wrap a hand around her mouth and the other around her waist. A muffled scream erupts from her mouth and I tug her back into the shrubs.

"Shhh. Don't scream little mouse. I don't want to have to tie you up. Unless you'd like me to." I feel her heart slam against her chest and her body shake. "If you promise not to scream I'll remove my hand. Think you can be a good girl?"

Dagen's head nods rapidly and I drop my hand. I hastily spin her around, thwacking her back against the harsh stucco house. I forget about the scratches that already line her back when she winces and I change my plans slightly.

My eyes adjust to the dark and see hers large and wide with only a thin ring of green circling her midnight black pupil. Her chest heaves with brisk breaths and I see the pulse in her neck jump with fright.

"Little mouse, little mouse, you look so delicious. And I'm the big bad wolf of your nightmares, sent to ravage you." My gloved hand slides down her cheek but she doesn't move. "Are you afraid of me?"

Her voice trembles when she says, "Yes. But what scares me also excites me."

A demonic laugh rumbles, joy spreading through my body that I've been able to infest this good girl with a taste of something sinister.

"I'm going to have my way with you, little mouse, but I'll let you tell me one thing. Do you want to feel fear or elation?"

Her lips quirk up and she whispers, "Why can't I have both?"

I hold her stare, her innocence to my nefariousness, and remove my helmet. I grip it with one hand and slowly lean in. She parts her lips, waiting for the kiss she thinks is coming and instead, swipe my tongue from her collarbone up the slender column of her neck and stop at her ear. I take the small lobe adorned with a diamond between my teeth. My hand clamps around her jaw and I angle her head to the side, giving me perfect access to nip back down her throat.

Her breath shudders and she squeezes her thighs together, warding off the desire that tingles between them. I suck in her delicate skin, breaking the blood vessels and digging my teeth into her. I realize she already wears the imprint of my teeth on her, but I figure she needs a matching set. Like eyes and ears. Two are better than one.

I release her with a pop and tell her, "Now you wear the mark that lets the world know you belong to me."

My helmet gets lowered to the cold dirt beneath our feet and I take her purse, setting it in the same place. I claim her mouth is a scorching kiss and when she moves to wrap her arms around me, I grab them and raise them above her head, trapping both wrists in one hand.

The muggy evening sets my body sweating with all of my clothes still on and zipped to my neck. "Take off my gloves," I order her.

She tries to pry her hands from my restraint, but I only tighten my hold on her. "Use your teeth."

I present my hand to her, holding it steady in front of her mouth. Her eyes waver between my hand and my eyes and I encourage her to do as she's been told. Gradually she opens her mouth and carefully bites down on one finger, catching a small sliver of leather between her teeth.

She stretches her neck back, working to free one finger at a time until I'm able to pull my hand free. I trade out one hand for the other, and insist she do the same with the other hand. I take my warm, calloused hands and band them tenderly around her neck. My thumbs rub circles on the side to soothe her worries that I may hurt her.

Inhaling and exhaling I tell her, "I really want to feel that soft mouth of yours wrapped around my thick cock." She bites her lips and her pulse jumps. "Oh you like that, don't you little mouse? You can't wait to feel the searing pain of my dick forcing its way down your throat. Fuck, I want to see those big green eyes staring up at me with tears pooling in them."

I glide my finger across her lips and she sticks her tongue out as it passes. This woman is feisty and it makes me want to see just how far I can push her.

The first finger slides into her mouth and she sucks it in willingly. Then I feed her a second and a third, pushing them further back in her throat. I can feel the way it spasms with a gag, but Dagen is a good little mouse and she doesn't pull away or tell me to stop.

"Get on your knees, Dagen." She languidly drops to her knees and strains her neck to keep her gaze focused on mine.

I wait for her to unzip my pants and pull me out, but she's frozen in her stance.

"I shouldn't have to tell you what to do. Pull out my fucking cock and choke on it, Dagen. Swallow it down."

With trembling hands, she undoes my pants and works her hand into my boxer briefs, running her hand up and down my shaft before pushing the pesky fabric away and suctioning her mouth to my throbbing head.

A growl echoes through the crisp air and she drives down deeper until I fill her mouth. A gush of air billows out of her nose and I feel it against my groin. She moves back and forth, sucking and slurping as she goes. I break, not able to take this slow ebb and flow, and yank on her hair, pulling on the roots and locking her into place.

My hips thrust and I'm more forceful than I intend to be, but she feels so good. The sound of her gagging sends a chill up my spine and it sets my balls tingling and drawing up. I take no care yanking myself free from her mouth and hauling her to her feet. She heaves for air as she tries to catch her balance, placing her hands on my arms to steady herself.

"Turn around," I bark while pushing my pants to my ankles and choking my dick to stop it from exploding all over my unsuspecting flowers.

She stumbles over her feet as she spins around, and I grip onto her hips quickly unbuttoning her jeans and working them over her ass. When I yank her back to me, she tips forward and braces her hands on the wall.

I lick my fingers, soaking them with the saliva that builds in my mouth, and rub them between her dripping pussy. She moans when I play between her lips, wiggling her hips and silently begging for more. I give her more by slapping my hand over her tender clit and she yelps.

"Don't act like that didn't get you wet, Dagen." I plunge my fingers harshly inside of her.

They scissor and curl, pulling whine after mewl. I can feel the way her pussy convulses and spasms, and I need to feel it quake around my dick. I remove my fingers and replace them swiftly with my throbbing cock.

"Aaahh." She cries out and lets her head sag between her outstretched arms.

I place my hand back over her mouth and shush her. "Quiet, little mouse. You don't want the neighbors to know you're getting fucked like an animal in the wild."

She nods and her groans vibrate against my hand. I thrust harder and faster and her muffled cries continue to bounce off my palm. Her body begins to tremble and my guess is that she's close.

I let my hand fall away from her mouth and begin rubbing furiously over her nub. She goes rigid, pushing back and locking out her arms.

"Shhhhit," she cries and actual tears fall, landing in my arm with a soft drop.

Working her through the orgasm I don't ease up, slamming against her with fervor and fury until I'm pouring into her hot womb.

Together we make the sounds of savages, feasting on their conquest and relishing in their prize. My hand is gripped tightly around Dagen's throat and I feel it constrict as she gasps for air. Emptying the last of myself deep inside of her, I remove my hand and tug her upright. I grip her jaw and turn her head towards me, then take her mouth in a ruthless kiss.

My dick softens and I pull out of her then tuck myself back into my jeans and help guide Dagen's back up her legs and over her hips. I pick up the discarded items from the cold dirt and she finally turns to face me.

"Are you okay, little mouse?" I ask and she nods, completely out of breath and spent. "Did I scare you?" Another nod. "Did you like it?" This time a big and rapid nod.

I savor the sweet taste of my victory. No other man will ever be able to satisfy her craving for the demented that I've shown her, and in that sense she will always be mine.

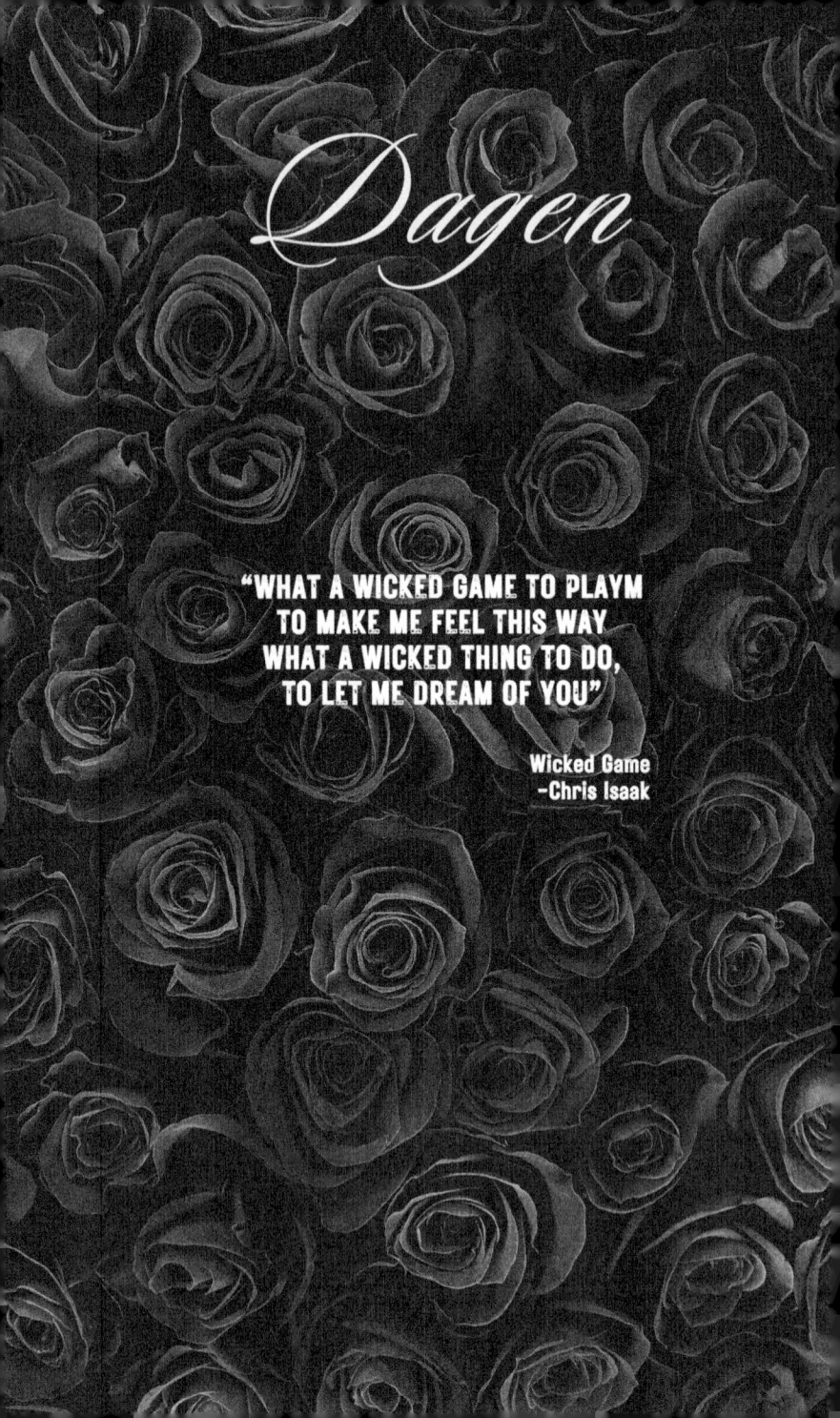

TWENTY-ONE

"SO ARE we doing bonfire and beers at the beach tonight?" Malik comes walking into Hendrix's house without any warning and I jump off the stool I sit perched on, screeching as I run to hide behind my tattooed wall of safety.

"Fucking christ, Mal. You really need to, oh I don't know, ring the goddamn doorbell." Hendrix shields my body, clad only in his white t-shirt and nothing else.

And when I say nothing else I mean *nothing* else. I'm positive my nipples peek through the thin fabric as does a hint of my bare ass.

"Why? I never have before. And if you didn't want me to just walk straight in, you shouldn't have given me your garage code." He walks over to the island and pulls a banana from the bunch that sits in a bowl. "Hey Day. Can I call you Day? Kins said that I could."

I peek my head out from behind Hendrix and tell him, "Hi. Uh, sure. Day is fine. It's what most of my friends and family back home call me."

"Cool. So I was thinking I'll go grab the firewood and the stones we usually use are still in my garage. Danté said he—"

"Malik! Get the fuck out! Dagen needs to get dressed." Hendrix's hands are balled into fists and I can feel heat radiate off his back.

I've noticed that aside from being an asshole, Hendrix has a bit of a short fuse when it comes to things that anger him. It was evident after last night at the bar when he hauled off and punched a friend.

"It's okay. Maybe you can just turn around or something, Malik."

He shrugs and smiles as best as he can with half a banana shoved into his mouth, and turns his back to us. I make like a bullet and fire out of the kitchen so fast I'm sure Hendrix saw everything wiggle and jiggle as I went.

When I get to his room, I don't bother putting on last night's clothes. Mostly because they're dirty from laying in the dirt and mulch as Hendrix fucked the life out of me. Not to worry. He fucked it right back where it's supposed to be in bed this morning.

I sort through my things to find my bra and slip on a pair of Hendrix's sweatpants that I find sitting on a shelf in his closet. I roll the waist over and over until my feet stick out and I can walk without tripping. As I enter the main living space again, I can hear Hendrix and Malik talking, so I plaster myself against the hallway and eavesdrop on their conversation.

"What were you thinking, punching Paolo like that? You know he's not a bad guy. He wouldn't have made the moves on Dagen."

"I know I shouldn't have. It was really Danté I wanted to punch but since I couldn't, the poor guy was the unlucky recipient of my wrath."

"What's his deal, anyhow? He's been a motherfucker even more than usual," Malik asks.

"He's still pissed about the whole darts and Dagen incident. I thought everything was cool yesterday when he called to tell me to meet y'all at the bar, but apparently it was just a bunch of shit. He knew exactly what to say to set me off. Especially seeing that I was already a hair trigger when I saw Paolo's hands on her."

They grow silent and I'm just about to make my presence known when Malik speaks up.

"You like her."

"Yeah. She's a cool chick and hot as fuck. What's not to like?"

A small laugh accompanies Malik's next words. "Nah, man. I mean, you *like* Dagen. Enough to want to tie her up in your basement and keep her here."

I think about being bound and what Hendrix would do to me. It's another one of my worst nightmares and greatest fantasies come to life. My body restrained while Hendrix has his way with me. It's a thought that shocks me at how much I want it.

When Hendrix doesn't respond I walk a little harder than necessary, slapping my feet on the tile to warn them I'm returning.

"Now that I'm dressed, I think we can have a proper conversation. So what was that you were saying about beer, beach and bonfire?" Malik's big, bright smile is wide and infectious.

He palms an apple, tossing it up in the air and catching it like Uncle Phoenix does with baseballs.

"That's right sweetheart. I think it's time you experience a Dare Night. You'll have fun." He takes a large bite out of the apple, crunching it.

"Do you not have food at your own fucking house?" Hendrix yanks the fruit bowl away from him and sets it down on the opposite counter. "It's not going to be a normal Dare Night. Right Mal?"

Malik's eyes volley between mine and Hendrix like one of us will tell him the correct thing to say. "I mean...maybe?"

"No. The correct word you're looking for is no." Hendrix's voice is stern and leaves no room for debate.

"Well wait. I want to know more about Dare Night. Is it anything like the game we played, Hendrix?" Malik snorts, choking on his apple as bits fly out.

Hendrix's face pales and I give myself an internal pat on the back for stunning him into silence. I get the feeling that not many people are able to one up this man.

"I just need to know if I should wear something better to protect my ba–" Hendrix dives over the counter and slaps his hand over my mouth.

Apparently Mr. Dare doesn't like even his brothers knowing about his proclivities. Or he's trying to save me from some type of inquisition from Malik that may end up in fists flying like last night. I stick my tongue out and lick his palm and when he doesn't remove his hand, I lick again.

"Quit you little brat. Do you want Mal knowing all the details about how you got those scratches on your back?" I immediately stop with the tongue bath I'm giving his hand. "That's what I thought."

Malik continues to watch our interaction as he wipes away the spittle that landed all over his black t-shirt. When Hendrix slowly drops his hand and arches his brow at me, I challenge him with one of my own.

"What should I wear to this beer, beach and bonfire night? Is there a dress code I need to adhere to?"

"Nope. But I would suggest you bring a sweatshirt. It can get chilly even with the fire. Other than that, just wear that pretty smile of yours." Hendrix groans and rolls his eyes and it makes me laugh.

He really is a grump. No one is spared from his sour mood. He makes it clear that he doesn't want to continue our conversation when he grabs Malik by the shoulders and steers him towards the door he came in from.

"See you tonight, Malik."

"Bye Day," he sings and it echoes through the house.

When the door is closed, Hendrix struts back into the kitchen and damn does he strut good. Defined, well toned chest and abs covered in beautiful art and his black boxer briefs sitting low on his hips, just on the border of obscene.

"You're gonna get it," he warns.

"Well I would surely hope so." I smirk and watch his eyes turn a torrential shade of blue.

With a wink, I sprint up the stairs rushing for my room. I don't really try too hard to not get caught. After all, it's the thrill of the chase.

We pull up to the beachside parking lot on Hendrix's bike and he comes to a stop. I'm almost a little sad that our ride is over. I don't have an excuse to have my arms wrapped around him in public when we're not on his bike.

After climbing off and peeling out of our gear, we walk down to the beach side by side. I want so desperately to reach out and hold his hand, but I don't think he's the holding hands with a girl type. So I keep my hands tucked into my pockets and let the most touching we do be our arms rubbing against each other.

As we get closer to the group of people gathered around the bonfire, we hear loud laughter and music playing. I scan the group, hoping and praying that Kinsley has come because I really need back up for tonight.

"Day! You made it." Malik calls out from where he stands with a few girls.

They all turn their heads towards us and Malik leaps over a couple of people seated in the sand. He jogs over and inserts himself between Hendrix and I, throwing an arm around each of us.

"You're just on time. We're just about to start the dance party." Hendrix bats his hand at Malik, smacking him in the chest.

"No dance party, no dares. Just a chill evening on the beach. Got it?"

Malik sticks his tongue out and jacks his hand. "Such a spoilsport. Remember when you used to be fun?"

"No," Hendrix answers, curtly.

"Yeah, me neither. Hey everyone! This is Dagen. My new best friend."

I spend the first several minutes being dragged around and introduced to various people whom I will definitely not remember their name. When they ask if I live in Cattywump Bay, Hendrix tells them I'm visiting then moves me right along.

At one point I ask about Kinsley's whereabouts and am told that she'll be joining as soon as she's done with the work she hasn't been doing since I crashed into town. Chairs get opened up along with blankets that get spread out, and I'm handed a beer from one of the guys that rides with the Dare brothers.

I think about the fact that there is one person in particular missing just as a deep voice laced with venom speaks up.

"Well look at that. If it isn't Henny and his new gal. How's it going, Dagen?" Danté slithers up to me and places a hand on my shoulder before squatting down to my level where I sit. "Hey, I want to apologize. I tend to push people's buttons a lot, and I think I pressed too many of Henny's last night. I don't like fighting with my brothers and I certainly don't like making pretty girls sad. Forgive me?" He smiles with a wicked gleam and the roaring fire behind him seems to be very fitting.

I'm not a person known to hold on to grudges with both hands. My parents have always taught me to give second chances when they're due. I've always tried to live by that. So I'd be a hypocrite if I turned a cheek to Danté knowing I would encourage someone to put discretions aside and forgive.

"Of course. I'm sure you were just looking out for your brother," I tell him and he glides his hand down my arm and stops when he reaches my hand.

"Actually dollface, I was looking out for you. Us Dare Bros are nothing but trouble. The last thing you need is to get twisted up with one of us. We'll only bring you down." He lifts a hand and taps the underside of my chin. "Can we let bygones be bygones?"

I pass him a small smile and agree. "Sure."

He jumps to his feet. "Alright. Now that we're all friends, how about we get the Dare games started now that the devil himself has arrived."

The group cheers and I feel the heat of Hendrix's stare on my face.

"We aren't playing," he tells me very matter of factly when I look at him.

"Why not? If everyone else gets to, why can't we?"

He grows agitated and leans in close to me. "Please just trust me."

I've known this man for a whole seven days and he thinks he can tell me what to do? My mom and aunts raised a free-thinking, independent woman and I'm not about to bow down now.

"I'm playing, so let's go." Hendrix's eyes fill with fire and I turn away, not really caring how he feels.

The night really just starts out as drinking games, many

that I've never heard of. Pizza box was the first game where everyone wrote their name on a box –in this case an empty beer case– and drew a circle around it. One person tossed a quarter and the name it landed on had to take a shot. Then that person threw a quarter and it continued until everyone was pretty knackered. Luckily I only got saddled with two shots. No surprise, the grumpy old man Hendrix didn't play.

Next we played Thumper, which required one player to continuously make some type of hand motion or tick. When a person picked up on it, they took a swig of their drink each time the motion was repeated. This had people tapping out.

After that, things turned a bit racier. One person was dared to jump over the fire pit. Thankfully he avoided catching fire. Malik was dared to run naked into the ocean and while I tried to redirect my attention, I admit to taking a small peek. Not even a little guilty that I did.

Now I sit close to Hendrix who has participated in nothing to do with drinking, sipping on a beer of my own.

"Henny," a girl who is quite inebriated and wearing the smallest shorts known to man, calls out from across the fire. "I dare you to play the game with us."

He sighs and leans back into his chair, throwing his arm over the back of my chair. "Fine. I'll play your fucking game but no drinking. I'm on my bike with Dagen."

The woman gets a sly smirk on her face as does Danté who sits next to her.

"Good. First dare...I dare you to kiss me."

Hendrix rolls his eyes. "I'm not doing that, Soria."

"Why not? It's not like you haven't done it before," she purrs, obviously trying to make me jealous.

"Henny, you gotta take the dare. Otherwise, you know what happens next." Danté lifts his beer to his pink lips and throws back a swig.

"Kiss her. Kiss her," the group starts chanting.

Everyone, but Malik.

"That's a lame dare. We're not thirteen anymore."

Soria –as I have come to learn is her name– slinks her way over to us and stops directly in front of Hendrix's chair. I see his jaw clench with tension and his nostrils flare.

"Exactly. Which is why this isn't a typical kiss."

"Bro," Malik says, a little bit of torture in his voice. "Just do it. You don't want the alternative."

Hendrix looks from Malik to me to Soria, his chest heaving and teeth grinding together. He lowers his head, exhaling a defeated breath, then lifts it to look up at Soria. Once his attention is fully on her, she begins to roll up the t-shirt that is suctioned to her body, exposing her flat stomach inked with a dragon that wraps around her torso.

I swallow down a lump of anxiety as I continue to watch them. Next she unbuttons her shorts and pulls them open, just enough to hint at the ladybug tattoo that sits just above her pubic bone.

"Lick it," she purrs.

"You said kiss, Soria," Hendrix protests.

"Kiss the ladybug, then lick your way and kiss Falkors face." I presume her tattooed dragon is Falkor and I think it's a bit pathetic she named it, but whatever.

Hendrix's eyes close in agony and I wait for him to refuse. In my head I'm begging him to say no and take whatever consequence they'll dole out.

But against my silent pleas, he leans forward and places a chaste kiss on her small tattoo, getting dangerously close to a place that should only be explored in private, and licks all the way up her lower abdomen, up her ribs, and stopping at the dragon's head that sits just below her breast. My stomach turns with jealousy and I simply cannot stand to watch one more second.

I stand up abruptly, dropping my beer to the powdery sand, and stomp off towards the wooden boardwalk that leads back to the parking lot, far from the watching eyes of the people enjoying their gluttonous pleasures.

My eyes sting and I work hard to ward off the tears that threaten to fall. This is stupid. He's not my boyfriend, he's not my anything. I have no right to feel any sort of possession over him.

I prop my hands on my hips and take deep breaths, working to calm myself down. I look like a fool and there is no way in hell I'm walking back down to that beach to sit and act like I didn't just stomp off like a child who was told no by her dad. I search for my phone in the front pocket of Hendrix's hoodie and pull it out.

My only chance at getting away from here is Kinsley. I feel bad for relying on her so much over the last week, but this genius forgot to get the actual address of Hendrix's house, so getting an Uber isn't going to be an option.

I open my phone and pull up her number, but just before I touch her name, my name is shouted out behind me.

"Dagen!" I look over my shoulder to see Hendrix jogging up the wooden bridge.

I turn my face away and let my shaky thumb hover over the phone screen.

"Don't act like you didn't see me. I saw your big greens." He walks up behind me, the heat of his body warming my back, but I don't turn around or acknowledge him. "Stop it you little brat. Look at me."

My head whips around and anger washes over my face. "Do not tell me what to do. I'm not your dog, your friend or your girl."

"Then why the fuck did you march off like a jealous girlfriend?" He bellows.

"Because...because I didn't want to sit there and watch the guy who was kissing me just this afternoon lick the body of one of his previous conquests."

Hendrix hangs his head and his shoulders rise and fall with exaggerated sighs. "I'm sorry."

"If you're sorry, why'd you do it!" My arms wave in the air and my voice begins to turn up an octave.

"Because it was better than the alternative."

I roll my eyes with a scoff. "Oh yeah, sure. What, were they going to make you sing and dance like a chicken? Poor Henny."

"No, it wouldn't have been anything embarrassing. The alternative would have been to give you to one of the guys. If you bring a date to the bonfire and pass on a dare, you forfeit your date. It's the only reason why I slept with Soria."

I let all of what he just said process and it just seems totally unbelievable. Too ridiculous to be true.

"What a crock of bullshit. You really expect me to believe that?"

"Go ask Malik if you don't believe me. Call Kinsley. She'll tell you the truth. She knows what goes on down here. She never plays, but she's witnessed it all."

I stand there with narrowed eyes and my phone clenched tightly in my hand.

Hendrix pulls out his phone and taps the screen. A loud ring sounds from the speaker and I wait to see who picks up the other end.

The ringing stops and the sweetest southern voice booms. "For cryin' out loud, I'll be there soon."

"Kins. What happens when you pass on a dare?" Hendrix asks, wasting no time with pleasantries.

"Wha–why? Am I on speaker?"

"Just say it. Please Kinsley. If you say no to dare, what happens next?"

The phone is silent for a beat then Kinsley says, "You have to pass off your date. Man or woman, you hand them over to someone of their choice."

My mouth drops as does my stomach. "Thanks. See you later."

"But wait. W–" Hendrix cuts her off by ending the call and slipping the phone back into his pocket.

"Believe me now?"

I cross my arms over my chest to stop my hands from trembling.

"Whatever. It doesn't matter anyway. We're just fucking anyhow, remember?" I flip my head away, but it's quickly returned to face Hendrix once again.

"Cut that shit out, Dagen." My cheeks are squeezed in his grip and if I thought his eyes were stormy before, they're a full on cyclone now. "I already told you I didn't mean it. I just did that to get Danté off my back."

He drops his hands and I throw mine up. "Then what are we?"

"I don't know!" We shout at one another like two lovers caught in a quarrel, drawing the attention of everyone in earshot.

We're in a standoff, waiting for the other to make the first move, whatever that may be. My body tingles while his eyes drink me in. With the passing of another tense moment, we both lunge and grab for each other. Our lips crash and our hands feel their way around like a blind person trying to make sense of what lies beneath them.

Hendrix circles his hands around my waist and boosts me up, my legs immediately wrapping around him. I feel his fingers dig into my ass and he groans into my mouth. I'm so wet right now that if I stood up, I'm sure it would puddle to the ground.

He rips his lips away from mine and pants, "Get that fucking helmet on your head now."

Still in his strong hold, he removes me from clinging to him, sets me on his bike and tosses the helmet at me. He yanks his off the handle it hangs from and tugs it on, then quickly shoves his arms into his jacket like it pissed him off.

With the pop of his clutch and push of a button, his bike fires up and we're peeling out of the parking lot with a screech and trail of dust.

I look over my shoulder and see the faces of those still on the beach. I can't make out any of their expressions, but some of the men have their hands raised in victory. Danté is not one of them.

I'm over what he thinks of me. Right now I'm on fire and only Hendrix can cool the flames.

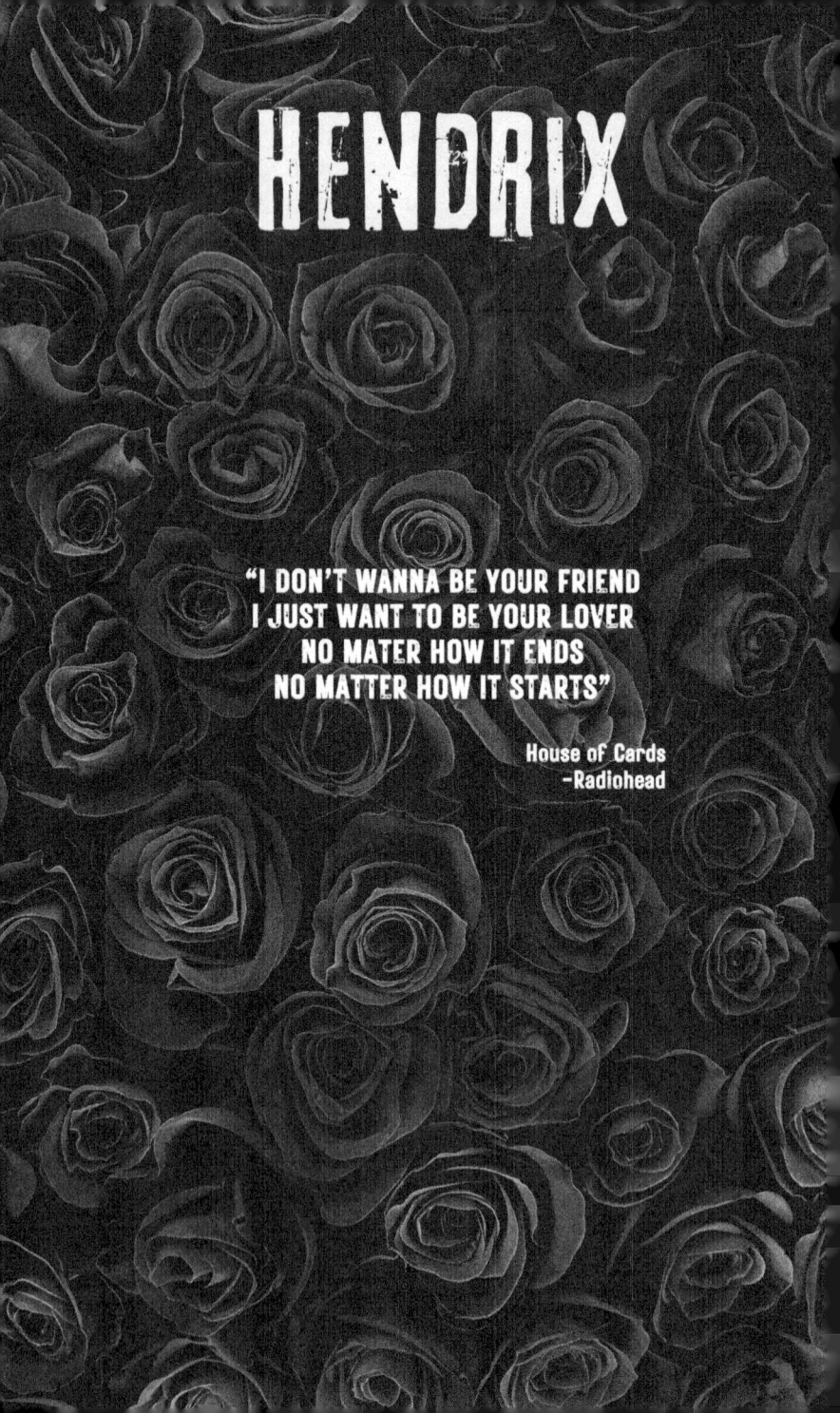

TWENTY-TWO

HER HANDS ROAM UP and down my chest and every opportunity I have, I reach back and stroke her leg.

I knew that fucking game would be a disaster tonight. A beach night never ends innocently. But tonight I prayed that it would. Then Soria had to go and give me that bullshit dare. What's worse is that I have a feeling Danté put her up to it.

Whatever he was or wasn't a part of doesn't matter. What does matter is getting Dagen to a place where I can let my carnal cravings loose. And since my house is more than thirty minutes away, the shop it is.

Neither of us speaks as we ride. The sound of the wind whipping past us as I drive eighty miles an hour, weaving in and out of cars, is the only thing we hear. But when we pull into the garage amongst the cars still being worked on, Dagen tenses.

"I thought we were going back to your house?"

I walk my bike to a stop and drop the kickstand. "Too far. I needed you ten minutes ago."

I turn off the motor and quickly jump off, pulling Dagen with me. It's another frantic grab at clothing to free ourselves.

T-shirts here, shorts there, shoes wherever, everything is tossed until we both stand naked.

I advance on Dagen, pushing her back until she runs into her silver BMW that is parked conveniently right beside where my bike is. She falls to the hood and surges from the cold. My hand slides into her hair and I rip her head back.

Her lips part, begging to be kissed. "What are you waiting for, Mr. Big Bad Wolf? Aren't you going to gnash and claw at your scared little mouse?"

"Is that what you want Dagen?" She spreads her legs, wrapping one foot around me and tugging closer to where she wants me.

Her head nods as she bites her lip, and she arches her back offering her tits to me. I dip my head and flick each nipple with my tongue. Her breathy moan is music to my ears. I kiss my way down her body, circling my tongue around her belly button before moving further down. She tries to clamp her legs shut and I lift my head to look at her.

"Open up, Dagen."

"You don't have to do that. Let's just skip it." She wiggles her fingers, trying to get me to climb my way back up.

"Fuck no. I've been dying to bury my face between your thighs and drink from your sweet pussy. There's no stopping me."

She stares at me, her chest heaving with apprehension. With our eyes still glued to each other, I descend her body and inhale the delicious scent that floats and drowns my senses. I spread her legs wide with my hands on her thighs, and I slip my tongue between her drenched lips.

My eyes roll when her nectar floods my taste buds. She's better than I remember. My tongue swipes up and down her seam like a hungry cat lapping up milk. If this was my last meal, I'd happily die right between these creamy thighs.

I move my head side to side, trying to crawl inside of her

as deep as I can. My tongue plunges in and out, drawing more from her.

"Fuck me. Fuck me now, Hendrix," she begs and reluctantly I pull away.

I replace my tongue with my dick and we both moan in pure content. It's a relief to finally settle into where I belong. Where I've belonged all along. I just never knew it.

Dagen's back sticks to the hood of the car as she tries to anchor herself to something solid to stop from climbing the walls.

"I wonder what daddy would say if he knew I fucked his little girl on the hood of his car," I grunt, slamming into her. "He doesn't know his princess is a dirty vamp who likes to get fucked hard by a bad, bad man."

I pin her down by her throat and feel the way her pulse jumps. She loves the danger I bring into her life. Her new hunger for pleasure and pain will never be satisfied by anyone but me. I'll make damn sure of it.

She reaches up and grips my face, urging me closer until our mouths mimic the movements of our bodies. Her mewls echo in my cavernous mouth and I swallow them down. She feeds my mind and body and I don't think the desire will ever fade.

"Oh shit," she hisses. "Right there. Harder."

With a growl I lift her legs, pushing them up wide by her ankles. I slam hard, reaching depths I hadn't before.

"Yes." Her eyes close and her neck arches, pushing her head harshly against the hood. "I can feel you everywhere."

"Because you were molded just for me. We fit together like a lock and key." I tilt closer and whisper, "My name is etched inside of your pussy. It's mine."

Her wails ricochet off the vast space. I yearn to have her between my teeth and draw her breast into my mouth. My teeth sink into the tender flesh and her screech pierces my ears. The way her pussy clenches when I do, is all the indication I need to give her more.

I suck brutally hard, practically ripping her nipple right off her tit. And when her nails rip into my scalp, I shoot off like a rocket. Groans and moans and foul words fall from my mouth, and I pump ruthlessly until I'm drained.

Her legs tumble from my grasp and slap the metal beneath us. I rest my forehead against hers and she runs her short nails up and down my spine.

"Do you think it's possible to know you won't be able to live without something after just finding it?" she asks.

I push up on my hands and fix my eyes to hers. "Completely."

It's a fact I know to be true. Just like I know I'll be an incomplete man once she's gone.

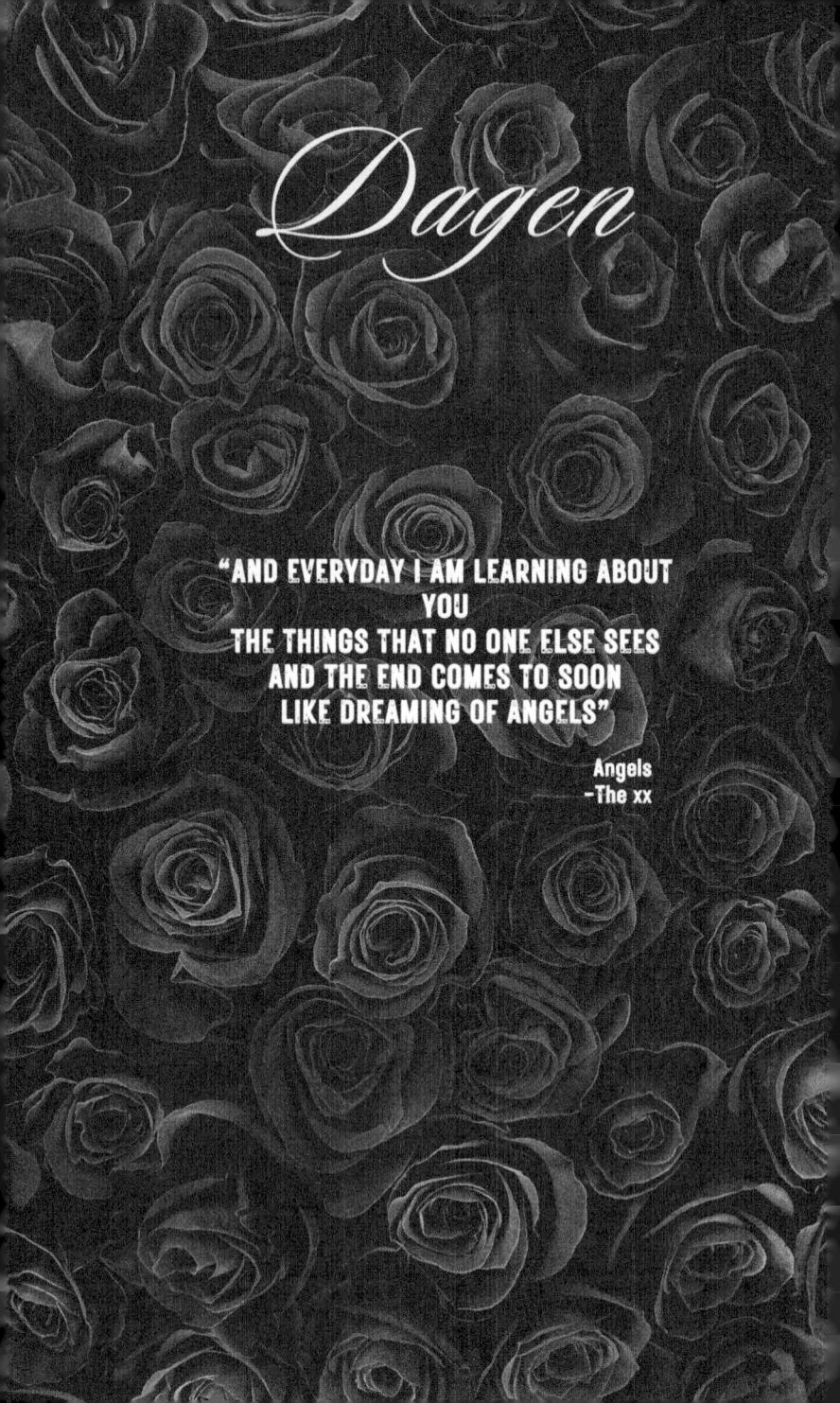

TWENTY-THREE

"WHY DO you have so many tattoos of skulls and roses and snakes and...and naked, evil women?" I straddle Hendrix, soaking up the warm afternoon sun as we sit out on his deck.

His friends will all be descending on his house soon, so we decided to enjoy some time alone before the madness – and possibly fighting– commences. I say fight, because after returning home from our rendezvous at Hendrix's shop, he spoke with Malik and found out Danté was the one who pushed Soria to make that stupid dare last night, and I'm still trying to figure out why the guy hates me so much that he'd do anything to drive me away.

I can't imagine that he's that pissed over losing darts. There has to be more to it because that just sounds ridiculous and childish. Malik seems to be everyone's best friend, so maybe he'll be willing to give me some information and clue me into why Danté's treating me like I'm Yoko Ono.

"What else am I supposed to get? Rainbows and four leaf clovers and unicorns?"

"No, but maybe something not so doom and gloom." My fingers ghost over one tattoo in particular between his pecs, tracing the twisting thorns that circle the blade of a dagger.

"Baby," he says, resting on his elbows and pushing his jet black sunglasses up. "My middle name is doom and gloom. And when that's all you ever known, you go with what feels like home."

I examine the grim reaper on his chest that is the most villainous figure I've ever seen. The head of Medusa sits on his collarbone, and her snakes crawl up his neck. Melting skulls, rotting roses, black widow spiders and pure malevolence cover his body. All in black, not an ounce of color in sight. They tell the story of a sad, dark, lonely life and I hope I can shed a little light for the short time I'm here.

"Looks like you have an empty spot right here." I circle my finger over the small space over his heart that remains untouched.

"That's reserved for something special."

"And what would that be?" I lean forward and rest my arms on his chest, propping up on my forearms.

"I haven't found it yet. When I do, I'll have the perfect place for it." His face looks so at ease, the strain that lined his forehead the first time I met him has vanished.

At least around me it has.

Hendrix's hands crush my ass and I move in to kiss him. He tastes like summer sun, ocean and carefree. I want to live wrapped in his warmth and play in his darkness. He's a complete juxtaposition that seems to only appear for me.

I roll my hips, grinding down on his hardening erection, and his fingers pinch my skin.

"How much time until everyone gets here?" I ask, my lips pressed to his and eyes closed.

"Soon. So we better hurry." He slides his fingers around and teases the edge of my bikini bottoms.

"Maybe we outta just wait." I attempt to pull back, but my body slaps against Hendrix's when he wraps me up.

"Little mouse. You can't just tease a hungry wolf then

walk away. You've awakened the beast and now I need to feed."

One of his hands slips inside the back of my bottoms and his fingers run up and down my seam. He toys with my puckered hole and glides down to my clit that buzzes with anticipation. Adrenaline courses through my veins waiting for the moment he does what only he can do so well.

His hand clamps around my throat and my eyes pop open. "I love the way you taste, little mouse." He inserts his finger in me and my body shivers. "Have you ever tasted yourself?"

"N-no," I croak, pushing the words past his firm grip.

He swirls and plunges his finger in and out before extracting it slowly and steady.

"Open. Taste the paradise that I do every time I bury my face between your legs." A long finger pushes through my parted lips and I close around it. Just like he did with my pussy, he slides in and out leaving a sample of me on my tongue.

My mouth pops when he pulls away and immediately brackets my face, swallowing me in a kiss. We both savor the tangy aftertaste, moaning into each other's mouths and rubbing our bodies together like kindling to a fire.

"Eh em." A loud clearing of a throat causes us both to jump and knock foreheads.

Rubbing our heads, we look and find Malik standing with a giant grin and foil covered tray.

"Sorry to interrupt. As much as I'd love to hop in and make that twosome a fire threesome, I don't think we have time." Malik holds the tray up with one hand, showing off his thick muscles.

"Like hell you'd join in. Give us a goddamn minute. You're early," Hendrix gruffs and wraps me up in his arms, trying to shield me from Malik's eyes.

"Thought I'd come help y'all out…in more ways than

one." His brows waggle up and down and that smirk grows to an alligator grin; wide and naughty.

"I'm gonna fuck you up if you don't get out of here, Mal." Hendrix swiftly rolls me over so that I'm on my side.

Over his shoulder I can see Malik laugh and jog back into the house, a playful gleam in his eyes.

Hendrix looks into my eyes and kisses my lips chastity. "I'm going to kick his ass real quick. Put some clothes on and meet me inside."

"Wait. Why do I need to put clothes on?" I ask, gripping onto his arm as he rises from the chair.

"Because if you don't, one, all the guys are going to want to fuck you. And two, if that happens I'm going to have to knock some skulls, then beat that little pussy of yours to remind everyone you're mine." He smacks my butt with a harsh snap of his wrist and runs off, leaving me to rub out the pain and process his words.

You're mine. But for how long, Hendrix Dare?

Kinsley and I sit in the hot-tub while the guys play a riveting game of cornhole. Hendrix has really cut loose with his drinking tonight since he doesn't have to drive and his affection has been dominating and possessive.

His kisses have been rougher and his touches have been all consuming. He has definitely let his actions speak louder than words, warning Danté and Malik away from me.

"I can't believe you'll be gone in a few days. The one time Henny's workers could have slowed their roll and they just went on and did ya up quick." Kinsley's face falls and I reach over and squeeze her hand.

"Don't be sad. I'm going to text you daily, and soon you'll come visit me. I'll drive down to Magnolia Creek and we can spend the weekend at my family's ranch."

She twists her mouth to the side and shrugs. "I guess that'll be alright. But I'm not the only one who's going to miss you."

I look over at Hendrix who sits on a lawn chair, drinking a beer and watching Danté and Malik battle it out. My lip gets trapped between my teeth and as if he feels the weight of my stare, he drifts his gaze to mine. Our draw to one another is electric, like one current flowing between us. It's like I've always had this live wire in me, charging with nowhere to go. Then I found Hendrix who had the same fragmented circuit, our loose ends joined to form a powerful force that could only exist between the two of us.

"You like him, dont'cha?"

"Yeah," I admit, never tearing my gaze away from the man who is going to break my heart.

What kind of person would willingly lay themselves in front of a beautiful monster knowing they'd only destroy them, never to be whole again?

Me.

I'm that kind of person.

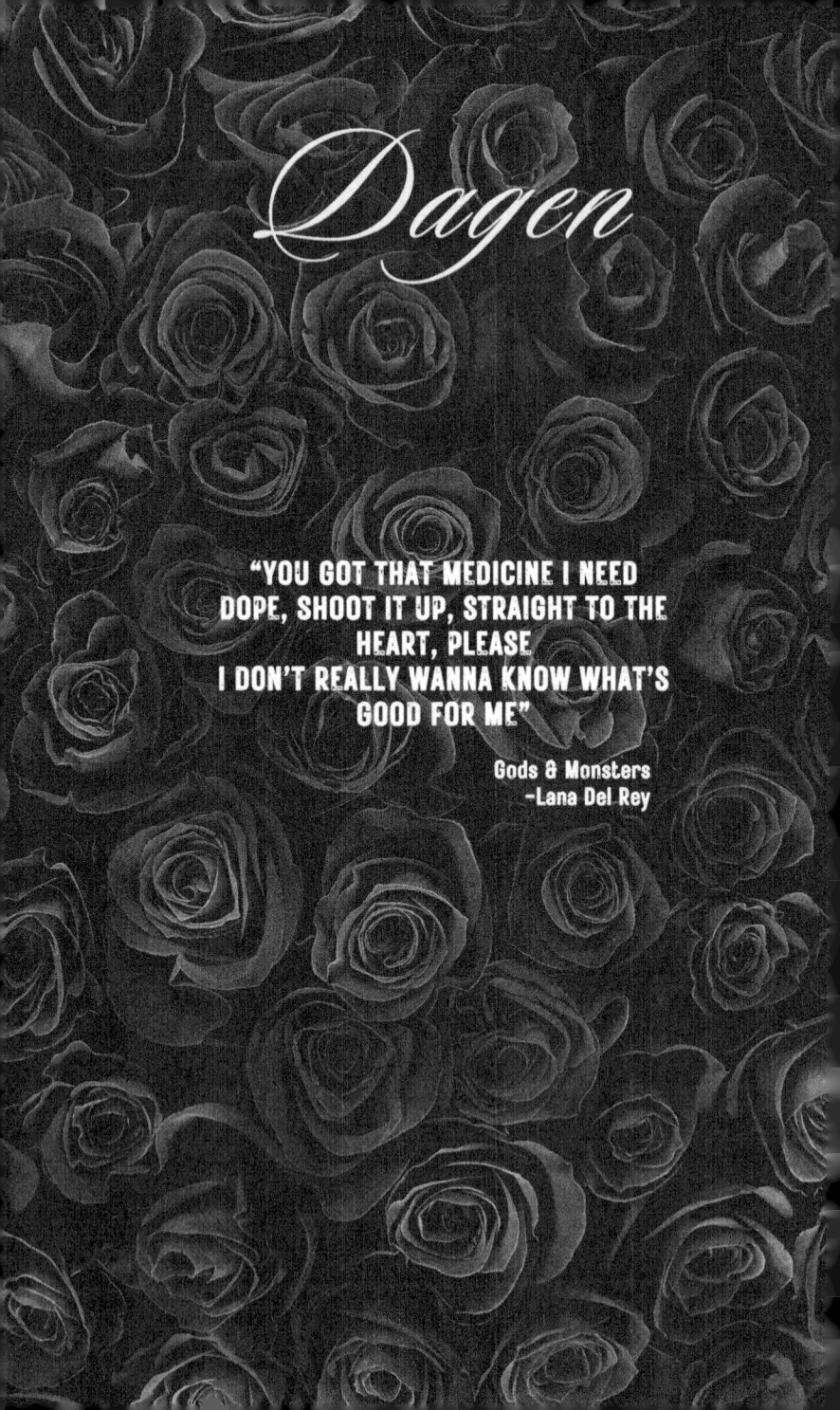

TWENTY-FOUR

"YES, I promise to drive carefully. Stay only on I-10, no detour and only stopping for gas, pee break and food." I sit on FaceTime with my parents, while in my home for the last nine days, while I gather all of my belongings.

"And check in with us every hour," Dad adds.

"Good grief. Okay. Seven phone calls. Maybe six if I can speed through Baton Rouge without all the traffic."

"No speeding!" Mom shouts. "Drive the speed limit. *Below* the speed limit."

I roll my eyes and sigh. "Okay. I'll drive twenty-five miles an hour. See you in five days."

"Smartass. Just make it home safely, baby bird."

I hear the worry in Dad's voice and I feel horrible for what I've put them through over the last two weeks. I'm not a bad girl. I don't step a toe out of line...*ever*. I graduated at the top of my class in high school. I've already been accepted to grad school, and I'm the best big sister you'll find. My family always comes first so the fact that I left everyone high and dry without a word is very unlike me.

But as much as I love my family, I just needed to breathe

without fifty people in my face. Their love can be a bit suffocating at times.

"I will, Dad. I promise. I'm really sorry I've put you all through so much lately." My face falls and my heart stings with guilt.

"Oh honey, it's okay." Mom's face falls soft and loving and it looks like she's trying to climb through the phone. "You had a lot thrown at you. It's understandable that you would need to be alone to process it all. We can be a bit much, sometimes."

I squint one eye and hold my thumb and forefinger just a millimeter apart. "A little."

"You better get on the road. I don't want you driving in the dark. Please be sure to thank Mr. Dare for his kindness. I worried a lot less knowing he was looking after you." Mom's eyes widen and I bite back my smile, both of us knowing Dad wouldn't appreciate the way that Mr. Dare cared for me.

"I will. Love you guys."

"Love you," they sing out together, like an expertly practiced chorus.

I press end and flop back on to the bed that I have stripped of its sheets in anticipation of them being laundered. I offered to wash them, but Hendrix wasn't having it. His maid is coming to take care of it all.

The door creaks open and Hendrix slowly steps in. "Everything good?"

I turn my head and smile. He's so gorgeous, my eyes have never seen a more beautiful man. And despite the black exterior he shows the world, inside he's a bright light.

"Yeah. They're just worry-warts. And not just because of the accident. They've always been that way."

"I could tell when your dad interrogated me," he huffs.

I prop myself up on my elbows and watch as he swaggers over. My eyes eat him up and my body already feels the loss of his touch.

"Can I say something without you thinking I'm some clingy, silly girl?" I ask him just as he leans over me, framing my face with his outstretched arms.

"Yes. You tell me and then I'll tell you what I came in here to say."

I nod my head and swallow, my throat scratchy and feeling like thorns line it. "I'll never forget you Hendrix Dare and I'm thankful for that."

His eyes search mine and I work hard to not let him see the tears that build behind my eyes. The look on his face is thoughtful and I can't decipher if he's about to kick me out on my ass or…or I don't know.

I'm surprised when he kisses me, hard and unrelenting. I circle my arms around him and hold on with every fiber of my being, memorizing what he feels like. My nose starts to tingle and a lump builds in my throat. Hendrix rests his forehead against mine and sighs.

"I'm coming with you," he tells me, his eyes still closed.

"Say what?" My eyes fly open and he rises to his full size.

"I said I'm coming with you."

"Like…forever?" I am so confused right now and apparently it's amusing to him.

"No, little mouse. I can't stay forever." My heartbeat that was pounding at triple comes to a hard stop. "I want to make sure you get home safely, so I'm coming with you. I'll fly back tomorrow."

I blink over and over, not really knowing what to say that doesn't make me look like a childish teenager. I want to jump and scream and cling to him and never let him go. Instead of the insane woman that wants to break free, I tell him, "Okay."

He reaches out, asking for my hand, and I give it to him. He pulls me to my feet, my chest crushing to his, and I circle his waist with my arms.

"What did mommy and daddy have to say?"

"My Dad told me to thank you for your kindness. I don't

think he'd be saying that if he knew the extent of your kindness."

A small tick of his mouth sends flutters swirling in my belly. "Yeah, we better not tell him. Come on, little mouse. Let's go."

He kisses my nose and zips up my duffle bag, then throws it over his shoulder. Grabbing my hand, he pulls me from the room and I give one last look at the place that may have changed my life.

"You're killing me with the music, little mouse." Hendrix wears black wayfarers and drives oh so cool with his hand hanging on the steering wheel.

"You were the one that said you wanted to drive to make sure I didn't 'accidentally' kiss anymore light posts. And I informed you that the navigator controls the music. Want a different song? Give me the keys." He looks over at me, a crooked grin on his stupidly handsome face, and shakes his head no. "Fine. Then Lana it is."

I set my phone in the cup holder and turn up the volume as Lana Del Rey croons about races and Bacardi chasers.

He sighs and asks, "How much longer until we're at mommy and daddy's house?"

I tap the map icon on the touchscreen and read off the estimated time of arrival. "Five thirty-six."

"And what time is it?"

"One thirteen."

His head falls back against the headrest. "Can you at least throw one song in for me every now and then?"

I clamber up on my knees and turn my body to face him.

"Tell you what, Mr. Wolf. If you can tell me the name of my Mom, Dad, brother and sister, I'll not only play whatever songs you want I'll lean over the center console and help you relax a little."

His jaw clenches and clicks and he grips the steering wheel with white knuckles. I watch him, waiting for the moment he gives up and I can go back to playing every song Lana has sung which will almost last the remainder of our drive.

"Vaughan, that's easy," he says and my eyes grow wide. "Your smoking hot mom is Camille."

"Hey! Don't look at my mama like that." I smack his arm and he laughs.

"Sorry baby. I can't help it. A blind man could see how beautiful she is." I pinch his nipple and he barely flinches.

Masochist.

"Then you've got your little sis that has initials. A...AD. No. A.J. I can't remember what it stands for."

"Autumn Jade."

"Right. Then the little man is Sloane, aka Sloaney Baloney. That name is unforgettable."

"And why's that?" I ask, genuinely curious.

"It's just a cool name. At one point in my bleak existence I thought it would be a great name for a kid if I ever had one. But reality punched me in the face to remind me that would never happen."

I tilt my head, studying his chiseled profile. "Please don't say it's because you're too old. My Mom was in her thirties when she had Sloane. And my Uncle Bishop was almost forty when he and his wife had their second kid."

"Nah. I know I'm not too old. I just recognize the fact that I'm not father material."

"Hendrix...that's not true. I'm sure you'd make an amazing father."

He shrugs and passes me a quick look. "I never had

anyone to base what being a good father means. My foster dads were all pieces of shit and much like my mom, my dad never stuck around to be one."

Guilt settles in my belly like a boulder. Guilt for being such a brat and causing my Dad to worry so much. Guilt for having a dad which is silly, but when you've been spoiled by the best one ever, you forget that so many people have never had the satisfaction of feeling so loved.

"Well I wouldn't rule it out, if I were you. I see the way you care for your brothers, even if one of them is a jerk face," I add, thinking about Danté and his foul mood. "And the way you baby your cars and bikes would surely translate over to a child."

He reaches over to squeeze my cheeks. "Sure. We'll go with that."

I smack at his hands and he laughs when I stick my tongue out. I flip through the songs on my playlist to find something that would satisfy his musical preferences and find a song by Godsmack that seems like his style. I press play and a devilish voice growls through the speakers.

"Are you forgetting about something, little mouse?" I look over at him and he points his finger down at his empty lap.

Apparently where my head should be.

"You aren't really going to hold me to that, are you? I changed the song. Shouldn't that be enough?"

"Baby. You're the one who made the deal. Not me. I'm just adhering to the rules." I pretend like what I'm going to do is such a hardship for no other reason than I like to poke the bear.

"Fine. You held up your end of the bargain, I'll hold up mine." I flatten my hands to the center divider and push myself up, reaching over as far as my seatbelt will allow.

I run my nose up his neck, kissing the spot below his ear and flicking his lobe with my tongue. "Ready?" I whisper in a breathy tone and he nods.

My fingers glide up his stomach, his hard abs tensing under his thin t-shirt. I play with the button of his jeans and I see the way his hardening dick twitches under the thick denim. I place my hand on his shoulder and begin rubbing his shoulder.

And that's it. I just rub his shoulders, alternating between each side. Hendrix doesn't say a word. He stays staring out of the windshield, focusing on the road and not the fact that I've left him wanting more.

"Feel good?" I ask him, but he stays silent. "Hopefully that helps you relax a little."

I plop back down in my seat and rest my head back. The god awful music blares on and I sit with a smile on my face.

"Woman, you better climb that ass over here and choke on this dick before I pull over on the side of the road and fuck that sassy mouth of yours." My jaw drops, utterly flabbergasted by what he's just said. "Yes. Just like that. Bring that mouth over here, little mouse."

He grips the wheel with his left hand and holds his right arm out wide, welcoming me like he's going to give me a warm hug. I stare at him for another moment, still not believing his audacity, then climb over the seat because come on, let's face it. Like any woman could resist a man like Hendrix Dare.

HENDRIX

"WIDE EYED AND HOPEFULLY WILD
WE BARELY REMEMBER WHAT CAME
BEFORE THIS PRECIOUS MOMENT
CHOOSING TO BE HERE RIGHT NOW
HOLD ON, STAY INSIDE"

Parabol
-TOOL

TWENTY-FIVE

WE PULL down a dirt road as the sun begins to dip below the horizon. After Dagen properly helped me relax, we took turns picking out songs to listen to and talking about things I never thought I would.

Life. Hopes. Dreams. Things I've never allowed myself to talk about with anyone. Not even my brothers. But something about this girl has me spilling all the things locked up in my dark heart.

Now, here I am, nervous as hell because I'm about to meet a man who has no idea I fucked his sweet daughter in ways he couldn't even dream of, and not just fixing her car like I told him.

"Take a left into that house with the big magnolias," she tells me, pointing to a massive stone and brick home.

An iron gate with the letter M in the center of each side closes off the home from the street and I wonder how we're going to get on the inside. Just then, Dagen reaches up and pushes a button on the underside of the rearview mirror and the right side of the gate begins to slide open.

I turn onto the long gravel driveway and Dagen tells me to drive to the garage that sits off to the right of the mansion —

because it is not a little ranch style home like she tried to tell me– and just behind it. I do as she has instructed and suddenly want to jump out of this window and run my ass back to Mississippi.

What the hell was I thinking? Driving all the way with a girl to Texas just to make sure she made it home safely? Her dad is going to blow a gasket when he sees me driving his wife's car with his daughter right beside me, my cum still lingering on her tongue.

Jesus, I am fucking scum right now and I don't have any idea how I'm going to get out of this.

A woman who I recognize as her mom comes running out from the back of the house followed by her father who holds a little girl in his arms and a little boy running right beside him. Her family looks excited to see her and I breathe a little sigh of relief seeing that her dad isn't billowing smoke from his nose when he sees me.

"My parents are amazing so there is nothing for you to be worried about. Okay?" Dagen touches my hand softly and swiftly, soothing away my fears.

I throw her a wink and put the car into park before turning off the engine. The garage is massive and looks like it houses several vehicles. I actually itch to take a peek inside at the vehicles Dagen has told me so much about.

Her door gets thrown open and she jumps out. Her little sister who was held up in her father's arms wiggles until he sets her down, and she tears off running towards Dagen. Her little brother follows with her parents trailing right behind. I push open my door and cautiously step out.

"Sissy," the little girl shouts and Dagen squats down to scoop her up.

"Autumn Jade. Did you get a haircut?" She asks and the little girls cheeks turn bright red.

"I gives myself a hairs cut. Momma got mad." Her voice is

sweet and innocent and everything I imagine Dagen was at that age.

"Yes. Little Miss decided she wanted to try out some bangs. And then hid the hair in Sloane's backpack." Her mom walks closer and stands with her hands on her hips.

"It was in my homework folder, Day. She put it in there." Her brother Sloane throws his hands up as if to ask *can you believe this shit*.

"You must be Hendrix." Vaughan walks up to me at that very moment, a big smile on his face as he offers me his hand.

The fact that he is Dagen's dad is undeniable. They share the same green eyes, the same smile and the same nose. Her hair is darker than his that is sprinkled with grays.

"Yes, sir. Hendrix Dare. Nice to meet you." I shake his hand and pull out every ounce of manners Miss Shirley tried to drill into our thick skulls. "I hope I didn't overstep by accompanying Dagen. I wanted to see to it that she made it home safely, and to make sure the repairs are to your satisfaction."

He pats my shoulder then grips it with a strong hold. "Well, thank you. I really appreciate that. I'm sure you could tell how worried I was about my girl."

"Just a little, sir," I smile.

"Woah. You have lots of pikturs on your body. More than Uncle Nix." Sloane comes walking over to where I stand with his dad, his big whiskey eyes tracing all of my ink.

"You must be Sloane." I hold my fist out for him to dab and he does so happily.

"Yup. Sloane Robert McCallan. And that's my sister Autumn Jade. You can call her AJ."

"Nice to meet you, Sloane." I pass him a small smile then stand up to my full height to find Dagen's mom right behind him. "Hello, ma'am. You must be Mrs. McCallan."

"Oo. Ouch. Ma'am and Mrs in one sentence," she laughs

then pulls me in for a hug. "Camille, please. And thank you so much for taking care of Dagen."

My hands don't know what to do. From what Dagen has said, her father would cut a man's eyes out with a rusty butter knife for looking at his wife, so my fear is quite great. I end up air hugging her, not fully touching her back.

Dagen laughs as our "hug" breaks. "Dad's not going to murder you Hendrix. He only wants to do that to men who want to steal mom away. I think she's safe around you."

Vaughan laughs as does Camille and I relax.

"Come inside and eat. Dagen said I better have food ready for you two, because she was starved since you didn't want to stop to eat," Camille tells us, ushering us to the side of the house.

Before I follow behind her, I turn around and go to the trunk, grabbing Dagen's bag from it and handing it to her.

"Here you go, lit–Dagen." I quickly release it once she takes hold of the handles and take two steps away from her.

She rolls her lips between her teeth, holding back a laugh, but I'm not taking any chances. I look at the land sprawled out behind and to the side of their property, and see a vast amount of space where a body could be buried.

"Hey, mister," Sloane calls.

"You can call me Henny," I tell the little guy.

He smiles wide. "Henny. You wanna see my new bow and arrow? Day bought it for my birthday and she's gonna show me how to shoot a deer."

"One day, Sloaney Baloney. First we'll start with shootin' at hay bales. It'll be a few years before we start hunting bud."

His face falls and he drags his feet as they walk into their home. The five of them laugh and smile and hug as if they haven't seen one another in several years and not days. I grow a little uncomfortable as this is all so foreign to me. Hugs weren't handed out freely when I was growing up, and by the time we got to Miss Shirley's we were way too "cool" for affection. At least in the motherly way.

I feel a tug on my hand and look down to see AJ standing there, her very uneven bangs falling to the side. She smiles and pulls on my hand.

"We hafta go inside. Momma made food."

"Oh. Sorry. I forgot." She doesn't let go of me and I follow her in.

Something about this moment strikes me, but I can't put my finger on it. I don't know what it is about a simple walk with this little girl, but I get a feeling it's big.

"Vaughan, I really don't want to intrude. I don't have a problem staying at a hotel near the airport. This was so last minute I didn't even have time to book a flight. I was planning to just show up in the morning and take the first one out to Biloxi."

We ate an amazing meal prepared by Camille where we had the chance to talk. Vaughan asked me about cars and bikes and the businesses I own –someone did their homework, or rather background check– and Dagen spoke more about their ranch. After dinner, Vaughan let me take a look at his Camaro and I just about begged him to let me buy it. It was absolutely pristine and gorgeous. I showed him a photo of my Dodge and he drooled equally over my green girl.

After all of that, I informed them I would be getting an Uber to a hotel in order to catch a flight out in the morning. Dagen's face fell and I could hear her heart breaking. To be honest, I felt an ache in mine too. Camille wasn't having any of it and insisted I stay the night at their home and someone would take me to the airport tomorrow.

We went back and forth for a few minutes, but Vaughan insisted and said he wouldn't open the gates to let anyone in or out if I decided to leave. I felt like I couldn't say no after that, so here we are, Vaughan showing me to the guest room for the night.

"Well my daughter intruded on your life for nine days so one night is the least we can do." He pushes open the door to reveal a very ranch-like room.

A wood four-poster bed is the centerpiece with coordinating accents including leather and iron. I look around for a deer head but that seems to be the only thing it lacks.

"You know where the kitchen is so feel free to help yourself if you need anything. The bathroom is right there," he says, pointing to a door on the far wall. "And breakfast will be on the table by seven. Cami has a very strict schedule when it comes to the little ones. There's never a sleep-in day at the McCallan house. Lord, I hope that changes one day."

I laugh a little and hold out my hand to shake his again. "Thank you, again. I really appreciate your hospitality, Vaughan."

"No. Thank you. Truly. Knowing there was a decent man looking out for my little girl put me at ease. She could have run into some slimeball and who knows what they would've done."

I keep a tight smile on my face, but gulp down a ball of *I'm such an asshole.*

He pats my arm with a nod then leaves me to sit in my tub of guilt over how I violated his daughter. He'd be even more pissed to know she liked it.

I walk into the bathroom and flatten my palms to the brown marble countertop, hanging my head between my sagging shoulders. *How am I going to do this?* Leave here and act like that girl didn't completely decimate my life as I've known it.

A faint knock sounds at my door and I scrunch my brow, wondering if he forgot something. I pad over to the door and open it to find Dagen in a small nightgown standing there with wide eyes and a plump lip caught between her teeth.

"What are you doing here?" I shout at a whisper volume.

She pushes on my chest, causing me to stumble backwards, and closes the door behind her.

"I needed to be with you. One last time before you leave and...and I never see you again."

"Little mouse, we are not doing that with your parents just downstairs and your siblings feet away." I grab a hold of her wrists and stop her from advancing.

"My Dad sleeps like the dead, and Mom knows. Well, she suspects."

"Are you fucking kidding me?" I feel a roil in my stomach, and I watch the door to see if Camille is going to burst in with a shotgun.

"I didn't tell her, of course. She saw you that one day I was on FaceTime and you walked in and she pretty much knew. I didn't say a word."

"Fuck my life." I drop her wrists and drop down on the bed.

"Don't worry. She won't say anything to my Dad. It's over after tonight anyway, right?" Her chest rises and falls with a deep breath and her eyes glisten.

I reach out and pull her to me and her hands fall on my shoulders. "I guess. You're seven hours away so it's not like I can pop in and see you whenever I want."

"Ten," she replies.

"Ten, what?"

"Ten hours. School is about three hours from here, so it'd be ten from you." She looks sad and defeated like she's realizing there isn't a way to make this work. "I don't want to let you go."

My hands roam up and down her back and I watch as a single tear trails down her face.

"I don't want to let you go either, little mouse." I place my hand on the back of her head and draw her in.

I kiss her lips, tasting the salt of her tear that has landed there, and my inner demon takes over, overriding my good sense to end this here.

I lay back on the bed and pull her with me. She crawls on top of me and straddles my lap. Sitting tall, she pulls the thin nightgown up, revealing her gorgeous body. Her breasts fall heavy and her nipples harden with desire.

I glide my hands up her stomach to her breasts that I cup, rolling my finger over the peaked points. She responds with a breathy moan, a sound that will live in my brain forever. I own her moans and if I can help it, no other man will take pleasure in hearing them.

"I'm going to ruin that tight little cunt. Don't you make one fucking sound. Understand?" She smiles with a nod, but remains silent.

Her hands fall to her tits and she begins massaging them, letting her head fall back. The ends of her hair brush against my denim covered thighs and I first need to fix that obstacle.

"Take off my clothes, little mouse." Her head pops up and a saucy smirk exposes itself.

She slithers down my body and begins with pulling off one shoe and then the other. Socks are tossed and she slinks back up to unbutton me. When she slides her hands under my waistband of my boxer briefs, her fingers brush lightly against my throbbing dick.

I hiss, needing more. She licks her lips and drags my jeans and boxers down until I'm free of them. She looks up at me from between my legs, her plump lips parted ever so slightly.

"Get up here and suck my dick, little mouse." She bites the corner of her lip and gleefully works her back up.

Her long brown hair falls in her face and I reach down, gathering it in one hand and gripping it tight. "Let's see how well you can do it without any hands."

She presses her palms down on my bare thighs and dips her head, her eyes still laser focused on mine. Her pink tongue flattens wide and she licks my already dripping tip. Her eyes close when she does it again and I do the same, clenching my jaw with restraint not to force myself in her small mouth.

Watching Dagen wrap her lips around my engorged head and suck me in is the sweetest paradise. I could close my eyes and stay like this forever. We could tell the world to fuck off and live in our little slice of heaven.

As she swallows more of me, I watch her slender throat work and heavy breaths fall from her nose. Her cheeks hollow as she moves up and down, trying with all her might to fit me all in.

"Fuck you look so beautiful like that. On your knees stuffed full of my cock with tears in your eyes. Do you like it when it hurts?" I can feel her jaw straining to stay open and I tug at her hair wrapped in my fist, pulling her off of me with a pop.

"Yes," she pants, her cheeks flushed and her mouth covered with saliva.

"Ask nicely, little mouse, and I'll fuck the tears out of you."

She swipes her mouth with the back of her hand and moves onto the bed, resuming her earlier position. "Hendrix. Please make it hurt so good, the way only you can. Fuck me until my tears run dry and I see heaven. Fuck me until I can't breathe and you bring me back to life. Fuck me and never stop."

Dagen isn't a scared little mouse anymore. The woman is a goddamn minx.

She pulls the remaining piece of clothing off of me, and tosses my t-shirt to the floor. I watch as she inches her way up, passing right over my face and dragging her soaked pussy right along my open mouth. Before she can move, I capture her and suck her swollen lips into my mouth. I shove my tongue inside of her then bite down on her sensitive clit. She whines, jumping when the pain hits every nerve in her body.

When I free her I look up to find her watery eyes. How demented is it that her tears excite me? I'm fucked up, but apparently Dagen likes me that way.

"Put your hands on the headboard. Let me see that beautiful ass of yours." She finishes her ascension and braces herself on the dark carved wood.

I bet daddy Vaughan didn't think this is how his precious bed would be used when he put it in here.

I move to kneel behind her and run my hands over her perfect skin. Her creamy flesh is soft and unblemished. I bet she never got a spanking as a child, the perfect little angel she was. That changes tonight.

Pulling back my hand, I land with a hard thwack. She cries out and I wrap my hand around her mouth.

"Nuh uh, little mouse. You promised. Now...do I stop or are you going to be quiet?"

She nods and I drop my hand. "I'll be quiet."

I lean in, whispering in her ear, "You've been a bad girl, Dagen. You need to be punished for the dirty things you've done."

I place my hand back over her mouth and spank her again. Her body tenses and her teeth bite into my rough skin. Another smack lands with a resonating thwack and her teeth sink further in.

I quickly switch out my hands and spank the other firm

globe, making sure to give both equal treatment. Two on this side, one on the other, and four more split between them.

"Nine spankings. One for each day you tortured me with your beauty."

I kiss the now flaming red cheeks and remove my hand from her mouth as she heaves for air. She's broken through the thin skin in the crook of my thumb, and a drop of blood rests there. I suck it clean then use my hand to spread her open. My tongue runs from her clit to her tight hole and I bury my face between her throbbing ass.

Reaching down, I fist my cock, stroking and readying it to plunge into her dark paradise. When I do so with force, the headboard bangs against the wall and I quickly lean over to stop it from doing it again.

I use my grip on the headboard as leverage and begin working her over, hard and fast. I'm grunting and she's whining, taking my pounding like the good girl she is.

"Hendrix. I'm....oh fuck. I'm going to come," she cries out.

I roll my hips, hitting her in all the places to make her fly off the cliff she stands on. Short, high pitched mewls begin to fall from her mouth and I reach back to grab her nightgown that lays on the bed, and shove it in her mouth.

"Now you can scream, little mouse." She lets go, her cries muffled by her nightgown, and I feel her convulse.

I keep pumping and her moans grow louder and louder until her body goes limp and she falls silent. Removing the nightgown from her mouth, she heaves and gulps in air and I roll her over, placing her gently on her back.

Her eyes are dilated and sweat beads at her hairline. I trace my finger across it and down her cheek.

"Are you okay, baby?" She nods and her mouth moves open and close like a fish yearning for water. "What?"

"Finish. You," she forces the words out and I shake my head *no*. "Yes. Now."

Her voice is raspy and it sounds like she's in desperate need of water. Dagen manages to lift her hands and legs and wraps them around me, dragging me down to her until our nude bodies tangle together.

I stare into her eyes in probably the most intimate moment I've ever had and decide this just isn't the time to be my usual brutal monster.

Slowly, I dive back into her, tighter than she was just a moment ago. Her face contorts and I stop, letting her body readjust to having me invade once more. Soft hands slide up my back and I move in measured strokes, drawing in and out of her with care.

Peace washes over her face as I keep up this languid pace. My hand caresses her hourglass torso, memorizing the curves like a roadmap. I don't think I've ever had sex like this. I usually fuck women. For as long as I remember. But sex, intimate and close, is not something I've experienced before.

But like with everything, Dagen is different. She's special in a way that takes me by surprise because of how she makes me feel. The crazier part of it all is that it's not scary like I always assumed it would be. It's why I've tried so hard to avoid intimacy. I guess your heart doesn't always abide by the rules your brain has told it to.

Dagen sighs and melts into me. When the familiar tingle begins to build, I take her mouth in a tender kiss. She buries her fingers in my hair, scratching at my scalp the way I love. A sweet whimper floods my mouth and then the feel of her walls growing tighter around me. Her legs lift and hang over my hips and when I release her from our kiss and open my eyes, I see that she's ready to let her body fall again.

She lays her hand over my heart and falls apart. Her nails dig into the blank space on my chest just as her eyes seal shut.

When her teeth sink into her lip, I lose it. My teeth clash

and I empty into her, my orgasm, my soul, my heart. I give her everything.

"Wow," she whispers when we've both finished with silent flourish.

"Saying goodbye tomorrow doesn't mean it has to end." I spill the truth just as it hits me. "We can make this work."

"Make what work, Hendrix?"

"Us. Me and you. We don't have to be over." Her eyes grow wet turning the green into a watercolor painting. "I don't want this to be over. I want to call you mine."

Her lip trembles and her voice shakes when she says, "I want to be yours. So very much."

And with that, another ray of Dagen's bright light pushes away my darkness.

TWENTY-SIX

I WALK into the kitchen at seven a.m. with a smile on my face and a full heart. Last night with Hendrix was more than I could have hoped for. Knowing that he feels like I do and that he wants to continue what we've started makes me happier than I've ever been.

"Good morning," I sing, seeing Mom rummaging through the refrigerator for breakfast ingredients.

She pops up and spins around, arms full of eggs and bacon. "Good morning, sweetheart. You're chipper this morning."

Taking the ingredients from her, I kiss her cheek and say, "Just happy to be home. Let me help with breakfast this morning. I'm sure Sloane is giving Dad a hard time about getting ready for school, and we both know you have the magic touch."

"Yeah, he's not too happy about school this morning," she chuckles and squeezes her arms around my neck. "Mmm. New body wash?"

"Oh, yeah. Just something I picked up." I quickly turn away so she doesn't see the lie written across my face that it's actually Hendrix's body wash from last night. "What's the excuse this morning?" I place everything down on the large kitchen island and start sorting through everything. "Breakfast pizza?" I ask.

She nods and digs back in to retrieve tortillas, cheese and salsa. "Apparently Sloane says he is the smartest one in class and doesn't need to go to school anymore. He said he can skip straight through to helping on the ranch."

"To be fair, he did school me on cost principle, does he really need to know much more than that?"

Mom shakes her head. "I'm assuming that little accounting fact was courtesy of Aunt Cat."

"If he doesn't want to work on the ranch, I'm sure Malik could really use some help in the financial aspect of our company." Hendrix comes swaggering in and I think to myself *who needs breakfast when he looks like a whole meal*.

"Good morning, Hendrix. I hope you slept well." Mom walks over to him and gives him a hug, which is pretty typical for her.

She pulls back slightly and scrunches up her brows, taking a whiff of him.

He tenses, but relaxes enough to pat her back gently. "Very well, ma'a–Camille. Thank you for having me."

"I'm going to get breakfast going while Mom gets the rugrats moving. Would you like juice or coffee? We don't have that black tar stuff that could pass for crude oil, but there are some others you may like." I reach up and open the mug cabinet, grabbing one for him and setting up the coffee machine. "Or there's an espresso machine. That probably has enough caffeine to get you through the morning."

He smiles at me and I see Mom's eyes volleying between us. When he walks over to where I stand and touches my side ever so quickly, I hear Mom say, "Dagen. Can I speak with you for just a moment?"

We both freeze and I hear Hendrix whisper, almost indecipherable, "Shit."

"Um sure. Give me just a minute to pop the bacon in the oven. Hendrix, help yourself." I work quickly, lining the baking sheet with foil and laying out strips of bacon.

I stick the bacon in the oven, only for Mom to remind me, "You need to start the oven first." She presses the buttons and gives me a side eye.

Setting the sheet pan on the counter, I follow mom into the mudroom.

"What in the hell, Dagen Rayne?" Her voice is hushed and stern.

"I don't know what you're talking about?"

"You and Hendrix seem to be wearing the same scent this morning." She crosses her arms and pops out on hip.

"It just probably seems that way because the body wash I bought is a bit more musky than usual. But the store di–"

"Cut the bullshit. I'm not a dumb woman." I chew on my lip, my eyes filling with tears and my body with nerves. "Oh, honey."

She quickly pulls me into her arms and smooths my hair.

"I'm sorry," I whisper and wrap my arms around her.

With a sigh she tells me, "It's okay. I just wish, lord help me, you could have held yourself back while your Dad and I were here. Now I have images in my head that I really don't want there."

Pushing back I explain. "I thought it would be the last time I saw him."

"What do you mean *thought*, Dagen?"

I swipe at my running nose and stare at my feet. "We decided that we want to have a relationship beyond…you know–"

"I know." She holds up her hand and closes her eyes. "You understand you're going to have to speak with your father, and that he is going to have a lot to say about you dating a man."

"Mom, I'm pretty sure anyone I was to date over the age of twenty is a man."

"No, Dagen. I mean, that man is a *man*. Not a young one figuring out life, but one who has years of experience on you." She exhales, waiting for me to say something. "Just..don't let this get out of hand. And please b–"

"Hello. Are y'all going to stay locked up in there, or are you going to come out and greet us?" Mom groans and drops her head and I do the same.

The crew has ascended. Aunt Viv's voice is very loud and clear as are the giggles of little girls.

Blowing out a frustrated breath I say, "Let's get this shit show over with."

Mom nods and we open the door to find a mass of people in our kitchen, and Hendrix being bombarded with looks and questions.

"Bacon's in the oven, eggs are being scrambled, and dads are on school drop off duty." Aunt Viv stands with little Sutton in her arms while Uncle Phoenix grabs the other two, Cassie and Genie, as they run around the kitchen.

"We're so happy you're home, Day." Aunt CeCe walks over, an apron over her sleek black skirt and plum colored blouse, and kisses my forehead. "You really had us worried."

"I know. I'm really sorry about it all." She gives me a small, warm smile and touches my cheek.

"Piccola bellezza." Zio Luca approaches me with wide arms and I step into them. "You are okay, yes?"

"Yes, Zio. I'm fine."

They may be crazy and loud and an absolute mess, but I wouldn't want my family any other way.

I look over at Hendrix whose eyes beg me to rescue him and I wiggle out of Zio Luca's arms.

"Alright. Y'all are scaring the poor guy. Give him some room to breathe." I push on Dad's and Uncle Bishop's chest, standing between them and guarding Hendrix. "I would introduce you, but it appears you have already scared our guest."

"Girl, you better not ever pull a stunt like that again." Uncle Bishop pats my head with his giant paw, then kisses it.

"I know. I won't. Sorry." I pass him a half, apologetic grin and leave it at that.

"Welp. We better get the kids off to school. Get that food done so they can fill their bellies. Hendrix," Dad says, turning to look at Hendrix. "You think about what I said. You're more than welcome to stay and we'll get you home whenever you're ready. Sloane, Naveen, Cassie, Genie! Eat up," he shouts, calling all the kids like he's corralling cattle.

Mom quickly places scrambled cheesy eggs and toast on a plate and apologize to Sloane that the bacon isn't ready. The other kids grab toast, having already eaten at home.

"Time to go," Uncle Bishop calls, his hands cupped around his mouth.

"We're just missing Mav and Burton," Uncle Phoenix points out just as a bustle flies through the back door.

"They're here. Sorry. Maverick insisted on wearing his boots with shorts today." Aunt Cat walks in holding the hand of one boy dressed in shorts, sneakers and a t-shirt, and the other sporting basketball shorts, a collared polo and brown boots.

I snort at the vast difference between my twin cousins. It's quite a riot to see them. Mav is definitely Uncle Hayes to a T. In looks and behavior. And speaking of Uncle Hayes.

"C'mon kids. The school train is ready to leave the station." Uncle Hayes pulls off his cowboy hat that has an almost permanent place on his head. "Hey darlin'. We missed you."

"Oh my god, you guys. I was literally gone for eleven days. Y'all are acting like I flew to the moon." My hands raise high then drop back down to my sides, landing with a smack.

The kitchen grows silent with more than a dozen eyes staring at me. Everyone passes looks before erupting again.

"How are we getting all these monsters to school?"

"Hayes said he'll hook up the horse trailer to his truck and throw them all in there."

"We better take two vehicles. Vaughan and Luca, you two are with me. Nix and Hayes, you take the truck." Uncle Bishop starts grabbing hands of kids.

The women kiss their kids and husbands goodbye, and the men hustle all the kids out the back door, backpacks on and lunch kits in hand. When the door clicks shut, the moms all breathe.

I look over at Hendrix, standing at the counter with a coffee mug in hand and looking shell shocked.

"Do you see what y'all did? You scared the shit out of Hendrix." I glare at each one of them before walking over to him and asking if he's okay.

"Yeah. I'm fine. That was just...a lot." He scratches his forehead, probably trying to ward off a massive headache.

"We're so sorry, Hendrix. I'd like to tell you this is a rare occasion, but this is our life. Day in and day out." Just then, we hear the cries of a little girl followed by another. "Oh boy. And there is round two. I'll go grab them."

Mom scurries off to the upstairs playroom where AJ and little Farah are playing.

Anais works to get on her feet and Aunt CeCe tells her, "Ana. Please sit. You're not going anywhere with that big ole belly of yours. Let Cami handle it."

She lowers herself back down with a puff of air.

"So," Aunt Viv interjects, still holding Sutton on her hip. "Tell us about yourself, Hendrix. How old are you? What do you do for a living? What's your credit score? Any kids? Criminal record?"

"Lord, will y'all stop." I place my hand on Hendrix's arm and tell him, "You do not have to answer any of that."

The oven dings and Aunt CeCe grabs a potholder, pulling open the door and removing the cooked bacon. "Why don't we finish breakfast before the men get back and leave poor Hendrix to catch his breath."

Aunt Viv sets Sutton in a chair at the table by Anais, and Mom walks in carrying two little girls with tears in their eyes, one in each arm. She places them next to Sutton and Anais, then walks to the fridge and reappears with an applesauce pack for each girl.

"I'm sorry," I apologize to Hendrix, my voice low so that the rest of the chickens won't hear me. "Let's go sit out on the back porch while they finish."

"Don't you need to help them?" he asks, bringing the mug to his mouth and wrapping his pink lips around the edge.

"I think they can manage." We both look over at the three ladies buzzing about the kitchen to finish breakfast, while Anais talks to the girls to cheer them up.

I push on his shoulder, urging him towards the sliding doors, and follow him out. We take a seat on the couch and I cross my legs facing him.

"That's quite the family you have." He chuckles then takes another sip of his coffee.

"And this is my life. For the last ten years. It's a circus, for sure, but I love it." He nods with a solemn smile. "What was my Dad talking about? Oh, and my Mom knows we were together last night."

"What the fuck, Dagen. You can't just add that in like you're telling me it's going to rain today. How does she know?"

"I think the fact that you and I smelled of the same body wash and me knowing how you take your morning coffee clued her in."

He hangs his head and I touch his hand. "It's okay. She basically just said to be careful, because you're a *man* man, and to tell my Dad sooner than later."

"What's a *man* man?"

"Apparently you're old enough to know things." He snorts and practically chokes on his coffee. "Don't worry. I didn't tell her you gagged me with my nightgown last night."

This time he does choke and I pat his back. Soon my pats turn into rubbing his back and I move in closer. Hendrix watches me and slowly leans in. Our lips are inches apart, but our bubble is burst in the worst way.

"Breakfast is ready." Aunt Viv stands at the edge of the door and patio with a knowing smirk on her face.

"C'mon," I tell him. "Let's just get this over with."

I grab his hand and pull him back inside and say a prayer that these women don't have him running for Mississippi without ever looking back.

HENDRIX

"WANTING YOUR LOVE TO COME INTO ME
FEELING IT SLOW, OVER THIS DREAM
TOUCH ME WITH A KISS, TOUCH ME WITH
A KISS"

Heavenly
-Cigarettes After Sex

TWENTY-SEVEN

THE SPANISH INQUISITION I endured from the ladies was cake compared to the growls and narrowed looks I got from Dagen's uncles. My heart was pounding in my ears and beads of sweat gathered at my hairline. If it wasn't for Vaughan and his friendly disposition, I would have been shit on a shingle.

Now I stand on a private tarmac getting ready to board Luca Amato's private jet that will take me back to Mississippi. The difference between billionaire's and millionaire's is great.

When he offered to fly me home, I protested about it for about five minutes before Luca said there would be no more discussions on the matter. And when the rich Italian with possible mafia ties insists on something, you just go with it.

Dagen had already told me she would bring me, but once again, Luca offered his chauffeur. And with that, Dagen said she'd accompany me and Vaughan thought it would be more time for us to talk about cars and bikes. So here we sit, me stuck in between the two of them, talking to Vaughan about visiting my shop and wishing I had time alone with Dagen. Who knows when I'll get to see her again.

"Whenever you're ready, just let me know. I've got a room

for you." Vaughan shakes my hand with a pat on the shoulder and smiles.

"I'll hold you to that, Hendrix. Thanks, again, for taking care of my girl. I really appreciate it." Vaughan slides out from the back seat and I follow.

Dagen steps out behind me and I offer her my hand. "Sure thing, Vaughan. And thank you. It was a pleasure to meet your family."

I shake Vaughan's hand with a big smile on my face, figuring I need to soften the blow as much as possible when Dagen talks to him about us. I told her that we should do it together, but she said she needed to be alone with him.

An attendant stands at the top of the stairs leading into the private jet, and I take a look at her knowing it's time for me to go.

"Dagen, stay away from light poles," I joke and pass her a wink.

She laughs, sadly, with moisture building in her eyes. I lift my hand and give them both a short wave, hoping the longing in my eyes for Dagen isn't too visible to Vaughan. Hefting my bag on my shoulder, I turn and begin the walk to the plane that seems impossibly far. Just as I reach the bottom of the stairs, a voice stops me in my tracks.

"Hendrix! Wait!" I look over my shoulder and see Dagen break free from her father's arms and come sprinting towards me.

Fuck it. If he's going to hate me, a ready jet seems like the best getaway option.

I drop my bag and turn to her just as she launches into my arms. With my hand on her head and her legs around my waist, I kiss her incredibly inappropriately in front of her dad. I hold her tight to me and her hands bracket my face, pulling me to her like I might fade away if she doesn't.

When we separate, our foreheads press together and we breathe each other in.

"Your dad is going to murder me, little mouse."

"I won't let him," she whispers then drops her legs. "Travel safely, Mr. Wolf."

A small tear rests on the corner of her eye and I swipe it away. "I'll call you tonight?" She nods and I give her one last kiss. "Be good, little mouse."

I reach down and pick up my bag and take a glance at Vaughan who stands there with his hands balled into fists and his face red with anger. I hurry up the stairs and see him arguing with Dagen, his hands shaking and his words coming fast, just before the door closes.

I wonder if Mr. Mafia will let me take his jet for a second ride to save my little mouse if she needs rescuing.

"Thanks for picking me up," I tell Danté, as I drop inside his car.

He was my third option since Mal has parent-teacher conferences this evening, and Kins had a lot of work to make up for after missing so much to be Dagen's personal tour guide. As much as I didn't want to, Danté was my last choice with Miss Shirley running the shop.

"Yeah," he grunts and speeds away. "So you drove all the way to Texas just to see your houseguest home, then get flown back in a private jet. Quite a perk. I wish I had known about that. I would've tried harder."

"Don't fucking start, D. What the hell is your problem? Are you seriously that pissed off, because she chose me and not you? Grow the fuck up man."

His tires squeal as he pulls on the expressway and slams

down on the gas. "You think I'm pissed because your little rich girl decided to fuck you and not me?"

"Watch your goddamn mouth when you speak of her." My blood boils and if we weren't going eighty on the freeway, I haul off and ring his bell.

"Oh-ho. Did someone get attached? What an interesting development."

"I am sick of your attitude, bro. You've been acting like a little bitch, all because you got turned down. Setting up that shit with Soria. Fuck you, Danté. You're supposed to be my brother, but you've done nothing, but stab me in the back."

"Oh yeah, *brother*. You weren't acting like one, ditching your family for fresh pussy."

"Get off the fucking freeway. Now!" I'm going to beat his ass on the side of the goddamn road and not feel any type of way about it.

He cuts across all the lanes of traffic, practically hitting cars along the way, and speeds down the exit ramp. He screeches to a stop in the parking lot of a convenience store, and I jump out of the car, rushing over to his side.

"I told you to watch your goddamn mouth," I growl.

"You gonna fucking hit me? You really want to fight your brother? The only one who's been there for you. Long before some bitch."

Sirens blare in my head and my vision blurs. Rage courses through my veins and the adrenaline surges. I cock my arm back and throw a hard punch straight to his face.

His head flies back and he stumbles. I get my hands up, because I know he's mad as a bull and will fight right back. He gathers himself then comes right at me.

I match him punch for punch, throwing an elbow when he comes at me from behind, and kneeing him in his ribs when he folds over. He charges for me, ramming his shoulder straight into my gut and we both fall to the ground. We start grappling, cuts piling on top of cuts, and skin getting scraped by the rough gravel.

I don't know how long our fight lasts, but I know it's long enough for a crowd to gather and for the cops to pull up. This time there are real sirens blaring and it takes several of them to pull us apart.

I spit at Danté when they yank the two of us away. Blood drips into my eyes and I see a large cut on his cheekbone.

"Calm down. Now. Do not resist." The officer holding me yells and slams me onto one of their cars.

My arms are twisted painfully behind my back and I feel handcuffs slap on my wrists.

"Fuck you, D. You're not my brother. Stay the fuck away from me."

Danté tries to get away from the cops and he gets wrestled to the ground, a knee jamming into his neck. "Go to hell. Picking some chick over your family."

His words are choked and I'm barely able to understand him. He gets cuffs that match mine, then he's lifted and thrown in the back of a car. I get tossed into another and my chest heaves with exertion. Blood continues to drip down my face and I hang my head to see how it stains my white t-shirt.

I curse myself for not being able to control my temper. But hearing Danté talk about Dagen like that lit the fire keg that exploded in me.

An officer sits in the passenger seat and begins typing away into the keyboard that extends from his dash. After calling something in on his CV and speaking with the other police officers, he speeds off towards the police station where I'm booked and thrown into a cell where I remain for hours.

I never get to call Dagen to let her know I'm home and that I'm thinking of her. My one phone call goes to the only brother I have left. Apparently Danté makes him his one call, too. Fucking great.

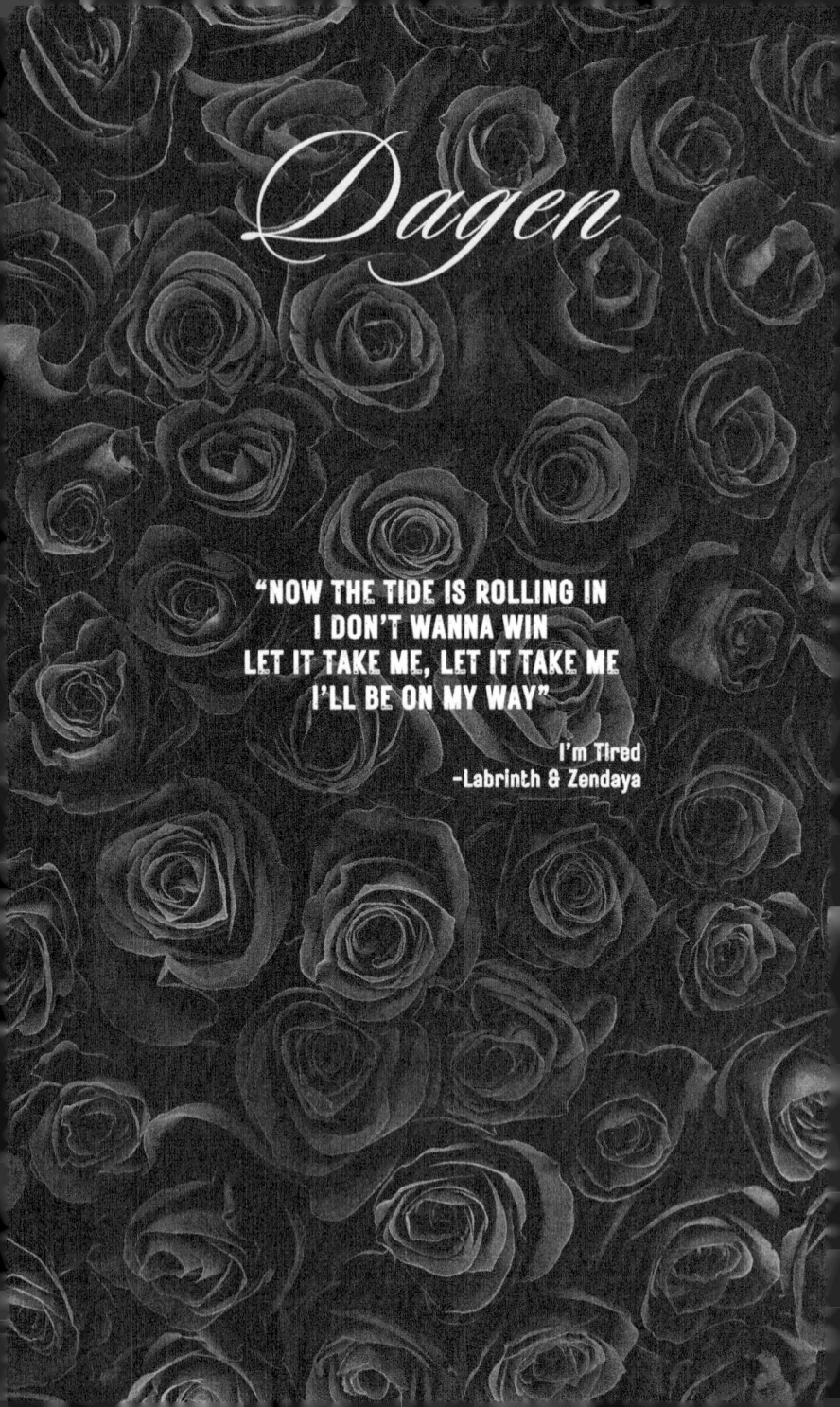

TWENTY-EIGHT

"DAGEN RAYNE. I cannot believe you. I have no words." Dad and I sit in the back of Zio Luca's car while he lectures me on my newly discovered relationship. "That man is almost thirty years old." Apparently he does have words. "And he is definitely not the kind of man you should be forming a relationship with."

"Not the kind of man. That's a horrible thing to say. Especially after you thanked him profusely for taking such good care of me." I cross my arms and turn to stare out of the window.

"Well, had I known the kind of care he was giving you, I would've flown my ass out there and dragged you home by your ears."

"I'm not a child anymore. You can't just force me to do what you want." My eyes and ears are burning with fire.

"You sure as hell are a child. You're my child. Whom I support. So if you think for one minute that you are going to use my money to go and see that boy, think again." Dad's voice continues to climb.

"Wow. Okay. Well, don't worry. I won't use one dime of your money. I'll figure it out on my own."

"And your trust is off limits." My jaw drops, fury turning into tears.

"What? You can't do that. That's my money. You can't stop me from using it." Both of us are now screaming at full volume.

"I'm the executor so I sure as shit can. Wait until I tell your mother. I can only imagine what she'll have to say about this."

I smirk. "She said to be careful." His eyes are full of rage and his jaw clenches. "Mom figured it out because she's a bit more observant. She also said Hendrix was hot."

Hot breaths billow from his nose and he digs into his pocket, retrieving his phone and stabbing at the screen. He lifts it to his ear and waits for the other end to pick up.

"You knew about Dagen and that man and didn't say anything to me?...I don't care when you found out, you should've told me immediately...Oh, and Dagen told me you think he's hot. Really Camille? He's a child...To me he's a child...We'll talk about this when I get home."

Dad's face grows pale as I hear mom shouting, "Don't you dare threaten me like that Vaughan Asa McCallan. I'm not your dog and if you want to raise your voice at me again, you better have a fucking bag packed and ready to run your ass out of this house."

Dad gulps and his hand shakes. "I'm sorry, Sunshine. We'll be home soon." He listens for another moment then says goodbye.

Well, he tries to say goodbye but I have a feeling Mom hangs up without another word.

He sticks his phone back in his pocket and I scoot as far away from him as I can, practically melding into the car door, and don't speak another word until we're home.

When we arrived home after our blow up car ride, Mom was waiting with her hands on her waist and a scowl on her face. We stepped through the front door and she told us Sloane and AJ were with Uncle Hayes and that we were having a family meeting immediately.

We followed her to the dining room, both with shaky steps, and we each sat on our side of the table with mom at the head.

"I know this is not what you expected to find out, or how, but it's happening and the best we can do as parents is support our daughter and ensure she is being safe." Mom was very diplomatic in her speech while dad and I sat ready to return to our screaming match.

"Ensure she's safe? Aw Christ, Camille. Are you saying that she needs to go on…on–"

"Birth control? News flash, Dad. I'm already on it." Dad's head dropped to the table with a groan and I took great satisfaction with that.

We continued to argue back and forth, each of us throwing out an accusatory comment which Mom would quickly shut down. At the end of it all, we were nowhere near a truce and I stomped off to my room where I began to throw all of my clothes in my bag, and readying myself to return to school.

Then I threw myself on my bed and waited for Hendrix to call.

And waited.

And waited.

Now it's ten o'clock and I still have yet to hear from him. I don't want to be that girl, but I'm growing worried that something horrible could have happened to him. Deciding I can't wait any longer, I call up Kinsley.

"Hey sister. I miss you already. Please come back."

"I miss you too, Kins. I have a question that hopefully you can help me out with. Have you, uh," I blow out a big breath. "Have you heard from Hendrix? He said he would call me when he got home and I don't want to seem like a jealous girlfriend –because I am so not– but I'm kind of worried."

"I haven't. Did you try callin' him?"

"No."

"And why not?" The rumble of her truck blares, almost drowning out her voice.

"I don't want to seem needy. What if he just told me he wanted to be with me, but really didn't mean it?"

"Wait. Hold up a doggone minute. Henny said he wanted to be with you? Like boyfriend and girlfriend?" I nod my head. "Your silence makes me assume you're nodding your head. All I have to say to that is, eeeekkk! Oh my gosh. I am so happy. Y'all are gonna have babies and live happily ever after and we'll all be the best of friends."

"Just hold off on buying neighboring houses. I still need to find out if this is real or not." I roll over on my back and stare up at the ceiling fan that spins round and round, much like the nerves in my belly.

"Well I haven't heard a thing. Did you try King? I mean Mal?" I still want to know the story behind the nickname King, but we'll leave that for another day.

"No. I don't have his number. Do you think you could call him for me?"

"Sure thing buttercup. You just sit tight. We'll find out what's going on." She hangs up and I chew on the inside of my cheek, forcing my tears to stay at bay.

It must be twenty minutes before my phone rings, the caller is one I do not recognize.

"He-hello?" I answer, apprehensively.

"Day? It's Malik."

My nose stings and my heart hurts thinking Hendrix has sent Malik to tell me it's over.

"Hey. Um, Kins said you were waiting for Henny to call you when he landed?"

"Yeah," I choke out.

"Well he's home. But…" he wars with his words before finally blurting it out. "He got arrested for fighting with Danté on the side of the road. Disorderly conduct."

"What?" I shout, jack knifing up from my bed. "Are you serious?"

"As serious as a heart attack. I'm actually waiting to bond them out. I don't know if it's a good idea to take them both home since they can't seem to keep their hands to themselves, but they need to work it out somehow. They're brothers. I don't know what the hell they're fighting about, but this shit has got to stop."

My door bursts open and Mom practically falls in. "What's wrong? Are you okay?" She sounds out of breath from running up the stairs.

I must have been loud enough for her to hear me down the stairs and come running.

"Nothing Mom. I'm fine."

"That was not the screech of someone who is fine. Cough it up."

I sigh and tell Malik, "Will you let me know when he's home?"

"Sure thing Day. Don't worry, okay. They'll figure it out. See ya, tart." I hit end and look at Mom who stands in the doorway with her arms folded across her chest.

She arches a brow and purses her lips waiting for me to explain.

"That was Hendrix's brother, Malik. I was worried that he

hadn't called me since landing so I reached out to Kinsley – my new friend– who called Malik who called me."

"And?"

I twist my face and squint. "He got arrested."

"What the fuck, Dagen?" My head blows back like she punched me.

Mom very rarely curses and this is a big one. Especially with Sloane and AJ just down the hall. Loud stomps can be heard climbing the stairs and I just know the fight with Dad is going to hit a peak.

"Sunshine? Are you okay?" he asks, walking over to her and placing his hand around her waist.

"I'm fine, but why don't you ask your daughter about the news she just shared with me." Dad looks at me and I shake my head, my eyes large and panic stricken. "It seems her new boyfriend got arrested shortly after landing in Mississippi."

"What the fuck, Dagen?"

"Jesus. Do you guys know any other words? There is more than one curse word in the English language."

"Yeah, but it's the only one that fits this situation." Dad's chest rises and falls and he shakes his head slowly. "I knew that boy was bad news. I could just tell."

"Oh whatever, Dad. You were practically kissing his feet just hours ago." I jump up from my bed and stand in front of the two of them.

"That was before I knew he violated my daughter and before he was arrested," Dad yells back.

"What was he arrested for? You failed to give us that information." Mom's expression matches Dad's and it hurts my heart to see it.

I don't think I've ever disappointed her, but it's obvious I've done more than disappoint.

"He and his brother got into a fight. I guess it was bad enough that people called the cops."

"For Christ Sake." Dad throws his hands up in the air and

paces the hallway. "That's it. You are never allowed to see him. Never, Dagen, and you will not defy me." He points his finger at me with a hardened face and the tears burst free.

"You can't tell me what to do. I'm twenty-one!"

"I just fucking did, so try me." He huffs and I do the same.

Without another word, I scurry to where my bags lay in my small sitting area and start throwing them over my shoulders.

"What-what are you doing?" Mom asks, her voice distraught.

"I'm leaving. I was going to wait until tomorrow to go back to school, but I can't spend another night under the same roof as him." I look around for a pair of shoes and find my Berks at the foot of my bed.

I slide my feet in and snatch my phone from the bed as I pass by. I try to squeeze between the two of them but they refuse to move. Still defiant and still angry, I turn and walk over to my balcony doors.

"Where are you going?"

"If you won't move, I'll jump out of my window." I glare at Dad and yank my french doors open.

"Stop it! Just stop this." I freeze when I hear the emotion that laces my Mom's words.

Looking over my shoulder I see her crying, tears pouring down her face. A moment later, AJ begins to cry, no doubt awakened by our screaming match. Mom stands there, staring at me, then spins and rushes to AJ's room. Dad remains, a deep scowl on his face. With mom gone, I move to exit my room once more.

He grabs my arm as I try to move past him. "Don't do this, baby bird. Please don't run again."

I close my eyes, gathering myself and letting the sob in my throat fade away, and tell him, "I'm not running. This is you pushing me."

I pull my arm free and shove him, walking away from my

parents for a second time in two weeks. Crushed, yet again, by their words. My heart is so tattered, I don't know if there's any left to see me through the tough roads ahead.

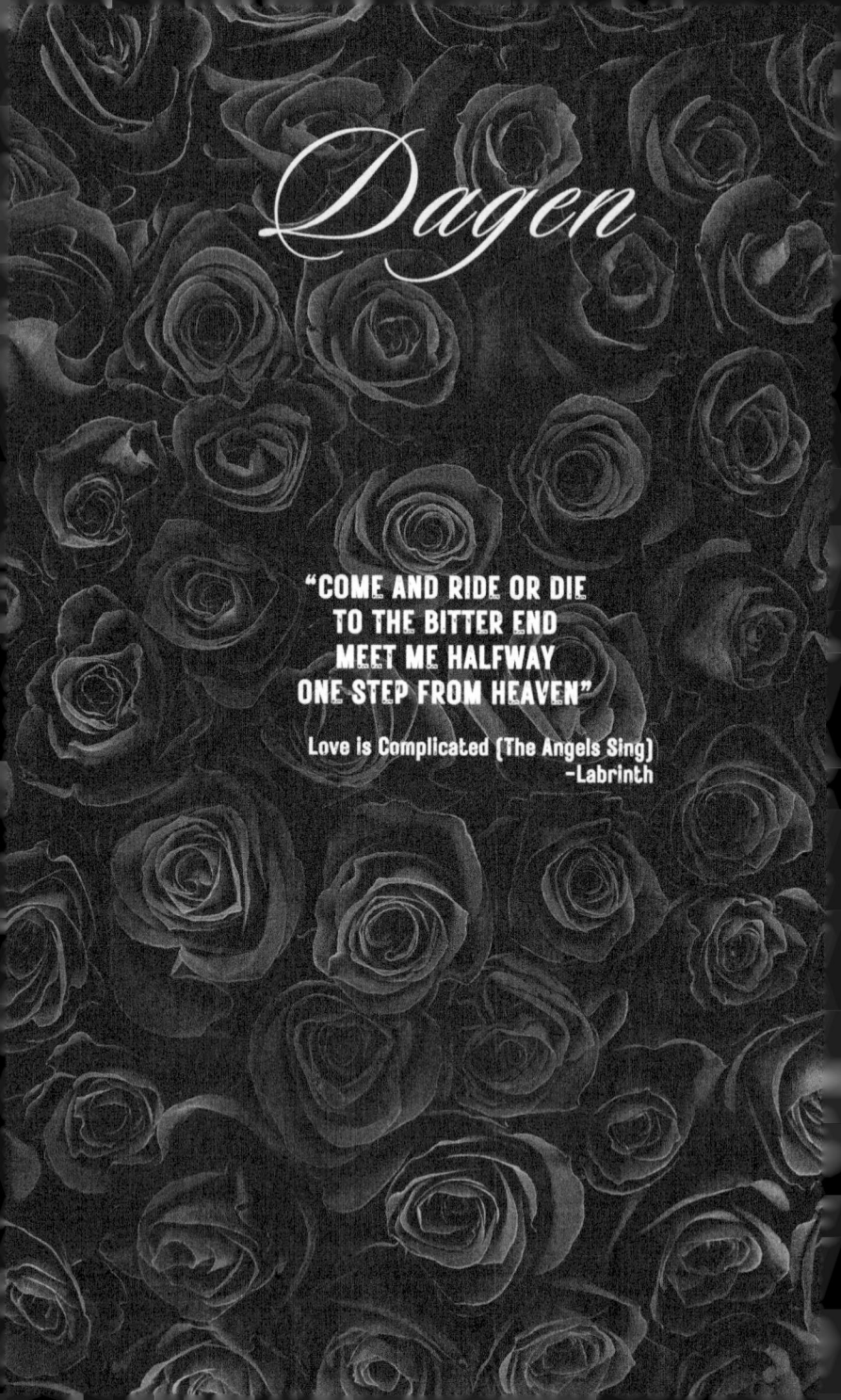

TWENTY-NINE

IT TOOK me longer than the usual three hour drive back to school after storming out of my house last night. The tears that wouldn't stop falling made it difficult to see, causing me to drive well beyond the speed limit. Plenty of people honked as they passed me, but I just couldn't gather myself enough to care.

I cried myself to sleep, completely ignoring Mara, Janelle, Sami and Lizzie when I walked in. I threw my things down on the floor, not bothering to take off my clothes, and fell face down to my bed.

I don't know how long I cried for, but I know it's definitely not morning time as my phone goes off. I'm groggy and my hands feel like they're on a sandy beach. Then I realize that it's not my alarm going off but my phone ringing.

My eyes pop open and I reach for my phone that is still tucked tightly into my back pocket. I pull it out to see the time read four-fifteen and Hendrix's name on the caller ID. My fingers fumble as I try to swipe over and over, then take a deep breath to steady myself and try again.

"Hendrix?" I answer, worried that it might not be him.

"Hey little mouse." His voice is tired and gravelly, like

he's been trekking across a dry desert for days. "I'm sorry I didn't call you."

"It's okay. Malik told me why you couldn't." He grows quiet, only puffing out air. "What happened?"

"It's a long story that I really don't want to get into right now. Is that okay?"

"Yeah. Of course." I can tell his mind and his body are exhausted and the last thing I want to do is push him when he's already had such a rough day. "Are you alright? Aside from being arrested?"

"I'm a little rough for the wear to be honest. Danté wears this fucking ring that has a pointed end on it. He uses it for… stuff. Well the asshole sliced me right above my eye with it, so I'm definitely going to need stitches. It's my first stop in the morning."

"Oh my gosh. Does it hurt?" I sit up in bed and look over at Lizzie who is snoring away.

I decide not to wake her, and quietly tip toe out of my bedroom and out onto the back patio.

"It's fine. I'll just have a gnarly scar, but he should have one too. I caught him good on the cheekbone. We also have cuts on our arms from rolling in gravel and several bruises, but it's whatever. I just don't know if we'll be able to recover from this."

He sounds hurt, not just physically but emotionally. If I could reach out and take his heart in my hands and keep it safe I would. Something occurs to me and I just have to ask.

"Hendrix?"

"Yeah, baby?"

"Was your fight about me?" His silence tells me everything I need to know.

I pull my legs to my chest and hug them tight, resting my head on my knees. A chill blows in the early morning hours, and shivers roll through my body. But it's not from the cold.

"I don't want to be the reason you and your brother fall apart." My voice cracks and I sniff.

"Dagen, you won't be. Trust me. Danté has a chip on his shoulder and doesn't like when someone puts him in his place. He's stubborn and hard headed and doesn't know when to just shut up. He runs his mouth and it's the source of many of our fights. This one got a little more…heated." I can hear how worked up about it he is and I feel even more guilty.

"Well if you ever need a break from there, you're always welcome here," I tell him.

"Be careful what you say little mouse. I may drive up there and steal you away. Maybe hide us from the rest of the world."

"That would be perfectly okay with me. Just tell me when and I'll be ready." I smile, my heart feeling a little lighter than it was hours ago.

"You better go back to sleep. It's late. I'm sorry for waking you."

"Wake me any time you want. I'll always answer."

"I'll remember that. Good night, little mouse."

"Good night, Mr. Wolf." He laughs softly and the line goes quiet.

I stay up for the next hour, staring up at the navy blue sky and wishing I was back in Cattywump Bay, far away from the problems that chase me down.

A week passes with Hendrix and I talking every chance we get. He sends me texts while he's at work and I'm in class. Once the evening comes, we're on the phone until our eyes were weary and our yawns abundant. He spent little time out of his house aside from work, and my friends grew increasingly angry with me over my lack of communication.

They knew the reason why I ran from my house that day, and have since come to know about my time in Cattywump Bay and Hendrix. But I just don't have the energy to be the person they know me as. Something changed in me. I can't say whether it was finding out about Stephanie or meeting Hendrix, but I know that it shifted my life's trajectory.

Last night, we spoke about the possibility of me flying down for a weekend, soon. I'm trying to find a way to pay for it without my parents knowing about it, since we are still on very limited speaking terms. I mainly call to talk with AJ and Sloane.

Hendrix said he would buy me a ticket, but I don't feel right asking him to do that. I know he is not lacking for money, but I don't want him to think I expect things from him.

I'm staring at my laptop screen, finishing up the last of my project and waiting for Hendrix to call when I hear Lizzie yell out from the living room.

"Any of y'all expecting someone driving a sweet ass car to be making a visit tonight?" I pop up from my bed and shuffle down the hall.

Sami and Mara crowd around the window, peeking out of the blinds like the nosey neighbors they are.

"Where's Jenelle?" I ask.

Sami looks over at me and replies, "Lab. She said she'd be home around ten."

I look at my watch and see that she has another hour before she gets home, so it can't be that she got a ride with someone who is dropping her off.

"Holy fuck me hard. That is one morally gray glass of water," Mara moans.

"I call dibs," Sami shouts.

"You can't call dibs on someone you don't even know. What if he's not even–oh my god. He's walking up the sidewalk." Lizzie scrambles about, her hands flapping around.

Sami and Mara jump back from the window and scurry around the living room. I decide to take a look at this person they are in a tizzy about, and walk over to the window. When I look out and see the face of the man approaching our front door, I too turn into a horny chicken with her feathers on fire.

I hurdle over the coffee table and lunge for the front door, yanking it open and practically ripping it from the hinges.

"Hendrix!" I shout and fly out the door and straight into his arms.

"Hi, little mouse. Miss me?"

I grab his face and plant kisses all over it. Cheeks, nose, eyes, forehead, just everywhere. He holds me tight, squeezing my ass and snaking his arm around my back. He smells of cedar and motor oil, only a scent he can pull off.

"Can we go inside?" He mumbles into my neck.

Without lifting my head or letting go, I nod and he walks in.

"Hey. I'm Hendrix. You all must be Dagen's roommates," he greets, his voice so deep and so smooth.

"Yeah-huh."

"Yip."

"Us. That's us."

My three friends suddenly have tongues too big for their mouths and forget how to form complete sentences. His boots echo over the wood floors and the girls begin picking up various items that are laying around.

"You can sit on that leather chair," I tell him.

"Okay, little mouse. Are you going to let go?" I shake my head that is still buried in the crook of his neck. "Good."

He gently sits in the comfy chair and readjusts me, my knees bent and tucking in on either side of his lap.

"What are you doing here?" I finally ask.

"I missed you. Figured I'd visit for a few days. Is that okay?"

I lift my head and stare into his blue eyes. "More than okay. Thank you. I don't think you realize how much I was needing this. Needing *you*."

"I think I do because it was the same way I was needing you." I bat away my tears because dammit, I'm tired of crying all the time. "Is there somewhere private we can go?"

"Kinda. I share the master with Lizzie, and the other three have their own room. Maybe I can see if we can borrow one of the singles."

"Nah. Don't do that baby. How about I just get a room and we can stay there for the weekend?"

I sit up tall and place my hands on his shoulders. "You don't have to do that. I don't want you to waste money when we can stay here for free."

He raises a brow at me with a smirk. "Dagen...I think I can afford to get a hotel room with my girl for the weekend."

My stomach erupts with a swirl of butterflies in it hearing him call me his *girl*. "I know. You just drove such a long way, and now we have to find a hotel."

He wiggles around, still holding me to him, and digs for his phone. With one hand, he slides his thumb across the screen. I try to sneak a peek at his screen, but he holds it higher and out of my view.

"Done. Go pack a bag," he orders.

"Bossy."

"Don't act like you don't like it. Now hurry up." He kisses my forehead and smacks my butt, urging me to get up and do as he's told me.

I fidget, working to free my knees, then hurry off to my bedroom. My Louis duffle seems to be getting quite a bit of use as of late. I run into my bathroom, snatching my toothbrush and toothpaste from the holder, and pull open the cabinet under my sink to retrieve the toiletries I just unpacked days ago.

Rummaging through my dresser, pajamas, leggings, t-shirts, shorts, undergarments, all get tossed into my bag. I slip my feet into a pair of shoes then run back into the bathroom to grab a brush and my makeup bag. Five minutes of tornado-like chaos, and I'm back in the living room.

"So your last name is Dare? That's not like a pen name, or whatever?" Lizzi, Sami and Mara all sit on the couch, their chins propped in their hands and all staring at Hendrix like he's a greek statue come to life.

I won't lie, he's pretty amazing.

"Nope. It's my real last name. My brothers and I changed our names when we were eighteen," he tells them, a kind smile on his face.

It's a very strange look as all I've seen when he speaks with people outside of his friends is a scowl that says *fuck off* to anyone who dares to speak to him.

"Cool cool. So you have brothers? How many and do they look like you?"

A small, muffled chuckle vibrates in his chest and I hurry over to save him.

"He has two brothers and they do not look like him. I'll be gone for the weekend so y'all better not die of alcohol poisoning." I step to each friend and kiss their forehead. "Do the dishes. Go to your Saturday class. No, you do not need to buy another book. Love you."

I give them each a little piece of advice before leaving and grab Hendrix by the hand, tugging him to his car, more than ready to spend some time with him.

Once we are both tucked inside his car and belted in, he reaches over to me and pulls my face to him. His lips land on mine, hard and lustfully, and finally delivers a real kiss. My mouth opens and a moan escapes, tasting him like he's my favorite dessert. His fingers tangle in my hair and tug at my strands, and his teeth nip at my bottom lip.

"How far away is Hotel Gatsby?" He asks me, mouth still glued to mine.

"Ten minutes. Straight down Franklin Street."

"I'll make it in five," he says and pulls away. "Hold on tight." The engine revs and he throws it into drive.

A blaring screech fills the night air, but Hendrix Dare has filled my heart.

THIRTY

DAGEN SITS on the edge of the bed, her chest heaving with labored breaths and her eyes large as baseballs.

I walk over to the window and push open the drapes, letting in the glow of the moon and city lights to illuminate the room. I turn and lean up against the cool glass and fold my arms over my chest, one leg over the other.

"Take off your clothes, little mouse." Her arms and legs tremble as she stands up, and I watch the way she rolls her shirt over her head with fingers that shake like tree branches in the wind.

She reaches behind and unclasps her bra, then lets it slide down her arms, freeing her full tits to me. Her black shorts fall to her feet followed by her thin white panties. Stepping out one foot at a time, it only takes her moments to stand bare before me.

"Rub your nipples. Get them nice and hard." Her hands glide up her body, softly caressing her curves.

Her fingers roll her nipples, tweaking them and pulling them into hard points. Her mouth falls open on a sigh and her eyes glaze over. The way she toys with her nipples sends a shock to her pussy. I can tell by the way she presses her thighs together.

"Lick them." When she hesitates, I arch my brow at her to let her know this isn't an ask. "Do it. Now."

She slowly sticks her tongue out and lifts her breast to meet her mouth halfway. With her eyes locked on me, she laps at her brown blossom like she's tasting the sweetest nectar. And oh how sweet it is.

"Suck on them." This time she doesn't stall and sucks as much of her breast in her mouth as she can.

Her eyes close and I see a shiver roll through her body. Her toes wiggle and she whimpers.

"Taste good?" She nods and alternates between licking and sucking. "Now stop."

With her mouth still clamped tight onto her breast, she pops open her eyes and stares at me. Almost comically, she lets it fall with a plop and drops her hands to her sides.

"See my bag? Go over there and open it up." She pads gently to where my black leather bag sits and sluggishly unzips it. "There's a long black piece of satin. Take that and sit back down on the bed."

With a deep breath, she does just as she's told and sits nervously on the bed. Unfolding my body, I stride with heavy steps to her. She cranes her neck to look up at me. That frightened look in her eyes returns and she's every bit my scared little mouse.

I slip the fabric from her hand and wrap it around her head, covering her eyes in darkness. She shudders when my fingers trace over her collarbone. I unbuckle my belt and whip it free from my jeans. Her body jumps, startled by the snap of the leather, and she sucks in a breath.

"I'm very upset with you, Dagen."

"W-why?" Her voice shakes with the mix of fear and adrenaline she loves so much.

"Because you made me feel something I told myself I

never would. You've put images in my head that aren't supposed to be there." I thread the end of my belt through the buckle, and loop it back around, then loop again until it looks like a figure eight weaving in and out of the buckle. "Hold out your wrists."

Apprehension races through her body, but she holds her arms out, presenting her thin wrists to me. I slip the belt over them then pull the tail, tightening it into cuffs. The action draws the air from her lungs and I wrench her to me, her naked body colliding with my fully clothed body.

"I'm sorry," she whispers.

"No you're not." I reach around and slap her ass with a sharp flick of my wrist. "But it's okay, baby. You can make it up to me. Want to know how?" She nods. "You're going to make it up to me by doing every-thing-I-say."

Her body begins to tremble in my arms and I dip my fingers between thighs to find her pussy dripping. I soak my fingers then bring them to her mouth. "Stick out your tongue."

When she does, I swipe my fingers coated in her to her wet pink tongue. With her mouth still hanging open, I press my tongue to hers and suck, tasting her pussy and now I need more. Wrapping my hands around her thin waist, I pick her up and throw her down on the bed. She yelps and I watch her tits bounce.

My hands grip her ankles painfully hard and I anchor her to me. She stretches her arms above her head and clasps her hands in prayer. I swipe my tongue up and down her seam, letting my nose inhale her smell and burning it into my lungs. She wiggles her hips and kicks her legs, trying to break free from my hold but my grip is too tight. I calm her by burying my face in her pussy and eliciting begs and pleads.

"I'm coming," she mewls and clamps her legs around my head.

Her cries and convulsions make my aching dick start to

leak. Dagen's beautiful voice, sweet and painfully raspy makes my body sweat with longing. I peel off my clothes as she recovers from the first of many orgasms I have planned for her tonight.

I lift her feeble arms and pull one free of her constraints, then flip her to her stomach. I carefully take both hands and lower them to the small of her back, securing them once again.

"Ready for more?"

"Yes."

I prop her knees up and push her head down. With her spread legs, she looks like the main dish on a silver platter.

"I fucked my hand all week thinking about you pinned against that tree in the dark woods. The way you cried was like a sonnet written just for me." I rub my hand over her smooth skin, creamy and unblemished.

I let my fingers walk their way to her still spasming core, and roll my hand over her clit. Rubbing faster and faster, she begins to whine and detonates once again, leaving her body sweat soaked and quivering, as I lick away what she left behind.

"God I love the way you cry. I bet you've only ever cried for me. Isn't that right, little mouse?"

She makes a small imperceivable squeak in response, and my craving for her is now an insatiable hunger. I line my dick up with her opening and push in nice and slow, my head immediately falling back on first taste.

My hips move and I pump in and out of her, drawing back with long pulls. Each one brings another whine from her. I grip the belt in my hands and tug. Her body arches like a goddess on the bow of a ship. Madness fills my chest and the inclination to see her skin red and hot washes over me. I grab the tail of the belt and use it to pink her ass.

"Oh gaah." Her moans are laced with tears and I push harder and faster.

One of her arms breaks free from its constraints and she fists the sheets in her hand, searching for purchase. I don't know what it is about her that makes me want to taste every inch of her, but I can't help myself and end up with my teeth digging into her shoulder.

The act rips a scream from her mouth. One of ecstasy and agony, and she quakes with another orgasm. It isn't long before I follow her over, howling in rapture. I drop the makeshift cuffs and sink my hands into the mattress, barely able to hold myself up.

My eyes examine Dagen's tarnished skin. Red welts on her ass, angry rings around her wrists, and the imprint of my teeth on her shoulder.

"Shit, baby. I'm so sorry." I map the marks that add to the fading lines from the tree. "I don't know what comes over me. I feel actual hunger when I fuck you."

She gasps for air and musters up what little energy she has to turn her head. "I didn't feel anything. At least I don't remember."

"It's like I need you to live. I'm afraid if I don't have you… I'll die."

Languidly, she rolls over and reaches up to touch my face. "I know the feeling."

My fierce starvation fades and my burning need for her takes over. I lean down and kiss her like I've never kissed another woman.

And probably never will again.

"I want to do something crazy. Wanna come with?"

I throw her a side eye as we walk down the sidewalk

towards a row of shops and restaurants. "It depends on what it is."

She freezes in her tracks, jerking my arm back when she does. "Hendrix Dare is skeptical of a spontaneous outing? Is it the old age catching up with you?"

Our hands are laced together –another thing I never thought I'd do with anyone– and I tug her to me. She yelps and wraps her hands around my biceps.

"I'll show you old when I paint your back porch red." Her hands slide up my shoulder and she twines her fingers behind my neck.

Lifting to her toes, she whispers, "Careful, Mr. Wolf. Don't want you throwing out your back trying to punish me," then kisses my lips.

I let my hands fall to her ass and I squeeze, digging my fingers in with a pinch. "What is this crazy thing you want to do, little mouse?"

Like the Joker, a wicked gleam spreads. "Follow me."

She drops back down and pulls me down the street until we stop in front of a shop that reads *Stitched* on the windows and doors. At first I think it's some kind of clothing store, but a closer look tells me it's a tattoo parlor.

Leather chairs, the buzzing of guns, hard rock music. All telltale signs of people getting inked.

"Dagen." I turn to face her to study her face. "Are you sure about this? This is permanent, you know."

"What?" she gasps, slapping her hands on her cheeks. "You mean I can't wash it off when I'm done."

She smirks and I pinch her nose. "Okay smartass. You want a tattoo, let's get you one."

I pull open the door and escort her in. The men immediately greet us, but a couple let their eyes linger on Dagen in her denim shorts and tank top a bit too long. Wrapping my arm around her waist, I glue her to my side, making sure to send that loud and clear message that she's mine.

"Hey. How are you?" A beautiful woman stands behind the counter, her skin fair next to her dark brown hair, making her green eyes pop.

Her features resemble my Dagen, but nothing or no one can compare to my girl.

"Hi. I want to get a tattoo. Are any artists available?" Dagen hops on her toes, excited to endure a little bit of pain for a permanent memory.

"Yo Oxy!" she shouts and one of the men who was licking his lips looks our way. "You free?"

"A tattoo?" he asks, and the woman nods. "Absolutely."

The woman behind the counter asks Dagen some questions, passes her papers to fill out, then takes her ID and makes a copy of it. After five minutes, she escorts us over to his station and I sit down facing his chair just out of the immediate area. I'm close enough to see and hear them, but not enough to witness the lines as they are scribbled into her skin.

Dagen sits down and begins telling him what she is wanting. Her voice is too low to hear and I have a suspicion it's on purpose. She then looks down at her chest and runs a finger in the valley of her breasts.

"The fuck you are," I growl and jump from my seat.

I stomp over to them, not caring that I'm not allowed to be in their sanitary station.

"Does it hurt there?" She asks him.

"No," I bark. "Because you're not getting a fucking tattoo there."

Her face grows hard and her eyes spit fire. "Don't tell me where I can and can't get one."

"I'm not telling you where to get one, I'm telling you who you're not getting one from. Want it on your arm or ankle, fine. Have it at, bro. But *there*," I say and point to the spot that only I belong. "Is not fucking happening."

"What are you, her dad?" he asks.

"I'm more than her dad. I'm her man, and you aren't touching her there." I look over at the woman who is now gawking at our interaction. "Is there a woman who can ink her?"

"Uh, yeah. I can," she stutters.

"Cool. Dagen you go with her. Don't worry, man. You won't lose the money. I'm getting one, too. And so help me, if you purposely fuck it up, I'll fuck you up."

"Jesus. Don't be an asshole. I take my art seriously."

"Good." I walk over to the counter, do the same paperwork as Dagen and go back to sit on the chair that my girl once occupied.

I tell him what I want and where, pull off my shirt, and sit back. The guns buzz and I close my eyes, wondering if this is just a little too much.

Who fucking cares?

Dagen

"I NEED REAL LOVE
FUCKING IN THE BACK SEAT
REAL LOVE
JUST LIKE SID AND NANCY
REAL LOVE
NOTHING MORE BUT YOU AND ME"

Summer Song
-Remy Bond

THIRTY-ONE

I TAKE A DEEP BREATH, swiping at the small tear that has leaked from the corner of my eye, as Mollie, my tattoo artist, wipes away the last of the ink puddled on my skin.

"You okay, little lady?" she asks me.

"Yeah. I just didn't expect it to hurt so much." I puff out a small laugh.

"That spot does hurt like a bitch. I just didn't want to tell you because then you'll be anticipating the pain and it makes it so much worse." She swipes and ointment across the fresh tattoo then hands me a handheld mirror. "What do you think?"

I take it and stare at the reflection in absolute awe at the masterpiece she has painted. It's a simple line tattoo but it's elegant and exactly what I wanted. A beautiful rose blooms and the stem consists of elegant writing and words I never want to forget, as insane as that may seem. What type of person wants a phrase branded into them that reminds them of fear?

Me.

Run run run, little mouse takes the place of the stem in a flourished scroll. It stretches between my breasts and there aren't many people who will know it's there. I really only got it for one person and one person only.

"Did you want to show your guy? Or do you think that will set him off?" Mollie ponders.

"He may get a little pissed if I walk over there without a shirt on. Maybe I should just wait."

She winks. "Good idea. Let me get the wrap and then you'll be ready to go."

I continue to look at it from different angles until she covers it with a thin almost plastic wrap like film she calls second skin. I carefully pull my bra and shirt on, and Mollie begins folding the screen that she placed around her station to block the view of those around the shop. I can see now why Hendrix didn't want a man tattooing me. I assumed I could just lift my bra a little, but Mollie told me I would need to completely remove it so that the skin didn't fold.

"How do you prefer I pay you? Credit card or transfer?" I grab my purse from the chair and pull out my phone.

"Oh baby, it's taken care of." I look at her questioningly. "Your man already paid for it. He asked how much then paid me double."

My jaw drops and I look over to Hendrix who sits in the leather lounger, the artist hunched over his chest, working on a new piece. He looks relaxed like he's getting a hot stone massage with zen music in the background. I guess at this point for him it is relaxing.

"You almost done there, Mr. Wolf?"

Hendrix opens one eye and looks over at me. "No. I think he has quite a bit more to go."

"Oh. Okay, well I can just wait over there."

"Do you want to take a look?" He asks.

"Can I? I mean, I don't want to be in the way."

The artist who was originally going to tattoo me looks over and says, "Come take a peek."

He stops the tattoo gun and I walk over cautiously, like

what's been inked will somehow come to life and attack me. Hendrix outstretches his arm and smooths his hand up the back of my leg, pulling me closer.

When I look down I'm speechless at what I see. It's mesmerizing and I itch to run my fingers over the lines.

In the empty spot on Hendrix's chest are the outlines of what looks like his skin being torn back. Underneath is a heart –anatomical heart– sprouting flowers. While his existing tattoos are all colorless, this one is a mix of black and white lines and vibrant flowers. The colors are still being filled, but the pinks and blues and purples are clearly visible.

"Wow. That's beautiful," I tell him, letting my eyes trace every detail.

"It's my Dagen tattoo," he rasps.

"What?"

With a cocky smirk he explains, "Dagen means to be cut open in Hebrew. And that is what you have done to me, Dagen McCallan. Cut me open and helped my black heart beat again. My world was black and white and now with you in it, there's a world of color I didn't know existed."

I swallow a hard lump but it does nothing to keep the tears at bay. This grumpy man, hardened and jaded by life, just poured his heart out and revealed a side of himself that most have not seen.

"Honey if you don't marry that man, mind if I take a shot?" I look over my shoulder with big puddles in my eyes and see Mollie standing there with a smile.

She reaches out and squeezes my hand before turning and walking to her station to clean up.

"I...I don't know what to say," I whisper.

Hendrix takes my hand and brings it to his mouth, softly kissing the back of it. "Don't say anything. Just know it's true."

I nod then run my fingers through his golden strands, and place a kiss on his forehead. "Back at ya, Mr. Wolf."

"I can't believe we each got a tattoo for the other without knowing it." It's Sunday morning and as much as I wish it didn't have to be over, I know Hendrix needs to get back home.

It's a long drive from my house in Waco to his, and I worry about him driving so late.

"Great minds," he tells me with a wink.

Our fingers are laced together and sit on the center console of his car.

After tattoos and lunch, we spent the rest of Saturday wrapped in each other's arms, lost in the feel of warm skin and tender kisses. And equally, we basked in gluttonous pleasure with moans and lascivious touches. I prayed for it never to end, but reality sat knocking on our door.

Three weeks of this man and I'm ready to sing that I've found the one. Maybe my age makes me naive, but a man doesn't get a tattoo for a girl if she's a flash in the pan.

"Do you think we're moving too fast?" I ask.

"One hundred percent. But ask me if I fucking care. No one is going to get in the way when it comes to you and I. Promise." We pull up to my house and he stops his car, then turns to look at me. "When someone shines a light on the darkness you've been living, it helps you see truths that you didn't realize were waiting for you. Once you see them, it's impossible to go back to living in a world of black."

"I didn't know you were such a sap, Hendrix Dare. I thought I got myself a tough biker when really, it seems I've been gifted with a tender poet." I bite my lip and wait for his response.

It comes in the form of him ripping me from my seat and yanking me to straddle him in the driver's seat.

"You are such a brat, you know that." His fingers dig into my sides and I screech as he tortures me with tickles.

"Oh my god. No. I'm sorry. You're gonna make me pee my pants," I laugh.

He buries his head in my neck and nips at my thin skin, growling and pretending to eat me like the big bad wolf he is. A knock bangs on the window and we both jump. I look up to see my Dad standing very close with a stern look on his face.

"Can he see in?" I ask him, because from the outside, the tint is a dark ebony and I assumed it was impossible to see in.

"If he looks close enough he can. Come on. Climb over and let's get out. Better to face him now than draw it out."

My insides shake and it pours out of my fingers and toes as I shakily move to exit on the passenger side of the car. When I emerge from the midnight black car, I find my Dad fuming with my Mom right behind him.

"Get in the house Dagen," he rumbles through gritted teeth.

"Vaughan. Could I talk to you for a moment? Just to exp–"

"Mr. McCallan. And no, we cannot talk. You need to get back into your car and drive away and don't come back." Dad's eyes shoot lasers into Hendrix but the man doesn't cower.

"Respectfully Mr. McCallan, that's about as likely to happen as a heifer sprouting wings and floating over us."

"Vaughan, honey. Why don't we go inside and wait for Dagen." Mom touches his arm and he flinches like she's touched him with hot coals.

"Dad, can you please just listen for a minute before you start freaking out."

"Dagen! Go inside."

"Hey, don't speak to her like that." Hendrix takes a step in front of me, blocking me from Dad's view.

"Hendrix, get away from my daughter before I call the cops."

I place my hand on his back and he chortles. "Call the cops with what reason? Your daughter is twenty-one and with me of her own will. I'm not holding her captive, or forcing her to do something illegal. You can't just call the cops because you don't like me."

I hear the anger building in my Dad's chest with each breath he takes. I need to snuff out the sparks before this goes up in a ring of fire.

Taking Hendrix's hand in mine, I tug on him and move to the other side of the car. "Hey," I whisper, getting his attention. "Maybe you should just go. You need to get on the road anyhow. I'll talk to him. Okay?"

His nostrils flare and his jaw clicks with anger. My hand touches his chest where his new tattoo is, and it instantly calms him. A large, warm hand covers mine and squeezes. The black in his eyes fades, making way for the blue to shine.

"Okay, little mouse. I don't want to cause any more problems. I'll call you in a couple hours." I nod my head and he steps to the back of his car, opening his trunk and coming away with my bag.

Without a word, he walks up the sidewalk and sets the bag down by my front door, then strides right back to me. With his eyes lasered in on where they stands, Hendrix cups the back of my head and angles in towards me. His kiss is grueling and intense and I can hear my Dad's knuckles crack as he balls them into fists.

Hendrix releases me from our kiss and taps my nose. "Take care of that tattoo."

He walks around the car, watching my Dad who watches him, and slides into the driver's seat. The engine roars, shattering the uncomfortable silence around us, and he slowly pulls away from the curb, only to speed off in a cloud of dust when he's far enough away.

I blow out a breath and ready myself for the blowback that's about to come.

The three of us stand facing each other, Mom and Dad in the middle of the street and me on the sidewalk, no one making the first move. Dad's eyes waver between wanting to cry and wanting to shoot fire. I feel a small pang of guilt, but he's really blowing things out of hand when it really doesn't need to be anything but understanding.

"I'm sorry, Dad," I finally say. "I'm going to continue seeing Hendrix. There isn't anything you can do or say that will change my mind. I really want you to be understanding of the fact that as an adult, this is a decision that is only mine to make. If you can't...I don't really know what there is for us to discuss."

The palms of my hands sweat and my heart pounds like a bass drum, vibrations pulsing from head to toe. He takes Mom's hand in his, inhales and exhales with a deep purpose, then turns and walks to where their truck is parked. A truck that I should have noticed when we pulled up, but I was too lost in Hendrix to notice anything else, but him.

Mom looks over her shoulder at me with big tears in her eyes and I just want to run to her and pull her in my arms, but I have to stand on my own. I won't back down to Dad's demands and doing that would have me bending to his will.

I stand on the sidewalk, watching Dad help Mom into the passenger seat before moving to his side and driving away.

Nothing speaks louder than words unspoken. And those words cut like a knife.

HENDRIX

"SOMEONE FINDS SALVATION IN EVERYONE
ANOTHER ONLY PAIN
SOMEONE TRIES TO HIDE HIMSELF DOWN
INSIDE HIMSELF
HE PRAYS"

Be Yourself
-Audioslave

THIRTY-TWO

IT'S BEEN two weeks since I saw Dagen last, and I feel like an addict whose high has faded and the itch is back. We talk daily –several times– but it's not the same as seeing her face and tasting her skin. I need a fix and I need it soon.

"Yo Henny. You ready?" Malik barges through my front door, yelling into the vast space.

"Bedroom," I shout back and continue to pack my bag.

His steps echo as he crosses the tile and they turn into a whisper when they reach the carpet of my bedroom.

"I appreciate the invitation, Henny, but you know my dick don't play like that. I'm flattered. Truly." He comes in and collapses on my bed, wrinkling the neatly made bed. "What are you doing? We're just going for a ride. I don't think you'll need your toothbrush."

"I'm going to see Dagen," I tell him, while continuing to pile items into my bag.

"Woah. Hey. It's Thursday night ride. You're not missing it again. It's time for you and Danté to squash this shit. I can't take any more of you two ignoring each other and putting me in the middle."

Danté and I haven't spoken since the day we ended up in

jail after fighting like two wild dogs. He has yet to apologize, and I have nothing to say I'm sorry for. I do feel bad for sticking Malik right in the thick of it.

"I'm sorry, Mal. I really am. I just don't think I can face him without punching his front teeth out." I decide to pack a pair of swim trunks in case we want to go down to the pool at the hotel for a dip in the hot tub.

"Man, you don't have to talk to him. I'll ride between you two and words, or fists, don't need to be exchanged. Please, Henny. I just want to have a nice ride with my brothers and to pretend that everything is normal."

His eyes plead with me to fold and I know it's going to take me being the bigger person to at least be civil enough to ride. Malik is right that we don't even have to talk. Once my helmet is on, it's just me and my bike.

"Alright. Let me change." He jumps off the bed and raises his arms in the air like a kid who just beat a tough level on a video game.

I huff and shake my head, then get my black riding pants and meet Mal out in the garage to suit up. With the push of a button, my bike comes alive and we peel out of my driveway to meet up with brother number three. If you can even call him that. Right now he's more like a guy I don't know. One I wouldn't want to know.

The highway stretches out in front of us and the world passes us by as we speed down the open road. The sun set about twenty minutes ago and the lights have come alive as the sky turns navy blue.

When we drove to Danté's house, I sat parked on the curb

while Malik got him. I didn't take off my helmet, I didn't stop my bike. I just sat with my bike idling, waiting for the two of them to come flying out.

Danté didn't even acknowledge me. At least I don't think he did. I barely passed him a glance as they approached, then quickly focused back on the quiet street. D headed out in front and I fell into line right behind Mal and we were off.

The ride has been everything I've needed. Aside from Dagen who seems to calm the riot in my head, I've had nothing but worry on my mind. She's barely talking to her parents –her dad not at all– and I can tell it's really affecting her. I can hear the despair in her voice every time we talk.

Sure, she's always happy to talk to me, but some of the joy is missing. A little bit of her light has been dimmed and I need to do something to fix that. I have an idea, I'm just hoping it doesn't land me in the hospital with a bullet hole in my body.

The warm air sneaks into parts that are uncovered by my gear, and it only serves to heat my already hot flesh. The cars come and go and we take turns speeding up and slowing down as we run into traffic. I need a little more room to just breathe, and speed up past both of them, finding a long stretch of open road. I rev my engine, the loud wail drowning out the turmoil still lingering thick between D and I.

The speaker in my helmet plays one of Dagen's Lana Del Rey songs and I don't care if it seems like I'm a whipped bitch. It's a piece of her that brings me solace. I know the feelings I have for her are more than lustful. I need her more and more with each passing day. And every day we spend apart is like a hot knife into my gut.

I can't explain it, but there's this feeling in my gut that has sat heavy for weeks.

Malik switches lanes to be in front of me and he points his hand towards the exit. Danté and I follow, quickly seeing what pulls him from our ride. The bright lights of our favorite burger stand, Griffin's, beckons him in. I'd like to argue and tell him I'm going home, but my stomach is gnarly right now.

The parking lot is full of cars at this little stand that has only a couple of picnic tables and a small order window. Our bikes are lined up in a row and we all remove our helmets, hanging them from the handles. I keep a bit of distance between myself and the other two, looking around at the guests who are either eating, or waiting impatiently for their order.

Malik bounces on his toes, rubbing his hands together and licking his lips just thinkin' about the food he has yet to order. I scan the menu despite knowing what I want, but it's a decoy so that I don't have to engage with Dante.

"Mal said you're going to see Dagen in the morning? Are you planning on moving there?" Danté sneaks up behind me while I stay laser focused on the menu and catches me off-guard.

With my attention still diverted, I answer. "Yeah. I'm leaving tonight and stopping half way. I need to make it in early and stop somewhere before I see Dagen. And no," I finally look at him. "I'm not moving there."

I shove my hands in my pockets and work my hardest to hold my tongue.

"But you'll probably move there, eventually."

I commend myself for keeping my trap shut as long as I did and let it just fly.

"What's it to you if I do or don't? You've been very clear on your dislike for Dagen, and if being with her means having to move away from Cattywump Bay, then so be it."

"I never said I don't like Dagen," he counters.

"You didn't have to say it! You made it abundantly clear. Message received." I spin on my heel and decide food isn't worth the high blood pressure and possible second stint in jail if I stay here and argue with him.

"I don't want to lose you," he shouts, and I freeze in my steps. "I know you feel something big for her. You're going to end up marrying her and leaving us behind. I fought too hard for this family, Henny, and I'm not about to lose it without a fight."

The crowd around us falls to a hush, waiting for the next part of their impromptu soap opera.

I look over my shoulder and see a man who is more vulnerable than he was when he was just a punk kid who ended up in foster care when his dad killed his mom, and none of his family wanted to take him in.

"We'll always be family, D. You're my brother. Nothing can take the place of you and Mal." I take a few steps closer until I'm toe to toe with him. "I won't lie and say that Dagen doesn't change things, but being with her doesn't mean I can't have you in my life."

Danté's face hardens, but not in anger. He steels himself from showing any emotion. The Dare brothers don't do emotions other than anger. Danté most of all.

"We've been through too damn much. You, me and Malik. No one else has the bond we do, as fucked up as it is, and no one ever will."

"Guys always say they won't change when a woman comes into their life, but in the end, nothing ever stays the same. Soon it'll just be me and Malik and you'll be off, having a life and family of your own."

"Danté…you're my family. And wherever the future takes me –be it with Dagen or someone else– they'll have to realize that you and Mal and me are a package deal. You want one, but you get all of us." I clamp onto his shoulder with my hand and squeeze it.

His black eyes are turbulent and I feel a pang in my stomach and my heart. I never thought that he would have a reaction like this. Ever. He's the brick wall that nothing can penetrate and the fact his wall is showing a crack is huge.

"Is that why you pulled that shit with Soria? And the fight?" When he doesn't say a word, I know I've hit the nail on the head. "I'm not going anywhere. Physically, I don't know where life will take me. But as far as I'm concerned, you're blood. You'll always be here. The three of us, we need each other to live."

His chest expands with air as he inhales and his jaw clicks with tension. His head nods and he holds out his hand in the best apology he knows how. Normally that would be good enough for me. But Dagen has changed me and this moment calls for something bigger.

I grab his hand and step closer, giving him a pat on the back in a hug that only men do. It takes him by surprise, but he quickly goes a step further and wraps me in a hug. The kid that needed family to hug him and reassure him they'd be there for him has been waiting for so long for that moment. And now it's here.

Another set of arms clamps onto us and a sappy voice speaks. "Aww. A family hug. I've waited so long for this moment." Malik pretends to sniff and Danté smacks him in the gut. "Does this mean we can go back to normal? No more sticking me in the middle of your fights?"

We all drop our hold and take a couple of steps back.

"No more putting you in the middle. Promise," I tell him.

"Cool," he says with a huge smile. "So then can we eat? I need a triple greasy Griff before we go back home. School has been kicking my butt lately and those little petri dishes love sharing their germs. I can't stand to eat anything at school for fear that I'll ingest strep throat."

"Or the cooties," Danté adds.

"Hey. Cooties are a real thing. And Hendrix has tons of girl cooties." He shakes his hands like he's trying to rattle away clinging germs.

"So, uh, is it serious with her?" Danté turns his head to look at the passing cars.

"I mean...I think so. I've never felt anything like this before, so I think that means it is."

Malik smiles, and there goes another arm around the neck. "Henny's in love. D, it looks like we have a new sister."

"Oh Jesus. That's not what it means. It just means that I like her more than a temporary fling. That's all," I explain, not fully convinced myself.

"K-I-SS-ING. Henny and Dagen sittin' in a tree." Malik begins to sing and I punch him in the shoulder.

He winces and rubs it out. "C'mon. I thought you were hungry?"

"Yeah. Hen's got a girl to go see . Let's eat." Danté walks past Malik, bumping into his other shoulder.

"Damn, y'all. What is this? Beat up on the nice guy day?" he asks.

"Yes," we both say and pass each other a smirk.

Things are right with the world again. Now I just need my girl in my arms and life is perfect.

HENDRIX

"NOTHING'S GONNA HURT YOU, BABY
AS LONG AS YOU'RE WITH ME, YOU'LL BE
JUST FINE"

Nothing's Gonna Hurt You Baby
-Cigarettes After Sex

THIRTY-THREE

I PULL up outside the McCallan residence at eight thirty in the morning. I took a guess that the kids would be off to school since last time I was here, everyone was out the door by seven forty-five like a whirling dervish.

The gates are closed so I have to use the buzzer to request access. There's no intercom so I don't quite know how they'll see who is wanting in. I press it, the buzzer sounding, and wait for something to happen. My eyes wander and I finally spot a camera planted on the juncture of where the fence meets a brick pillar. I gulp knowing that someone is going to see my face, and that's it's possible I won't be allowed in.

My fears are squashed when the gates begin to slide open, and I slowly move my car forward. The tires crunch over the pea gravel and I park just shy of the front door. I blow out a big breath and wipe off my sweaty hands on my jeans. Just then, the door opens and out steps an angry looking Vaughan.

"It's now or never, Hendrix," I tell myself and pull on the handle to let me out.

I slam the door shut behind me and keep eye contact with

Vaughan, who I realize is now holding a gun, and stumble back against my car.

"Woah. Mr. McCallan. I just want to talk to you. What's the gun for?" I hold my trembling hands out in front of me.

"To protect what's mine. And I don't mean my house."

The patter of tiny feet echoes across the tile and I see a bright little face peek out from behind him.

"Hey! I know you." AJ bounds down the front steps and comes running over to me. "Where's my stister?" she asks, presumably asking about Dagen.

"Hi AJ. I'm actually going to go visit your sister soon. I just want to talk with your mommy and daddy real quick."

She pouts, but then shrugs and pulls on my hand. "Okay. C'mon. I wanna show you my new doll. Do you wike dolls..." she searches for my name, but she's like three years old and probably can't remember what she had for breakfast, much less the name of a guy she met once.

"Henny. You can call me Henny, little lady." Her eyes light up, a glowing amber tone and something hits me like a thunderbolt.

"Henny," she giggles. "Thas funny. Wike a chicken."

Her little face breaks into more laughter and it makes me laugh.

"Yeah. I guess so." I look up at Vaughan who watches our interaction with the same stern look he greeted me with. "Is it okay if I come in? I'd really appreciate it if you and your wife could give me just a few minutes of your time."

"Vaughan," a voice calls. "Who is at the–Hendrix?"

Cami pushes past Vaughan to find me standing next to her daughter who still holds my hand.

"Good morning, Mrs. McCallan. I apologize for interrupting your morning. I was hoping I could speak with the two of you."

She looks at Vaughan then notices the gun hanging from his hand.

"Are you kidding me, right now? Give me that goddamn gun, Vaughan." A spell is broken when he hears his wife's voice and she yanks the gun from his hand.

Pointing it down, she opens the clip and finds it empty. Her eyes spit fire and I see the man visibly cower. It sends chills down my spine.

Tucking it in the back of her pants, Camille says, "Please come in. And it's Camille. Remember?"

"Yes ma–Camille." AJ pulls on me once more and this time I let her lead me into the house.

We reach the front door, which Vaughan still blocks, and Camille tugs him back by his arm, opening up enough room to let me by.

"Cut it out, dammit. Move out of the way," she bites out

"Aaumm. Mommy. You say a bad word."

"I know sweetheart." Camille squats and lifts AJ up in her arms. "Sometimes it's the only word I can find when Daddy's being a turd head."

AJ lets loose another one of her sweet little giggles and Vaughan's face turns red as Camille walks to the living room and sets her down. A snack and a puzzle gets sat on a small table, and the tv gets turned on. Once the cartoons have stolen the toddlers attention, Camille motions for Vaughan and I to follow her to the kitchen. We do so without question and sit at the kitchen dinette table, the two of them on one side and me on the other.

I fold my hands on the table and inhale some courage. "I owe you an apology for not coming to you once Dagen and I decided we'd like to try a relationship beyond..." I struggle to tell him *beyond fucking*, but I think he understands. "I promised to look out for her, and that was my full and only intention. But sometimes life doesn't always follow the rules."

Vaughan huffs and turns his head, while Camille pats his shoulder and says, "I think we more than most understand."

"I'm sure there's a list of things you find that are wrong

about me. I'm older. I'm not so perfect. I live two states away. But all that should really matter is that I want to be with your daughter."

"Do you love her?" Vaughan snarls.

"It's headed that way." The honesty is shocking to both of our ears. "Look. The distance between you three is killing her. Every day, the hurt takes over the joy a little more. I hate that I can't be there physically to reassure her, but that's your job. I'm not her parent, just the man who's going to fall to pieces if she ever leaves."

Camille's eyes blink rapidly as she bats away the tears that build, and Vaughan's throat bobs as he swallows.

"She's hurting?" he asks.

"She is. Dagen won't tell me as much, but I can hear it in her voice. She misses you guys. She misses Sloane and AJ, but she's afraid to call because she sees it as caving to your demands. You don't have to like me. That's fine. But she does. Did you ever think that there may be something redeeming about me to have your daughter so blatantly disobey you? She's the most pure and loving person I've ever met. I don't think she'd fight so hard for something so evil." My body sags in my chair as I breathe out the last word.

A tear falls over Camille's lid and Vaughan's breathing turns more labored. They both are flimsy dams waiting to burst. It's obvious they feel the same pain and distance Dagen does.

"I'm going to be here for her as long as she'll have me, but I won't come between a family. If you can't find a way to accept our relationship then…then I'll have to break her heart. What's something you can see yourself living with and being okay with? Me in your life, or a broken daughter?"

Neither one says a thing as they stare at each other. My nerves are warring with my anger. I want to bang on this table and scream at them to wake up. If they can't see what harm they're doing, one of us is going to lose Dagen and I don't think any of us will survive a life without her.

After another minute passes in silence, I slowly rise from my chair and walk over to where AJ sits. I squat down and she smiles at me.

"I have to go, AJ. Be a good girl?" She nods, a food pouch still attached to her mouth. "Can I have a high five?"

She puts down her pouch and holds her chubby hand up to mine, giving it a hard smack.

"Bye bye, chicken," she giggles.

"Bye bye." I tap her little nose and brave myself to make the drive to Dagen's house. I don't know how she's going to feel about this. I'm worried I may have just made it so much worse.

"Hendrix. Wait please." I freeze in my tracks, terrified that Vaughan may be hiding another gun that has a bullet with my name on it.

He steps toe to toe with me, his face still hard and unreadable, then holds his hand out. I gawk at it, wondering if it's going to rise and wrap around my throat. When he holds steady, I take it cautiously with my hand.

"That took some balls to come here. Not many men would be brave enough to face the unapproving father of the woman they'd move mountains for, and I respect that. It's just…it's hard for a dad to admit he's not the number one man in his daughter's life. It hurts like hell, but I hate that I've brought her so much pain."

He drops my hand and Camille stands beside him, supporting him with a gentle touch. I get a flash of what life with Dagen could be like. The stubborn and the strong part. I feel like maybe Vaughan and I have some things in common. Mainly how we each want to protect Dagen from things that threaten to break her.

"I just want to see her happy, sir. She makes me happy so I think it's the least I can do for her. And right now, she could use some more happiness in her life. I'm headed up to see her. I should be there just after her last class and hopefully before her study group."

"You know all of that?" Camille asks.

Nodding I tell them, "I know when she wakes and when she eats. I know what she dreams about and what makes her smile each day. This isn't some momentary fascination for me. I don't know where this relationship is headed, but I'm traveling down this road wherever it may lead."

Camille gives me a warm smile and rests her head on Vaughan's shoulder. "Have you eaten, Hendrix?"

"No ma'am. I grabbed coffee and headed straight here. I wanted to be sure to catch y'all before you got busy with your day."

"AJ," she calls. "Want to help me make Hendrix some breakfast?"

Little arms raise high up in the air and she pops up from her chair, abandoning the puzzle and cartoons.

"Chicken. His name is chicken, Momma." We all laugh as she rushes into the kitchen, dragging a stool over to the stove. "Are we gonna cook or what?"

Vaughan pats my shoulder and passes me a look that I interpret as an approval. A silent one, but one nonetheless.

Dagen

"GO AND SNEAK US THROUGH THE RIVERS
FLOOD IS RISING UP ON YOUR KNEES
OH, PLEASE
COME OUT AND HAUNT ME
I KNOW YOU WANT ME"

Apocalypse
-Cigarettes After Sex

THIRTY-FOUR

MY PROFESSOR DRONES on and on and I watch the clock as each second passes. For two days I've been battling a stomach bug and right now, I just need this class to be over so I can rush to the bathroom and empty out the granola bar I had before walking in here.

"You okay?" Lizzie asks from her seat beside me.

I blink, tearing my focus from the clock and turn to her. "No. My stomach is still bothering me. I must have caught something."

She rubs my shoulder and gives me a sad look. "Maybe you should skip study group and just get some rest."

I nod my head and go back to watching time move at the speed of molasses. I zone out and before I know it, the professor is dismissing us. I gather my laptop, shoving it in my bag, and draping it over my shoulder. Lizzie follows me out of the classroom and down through the lobby of the business school.

My head hurts and my mouth is parched. The need to drink water is heavy, but my worry that it will do anything other than make me sick is greater. We walk down through the plaza to the parking lot where Lizzie's car waits, holding my stomach as if it will make the roil go away. When the crowd in front of us parts, I see a sleek black car with a devilishly handsome man leaning against it.

Girls pass and they give him a second, third and some a fourth look, ogling him as they go. Lizzie bumps my shoulder with hers and grins.

"I bet your stomach doesn't feel so bad now. See ya at home." She pats my butt, jokingly, and waves at Hendrix on the way to her car.

His blue eyes shine in the early afternoon sun, and his smirk is one that sets my body on fire. I walk towards him slowly at first and move faster with each step. When I come to stand right in front of him, it takes all my might not to accost him in front of dozens of people.

"Hey you," I purr. "Don't you look like every girl's Jake Ryan fantasy come to life." My hand smooths across his chest, and his hand finds my waist.

"Who's Jake Ryan and where can I find him so I can kick his ass?"

With a small laugh I tell him, "Jake Ryan is a fictional character from Sixteen Candles. Haven't you ever seen that movie?"

He pushes away a wayward lock of hair from my face, and glides his finger down my cheek. "You forget that you and I had very different childhoods."

For some reason, hearing that causes a bubble to rise up in my throat. It travels higher and pushes a tear from my eye. The others follow quickly and I press my forehead against his chest, sobbing softly.

"Hey hey hey. What's wrong baby?" He wraps me in his arms and kisses the top of my head.

"I haven't been feeling g-good, and my head hurts, a-and I threw up twice, and you're he-here." My words are a mess of garbled hiccups, and I'm surprised he can even understand me.

"Oh, my little mouse. Let me take you home. First we'll stop to get you some medicine and a few other essentials. Then it's bed and rest for you." I don't have the energy to argue and only nod my head.

He helps me into the passenger seat, buckling my seatbelt and takes my bag from me. I rest my head back on the seat, closing my eyes and breathing deep. With the close of his door and the roar of his engine, Hendrix pulls out of the parking lot and quickly grabs my hand, holding it all the way to the store and back to my house.

Luckily it is roommate free and blissfully silent. Hendrix pulls my laptop bag onto his shoulder, then grabs the bag with ginger ale, crackers and soup in one hand. We barely make it through the front door when I feel my feet fly out from under me and I'm cradled in Hendrix's arms. Once again, I don't protest and let him carry me to bed and pull off my shoes.

He leaves me to climb under the covers and brings me a small plate with crackers and a glass of ginger ale with a straw. Very first class nursing.

"Let's nap. I could use one too, and then I'll tell you about my night and morning." He scoots in right behind me on my small bed and spoons me.

"Okay," I whisper, a whimper clogging my throat.

My eyes fall heavy and I fade into a tormented dream.

I take small sips of my ginger ale as Hendrix explains his night with Danté and the surprising conversation he had with my parents this morning.

"It was really funny. AJ kept calling me chicken. I'm assuming, because Henny reminded her of hen."

He leans against the headboard and has me nestled between his legs. I close my eyes as he runs his fingers through my tangled strands after he pulled it out of the ratty bun I put it in this morning.

"I've never liked kids much, because the ones I had to deal with growing up in foster homes were all pretty bratty. But AJ and Sloane are cool kids."

He says *kids* and my stomach turns. My mind races with the day of my last period and suddenly I'm feeling dizzy. Two months. It's been two months since my last period, putting it before crashing my car in Cattywump Bay.

My chest tightens and the urge to vomit is back. I scramble out of Hendrix's nook and slam my glass down on the dresser on my way to the toilet. I slam open the lid just as the two crackers and the few sips make their way back. Tears fall as I wipe at my mouth and rest my head on my arms folded over the seat.

A warm hand smooths circles over my back and Hendrix kneels next to me. "I hate that you're sick. I wish there was something more I could do. How about if I call your mom and ask her what I should do?"

I turn my head to look at him and shake my head. "No. I think it might be something else." He furrows his brow waiting for me to tell him my theory. "I think...I think I may need to take a pregnancy test."

His body goes rigid and he falls back on his butt. His face pales at the thought I could be pregnant and now I'm even more sick.

"I didn't have my birth control pills in Mississippi and we had *a lot* of unprotected sex. I haven't had a period since," I explain.

His eyes are distant and I see sweat begin to build on his forehead. I wait and wait for any type of response. The one I get was not one that made the list of what he may say. Because he doesn't say anything.

Hendrix stands, his legs trembling, and holds onto the counter for support. Slowly, he spins around and walks out of the bathroom, my room and out of the house, the door slamming behind him.

My body slumps to the floor and I cry until the tears are dry and my mind is weak.

HENDRIX

"LIFE, IT SEEMS, WILL FADE AWAY
DRIFTING FURTHER EVERYDAY
GETTING LOST WITHIN MYSELF
NOTHING MATTERS, NO ONE ELSE"

Fade To Black
-Metallica

THIRTY-FIVE

I DROVE around for over an hour, my thoughts running wild with shock and disbelief. It took a lot of scolding myself before realizing I needed to be a man and face my responsibilities. I had to get back to Dagen and be the support she needs right now. I remembered that this wasn't something that was happening to just me. I may have been scared, but Dagen had to be terrified.

I made a second stop at the convenience store and hauled my ass back to Dagen's house. I screeched to a stop in front of it and ran through the front door, not caring if anyone was on the other side.

When I walk into her room and see that she isn't on her bed, I begin to panic. I rush to her bathroom and find her sleeping on the cold floor rolled into a ball. Squatting down, I lift her up into my arms and her eyes blink open. They're swollen and red as is her face that laid on the hard surface.

"Hendrix?" Her voice is rough and scratchy.

"It's me, little mouse." I kiss her forehead and she lifts her weary arms around my neck. "I'm sorry. I freaked out a bit, but I'm here and I'm sorry."

I take a seat on the closed lid of the toilet and adjust her in my arms.

"It's okay."

"It's not Dagen. Don't excuse my behavior. I'm almost thirty fucking years old, not a punk kid who runs when things get tough."

Her body shakes with a soft cry. I hold her to me tighter and close my eyes.

"I bought you a test. Think you can wake up enough to take it?"

Her head lifts to meet mine and she nods. I stand up and set her on her feet, then pull the three different tests I bought.

"I didn't know which was best," I shrug and I'm rewarded with a small smile.

I open the boxes and together we read the instructions together. I kiss her cheek then leave her to take care of her business.

I sit on the bed, my hands knotted between my legs, and stare down at my feet while my thoughts spiral. What happens to us if she is pregnant? Will she move to Cattywump? She has school to finish so that isn't an option. But I have the garage and the bar and my brothers. It's just as difficult to pick up my life and move to Texas. So does that mean I won't get to see Dagen? Our baby? Do we get married? Do I buy a cemetery plot since Vaughan will definitely kill me now?

The panic sets in just as the door opens and Dagen steps out with cautious steps.

"Well?" I ask.

"We have to wait for fifteen minutes." I hold out my arm and she quickly tucks herself into my side. "What are we going to do if they're positive?"

I sigh. "I don't know, little mouse. I was just asking myself the same thing."

We sit in silence for what feels like days when the timer on her phone finally chimes. She looks at me, crying once more, and I touch her face.

"We'll figure it out," I assure her, but she doesn't seem convinced.

I take her hand in mine and guide her to the bathroom counter where three sticks lie, side by side. Together we look at the first one, and then the next and then the last one. I feel her body sag and catch her right before she hits the floor.

Positive. All three. Dagen is pregnant. And I'm going to be a dad.

"Holy fuck," I say, more to myself than to her.

"I'm so sorry." She buries her head in my chest.

"Shh. You have nothing to be sorry about. It takes two people to make a baby. This isn't all on you."

She wails and though I'm doing the same on the inside, outside I remain the support she needs.

Suddenly, all of the unexplainable feelings I had each time I saw AJ hit me. Maybe someone was trying to send me a hint. Maybe little AJ was letting me know I needed to prepare myself.

The blood in my face drains to my toes. In eight months, I could be holding a crying little AJ of my own in my arms. I have no idea how to feel about that, but I can say I'm not angry. I think what I'm feeling is more of Dagen's light in my life. I think what I feel is content for a life I never thought I could have, but now one I'm looking forward to.

All because of a girl who crashed her car into my town and my life.

"I need to tell my parents," Dagen whispers as she lays next to me, her arm and leg flung over my body.

"We will. I'll come back next weekend and we'll tell them then. For now, let's just take the rest of our visit for us. I still need to let it sink in more, you know?"

Her head moves against my chest. "Yeah. I know."

Her roommates returned home one by one over the last couple of hours. Lizzie came in once to see us lying here and probably assumed we were resting. The others haven't come in and they've been respectfully quiet.

"How about you pack your bag and we go to the hotel. It's the same one as last time. I think it will be good for us to have some privacy."

"'K." She starts to sit up, but I stop her, gripping the back of her head and bringing her lips to meet mine.

It's the first real kiss between us since I arrived at her school. I never thought my heart could break for someone else, but Dagen has been through so much in the last few weeks and it's all because of me. And it's only going to get harder.

"I'm sorry my little mouse," I tell her when we part.

Her fingers brush over the stubble on my cheeks. "Why are you sorry, Mr. Wolf?"

"For everything. Being an ass to you in the beginning. The distance I caused with your parents. Putting a baby inside of you. That one's kind of a biggie."

She smiles, her beautiful face lighting up. "Yeah, that one is a bit of a surprise. But I wouldn't want to be surprised by anyone else."

"You better not. If you ever leave me for someone else, I'll have to hunt down the fucker and pin his ass to a tree." Those words right there tell me that this, the baby, is only going to make life better.

"Well, try not to get him pregnant since I'm pretty sure that may have been the night you left me with this surprise."

She points to her belly and my eyes stare at the spot that will grow over the months.

Months that I will miss because I'm six hundred miles away. The thought of not being able to see Dagen grow, see her shine as she nurtures our baby inside of her doesn't settle well with me. I need to figure out a way to rectify that.

"I think I need to move here."

"What? You can't be serious. What about your house, your shop and your brothers?"

With a shrug I tell her, "You're more important than all of that."

"Um. Didn't you just tell me that Danté was upset, because he thought just that? That I'd tear you away from him and Malik?"

"He'll understand. Things are different. Plus, maybe he'll like the idea of being an uncle. I know Malik will." I throw my head back when I think of Malik. "Fuck. Malik is going to be even more annoying once he finds out. Yup. Moving is a good idea. I'm going to need room between me and his crazy ass."

She laughs and pulls my face to look at her. Our chests are pressed together and our hearts speak in a language only they can decipher. If I could, I'd reach inside mine and place it in her hands. She already owns it so she might as well hold onto it tightly. I know she'll always protect it. I hope I can do the same for her.

I run my tattooed knuckles across her pink cheeks. "What are you doing to me, Dagen McCallan?"

"Showing you what love feels like, Hendrix Dare."

That's it. The feeling inside my chest, that foreign emotion I couldn't pinpoint finally has a name. Love.

I love Dagen McCallan. As fast as it may seem, I have no doubt that it's true.

HENDRIX

> "LOSING MY SIGHT
> LOSING MY MIND
> WISH SOMEBODY WOULD TELL ME I'M FINE"
>
> Last Resort
> -Papa Roach

THIRTY-SIX

SAYING goodbye to Dagen this morning was pure hell. She cried fat tears that stained my shirt as I held her tight. Her arms were locked around me and for a minute, I didn't think she'd let me leave. Though it wasn't like I was trying very hard. I would have been perfectly fine staying there forever with her, but things need to be taken care of back home.

We stayed in the hotel all weekend and talked about our future, what it will possibly look like. We were in agreement that I need to be closer since she has school to finish, but she insisted that the move wouldn't be permanent. She knows my businesses are important to me, along with Malik and Dante, and Dagen thought it was best if we made our home there. She made the tough decision to withdraw from grad school and will look into the programs offered at University of Southern Mississippi. The drive from Cattywump Bay to the main campus is little more than an hour and that worries me, but it's a topic we'll revisit once we speak to her parents.

I get within thirty minutes of home and decide I need to clear my mind a bit.

"Hey Cherry," I call out, using the name I've given my car. "Call Mal."

The car echoes my request and the phone begins to ring through the car speakers after a short moment.

"Yo Henny! What's up brother?"

"Hey Mal. Wanna ride?"

"Hell yeah. You know I'm always up for a ride. I can be there fifteen," he says, already moving about his house.

"Nah. In about an hour. I'm almost home, but I could really use some fresh air." I run through the ways in which to tell my brothers.

I worry about Danté's response to this news making the weight on my chest even heavier.

"Cool. I'll call D and see you in an hour."

"Later," I reply and hang up.

The rest of my drive home is spent rehearsing lines and how to tell Danté and Malik that they're going to be uncles. I pray that the night doesn't end with me back in a cell. Who knows what's going to happen when D hears that I'm moving, too.

The night is warm as we fly along the highway. Malik is dancing like a fool, cars honking at him as they go by, and Danté is showing off with tricks, front tire high in the air as he stands on the tank. It's crazy, I know, but what kind of biker men would we be if we didn't pull at least one illegal death defying trick.

The engine of my Duc screams as I release the clutch and open up the throttle, zipping faster down the dark road. I wonder when the next time will be where I can just let go of any thoughts or feelings and ride. How many more nights like this will I have with my brothers?

I decide not to worry about any of that right now and let loose. I turn off wheelie control then power up in first, and quickly shift to second as I reach the top. My bike lifts up beautifully as I keep control of my elbows, staying nice and straight.

Putting her down gently, I speed up to catch D and Mal. I don't reach the full torque and power of the 998 cc V4 engine –I don't need to be opening up to two-ten on the freeway– but I give it enough to hit ninety, smoothly. I get a flashback to the night a distracted driver cut me off, causing me to veer and wreck my blue Yamaha YZF-R1. A broken arm and leg, bruised ribs and gnarly road rash had me off my bike for five and a half months. It worried Miss Shirley into such a panic that I didn't put up a fight when she insisted on caring for me.

Thinking of the look on Miss Shirley's face when she came to see me in the hospital is vivid enough to have me slowing down. I imagine that being Dagen's face and how she would have reacted seeing me like that. Then I think of something worse happening and my child never getting to know me.

My heart begins pounding in my ears and I feel like I'm about to fall apart into a fucking panic attack. The weight of everything that has happened in the last three days hits me like a freight train, and the shocked excitement turns to pure dread.

How the fuck am I supposed to be a dad when I don't even know what one looks like?

I place my toe under the shift lever, lift the gear shift to the next position, and release the clutch, sending me flying past Danté and Malik. I don't motion to them that I'm exiting the freeway, just hope that they follow.

I weave in between cars on the off ramp and barely make the yellow light before it turns red. I spot a strip mall up ahead and pull into the parking lot. I don't downshift or ease to a stop. I brake hard and hit the kill switch as my feet fall to the pavement, skidding to a halt. I flip the kickstand and jump off.

It gets harder to breathe with my helmet on, and I struggle to pull it off, making my chest tighten. I finally break free and toss it down on the ground, then bend over, bracing my hands on my knees and gulping for air. I hear the revving of engines and screeching of tires and assume it's the guys finally catching up with me.

The sound of what seems like a dozen horses grows louder.

"Hen! What's wrong?" Danté places his hand on my back and tells Mal, "Call 911."

"No!" I gasp. "No. I need...sit...down."

D lifts me to standing and Malik rushes over to bracket the other side. Together they guide me to a light pole and prop me against the concrete base. My head lolls back and my eyes are too weary to keep open.

"Henny. Talk to us. What's going on?" I crack open one lid to see the two of them squatting in front of me.

"Dagen. She's pregnant." Both of them jump to their feet with eyes wide as softballs.

"You serious?" Mal asks, and I nod my head.

Sweat beads along my forehead and upper lip, and my body feels weak. It isn't long before a cold sweat rolls over me, causing my body to quake. Danté rushes to me and scrambles to get my jacket off.

"I'm c-cold, not hot D," I explain.

"No, you're not. You're crashing. Get this off. You need more air." Malik scurries to help D, and they work to yank my arms free.

The jacket gets tossed and I feel my face being fanned.

"How do you feel?"

"A little better," I pant.

"Not physically feeling. How do you feel about the baby?" Danté clarifies.

I inhale a steady breath and open my eyes. "Up until about ten minutes ago I felt excited. Shocked, but excited for a future. Then the reality all came crashing down and I realize I don't know what the fuck I'm going to do with a baby. The only kids I've been around are the fosters and Dagen's little brother and sister a couple of times. I don't know how to care for a child of my own."

"It'll kick in. You'll hold your kid and instinct will take over." I arch a brow at Malik as does Danté. "So I hear. I don't know first hand."

"I bet Dagen feels the same way. I imagine caring for a child, twenty-four seven, is much different than watching a sibling for a few hours." For such an asshole, Danté seems to be tapping into his emotional side lately.

We grow silent, only the sounds of the passing cars filling the air.

"So I guess you're moving then, huh?" Danté's face falls, realizing the one thing he worried about most is coming true.

"Temporarily. We decided that I'm going to split my time between here and Waco –mostly there– until she graduates. Then we'll move here."

Dantè's melancholy eyes fill with a little light.

"Fucking sweet! I call dibs on babysitting." Malik, like I expected, is far too excited about this new development.

"I told Dagen you were going to be annoying about it." Mal sticks his tongue out at me, but returns to smiling.

"I know you're scared but I think it's really great." I hurt my neck with how quickly my head flies back at Dantè's word. "Yeah, yeah. Not what you expected me to say, but I mean it. If any of us are going to be a dad, it should definitely be you."

"Hey. I take offense. I'm a fucking teacher," Mal protests, crossing his arms like the children he spends his days with.

"Making flowers from coffee filters and story time are a bit different than being a responsible parent. Think about it,

Mal." Danté sits on the ground, knees bent and arms hanging over them. "Who's the person that has always made sure we have everything we need? Which one of us is the first to take the others to the doctors when we're sick? Who watched out for us and protected us when we were in trouble, even though it landed him in even more trouble?"

Malik nods his head, deep in reflection. "You got a point there, D. I kind of ick out thinking about changing shit diapers and throw up. And interrupted sleep? Yeah, not my jam."

"Well it's not really mine either, but it's happening either way," I add.

Danté grips my shoulder and squeezes. "We got you, brother. You won't go at it alone. I dare anyone to try us."

The three of us exchange a silent solidarity to always have each other's backs. Just like it's always been and always will be.

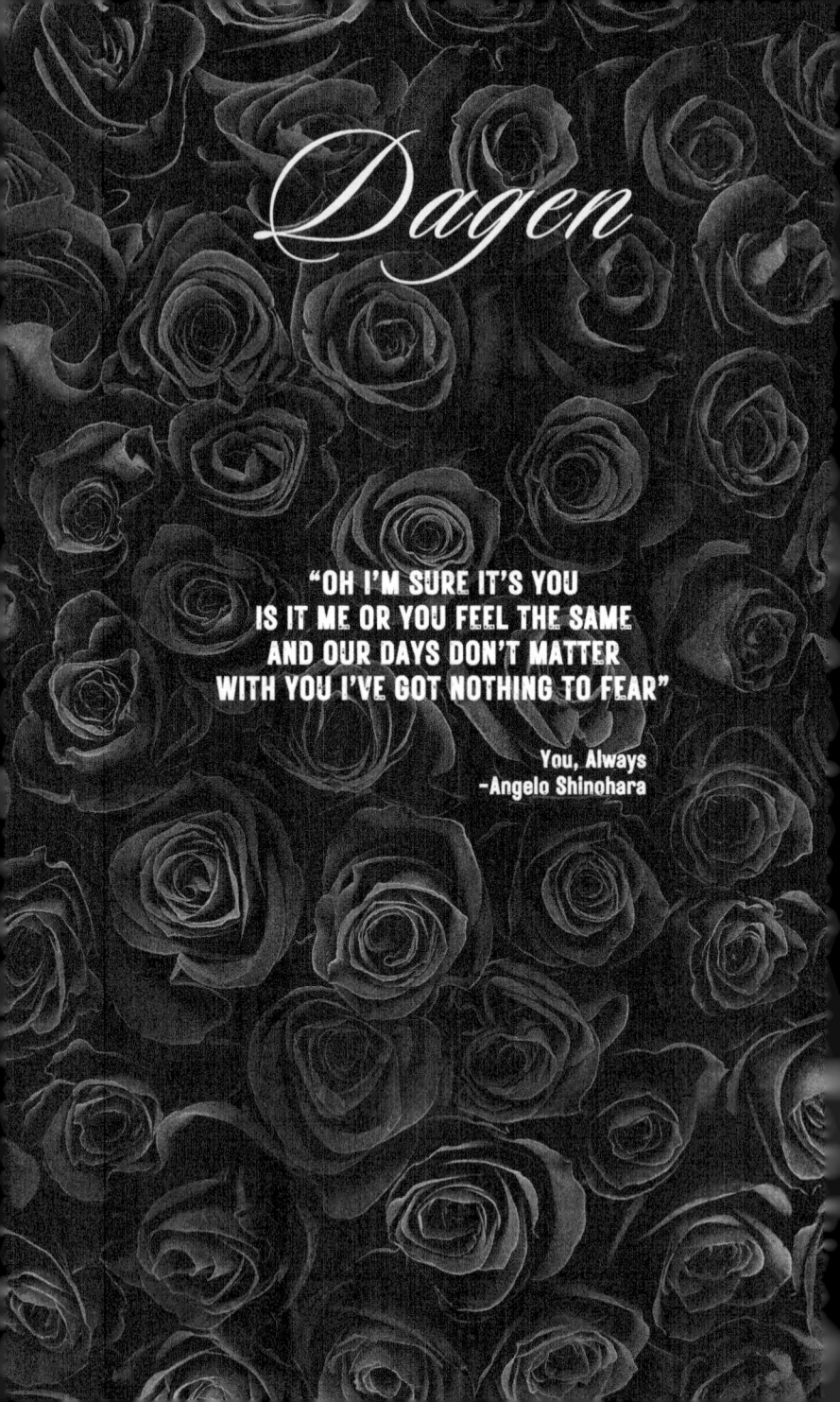

THIRTY-SEVEN

HENDRIX SQUEEZES my hand when we turn down the long dirt road that leads to my parents house. I picked him up in Dallas yesterday, where he flew in to, and took the evening to prepare for today's meeting with Mom and Dad.

I threw up –nothing new lately– he had a mild panic attack thinking my Dad's going bury him under a pile of horse shit, and together we promised not to let anything break us. Not even my parent's anger once they not only hear that I'm pregnant, but plan to move to Cattywump Bay after graduating.

He brings my hand to his mouth and kisses the back of it. "It'll be okay, little mouse. No matter what happens, you've got me."

A self-deprecating laugh falls from my mouth. "You say that. Just wait until daddy dearest takes the credit cards and financial support away. I hear I'm a bit of a spoiled brat."

He gives me one of his heart-stopping crooked grins. "One, you are a brat." I gasp and smack his arm with my free hand. "And two, I'll take care of you. You'll never want for anything and neither will T.D."

I screw up my face at him. "Who's T.D?"

"Tiny Dare. Until we know if it's a boy or girl, we're going with T.D. Then we'll discuss what his name will be later."

"Asa," I tell him without hesitation.

"Asa? Where the hell d'you get that name from?"

"It's my Dad's middle name." His eyes widen and he tenses.

"Asa Dare has a nice ring to it," he says with a shaky voice and I laugh. "And if T.D. is a girl, Gemma."

I tilt my head to the side, rolling the name around in my head over and over. "Hmm. That's…unique."

"As unique as *Asa*," I roll my eyes at him. "Gemma Dare. That sounds pretty fucking awesome to me."

"Yeah. I like it. Gemma. Wow. That was easy. Why do people always say that's the hardest part of having a baby?"

"No kidding. The hardest part to me seems to be the fact that you're going to push a bowling ball out of an olive."

I feel lightheaded visualizing that exact scenario. "Oh my god. I can't do this."

"Kidding. I'm sure it's not that bad." I drop my head back to the headrest and groan. "Welp. Here we are."

He turns into the driveway, the gate automatically opening when the sensor picks up my tag, and slowly pulls to a stop right in front. The engine is turned off and he turns to face me.

"It's going to be alright, my little mouse. I promise."

"Whatever you say, Mr. Wolf." I don't hold the same optimism that he does.

He leans over and frames my face as he kisses me. His affection drains me of my worry, and I fall into his universe. The one with the magnetic pull that I can't resist.

"Time to face the music," I mumble and go to unbuckle my seatbelt, but he clamps a hand over mine and shakes his head.

"Wait, dammit. How many times do I have to tell you?"

He taps me under my chin and unfolds himself from the driver's seat.

His swagger makes me wet as he walks in front of the car to my side, and I wonder if my parents have spotted my car on their phones yet. I could really use him to release the remaining tension in me.

"No. Stop it," he says, tersely.

"What? I didn't do anything."

He reaches over me and unclicks my seatbelt. "You're biting your lip. I know what you're thinking and just no. Not right as we're about to walk into your parent's house to tell them we're having a baby."

"Boo. You're boring. What happened to the dangerous bad boy who chased me through the woods?" He takes my hand and helps me from the passenger seat.

"He's still here, but he's hiding because your dad is for sure going to know I fucked his daughter."

I snort and cover my mouth. "And you think he didn't already know that I was sleeping with a thirty year old man when he saw me straddling you like a rodeo bull in your front seat?"

"Shh," he scolds, gently placing his hand over my mouth. "I'm going to tell him it was an immaculate conception. I need my balls for future kids."

My heart flutters when he says *future kids*. When all of this started, I was only hoping to make this last longer than two weeks. Now, Hendrix is talking about future children as we pick out names for the one that's already on the way.

I smile behind his hand then lick his palm.

"Dagen McCallan. That is uncalled for." He wraps his arm around my neck and tucks me under his arm.

"Look at you, practicing your dad voice already." We walk up to the front door and I press my thumb to the pad, unlocking it and pushing it open. "Hello? Anyone home?" I call out.

Hendrix shuts the door behind us just as Mom walks out from the den. "Hi sweetheart. Hi Hendrix. What are you two doing here?"

Here it is. The moment I've been dreading for a week.

With a deep breath I tell her, "Well, I wanted to spend the weekend on the ranch, show Hendrix around if that's okay."

"Of course it is." Mom meets us halfway into the hallway and wraps me in a hug and places a kiss on my cheek.

"And I," Hendrix clears his throat. "*We* want to talk with you and Dad. Is he here?"

"He is," she draws out with a curious eye. "Let me text him and we'll talk."

She knits her eyebrows and turns to walk back into the den.

"Where's AJ?" I ask.

"Nap. There's some banana bread on the island that I made this morning." She points to the platter with freshly sliced bread that I usually love.

Right now, the thought of eating makes me a little queasy.

Mom pulls her phone from her pocket to text Dad, and Hendrix leans in and whispers, "I better have a slice of that as it may be my last meal."

I smack his stomach with the back of my hand and he laughs. I get a napkin, place a slice of bread on it, and slide it over to him.

"So Hendrix," Mom calls out. "Did you drive into Waco?"

"No ma'am. I flew into Dallas yesterday and Dagen picked me up." He quickly shoves a chunk of bread in his mouth and moans.

"I know," I agree "It's the best."

"Are you not having any, sweetheart?" Mom looks at me with a piercing stare that makes me squirm.

"I, uh, had a big breakfast. I'll be sure to have some later." I pat Hendrix on the arm and walk to the fridge, opening it and getting water for the two of us.

I quickly crack mine open, and take a few chugs to quench my parched mouth. It feels like I've been sucking on balls of cotton, it's so dry. Mom continues to talk to Hendrix and I play over the words I've rehearsed a hundred times since last night. I just know that the minute the first one leaves my mouth, I'm going to choke and cry.

I zone out and only come to when I hear my name being called. "Dagen?"

I blink and look around the kitchen to see Hendrix, Mom and now Dad all staring at me.

"Sorry. I was just…I zoned out for a minute." I give my head a little shake. "Hi Daddy."

"Hey baby bird." He holds his arms wide and I slide into them.

His hug is warm and comforting, and he smells of fresh air and sunshine. I can't help the tears that begin to fall.

"What's wrong, Day?" The concern in his voice is evident.

I sniff and lie, "I just missed you."

He folds his arms around me and places his hand behind my head. "I missed you too."

We stand like that for another minute. "Want to sit down?" Mom asks.

I shake my head and Dad holds my hand as we walk over to the couch. I release his hand and grab Hendrix's, sitting us down on the leather sofa. I scoot close, gripping his hand with a white knuckle hold, and blink away my tears.

Mom and Dad sit on the chair facing us, Dad sitting with Mom resting on the arm of her chair and placing her hand on his shoulder.

"What's going on, Dagen? Is everything okay?" Dad wonders.

"Yeah. Things are, well I–they–" I look at Hendrix and he gives me a small nod, encouraging me to go on. "So, you know how when I left here after finding out about…*her*," I refuse to speak that woman's name ever again. "I didn't really take much with me. Thank god I already had my phone and my driver's license in my pocket or I would have really been in trouble."

Dad looks at me and rolls his hand, telling me to move it along.

"Well I didn't have anything but the clothes on my back. No makeup, not even a toothbrush. I also left behind medications."

My eyes flit between them, waiting to see if either of them pick up on what I'm trying to say. They both just stare, waiting for me to go on.

"I wasn't able to take any of my medication for almost two weeks that I was gone." I feel Hendrix shake beside me.

Or is it me shaking while he sits calmly?

The lights finally flick on in Mom's eyes and her hand covers her mouth, and I watch the blood drain from her face. I can see her heart breaking and it cracks mine, straight down the middle.

"Will someone please tell me what's going on?" Dad insists.

"I...I'm–" my throat is clogged with fear and I can't get the words out.

A strong arm is wrapped around my shoulders and Hendrix says, "Dagen is pregnant."

The room falls eerily silent. Not even the tick of the clock is heard. Everything freezes, all in fear of what's to come next.

"And it's mine, in case it wasn't clear," Hendrix adds.

Dad's face goes from passive to processing and finally to rage.

"I'm going to fucking kill you," he roars, jumping up from his seat and charging towards us.

Hendrix pops up quickly, and stands in front of me.

"Vaughan! No!" Mom screeches and I peek from behind

Hendrix's legs and see her rip him back by his shirt. "Sit down!"

His chest heaves and he reminds me of a beast, readying itself to obliterate its enemy. Red eyes burn holes at Hendrix, and his teeth are clenched.

"Dad. Can you please sit down? Please?" Full sobs are pouring from me, and it has Hendrix dropping to his knees.

"It's okay, little mouse. I got you." He runs his tattooed fingers down my face, trying to soothe me.

I breathe in and out in exaggerated puff.

"Get away from my daughter!"

"Sir. Please. You're upsetting Dagen and she doesn't need that right now. She's been sick with worry for a week–"

"A week? You've known for a week and you're just now telling us?" Dad's rage filled eyes turn on me.

"Look at how you're reacting. I barely had time to wrap my mind around it, much less have to deal with you. Don't you think the one thing I wanted to do was run to my parents and have them hold me and tell me it would all be okay? But I couldn't, Dad. I couldn't because I knew that you would freak out instead of hugging me like I needed." My chest heaves for air as my words become more and more unintelligible.

Hendrix turns my head back to focus on only him. "Do you want to go home, baby? We can leave right now. No one says we have to stay."

He gently runs his hand down my face, wiping away the tears that can't seem to stop. I inhale and my breath is stuttered. The crying that I have done in the last few weeks, starting with the bomb about Stephanie, is starting to wear on me. I'm so tired and weak and feel completely defeated.

"Dagen, sweetheart." Mom's voice is soft and cautious. "Have you taken a test or been to a doctor?"

Nodding, I tell her, "I took three tests. All of them were positive." Dad's nostrils flare. "I didn't plan this, okay. Nowhere in the neat and organized map of my future did I have *find out your birth mom is a rapist, crash your car and get pregnant from a man you've known for a month* penciled in. I'm just as scared and shocked as you are. Believe me. But all I can do now is roll with it. Are you in or are you out? Those are the only two choices."

Mom stands from her perch next to Dad and tiptoes over to me. The cushion dips as she sits and takes my hand.

"My sweet girl. I'm so sorry you've been going through this all alone–"

"She's not alone. I've been right here." Hendrix's voice is harsh.

"Thank you, Hendrix, for being there for her. Guess we look like big jerks, don't we?" Hendrix shrugs and I smack his leg. "We're here honey. We're not going anywhere. We'll be here every step of the way, offering whatever support you need."

Fucking tears.

I throw myself at her and sob into her shoulder. She squeezes me tighter than I think she ever has before, crying along with me. Leaning back, she takes my face in her hands and plants a hundred kisses on it.

"My baby is having a baby," she hiccups. "Can you please not let the baby call me granny? I'm not ready for that."

I laugh through my tears with a smile. "Sure, Mom. Whatever you want is fine."

She nods then pulls herself from me. Turning to Hendrix, her face drops.

"You're a good man, Hendrix." She stands and takes him with her, hugging his rigid body with the same strength she used on me.

Hendrix looks scared and awkward, not really knowing what to do with affection, and then something amazing happens. His big tattooed arms snake around her and hugs her back. It's not the kind of hug he gives me, but one you'd give your mom. A mom he never had.

When hugs have been handed out and tears dried, we all look at Dad who still sits there just staring. Expressionless. Emotionless. Completely void.

I rub my chest, my heart breaking with his avoidance. His eyes scan over the three of us and stop on Hendrix.

"Are you planning to marry her?" he asks, gruffly.

Hendrix swallows and looks at me. "We haven't discussed it yet, but I-I plan to. One day. Only if that's what Dagen wants."

"Dad, that's not something I'm really worried about right now. Let's just focus on one thing at a time. The first thing being that I'm pregnant."

"Dagen. I'm just looking out for you. You can't do this on your own. You–"

"She's not on her own. I'll be there. I'm buying a house in Waco for me. For *us*. I'll need to be in Mississippi sometimes for my businesses, but my plan is to be there for every doctor's appointment, every bump and kick and craving. My new job is to take care of Dagen and see to it that she has a safe and healthy pregnancy."

Dad looks at Hendrix like he's inspecting him. His eyes travel up and down, looking at Hendrix from head to toe. He tilts his head and narrows his eyes, evaluating every last inch of him. I scoot closer to him and grip tightly onto his flexed bicep.

As Dad moves closer, we both tense waiting for what comes next. And what does, shocks the hell out of both of us. Dad offers his hand out to Hendrix. He looks, then cautiously takes it. They shake and Dad pulls Hendrix in for a short hug.

Quickly, he releases him and grabs me, pulling me into a tight embrace. "I love you, baby bird," he whispers into my ear, his voice choked with emotion.

"I love you too, Dad."

I just know, everything is going to be okay. I can feel it.

Dagen

"OH, HONEY, A HEART THAT NEVER BREAKS
OH, TREASURE, A MARK THAT NEVER FADES
OH, DARLIN', LOVE ME THIS WAY
'TIL MY FEET TAKE ME TO THE GRAVE"

Love Is Complicated (The Angels Sing)
-Labrinth

THIRTY-EIGHT

WE TALKED with Mom and Dad for hours, telling them about our plans and what steps we need to take next. They weren't really all that excited about our decision to move to Cattywump Bay after graduation, but they understood why.

After making an appointment with my OB/GYN for next Friday, and many hugs and kisses, Hendrix and I make the drive back to Waco. We get closer to the hotel and suddenly my body is heating up and a familiar tingle rolls through my body.

"Can you drive faster?" I pant.

"What's wrong, little mouse? Are you going to be sick?"

"No." My eyelids are hooded with need.

His face is so drawn with confusion, trying to figure out what has me in a hurry to get to our room. Like a light switch, the realization for what I want flips and his foot slams down on the gas pedal, jerking us forward.

He plows through intersections, catching a few lights as they turn red, and screeches into the parking lot. I've learned my lesson when it comes to opening my door, so I stay put but ready my feet to run.

The door is flung open, practically off the hinges, and he

pulls me out by my hand. My legs scurry to keep up with his long strides to the elevator. He jams the button over and over, as if it will speed it up.

When the gold doors finally slide open, we're jumping in before they fully separate, and a woman rushes to hop in before they close.

Hendrix stands in front of me, and with a stern voice tells her, "You're going to have to wait for another one, ma'am. I need to fuck my girl and I need to do it now."

He holds the button to our floor down and blocks her from entering until we're tucked in all alone and rising.

A growl rumbles from his chest and in a flash, he's pinning me to the elevator wall. His mouth begins a journey, starting at my lips and traveling down my neck.

He spins me around to face the mirrored walls and says, "Take a good look at this face, little mouse. You won't be seeing it for a while because I plan to keep it buried in a pillow, screaming my name for many hours."

His inked hand glides up my ribs, over my breast, and circles my throat. Hendrix's thumb rubs over my pulse point that jumps with excitement. Fear has become an aphrodisiac and I can't get enough.

We reach our floor and this time I run to keep pace as he hustles to the room like a man on a mission. And what an important mission it is.

The door beeps, unlocking with the swipe of his keycard, and he kicks it open, scooping me up in his and carrying me to the bed. Instead of placing me gently on the mattress I'm flung through the air, landing with a hard bounce. He advances on me before my motion stops and pins me down.

"You are my light, Dagen. The only one I have in my life." His words are hushed but his eyes quickly turn black, and the Mr. Wolf I crave appears. "But now a bit of my darkness exists in you. You'll never be rid of me little mouse, and it drives me fucking insane to know that."

I'm ripped out of my clothes before I can respond, and watch with admiration –and drool– as he languidly peels out of his. The eye contact we keep is fierce and the electric current that passes between us is powerful.

Inch by inch, another sliver of his beautiful body is revealed, my tattoo the masterpiece. Until his pants drop, that is. I will never tire of seeing him naked in all his glory.

"Are you hungry little mouse?"

"So very hungry." My mouth waters and my heart pounds.

"Then I guess I better feed you."

He climbs up my body until his knees frame my face. Flat on my back, I look up at him as he strokes his hard shaft up and down. It grows with desire and my mouth waters as I recall the taste of him.

"Open," he commands, and I do without question.

The mushroomed head of his cock pushes past my lips, stretching them wide. Pain sears at the corners as I welcome him in and I feel my throat slowly relax. I breathe in deep through my nose, sucking in every last ounce of oxygen I can. Farther and farther he goes and my lungs begin to constrict. When he pulls out, I gasp for sweet air.

"Again, little mouse." I nod and prepare for him to breach once more.

He gets himself halfway into my mouth when he reaches down and cups my head, keeping me steady as he moves in and then out. He manages to do that four more times before he's gripping either side of my head and holding me still as he fucks my face.

My vision grows blurry when he goes deeper with each thrust. I grab at his thighs, my nails scratching at his hot flesh.

"Scratch me. Mark me. Make me bleed, Dagen." I sink my nails into him and hear him hiss.

The faster he goes, the deeper my nails dig. He grunts and groans and my gags mix with his feral sounds. He huffs like a rabid animal and drops my head back on the soft bed. He leans forward and his arms lock stiffly. My eyes fix on the tattoos covering his taut stomach and it's the last thing I remember seeing clearly before my eyes fill with moisture.

His hips roll as he continues to drill my head into the mattress. At one point he pushes so far down my throat I think it's possible he may get stuck that way. Black begins to close in on me as I turn weak. My hands are heavy and my mind is fuzzy. And right before I fade into nothingness, Hendrix pulls free and my lungs flood with air.

"Fuck. I bet you're soaked, aren't you." My words and thoughts are not clear yet, so he decides to find out for himself.

He slithers his way down my body and dips his tongue right down my seam that buzzes with urgency. My back arches and fingers tangle in his hair, pulling him closer and deeper. I grind my aching pussy on his face, trying to speed him up because I'm about to combust.

I feel the absence of his mouth and see his saucy grin when he emerges from his happy place. "Are you feening, baby?"

"Yes. Will you fucking hurry, already?" I reach out for him, wiggling my fingers and making grabby hands.

He lets out a deep, gravely laugh and smooths his hands up my thighs. Those calloused fingers of his tickle my belly as they glide. I wait for them to massage my tender breasts but he freezes, his hands laying motionless on my stomach.

"What's wrong? Hendrix. Don't stop. Please. I'm dying." I move my hips back and forth and hook my foot around his back.

I watch the way his throat moves and his eyes soften when they roam over me. The beast is instantly tamed and I just want to scream to bring him back. What he does shocks me into equal silence.

Hendrix rolls over onto his back, taking me with him so

that I straddle his hips. He lifts me gently and grips his dick, sliding into me at a tender pace. With his hands circling my waist and mine resting on his chest, I begin to roll my hips.

Our eyes barely blink, not wanting to miss a moment of what's happening. It's deeply intimate and nothing like I've ever experienced with Hendrix. He's hard and rough and dominating. But right now all of that has drained from his body and what's left is his big heart that he works so hard to conceal.

His fingers trace the lines of my tattoo, running over the words and circling the petals with grace. "My words are on your flesh and my seed is in your body. You're mine forever, Dagen."

Goosebumps erupt and I move faster, feeling my orgasm build, and run to the finish line. This one is different, though. While Hendrix is usually pulling the ecstasy from me, this one pours out, the bliss overflowing. It bleeds from me and into Hendrix, and this time I draw the lust that exists.

We both pant and heave as our bodies wake up, and I run my hand across his stubbled jaw before kissing him.

"I think I'm falling in love with you," I admit.

"I *know* I'm falling in love with you, little mouse. I don't ever want to step back into the dark now that I have you."

I don't think anything will bring me down from this high.

HENDRIX

"THIS IS MY LIFE
IT'S NOT WHAT IT WAS BEFORE
ALL THESE FEELINGS I'VE SHARED
AND THESE ARE MY DREAMS
THAT I'D NEVER LIVED BEFORE"

So Far Away
-Staind

THIRTY-NINE

I OPEN my eyes to bright light pouring in from outside and the smell of lavender fills my lungs. Dagen, my whole world, lays wrapped in my arms as early morning is upon us. We stayed the night in the small cottage that is attached to the barn on the McCallan property. It was a debate I didn't think Dagen would win. But Vaughan finally caved after realizing that I had driven all the way from Cattywump Bay to meet Dagen for her first OB/GYN appointment today. She was already nervous and an argument with him was just adding to it.

"Hendrix, you can take the room you had last time. Dagen you know where your room is." The night sky was dark as Vaughan rattled off instructions for our sleeping arrangements.

"Dad. Come on. That's ridiculous. Hendrix will sleep with me in my room."

"Like hell he will, Dagen Rayne." Vaughan's anger was slowly rising.

It seems like all Vaughan is around me is angry. Dagen has told me many times how affectionate and loving he is, but apparently I bring out a different side of him. Yay for me.

"It's not like you have to worry about anything. I'm already pregnant so he can't do that anymore."

"Jesus Christ," I mumbled.

That was definitely not the right way to go about the situation.

"This is my house, and what I say goes. Period. End of discussion."

"Fine. Then maybe I'll find my own house. Then I won't have to deal with you." Dagen crossed her arms over her chest and dug her foot in.

I had to say something. I was tired of being the strain between them. It was too much and I couldn't allow it to go on anymore.

"I think I'll just go to a hotel room and stay there. I can see that my presence is the root of all of these problems, and I don't want to cause any more stress on either of you. Most especially Dagen. I apologize." I grabbed my phone from my back pocket to search for a nearby hotel when Camille spoke up in a way that shocked everyone.

"No one is going anywhere! This ends now, Vaughan. I'm at my fucking breaking point with you. Dagen is an adult and you cannot continue to hold your thumb on her. She's having a baby, and you have to face the fact that she's not a little girl. Hendrix is a good man. He didn't have to stick around after finding out the woman he's known for a handful of weeks is pregnant. But he's here and he's done nothing but show support for the child you say you love. You either get your head and your heart right, or you're going to lose her. I will not lose my daughter because of your stubbornness, Vaughan." She turned to us with a sudden compassionate look in her eyes. *"Hendrix. Dagen. You two can take the barn cottage. I hope you'll be comfortable there."*

Vaughan's eyes were wide and somewhat frightened to be honest. Camille walked past him, bumping him hard as she did, and hugged Dagen with a strength only a mother possesses. She hugged me with the same affection and this time, I welcomed it.

She bore fire into Vaughan as she stomped out of the room and up the stairs.

Dagen cried herself to sleep and my worry about her mental and physical state grows a little more each day.

She's exhausted and I don't want to interrupt her sleep, so I carefully slide out from under her and pad quietly into the kitchen. I need some caffeine to ward off the headache that is lingering behind my eyes, so I search the cabinets for coffee. Finding some, I pop in a pod to brew and take a second one for Dagen. Then I realize that she can't have coffee. I look for juice or tea or anything she may want when she wakes up, but the fridge is barren of anything of the sort.

I spot the time on the microwave and see that the McCallan household is most likely awake and in full chaos with the kids. Slipping on my clothes and shoes, I abandon my coffee in search of something for Dagen.

The day is already warm and a slight fog hangs over the ranch. The property is expansive and in the morning sun, it looks picturesque. I understand why Dagen loves it so much. Her happy place is here, and I hate that soon I will be tearing her away.

Through the backdoor I see Sloane walking around in his underwear holding a small guitar and strumming it. From the look on Vaughan's face, it seems he's not doing so well. AJ sits at the table, swinging her feet and bopping her head like her brother is giving her a private concert. Her hair is a mess with tangles and she shovels sliced bananas in her mouth.

I watch the two kids, wondering if ours will be like them. Wild and carefree, loving and intelligent. My eyes focus on AJ, my heart feeling a special connection with her, and it tells me that's what I'm in store for.

I rap my hand softly on the glass and three sets of eyes

look at me. AJ begins clapping her hands and Sloane comes running.

He pushes the door open and smiles up at me. "Were you in the barn?"

I ruffle his hair and laugh. "Yup. Slept with the horses. It's pretty comfortable in there."

He laughs, shaking his head. "You're silly. It's stinky, not comfortable."

"Chicken!" AJ's little voice calls from the table and her arms raise in a V, one hand full of mushed banana.

Walking over to her, I squat down to eye level with her and wink. "You're the one that looks like a chicken this morning with all of that crazy hair."

She shoves her banana in her mouth then throws her arms around me, no doubt leaving behind remnants of it on my shirt.

"Autumn Jade. You just wiped your sticky hands all over Hendrix. Let go, little missy." Camille runs a towel under the faucet and makes her way over to us.

"Eh. It's okay. Definitely worth it for an AJ hug." I stand to let Camille wipe her hands and take a couple steps back.

"Good morning, Mr. McCallan." I've decided the familiarity of calling him Vaughan is over and go back to addressing him as I would a business associate.

"Mornin'." His face is riddled with guilt and I'm thinking Camille continued with the tongue lashing after we went to bed.

"Camille. Do you have juice or tea that I can take to Dagen? She's still sleeping but since she can't have coffee, I thought she'd want something to help her get going."

She smiles wide at me as she tosses the napkin in the trash.

"I have some decaf coffee she can have. I'll make her a cup of that and pour a glass of juice."

"And a 'nana," AJ adds.

"And a banana. She loves those, doesn't she." AJ nods with a big grin on her face.

"Thank you, Camille." I stand awkwardly, waiting for her coffee to brew.

I shove my hands in my pockets and stare down at my feet. I feel like I should say something, but I'm out of words and apologies to say to Vaughan. The only thing left to apologize for is simply existing.

"Hendrix," he calls over to me. "Do you think I can speak with you a little later? After you've finished your coffee?"

I gulp and feel thankful that my hands are in my pockets, otherwise he'd see how much they tremble. "Yeah. Absolutely."

One corner of his mouth lifts and he gives me a slight dip of his chin.

If that man packs his gun with him, I know his talk will be the last one before he drops me in a deep hole.

"Here you go." Camille breaks me from my contemplation over whether I'd rather see the bullet coming or close my eyes, and hands me a tray. "You two take your time. No rush. Dagen's appointment isn't until two."

I look down at the tray with a glass or orange juice, a cup of coffee, two bananas, two bowls of strawberries and blueberries and two bagels. In that moment, I'm jealous of Dagen and her siblings, getting to grow up like this. A real mother who cares for all of their needs. By the time we landed with Miss Shirley, we were teenage boys who just wanted to be left alone. None of us ever had a mom or dad to fuss over us.

Camille opens the door for me and before I can step out, AJ shouts, "I go with Chicken and Day."

"No, baby girl. Day is still sleeping. You'll see her later." Vaughan scoops her up and she pouts. "How about we go check on the horses?"

"Yes."

"Let me get my shoes," Sloane shouts.

"And clothes," Camille adds.

I walk out and turn to both of them. "Thank you. I appreciate this."

Camille smiles warmly, and squeezes my arm.

When I reach the cottage, I balance the tray and push the front door open. I'm greeted by the sounds of retching coming from the bedroom. I place the food down on the counter and quickly jog to the bathroom where I see Dagen hunched over the toilet.

I sit down next to her and begin smoothing circles on her back. "Are you okay, my little mouse?"

She nods, her head hanging into the bowl. "When will this stop?"

"I don't know, baby, but the doctor will hopefully give us some answers today."

Her back expands with a deep breath, and she reaches up to flush the toilet. I help her stand and run the water for her, letting her rinse her mouth. She grabs for her toothbrush but I stop her.

"Your mom sent juice and food. Do you want to try that before you brush? I read that sometimes brushing your teeth first thing in the morning can trigger vomiting. Maybe wait until after."

Her bleary eyes examine me like I'm a stranger who has burst in.

"You read that?" she asks and I nod. "Have you been… have you been reading about what to expect?"

Embarrassed, I admit, "Yeah. I want to be able to help you. I have no clue what being a parent or a partner looks like, so it's kind of like parenting for dummies. Gotta start somewhere."

She smiles and places her hand on my chest where her tattoo is etched and one teardrop falls over her lid.

"No crying," I remind her, wiping away the errant tear.

"I can't help it. This baby makes me cry one minute and then the next, I'm cranky and tired."

I pull her to me and she snuggles into my arms. Kissing the top of her head only makes her cry harder. My poor girl is a wound up ball of emotions. I hope that whatever talk Vaughan wants to have will help.

Or it could make it worse if he cracks me over the head with the shovel.

After we ate, Dagen only picking at her food, I showered and sat on the couch waiting for doom to come knocking. Dagen is laying with her head in my lap and I comb my fingers through her hair. I can tell she's falling asleep so I keep the television low.

I hear the tapping of knuckles on the door. Dagen begins to sit up but I hush her.

"Just lay down. I'll be back soon. You should take a nap. We have a big afternoon ahead of us." She nods silently and I slide a pillow under her head as I slip out from under her.

She immediately closes her eyes and I place the blanket on the back of the sofa over her and kiss her cheek. Inhaling and exhaling with a puff of air, I open the door.

"Hey," Vaughan greets. "Ready?"

"Yeah. Dagen is taking a nap so it's a good time." I quietly close the door behind me and turn to spot a golf cart sitting in front of us.

Yup. This is it. He's driving me to my resting spot. I should have sent a goodbye text to my brothers and Miss Shirley.

Vaughan sits in the driver's seat and I climb into mine with hesitation.

"I want to show you something," he tells me, and begins driving.

We're silent as he takes me across the property. Wide fields lead into a wooded area where I see some animals scurrying into. We drive past a small creek and circle back around, stopping at a large magnolia tree where a bench sits.

I don't see any large holes around, so I figure he's going to let me have a minute before I go.

"Why don't we sit on the bench," he suggests, pointing to it.

I clamber out of my seat and walk with heavy steps to the bench. When I get closer, I see a plaque with a name on it. I squint to make out what it says, but I don't have to wonder for long.

"Robert Stevens," Vaughan says. "That was Cami's first husband."

My face is pure shock when I look at him. At no time did Dagen tell me her mom was married before. I knew that Camille and Vaughan dated in high school and that her birth mother is the reason why they broke up. But she never told me that her mom was married previously, or that Vaughan most likely took him out, and now I'm going to meet the same fate.

Vaughan sits as do I, leaving plenty of space between us.

"Robbie died almost ten years ago. He, uh, he ended his life after battling deep depression. When Cami and I got back together, I made this bench for her after she spread his ashes here."

My jaw drops. I have no words and barely thoughts at this point.

"It was something I knew she needed. Every once in a while, I'll find her out here just talking about me and the kids, or simply sitting in silence. I never want her to forget him. He took care of her until we could find our way back to one another, and I'm grateful for that."

"Is Slo…did they ever have any…" Vaughan shakes his head, understanding the question I can't seem to get out.

"No. They never had any children. Cami said Robbie always made excuses as to why they should wait. She finally came to the conclusion that it was because he wouldn't be here to help raise them. I think it was because he was worried about passing on whatever problems he had to a child. I guess we'll just never know."

I look at the large tree and stare at the roots that protrude from the grass.

"But that's not what I wanted to bring you out here to talk about. I want to…" he pauses and closes his eyes. "I want to say I'm sorry. After a long talk with Camille –and by talk I mean she scolded me and I listened– she made me see what a first class asshole I was being."

I fold my hands together, handing them between my spread legs, a stare down at my shoes.

"I never meant for any of this to happen. I hope you know that," I explain.

"I believe that. Really."

"It's just…have you ever wanted something so much even though you know it would bring heartache?"

He looks at me with a slight grin. "Yeah. I do. As far as what you're talking about, no one can relate better than Bishop and Anais. They fought their feelings knowing what trouble would follow with their relationship, but love doesn't always listen to rationality."

"I've never felt anything so strong as I do for Dagen. No one has ever brought such peace into my life and I feel like, if I don't hold onto it with both hands, I'll never feel it again. We may not have planned this but now that it's here, I won't let anything steal it away."

"Now *that* I understand. More than most."

We both sit in shared silence, realizing we're more alike than either of us ever thought.

"All I ask is that you're a good man to my little girl and a good dad to my grandchild. Holy fuck, I'm going to be a grandfather." He shakes his head as if the final piece just clicked into place.

I breathe out a small laugh, relating to the same shock.

"I promise to always take care of them. I may need a little help with the dad part since I never had one. Hopefully you can guide me. After all, you raised an amazing daughter. That big heart came from somewhere."

His eyes glisten and he blinks it away as he places his hand on my shoulder and pats it.

"Deal." He suddenly seems lighter and maybe more like the man Dagen has told me about. "We better get back before Dagen thinks I buried you here."

Boy, if he only knew how true I thought that was.

FORTY

A LOUD WHOOSH and thump fill the small room that five people are crammed into.

When Mom helped me make my first doctor's appointment, I thought it was a me and Hendrix appointment. Not a me, Hendrix, Mom and Dad appointment. They might as well have invited all the aunts and uncles.

Then again, I don't even know if they all know. *Oh god*, I'm going to have to tell them.

"Is that…is that the heartbeat?" Hendrix asks, looking a little pale at the moment.

"It sure is," Dr. Molina tells us. "Nice and strong."

Hendrix grabs my hand and stares down at me. His eyes are wide and he mouths the words *"holy shit"* to me, and I couldn't agree more.

I hear sniffling coming from the corner of the room and look up to see Mom and Dad holding each other, both with tears in their eyes. The anger Dad held, and the fear Mom was festering seems to fade away.

"Well, based on the measurements, you appear to be approximately five weeks along. That puts your due date in December. Maybe even a Christmas baby."

"My birthday is Christmas Eve," Hendrix says.

"Really?" I ask and he nods with a mix of shock and disbelief on his face.

"Well wouldn't that be fantastic if you and your baby had the same birthday?" Dr. Molina smiles at us and turns off the fetal doppler. "I'll give you a minute to clean up and then will meet you at the appointment desk. Congratulations."

She walks out of the room, my eyes following her as she shuts the door behind her. My chin is tugged and my lips are instantly captured in a kiss. Hendrix's mouth locks with mine and he holds my face as if he needs the touch to assure him this is real.

He rests his forehead against mine and we breathe each other, and the moment in. "I love you, little mouse," he whispers and my eyes pop open.

My heart beats faster than the baby's that we just heard, and my bottom lip begins to wobble.

"I love you too, Mr. Wolf." It's a hushed moment between the two of us that I hope my parents don't hear.

Seeing as the room feels like a matchbox with all of us crammed in, I doubt that. But when I look over to the corner they stand in, I find it empty. I spin around to see if maybe they moved to stand behind me, but aside from Hendrix and I the room is empty.

"Where'd they go?" I ask him.

"I don't know, but how about you get cleaned up and meet the doctor at the reception desk." He kisses my forehead then wipes away the gel still smeared over my still flat belly.

"No sign of Mr. Wolf today." I bite my lip, hiding a cheeky grin.

"Oh he'll be along later. Be patient, little mouse." He leans in and takes my lip from between my teeth and into his.

I know he's itching to pierce my skin and taste me, but with my parents...somewhere, he refrains himself. When we walk out and find them standing near the wall, we see that they must have snuck out when we were lost in one another.

They both smile at us, and we walk to the check out desk, Hendrix holding my hand every step of the way.

"Hendrix. I'll be fine," I insist but continues to shake his head, arms crossed and standing in front of his bike.

After an adventure-filled weekend of sonograms and house hunting, Hendrix returned to Cattywump Bay alone and I stayed in Waco, crying and counting down the days until I'd be reunited with him again. I had already planned to go down for the weekend, so it was only a matter of four days until I saw him , but it was four days too long.

Now he's refusing to take me for a ride on his bike, saying it's dangerous for both the baby and I.

"No way, little mouse. You aren't getting on a bike ever again. Four wheels only."

"What? You're smoking crack if you think I'll just–" and then a brilliant idea pops into my head. "Fine. Four wheels it is. I want to drive Big Green."

His beautiful green dodge sits bright and shiny right next to where we stand in his garage.

"Dagen," he growls.

"Hendrix," I mimic. "It's either the bike or the car. What's it going to be, Mr. Wolf?"

His nostrils flare and he rests his hands on his hips, looking incredibly annoyed that I've bested him.

"Dammit. Fine. Let me get the fucking keys." I smile as he stomps towards where his keys hang, mumbling, "That woman."

With a laugh, I catch the keys when he tosses them to me and he smacks the button for the garage doors. The motor whirs and it opens slowly, revealing the warm spring day.

"Is it too much to ask you to take off your shoes and wear driving gloves?" He stands on the passenger side, a painful look on his face.

"Yes. Too much, Hendrix. Get in." He sighs and slides in while I gently sit and rub my hands together with a squeal.

I stick in the key and turn it, bringing the engine to life with a sweet, glorious purr. I adjust my mirrors, fasten my seatbelt and put the gear shift in reverse. Hendrix looks like he wants to jump out of his skin, so I decide to calm his fears and show him I'm a good driver.

I gently ease up on the brake and roll out of the garage. He clicks the button on the remote and we watch the garage door close. The tires are slow as I roll back and turn around once I reach the large driveway. I slowly shift into drive….then slam my foot down on the gas and haul ass onto the street.

"Fucking Christ, Dagen. Slow down," he yells while holding onto the dashboard.

"Oh for the love. Chill out grandpa. I'm only going," I take my eyes off the road for a moment to check the speedometer. "Fifty-five. You go like, one hundred on your bike."

"Yeah but that's me. And it's not my baby."

"I thought I was your baby," I pout, lip and all.

"You are but–watch that car. Fuck." He grabs at his chest like it hurts.

"Just relax, Henny. I've got this." I slow down until we're out of the neighborhood, then speed up once I'm on the highway.

I cruise along to I-10 and decide to take us to our beach. It technically belongs to the US Government, but it's the spot where we gave into our raging feelings for one another.

It only takes a few minutes to finally relax and see that I'm capable of handling his machine. Both of them, in fact. When I pull into the parking lot, he breathes a sigh of relief.

"See. Safe and sound. All your limbs are still intact and your baby is just fine." I turn off the engine and face him.

"Take off your seatbelt," he demands.

I roll my eyes and do as he says, figuring he'll be the one driving us home. The minute the belt slides back into the slot, I'm yanked over the wood paneled center console. I yelp as I'm lifted and come down hard in his lap.

His big hand holds the back of my head as he kisses me. My nipples harden and my core grows wet.

"Do you know how fucking hot that was? Seeing you take control like a goddamn badass." I moan into his mouth and begin rubbing up against him like a cat in heat.

Or like a horny pregnant woman.

"Think you can get us home just as quickly?" His mouth continues to devour mine between words.

"Yes. But you're going to have to let me go."

He groans at the thought of having to stop. He lets go of my head and before I climb back over, he slides his fingers up the inside of my shorts, dipping his fingers into my pussy. He brings them to his mouth and sucks.

"A little taste for the road." He throws me a wink and smacks my ass, urging me to get a move on it.

Life with this man is definitely going to be an adventure.

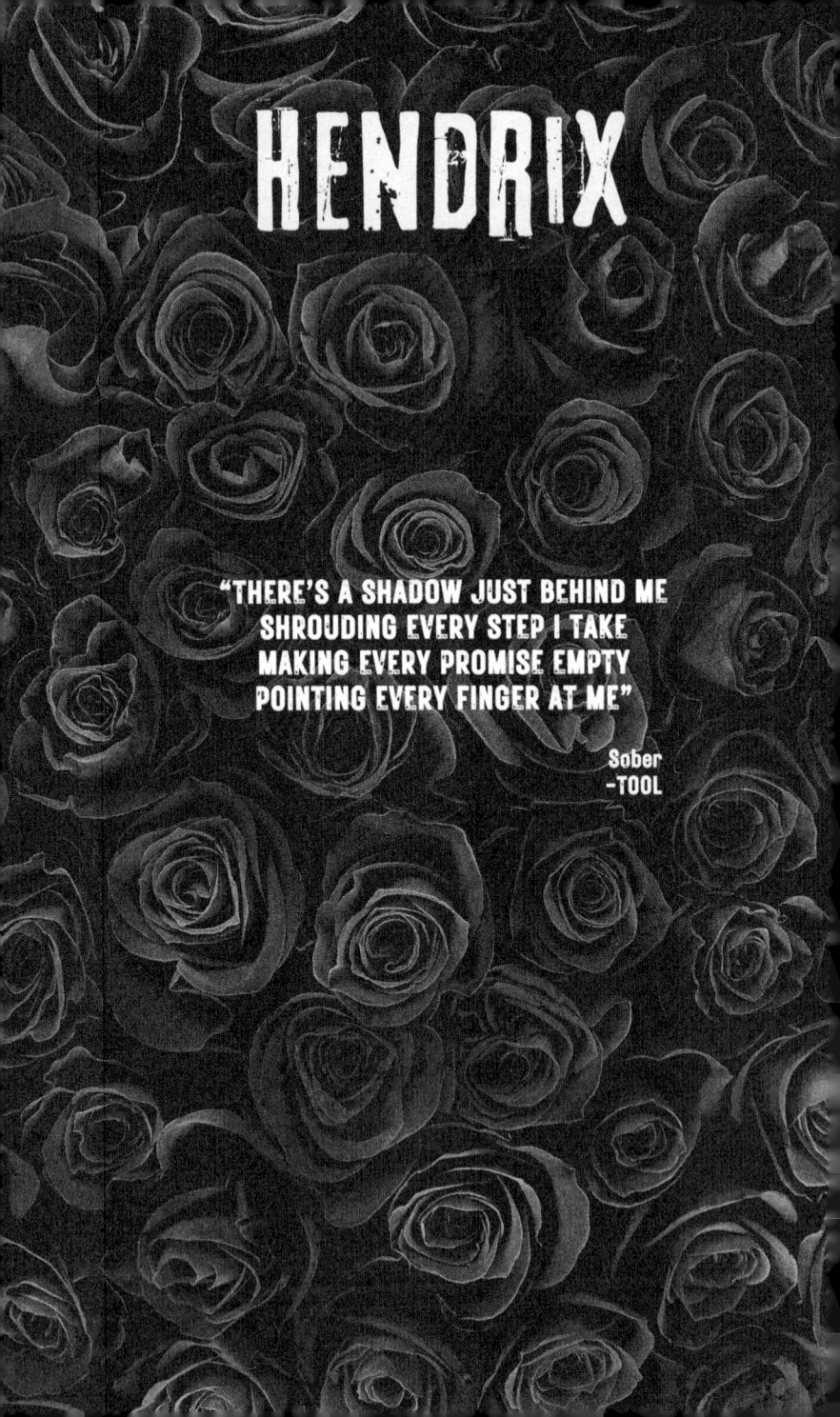

FORTY-ONE

THE MOVING truck parks in front of the house, and the guys and I walk out to meet it. It's moving day, and Dantè and Malik came up to help us.

I found a house not far from campus so that Dagen doesn't have to travel far, and something that will sell easily when it's time to go back to Cattywump Bay. It took a lot of talking, but I was able to make Vaughan see that it was best for Dagen to live here with me rather than at her house with her friends. On days I have to go to Mississippi, she'll either stay at the house with the girls, or one of them will come here. Kinsley volunteered to come live with us, but reminded her that her bosses may have a problem with that.

Just as the back gate of the truck rolls up, a caravan of trucks and cars comes pulling up behind us. Malik, Danté and I all watch as a hoard of people climb out.

The door opens and I turn to see Dagen standing there with her mouth hanging open.

"Hey baby bird. Hi Hendrix," Vaughan calls as he walks over to us. "We're here to help."

Behind him stands Camille, followed by all of her aunts and uncles. All but the younger one, Ana I think. I assume it's because she is very pregnant. Dagen is a whole ten weeks along so she has a ways to go before she gets that big.

"Dad. Is this really necessary?" Dagen holds her arm out wide, motioning to our unexpected help.

"Yes. It is most definitely necessary. Guys, you all help me. Ladies, you're on unboxing duty."

Everyone says hello and breaks off into their respective groups. Danté and Malik step into the truck and I hear the redhead say to the tall one, "Thank you, Jesus, for these beautiful specimens. I could eat those boys up."

I snort and cover my mouth.

"Viv, you have a husband. A very tall, very angry, very jealous husband. I'm pretty sure he'd have something to say about you eating those boys."

"But what a wonderful last meal they would be," she purrs.

"Vivian. Stop assaulting those boys with your eyes and dirty thoughts. Go!" Camille orders, pushing at her back.

"Fiiine. I'll go. But when the shirts start flying off, I'm going to need a bowl of popcorn and a glass of wine for the show."

Dagen shakes her head and pops up on her toes to kiss me. "Please tell Mal and Danté I apologize in advance for any inappropriate groping from my Aunt Viv. But remind them that she's married to that very large man over there." She points to Phoenix who picks up a heavy box like it's a box of cereal and not piles of shoes and books.

She hustles into the house with her mom and aunts, and I join the guys who are staring at the open end of the truck.

"You didn't really bring a whole lot with you," Vaughan points out. "Are you planning to let my little girl sleep on the floor?"

"No, sir. She won't be on the floor. I let her pick out whatever she wanted a couple weeks ago, and it should be delivered in the next few days. This is just the stuff I needed from my house and then we'll make a run to get Dagen's stuff from the other house that we already packed up. We'll stay at a hotel until it arrives."

"He's a goner," Phoenix tells Vaughan, jabbing at his side and pointing to me. "The man let her decorate the house. That's equivalent to an engagement ring."

"That is true," Luca adds.

I stare at him and wonder if the man is just on supervising duties today as he wears crisp jeans, a pressed white shirt and loafers. I don't know how they do it in Italy, but we wear ratty old clothes when moving.

"Alright. C'mon y'all. Let's get this unpacked so we can go grab the rest of Day's things. I need a beer and burger, but my wife said that's not happening until her daughter is unpacked and happy."

We all line up and take turns stepping into the back of the truck, grabbing a box and walking it to the house, where we drop it and let the ladies handle the rest.

At one point, my brothers pull me aside and ask, "Is this how her family is all the time?"

"Yup. Pretty much."

Danté shakes his head and laughs. "Lucky bastard. Did you see the ass on that little redhead?"

I smack his chest and figure I might as well give one to Mal. "Did you see the temper and muscles on that little redhead's husband? Or the fucking python arms of his best friend? You'd be wise to keep your eyes diverted from all of these ladies. From what I understand, none of them are above murder if you so much as smile at their women."

"Looks like you're in good company, Hen." Mal cackles then runs off to pester Phoenix.

The man is right. I would choke a man with a smile on my face if he looked at my girl too long. Luckily, it seems that I will always have an alibi and a willing hand and shovel if I need it.

It was a long day of moving and unpacking and chaos, but the extra hands were much appreciated since it made the task go by faster. The massive Mag Creek crew –the name which Dagen said they go by– left right after Vaughan treated everyone to dinner. The kids were all back home with the grandparents, and Bishop was practically in a panic without Anais. I swear that man called her at least fifty times while he was here. Dagen told me that she spoke to Anais and that she begged us to keep him an entire night. I guess she was feeling a bit smothered.

Malik and Danté got a room at the same hotel Dagen and I are at, so we decided it was a nice night to sit by the pool. We grabbed a six pack, got some snacks for Dagen, and now we sit in the hot tub relaxing the overused muscles.

Well, technically only Dagen's feet are in the hot tub because she shouldn't be in the hot water. She pouted a bit but stopped when I told her I'd rub her feet while they soaked.

I sit between her legs rubbing her feet as she massages my scalp with her talented fingers.

"Dagen, I don't know what is in the water down in Magnolia Creek, but your aunts are the hottest group of women I've ever seen. I'd include your mom in that but I don't want to be disrespectful." Malik rests with his arms propped on the tile surrounding us.

"Hendrix already told me and trust me, I've heard it all."

"Okay good. Because your mama is a fucking MILF. Damn Day. Your dad is a lucky sonuvabitch." Malik wipes his head when I splash water at his face.

"That man speaks the truth," Danté adds, looking a little more relaxed and happier than I've seen him in some time.

"Yeah, it's nothing I haven't heard before. At least you guys aren't as crude as my friends when they talk about my Uncles and Dad."

"I heard Vivian talking about Mal and D earlier and I about died."

"Oh god. She's the filthiest of them all. She puts the men to shame." Dagen scoots closer to me, her legs hanging over as if she sits on my shoulders.

"Just my type." Danté smirks devilishly and I can only imagine the thoughts that play in his head.

I lean my head back and look up at Dagen. Her eyes shine in the moonlight and I think about how dull and lonely my life would be without her.

"You feeling okay, little mouse?"

"Mhm. Just a little tired, but I'm good." She leans down and kisses my lips chastely, then strokes her fingers over my scruffy jaw.

We continue to talk and drink and laugh as the pool is empty aside from us. But that peace doesn't last long when a group of rowdy college boys stumble through the gate.

They're loud and annoying and I immediately feel like I need to call every teacher I ever disrespected. They flop down on several loungers and begin peeling out of their frat boy uniforms. One of them tosses a football as another jumps in to catch it. Water splashes everywhere when the rest of them dive in.

"Ah fuck. There goes our evening." Mal grows easily perturbed by their presence.

"It's getting late and we had a long day. I better get Dagen to bed." I drop her legs and rise from the hot tub, Mal and D doing the same thing.

"Oh okay *Dad*. I didn't realize it was my bedtime." She sasses me and it fires me up.

"Daddy's gon' tan that ass of yours if you keep it up," I growl in her ear.

I see a blush creep across her face, but hear no more protests. I give her a little pat on her ass as we grab our clothes and towels off the chairs. Dagen bends over to slip her feet into her shorts when a football slams into the back of her head.

"Ow!" She yelps.

I snatch the football from the ground and turn to face the guys with murderous rage flowing through my veins.

"Who the fuck threw that?" I bellow.

"Hey. Sorry man. It was an accident. We didn't mean to." The guys all watch Danté, Mal and I as we stand like a brick wall in front of Dagen.

"You just hit my girl. I should kick your fucking ass, you know that."

"Woah. Bro. Relax. It was an accident and he already apologized." One of the bigger guys wades through the water to speak up.

"Don't fucking *bro* me. You apologized to me, not her." My hands are clenched into white knuckle fists and I can feel them tingle with the itch to beat this guy's face in.

"Hendrix. It's okay. Let's just go." Dagen places her hand on my flexed bicep, trying to talk me down.

"We're not leaving until these douchebags. apologize for hitting you." My chest rises and falls with deep, hot breaths.

My brothers step a little closer to me, knowing that if shit is going to go down we need to be ready to guard Dagen.

"We're sorry, okay. Now can we have our ball back and you guys can go crawl back into the prison cell you broke out of?" Dagen's head presses against my back and I feel a gush of air across my skin.

"If you only knew who you were talking to, you'd be eating those words you little punk." Malik tries to clue them in on the fact that we could ruin their lives, but they don't seem to get it.

I stare them down then take their goddamn football and throw it as hard as I can, over the bushes that surround the pool area and into the parking lot.

"Hey asshole. That wasn't yours." The guys start climbing out of the pool and walking towards us.

"Hendrix. Please? Can we just leave?" Dagen's voice trembles with fear and I can tell she's on the verge of tears.

"Go get our fucking ball before we beat your ass to a pulp." The big guy stands at the center of the group, the other five right behind him.

Danté reaches into the pocket of his jeans that he lifts off the chair and pulls out the knife he carries with him everywhere. I hear Malik's knuckles crack and his neck pop as he rolls it out. Mal is the funny one of the group, but he's just as twisted and bat shit crazy as Danté and never backs down from a fight.

The three of us step forward to the pack and size them up. It's six on three but these assholes are soft and probably raised in a country club. They know nothing about trying not to break when the entire world is stepping on your neck, trying to keep her head underwater. We can take them and walk away with barely a scratch.

"You little pricks fucked with the wrong guys. If I were you, I'd gather up my shit and leave now. Open your mouth again and it'll be the last fucking thing you say." My eye twitches, praying they make one more sound so I can kick their asses.

They all stand with cocky smirks on their faces and big egos on their shoulders. It's clear that no one has ever knocked these guys down a peg or two. Or ten like we're about to do.

"Hey sweetheart. Just nod your head if you're in danger and we'll get you away from these psychos."

I lunge for the guy and hear Dagen screech, "Hendrix! No!" But it's too late. I've already got my hand wrapped around his throat while the other is punching his face. Malik and Danté jump in, beating up a guy of their own, and fists start flying.

One guy doesn't join in on the fight and walks over to Dagen who is now crying. I don't hear what he says, but when I see him touch her arm I see red. I break free of the guys who are throwing fists at me, and kick one in the gut.

"Don't touch her," I roar just as Dagen takes a step back.

And in slow motion, I watch as my world falls apart. Dagen's foot gets caught in the chair behind her and she loses her balance. The ground is wet and her other foot slips, unable to stabilize her. Her arms flail as I lunge for her, searching for something to grab onto. I hold my breath when her head slams onto the wrought iron patio table then crashes to the hard tile below.

"Dagen!" I scream and drop to my knees beside her. "Open your eyes. Wake up. Wake up!" Her eyes are closed and her body is limp.

Malik and Dantè come running over and the other guys stand around silently, the fight forgotten.

"Call. Call 9-1-1. Hurry!" Danté reaches for his phone and Malik stays kneeling beside us.

"Don't touch her, Henny. Don't move her neck. Keep it still, okay." Mal talks calmly to me but all I can focus on is her pale face, void of its usual glow.

Malik continues to talk to me, and the guys we were fighting with are now offering support. Sirens wail as they draw near and the world around me grows blurry. It's hard to see and I can't understand what's going on.

I rub my eyes to clear my vision and realize I have tears falling.

EMT's rush over and begin wrapping her head with something to keep it from moving, but her eyes don't open.

"She's pregnant. Please be careful." One of the emergency techs looks at me with a nod. "Call her parents."

I grab my shirt and pull it on, then take my phone and pass it off to Malik. He unlocks it with the code and scrolls through my contacts.

"Sir, what hospital are we going to?" I ask, slipping my feet into my sneakers and grab Dagen's shirt that still sits on the chair.

"Baylor Medical," he tells me and Malik confirms he heard.

She's hoisted up onto a gurney and buckled in. They move her to the waiting ambulance and lift her into the back. I climb in after them, sitting out of the way so they can work on her. The doors slam shut and I jerk when we drive away. My hands shake with the need to touch her, the words I said to Vaughan ringing in my ear.

I promise to always take care of them. I promise to always take care of them.

Never make a promise you can't keep.

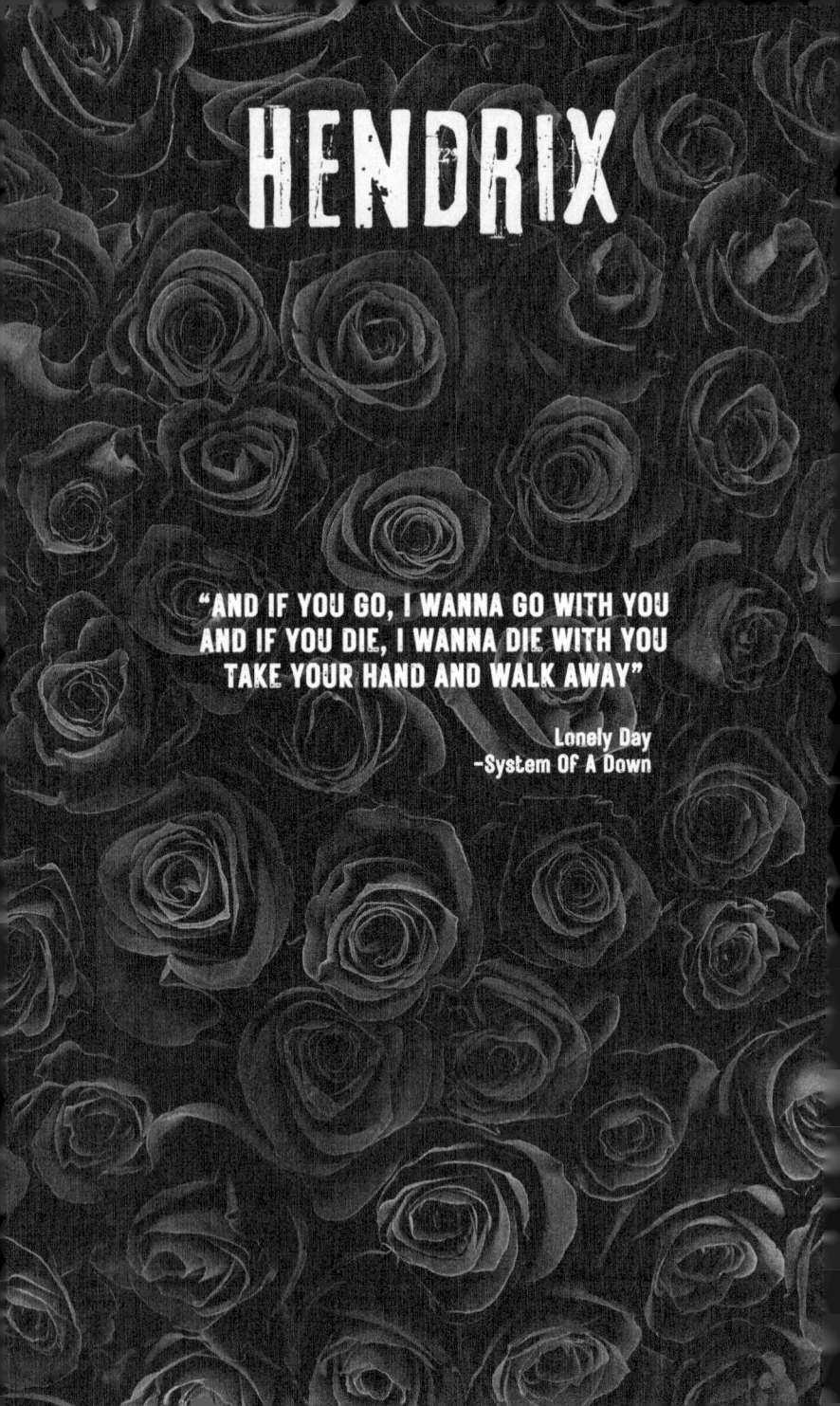

FORTY-TWO

VAUGHAN, Camille and I sit silently in the Dagen's room, each of us with a hand resting on her. It's like we need to feel her to know that she's okay.

The doctors are keeping her sedated as they continue to evaluate and monitor her. They tell us she has a severe concussion but will do additional testing once she's awake. For now, we wait for an obstetrician to come in and check on the baby.

We thought that the doctors treating her would tell us, but they just said that someone would be able to talk with us soon. I don't understand why we have to talk to so many different doctors when they're all in the same place and can relay messages. They really make it much more difficult than it needs to be.

"I wish they'd hurry already," I mumble.

"I wish you would've taken better care of my daughter."

"We're not doing that, Vaughan. Hendrix told you it was an accident." Camille's eyes are both hard and soft at the same time.

"An accident that could have been avoided if you had kept your temper in check."

"She was hit by a football that some asshole threw at her, Vaughan. Did you expect me to just sit there and shrug it off? Jesus Christ. Do you want me to protect her, or ignore her?"

"Stop it. Both of you." Camille's voice is terse and silences us.

We all go back to staring at Dagen, listening to the clock tick. It's just before midnight. Malik told me that Vaughan and Camille were about halfway home when he called them. They turned around immediately and were running into the hospital an hour later. They found me in the waiting room, my head hanging between my shoulders and guilt sitting on my back.

A light knock on the door draws our attention and a new doctor comes walking in.

"Good evening. I'm Dr. Newman." The woman walks in and we stand to greet her. "Are you the family of this young lady?"

"We are." Camille reaches for Vaughan's hand and I feel an instant emptiness.

"Is the baby okay?" I ask, not time for pleasantries.

"Are you the father?" The doctor asks and I nod my head.

"Those are her parents, so any information you have should be shared with all of us."

She dips her chin and stands at the foot of Dagen's bed. She opens a clipboard and reviews some papers

"I know you've been briefed on her condition, so I'll talk to you about the baby. Dagen has suffered a placental abruption. That means that the placenta has separated from the uterine wall. When that occurs, it depletes the baby of oxygen and nutrients. It is something that is treatable in most cases."

"What do you mean in most cases?" I ask her.

She breathes out and stones her face. "Because of the early stage of pregnancy she is in, the fetus was simply not strong enough to survive. I'm very sorry."

Camille lets out a hard sob and Vaughan wraps her in his arms.

"Wait. Wait, just…are you saying that she—" The word gets clogged in my throat.

"Dagen has, unfortunately, suffered a miscarriage. She will be okay however, we will need to perform a D and C. Since she is still sedated, we will…"

The doctor's voice becomes muffled as the ringing in my head grows louder. I stare down at Dagen and think about how crushed her heart will be. This is all my fault. I've killed my baby and she'll never forgive me.

I rise up from my chair and let my feet take me away. My name is called out but my body won't let my mind take the wheel. Like a robot on autopilot, it moves without instruction.

I reach the lobby where Malik and Danté sit. They begin asking me what's going on but like Camille and Vaughan, I can't respond. Nothing stops me from running away from the pain.

I walk out of the hospital doors and let my feet take me away. My brothers chase after me but I hold up my hand, letting them know not to bother.

I continue down a sidewalk and reach for my phone in my back pocket, where I stuck it after Malik gave it back to me once the doctors kicked me to the waiting room.

Pulling up the Uber app I order a car, then sit on the sidewalk until it comes. When it drops me off at the hotel, I find my keys, jump into my car and just drive. Destination unknown. What is known is that I need to get as far away from the pain as possible.

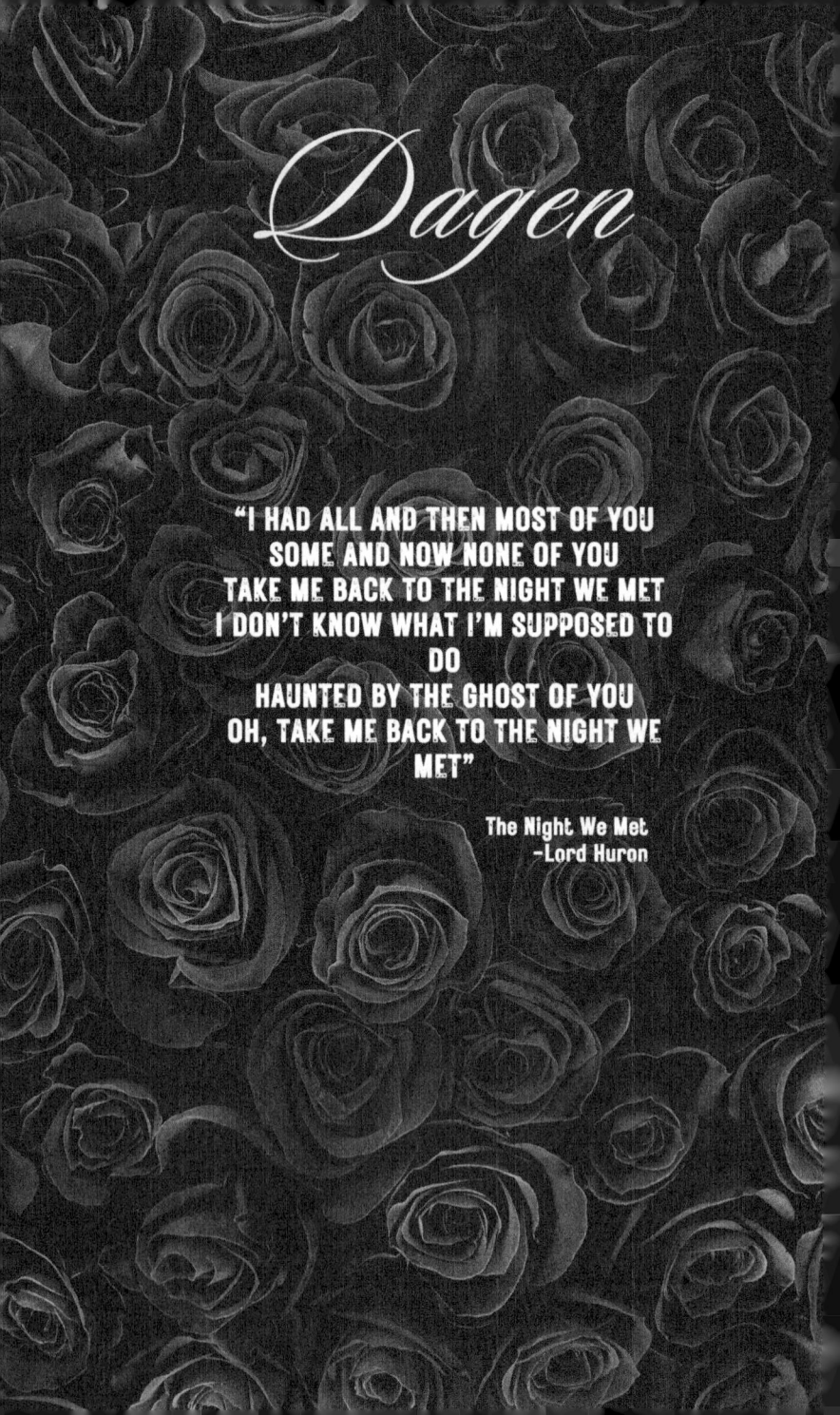

FORTY-THREE

MY EYES ARE SWOLLEN from crying for hours, and my heart is broken from the loss. Losing the baby, losing Hendrix, and losing my future.

No one has heard from Hendrix since he walked out of the hospital more than twenty-four hours ago. Mom said he just walked out and kept going. Malik and Danté said they tried to stop him also, but he didn't even turn his head in their direction.

The drive home to my parent's house was long and painful. Mom sat in the backseat and held me the entire time while I cried and played the words the doctors told me over and over.

"Ms. McCallan, can I speak to you?" Dr. Newman asked as she walked in my room.

I was already so confused because no one would tell me where Hendrix was and I just wanted to go home and find him.

"I am the on-call OB/GYN and I examined you when you came in. After performing the ultrasound, I was able to determine you suffered a placental abruption."

"What is that? Will it hurt the baby?" I asked, already in tears.

My head was pounding from the fall and I had yet to see the bruising my parents told me about.

"When you fell, the placenta detached from your uterine wall. It doesn't happen often from a fall like yours, so your doctor will want to follow up for additional testing. Just to make sure there aren't any conditions to be concerned or aware about."

"Okay. So the baby? Do I just need to rest or..?"

With a deep breath she explained, "If treated promptly, an abruption can be managed. While you were brought in soon after your fall, I believe the early stage in your pregnancy was not on our side. I'm very sorry, Dagen, but the baby did not survive the abruption. We will need to perform a dilation and curettage to remove the remains."

My lungs constricted and I couldn't breathe. I was sure everyone could hear the sound of my heart breaking. The scream that poured from my lungs filled the room and echoed down the hallway. It was a cry only those who have experienced this level of pain could understand.

I cried all the way back to the OR to perform the procedure. I cried as soon as I opened my eyes and realized where I was and what happened. I cried the entire way, wishing I could go back in time. And I cried myself to sleep when I couldn't reach Hendrix. I called and left messages until his mailbox was full, then drifted into sleep.

My dreams were filled with black nothingness and cold. I felt the way my teeth chattered in the cold of the dark space, and the ache in my bones felt so real. At one point I saw Hendrix walking towards me, arms open wide and eyes bright. Right before could fall into my arms, something gripped onto his shirt and began yanking on him.

I cried for him to come back, but the harder he tried to get to me, the more difficult it became.

Now I take the cold towel off my eyes and pull out my

phone, once again. I touch his name on the screen, *Sexy Baby Daddy*, and pray he picks up.

"The mailbox you are calling is full. Please–" I hang up the phone, already knowing how the script goes, and decide to call Malik to find out if he's heard anything.

"Hey Day," he says, answering after just one ring. "How are you feeling?"

His voice is cautious and tender, like what I imagine he sounds like when he talks to one of his students when they're sad.

After I returned from the OR and had some time to wake up and cry some more, Mom told me that Danté and Malik were on their way back from the hotel where they had gone to rest and get cleaned up. They stayed here long after Hendrix walked out until my Dad sent them away to rest.

When they walked in, I simply cried. Malik hugged me, being the tender hearted man he is, and Danté looked uncomfortable but touched my arm softly and supportively. It was more than I could have imagined from him.

With a sigh I admit, "Not good. I just don't understand where he is and why he left in the first place. Have you heard anything from him?"

"No word yet. I'm really sorry our brother is being an ass."

"I'm gonna fuck him up when I see him," I hear shouted from the background.

Danté, a staunch opponent in the beginning, is now a fierce supporter.

"I know he's hurt but," the sob works its way up my throat and I choke on my words. "I need him. He said he'd never leave again."

My head falls into my hand and tears that I thought had dried up pour from my eyes once more.

"We'll keep looking. The difficult part is that his phone is either off or dead, because we can't track him on *find my phone*. We know he loves you, Day, and I don't think he's given up on you. He's just…he's the kid whose mom abandoned him all those years ago. I don't think he really knows how to deal with all of this. He'll be back, though. I know he will."

"'K," I reply, the one syllable I can manage to say.

"We'll call you if we find out anything. Don't give up."

We hang up and I flop back onto my bed, covering my swollen eyes with my arm. I stay that way until a soft knock sounds at my door. It creaks open and the solemn face of my Mom appears.

"Morning my sweet girl." She steps in the room and quietly closes the door behind her. "The kiddos are already wild and asking if you feel better. I told them they're not allowed to bother you until your booboo heals."

"I don't think my heart will ever heal." She rushes to hold me and I cry into her lap. "Where is he, Mom? Why hasn't he called?"

Her fingers comb through my hair, freeing the tangles from last night's sleep. "Oh baby, I wish I had the answers. I saw how upset he was, so I don't think it's because he doesn't care. Men just process things differently than women. Take your father, for example. The man can't decide if he's angry or happy. It takes me smacking him in the head to get things to click into place."

I let out a soft laugh. The first one in days.

"Does anyone know?" I never got a chance to tell my family about the baby. All they knew was that Hendrix was moving to Waco and they assumed it was because he wanted to be near me.

I'm glad they don't know because I just could not handle their smothering right now.

"No. I would never share anything you don't want me to. It will be up to you whether or not you want them to know about this." I nod my head against her thigh, soaked with my tears. "Would you like to eat?"

"I'm not hungry."

"Dagen. You haven't had anything since the glass of juice the hospital made you drink before we left."

"Maybe in a bit?" She sighs and that's my sign that she gives in. "Mom?"

"Yes, sweetheart?"

"Does it ever stop hurting, or is it just always there?"

I hear a stuttered breath before she speaks. "I wish I could say it goes away but it lingers for a lifetime, I'm afraid. I felt it when Dad and I were apart, and I feel it even now with Robbie gone. Ten years later and I still feel a pain in my chest when I see or hear something that reminds me of him. But there are many things that make the pain not so bad. You are a huge part of that. And one day, you'll have someone that brings you the same amount of joy and will help you look back on the past, dulling the ache you feel right now. It's part of our story, Dagen, and it makes us stronger and more resilient. You just need to keep pushing. Don't ever give up. There's always a brighter day waiting behind the clouds."

She finishes and we both find ourselves in tears. I know she's right, but right now it's just hard to see beyond the grief.

"I love you, Mom. I don't think my life would ever have been as complete without you. Malik and Dante were right. Dad is one lucky sonuvabitch." She laughs through the tears, sniffling as she does.

"I'm the lucky one. You and your siblings are the greatest gifts of my life. I don't know that I'd trade those twelve years without your Dad because I wouldn't have you." She leans down and kisses my forehead. "I love you Dagen Rayne. Every day, always. From this life into the next."

We stay there holding each other, letting the tears heal a

small part of my heart. But until I have Hendrix, I'll never be whole again.

<u>VAUGHAN</u>

MY MIND IS weary and my body is weak. The last forty-eight house has wreaked havoc on my family. And the road ahead is still a treacherous one.

I've tried to get a hold of Hendrix at least a hundred times by now, but his phone stopped picking up hours ago. I feel that if there's anyone who is going to be able to get through to him, it has to be me. We have a shared pain now, though different, but it's one only another man could understand.

A woman doesn't understand what it's like to pretend you aren't affected by the everyday struggles we face. The biggest one being to provide and care for our family. In the blink of an eye, Hendrix lost that. Just as I lost Camille so many years ago.

I know I was hard on him in the beginning but in my eyes, no one will ever be good enough for my daughters. Or my son, for that matter. But deep down, I know Hendrix is the one for her. I can see it when he looks at her. A man so hardened by the world around him can perfect the look of callousness, but his eyes will never lie. And Hendrix spoke a million words.

My phone dings with a notification and I pull up the cameras. There's an alert that the edge of the property has been breached and I switch views to find out where it came from. I touch the screen, changing the direction. Off of the back of the barn, I see a figure stumbling beyond the fence and traipsing through the field.

I zoom in as much as it will allow, and I recognize the clothing that Hendrix was wearing from two days ago.

"Camille," I call out and she rushes into the office.

"What's wrong?"

"I got an alarm. I'm going to go take a look. Dagen okay?"

She shrugs. "As well as can be expected."

I rise up from my chair and take her face in my hands, kissing her like it's the first and last time.

"I'll be back, Sunshine."

She strokes my cheek and stares into my eyes. "Be careful. Call me if you need anything."

I kiss her nose then walk out to try and save the man that needs it most.

HENDRIX

"PROMISES HAVE BEEN TURNED TO LIES
CAN'T EVEN BE HONEST INSIDE
NOW I'M RUNNIING BACKWARD
WATCHING MY LIFE WAVE ME GOODBYE"

Running Blind
-Godsmack

FORTY-FOUR

I STUMBLE as I climb through tall grass and wind my way through the overgrown field, trying to remember the way Vaughan drove us.

My head hurts and the alcohol I've binged on has yet to find its way out of my system. I feel queasy and stop for a moment to let it pass. Or come up. I've teetered between both this morning.

After I drove off from the hotel the other night, I simply drove East. I didn't have a destination or know where I was going, I just knew I had to get away from the one place that was ripping me apart. My world was crumbling and it was all my fault. At this point, I didn't care if I drove myself into a ditch. At least it would put an end to the pain.

I drove until my fuel light lit up and I had to find a gas station to refuel. That led me to a nearby bar, that led to drinking for five hours straight. It was only after I fell off my stool that the bartender cut me off. A bar fly was quick to want to help me, in many ways, but I set her straight letting her know I had a girl and she needed to remove her hands before I broke them off. The bartender didn't like that and told me to get out.

I weaved my way to a small diner to eat and shake off the alcohol so that I could continue to drive. While inhaling a mountain of pancakes, I started to think about how broken Dagen must be. She would wake up and find not only me gone but our baby, too. I was a selfish son of a bitch, and I'd dug myself into a hole I didn't think I could climb out of.

I finished up my food, walked into the convenience store and bought beer and whatever alcohol they had before getting on the road again.

My phone was turned off because I just couldn't listen to it ring incessantly. Seeing *Little Mouse* or *Mal* and *D* on the caller ID was only driving the nail through my heart deeper.

I drove back to Waco and sat outside of our home, staring at it. The furniture delivery would be there soon, but I wouldn't. I called the store and told them to hold it because of a family emergency. I didn't tell them the emergency was that I lost my family.

I drove away from the house and stopped at a nearby park where I continued to drink, and eventually fell asleep in my front seat only to wake up with a screaming bladder. I had an early breakfast of Jack, then started driving again. I feel like I blacked out and only came to when my car stopped by the McCallan Ranch.

It's as if my heart was calling out to my brain, guiding it to the place where it laid. In Dagen's hands.

I knew there was no way in hell I could face any of them. So instead, I walked around until I found a way in and walked my way a damn long time before spotting the familiar barn. I thought of the last time we were here and remembered the talk I had with Vaughan by the big magnolia. It was peaceful and peace is what I need right now.

The walk to the tree seems impossibly long and I think about just dropping to the hard ground and passing out. Maybe the turkey buzzards will come and scavenge my remains.

The heat is really getting to me because I hear a low buzz coming from somewhere behind me. It grows louder until a rush of air sweeps by me. I turn to my right and see Vaughan sitting in his golf cart.

"Ffuck," I slur.

"Yeah. Fuck. Get in." His tone leaves no room for discussion, so I simply wobble to the other side and plop myself down in the passenger's seat.

"Are you taking me somewhere no one will find me?"

He looks over at me for a brief moment and I see how his eyes are rimmed in red.

"I should, but I'm not. That would be the easy way out, and this is not going to be easy."

My head lolls back and I close my eyes as we roll along. When we stop, I slowly lift my head and pry my eyes open, blinking in the harsh light and squint. I hear the soft trickle of water and surmise we're by the creek.

"Come on. Follow me," Vaughan orders, and I obey.

"You gonna drown me?" He looks over his shoulder at me with a glare. "Will you yell at me or hit me, or something? I can't take this impassiveness."

We reach the edge of the creek and Vaughan sits. I do the same but with less finesse. My body drops like a ton of bricks and has an *oomph* falling from my mouth.

He lets out a deep breath and says, "I'm sorry this has happened to you, son." The lump that gets stuck in my throat feels like a hand has snaked down it and taken hold of my heart. "But you need to remember that the same thing has happened to my daughter."

I drop my head in shame, and nod. "I know."

"Then what the fuck are you doing out here when you should be in there with her?"

I twist my head to look at him and offer up a shrug. It's the most I can manage.

"My daughter, the woman you say you love, is in agony.

And you should be the one by her side. Not me. Not Camille. *You*." He pauses but I still can't speak. "Her heart is broken, Hendrix, and I can bet yours is too. But you need each other. You can't heal on your own, and neither can she."

"I only bring heartache into her life. That's not what she needs." I fall back and stare up at the slow moving clouds.

"You also bring her love. That's how a relationship works. The light can't exist without the dark. It's a hard truth, but one nonetheless."

"What happens when the dark is too much? It will drown out the light. Dagen is light and I'm darkness. I can't stick around to snuff out that beautiful light."

"How do you know she won't rid you of the darkness? You promised me you'd always be there for her. Where are you, Hendrix?"

"I'm right here," I scoff.

"No. Where are *you*? Not physically, but here." He taps at my chest, right over the spot where Dagen's tattoo is inked for eternity.

"I can't do it! I don't have it in me. I'm no good for her. It's best I leave now before I cause anymore damage. It's best this way."

"You promised her," He reminds me. "Instead of running away, I dare you to stay."

My breathing turns fast and shallow as I try to fight off the sting. My nostrils flare and my eyes burn. I sit up, thinking it will push all this foreign emotion away, but it only serves to make it worse.

"Fight for her, Hendrix."

"I'm not strong enough."

"You are. You just have to get up and fight."

My body breaks as does the wall I've been holding up with a thin wire. I feel my chest crack as my heart bleeds out. Tears fall and I shake, sobs overwhelming me.

Vaughan wraps his arm around my shoulders and lets me

rest my head on him. I cry like I never have in my life. Not when I was dropped at the steps of an orphanage. Not even when I was passed over, time and time again by families and fosters.

I had finally found where I belong and I lost it all. I let it slip right through my fingers. And the man who should hate me is being the father I've needed in my life for so long.

"There's still time to fix this, but you have to want it. You're either all in or all the way out. What's it going to be?"

I lift my head and wipe my face clean. Alcohol still swirls in my head, but there's no doubt what I want. Nothing can dull the truth of how much I need Dagen to live.

"All in. I want to be all in."

Vaughan pats my arm and smiles. "That's what I was hoping to hear. Now," he pushes to his feet and dusts his pants off. "Let's get you looking and smelling better. You can't beg my daughter to forgive you smelling like a brewery and looking like you slept on a park bench."

"My car," I correct.

"What was that?"

"I slept in my car. A park bench probably would've been better. I could have used the fresh air."

"I wasn't gonna say anything, but since you did." He curls up his lip and waves a hand in front of his face. "Let's go."

Who would have thought that the person to save me would be the man I thought wanted to destroy me.

Vaughan took me back to the barn cottage and dumped my ass in the shower. I don't know what he told Camille, but he came back with clean clothes, food and a jug of water. He wouldn't let me leave without eating everything and drinking at least half of the water. I did so then made several trips to the bathroom to empty out all the food and water he practically forced down my throat.

I look at my reflection in the glass doors, noticing how damn much I look like the bad boy version of Vaughan. His creased Levi's and crisp white t-shirt is only missing the brown boots and cowboy hat. Thank god for the tattoos.

The door slides open, scaring me half to death, and a little head pops out. I struggle to push away the tears that Vaughan somehow turned on.

"Hi Chicken," AJ's little voice calls.

"Hi Autumn Jade."

She tilts her head to the side and studies me.

"Why you sad, Chicken?"

Fuck. Even a three year old can see how bad I am.

"I just miss Day."

"She's sick."

"Yeah. I want to make her feel better. Do you think she'll like these?" I hold up the large bouquet that was quite a feat to get.

I had to enlist the help of Vaughan who got Luca on the phone immediately. I don't know how that rich bastard did it, but he had the most unbelievable bouquet of black roses delivered an hour later.

"Bwack fowers?" she asks, very unimpressed with the color.

"Yup. But look," I hold them closer to her face and spread the petals of one open. "They're red in the middle."

Her eyes light up in wonder and she whispers, "Wow."

"Can I come in, little lady?" She digs her teeth into her lip and nods.

"You hafta be quiet. Momma said."

I wink and tell her, "Gotcha."

Her big eyes stay glued on the roses, so I carefully pluck one from the arrangement and hand it to her.

"Just for you, AJ."

"Fank you." She hugs the rose to her like it's the greatest gift she's ever received.

I can't help myself. Something comes over me and I reach down to scoop her up and give her a hug. She wraps her little arms around my neck and I breathe in her scent. Peanut butter and fabric softener.

"Okay," I say, putting her down on her feet. "I'm going to try and make Day feel better. Wish me luck."

"Wuck, Chicken." She holds out her hand and gives me a thumbs up.

I slowly make my way up the stairs and find Camille standing at the top. I pause for a moment then continue until I'm face to face with her.

"I–" my words are suffocated when Camille throws her arms around me.

She rests her head on my shoulder and cries. I would normally feel very uncomfortable in a situation like this, but things are different now. Vaughan broke my off switch and I can't contain it.

I circle my arms around her back and soak in the affection I've been missing for the last twenty-nine years of my life.

She pulls away and pats my cheek. "Your grovel game better be top tier. Day reads plenty of romance novels and she won't settle for less than begging and tears."

"Thanks, Camille. No pressure at all." She shrugs and moves past me, walking down the stairs and out of sight.

With one last breath of courage, I lift my hand and knock on her door.

"Come in." Her voice is frail and hoarse as if she's worn out her vocal cords.

I turn the knob with slow precision and push the door

open. She lays on her side, her back to me, and doesn't move. She probably assumes it's her mom or dad.

"Hi, little mouse."

She jackknifes out of bed and turns to look at me. Her beautiful face is marred with agony and anger. Her jaw is tense, but her eyes glisten with tears. I can already see how her breathing changes and I'm just waiting for the scream that works to free itself from her lungs.

But it never comes. I take slow steps towards her until I reach the edge of the bed.

"I'm sorry, baby." They're the first words that bubble to the surface.

"That's it? That's the best you can do? *I'm sorry, baby.* Seems like I've heard that before and it didn't mean shit. Try again."

"I-there's more. Just give me a second." Her face looks bored and annoyed as she crosses her arms over her chest. "I should have been there when you woke up. I should have doused my temper with ice water. There are a lot of things that I should have done, but I was a coward and ran instead."

"Coward seems to be quite fitting."

I clear my throat and let another punch hit me in the gut. "I made a promise to you that I wouldn't do that again, and now I'm faced with the challenge of convincing you it won't happen yet again."

"Of course it won't happen again because we're done. I won't have to worry about you running out on me if we're not together."

"Don't say that, little mouse."

"I'm not your little mouse," she bites.

"Yes you are. You'll always be mine. It doesn't matter where you go, how far or with who, you will be mine until my last breath. I'll chase you across the globe if I have to. And I will have to because I need you, Dagen. I don't think I can breathe without you."

"You left me!" Her screech is filled with sobs. "I woke up and you weren't there. The person I needed most was nowhere to be found. Then to find out that we lost our baby was like a knife to my heart. Do you know how scared I was? You should have been there, Hendrix, and you weren't. How am I supposed to forgive that?"

I hang my head, the guilt weighing heavy on me. "Let me earn it."

"And how the hell are you going to do that?"

"The only way I know how. Loving you like I'll never love another. If you say it's over, you have to know that there will never be another to take your place. Your side of the bed will stay empty, and the back of my bike will never have another occupant. You're the only backpack I want riding with me." I cautiously reach for her and she flinches when I run my finger down her cheek. "You're irreplaceable, Dagen McCallan. You're the light in my dark world and without you I can't see. It will only ever be you."

She clutches her fist to her chest and cries, a deep guttural sob racking her body. The flowers are forgotten as I drop them to the floor, and I jump on the bed, enveloping her in my arms. She gasps for air between her wails and I just keep holding her through it.

"I'm sorry. I'm so so sorry. I'll never leave again. Please, Dagen. Please forgive me."

She pushes me away with a shrill. A hand stings my cheek when it makes contact. Then my chest. She balls her hands and punches my shoulders, my arms, and bangs on my chest. I don't try to stop her. In fact, I welcome the pain. I want to feel just an ounce of the turmoil she is living through. Nothing will ever compare to what she's suffered, but if using my body helps to heal her one thread at a time, I'll let her use me until the end of time.

"I needed you!" She continues to hit and punch and I sit

with my arms limp at my sides, letting her use my body anyway she wants. "Our baby is gone, Hendrix."

Her arms grow weak and the punches stop. I pull her in and lay back with her tucked tightly. My shirt is tear soaked but my heart is healing. The feel of her skin on mine is like home and I don't ever want to be anywhere else.

"I wish I had been strong enough to save her," she whimpers.

"Her? It was a girl?" I suddenly feel like the air has been sucked from my lungs.

She shakes her head while circling her finger on my chest. "I don't know. I didn't ask. But I had this sense that it was."

"Can I confess something?" Her eyes look into mine, so wide and so sorrowful. "I thought it was a girl, too. Every time I saw AJ, something tugged at me. I think it was a sign."

Moments of silence pass and I'm grateful just to continue to hold her. My fingers run up and down her spine while her hiccups start to slow.

"I love you, Dagen. I'll do anything to show you that I'm not going anywhere."

She sniffles then pushes away from me. It's an immediate cold emptiness and I already feel like I'm dying inside.

"I need you to leave, Hendrix," she says with a hardened face.

"But wh-y?"

"Why? Really? I'm supposed to just forgive the minute you drop me a smile and an *I love you*? It's going to take more than that. And right now, that more is time."

My mouth falls open and I stare at her, hoping that she'll let out one of her glorious laughs and pull me into her arms with a forgiving kiss. When she doesn't, I feel like I'm choking on my own sorrow.

She sets her hands down on her bed and slowly pushes herself further and further away from me, until she sits at the edge of the opposite side.

I gather myself and stand on trembling legs. My eyes plead with her to please not do this. Her response is to turn away from me, stealing away the eyes that make my heart race.

I pick up the flowers that lay forgotten on the floor, and place them gently on her bed. My feet take to her door and my hand meets the cold metal for the handle.

Before leaving, I look at her over my shoulder and say, "The black rose has many meanings, all that I think really apply. Mourning. Strength and resilience. New beginnings. And the most important of all, eternal love. We're going to have it all and more. I promise."

This time, I won't let her down.

Dagen

"BECAUSE THIS IS WHERE I WANT TO BE
WHERE IT'S SO SWEET AND HEAVENLY"

Heavenly
-Cigarettes After Sex

FORTY-FIVE

THE DAY HENDRIX walked out of my room was one of the hardest moments in my life, right below losing our baby. But I need time, I need space without him. I need to be able to think without his words and his touches. They only break me down. I can't do that right now.

Once the door clicked shut, I let myself fall apart once again. Sobs choked the air that tried to work itself free, and my body crumbled to pieces. Mom came in, presumably seeing Hendrix leave, and Dad shortly followed.

"Sweetheart. What happened?" She gathered me up in her arms and rocked me.

"I need time to think. I just... I don't know." The consequences of my actions, forcing Hendrix to leave, was now settling like a boulder on my chest.

Dad sandwiched me between them, circling his arms around both of us, and letting me cry my body to sleep.

Later that night, I woke to another bouquet of the morbid black roses, this one sprinkled with red roses here and there. The sun had already set and they looked like ominous figures as they sat on my dresser.

The morning brought a basket of pastries along with juice

and coffee and a small bundle of red roses with petals that looked like satin ribbon wound round and round. A small note sat with everything and I read the words cautiously.

> Little Mouse,
> A basket of all of your favorite things and heart roses to let you know you have mine.
> Always.
> Mr. Wolf

I grabbed the coffee and left everything else sitting on the table. When I returned to my room after spending the early afternoon walking the stalls of the barn, the new roses sat nestled between the others.

Days three and four brought much of the same and just like the others, I ignored the gift and notes only to find them in my room later. It was beginning to look like a floral shop.

Between all of the notes and gifts came texts that went unanswered.

> Mr. Wolf: Little Mouse. Today I watched the sunrise and wished you were by my side to see the miracle. Another day that my soul feels empty without you. 🖤

> Mr. Wolf: People say absence makes the heart grow fonder. Mine grows deeper in love with you. 🖤

> Mr. Wolf: Your dad broke my faucet. Now all I can do is cry. I need you, Dagen. Please forgive me. 🥺

> Mr. Wolf: Today I tried to ride my bike but it didn't feel the same. I need you or I'll never be able to ride again. 🥺

At one point my Dad begged me to just *"accept the poor*

guy's apology." He said that bees were going to start pollinating in our house if he didn't chill with the flowers.

Finally after a week, I have decided it's time to meet face to face with him.

My hands shake as I touch my finger to his name on the screen and bring it to my ear. The phone barely gets through one ring when he answers.

"Dagen." My name sounds like a thank you to God for answering his prayers.

"Hi Hendrix." I'm nervous and it has me suddenly forgetting all of the words I rehearsed. "How are you?"

"Awful. Completely awful and miserable. I miss you, baby." His voice is thick with foreign emotion and it pulls at my heart strings.

I ignore the heavy weight on my chest and move on. "I was wondering if you would be willing to meet me?"

"Of course. Where? I can be to your parent's house in three hours. Or if you'd rather meet somewhere else I—"

"Three hours? Hendrix...where are you?"

I hear his shaky breath as he exhales. "Our house."

I sigh. "That's your house, Hendrix, and you only bought when I...when. You know."

"Yes. I know. And it's still ours."

"I just thought now that there's no reason for you to live here, you would sell it and move back to Cattywump. Or are you packing things up? Is that what you're doing?"

"Little mouse?"

"Yes," I answer without thinking.

"Why don't I show you. Think you can come up here tomorrow?"

I chew on my lip, wondering how it's going to feel walking into a home that would have been ours to start a family, but never got the chance.

"Sure. I need to go pack up some things from my house,

anyhow. All of my finals were online and I have clothing and books I need to get."

He's quiet before finally saying, "Okay. I can meet you there and help you pack up."

"No," I quickly blurt out. "I can do that myself. I'll just text you when I'm on my way over."

"Alright." His voice is small and distressed.

I end the conversation with a simple, "See you tomorrow."

"See you tomorrow. I love you, Dagen." His words hit me like an arrow to the heart, and I'm sure my lack of pierces his.

I throw myself back on my bed and close my eyes. I don't know what I'm going to say tomorrow, or how I'm going to feel seeing him. I guess I'll just let my heart decide.

I pull my dark green Mercedes in front of the house and see Hendrix's Maserati parked in the driveway. The engine silences when I press the button and I stare at the front door.

The drive up here early this morning was filled with racing thoughts and a pounding heart. Anxiety swirled in my belly, wondering what I would feel seeing his face. His stupid handsome face with that devilish grin and sinful body.

My hand rests on the tattoo between my breasts, the one I got for him and the one my parents saw and about flipped the table over. I find tracing the lines brings me comfort and helps the turmoil fade away. Maybe it's a telling sign of where my heart lies.

I step out of the car and close the door. When I spin around, Hendrix stands on the front stoop, looking better than I've ever seen. His blonde hair is a little longer and his scruffy face has a thicker beard. He wears one of his simple black tees and those damn jeans that hug his muscled legs and firm ass.

They're lethal and scramble my brain.

I walk slowly up the sidewalk and see the smile on his face grow and his eyes glisten. He wasn't kidding about my Dad breaking his faucet.

I reach the door, and come toe to toe with him.

"Hello," I breathe.

"Hi baby." He leans in and places a small kiss on my forehead.

I want so badly to reach out to him and dive into his arms. I want to get lost in a passionate kiss, but I have to stay strong.

"Come inside." He takes my hand and gently tugs me across the threshold.

I gasp when I see all that he has been doing. The living room that boasts rich wood floors is completely decorated with the furniture we picked out and more. Pictures hang on the walls and books are lined up on the built-ins that flank the fireplace.

"Are those my books?" I ask.

He pulls me further in and guides me to sit down on the golden mustard colored velvet couch that he let me pick out. His home in Mississippi is modern with sleek lines and cold stone and metals. This little craftsman home was far too cozy for decor like that.

"Well not *your* books per se, but books that you would like. I kind of took a peek at your wishlist." He smiles almost shyly, and takes a seat next to me, leaving a bit of space between us.

"You didn't have to do all of this. Especially if you're going back home."

"Dagen. I don't think you understand. You're my home. Wherever you are is where I want to be. If that means I have to travel to the moon just to be in your same orbit, I'll do it."

Tears build in my eyes and my throat clogs. "Hendrix. Don't say that."

"Why not? It's true. The small time I have had you in my life has been the best in my entire twenty-nine years. I didn't realize I was missing a big piece of me until I found you. Don't you see. Without you in it, I'm an incomplete man."

I let the drops fall over my lids. I'm not strong enough to resist this man. A man that owns every bit of my heart. A heart that will never belong to another. No matter what becomes of us.

He drops to his knees in front of me and takes my hands in his. "I am so sorry, Dagen. I will never be able to say it enough. I screwed up, in a big way. But if you forgive me, I promise to love you even bigger."

I let my eyes focus on our hands as tears splash down.

"I don't know. You broke me, Hendrix."

"I know. I'll never be able to forgive myself for that. But I'm willing to put in the work, day in and day out just to earn your trust back. And your love."

I swallow down the lump in my throat and admit, "You don't have to try to earn my love."

His face pales and I feel a little bit of his hold on me soften. "Why-why not?"

"Because you've always had it."

His chest moves up and down, shallow breaths flowing in and out rapidly. The muscle in his jaw clenches and one single tear tracks down his face. Reaching out, I wipe it away and let my thumb smooth over his cheek.

He leans into my touch and I see the way light fills his eyes. I bet if I could see inside his heart, I'd find the same glow.

"I'm sorry, baby. Please say you'll forgive me. I'll never let you down again."

With matching tears and full of a shared love, I nod my head and dive into him. Our lips smash together and our kiss is fervent and fierce. My hands roam across every plain of his body, remembering what it feels like to hold heaven in my arms.

His hands frame my face as his fingers tangle in my hair. "I love you, Dagen McCallan. You've made every one of my dreams that I didn't even know I had locked up inside of me come true."

"I love you too, Hendrix. Just please don't ever leave me again. I don't think I'd survive it."

"I know I wouldn't," he adds. "I dare you to love me forever, little mouse."

I bite my lip then smile big. "Dare accepted, Mr. Wolf."

EPILOGUE
SIX YEARS LATER

"GEMMA GAYLE DARE! What have you done?"

Gemma's little eyes grow wide hearing her mom's voice call from the entrance of the barn where we hide in the back corner. I hold my finger to my lips to hush her while my hands continue to try and wipe away the mud.

"Gemma Gayle. I know you're in here. I followed the muddy shoe prints. Show yourself." I peak around the stall and see Dagen, standing at the door with her hands on her hips looking every bit the delectable little mouse she was six years ago when she first crashed into Cattywump Bay.

"Gemma," she calls once more, baby Oliviana —Olive, as we call her— sleeping snuggly in the carrier that hangs from her shoulders.

"It's G.G., mama. Not Gemma Gayle." She pops up from where we hide, stamping her foot and balling her hands into fists.

My princess is a little too much like me at the young age of four. In fact, if she found out that I called her my princess she'd kick my ass. Getting her to put on this dress was quite a battle, but I had to remind her that it's for her Uncle D. And now we are getting ready to face the wrath of her mother who is not going to be happy when she sees what G.G. has been up to.

"Actually, it's Gemma Gayle and you are in trouble little missy. There is mud all over the back porch. Pops and Millie are going to be upset." The sun that filters in is bright and Dagen has to squint, working hard to focus on G.G.

"Nuh uh. Pops is never mad at me. He said I'm perfect. And so does Unc Sloaney. Auntie AJ thinks I'm a brat, but she's wrong." G.G. looks at me and says, "Huh, daddy?"

I drop my head, still squatting down, and sigh. This little girl loves to call me out, and now it's time to face the music.

I stand slowly, my muddy hands falling to my sides, and step out to face my fate.

"Don't be mad at G.G., little mouse. It's my fault."

Dagen takes slow steps towards us and says, "Come closer, Gemma Gayle. What are you hiding back there?"

G.G.'s chest begins to rise and fall quickly as her breaths turn shallow, and her nostrils flare with dread. I touch her back and urge her forward. Better to get it over with now.

She takes a few shaky steps forward, and then a few more. Dagen gasps and covers her mouth with her hand when she sees what we've been hiding.

G.G.'s light blue dress is covered with mud as are her fancy shoes. Well, just one shoe. We still don't know what happened to the other. My guess is that the other one is floating in the creek where she crashed her dirt bike.

"What did you do?" Dagen's face turns bright red.

Just like Olive's when she throws one of her famous tantrums. That little girl has the lung capacity of a swimmer and the shriek of a horror flick chick. Add in the sleep habits of an ER doctor on the night shift and it makes for a lot of sleepless nights.

"We thought we had time to take a small ride and had a little accident," I explain.

"A *little*? Hendrix...she looks like she walked through the swamps of Mississippi." Her voice raises an octave and it stirs Olive.

She rocks from side to side, rubbing circles over her back and giving her soft pats.

"Little girls who wear dresses don't play in the mud, Gemma." Dagen lowers her voice just as Olive begins to calm.

"I'm not a little girl. I'm a bad ass, mommy. That's different. Auntie Viv says so." I snort with laughter and it earns me a glare from my wife. My beautiful wife, I might add.

"Oh Jesus," she mumbles and smacks her forehead. "No more FaceTiming with Auntie Viv. She has a potty mouth. That dress is never going to come clean. Auntie Marcie is going to be so disappointed."

The worry that was building in G.G.'s eyes turns to tears, and they rush over her lids and track down her face, leaving clean paths where mud once was.

Dammit I'm a sucker for this little girl. I can't stand to see her cry. I reach down and pick her up, holding her to me as she sobs.

"Shh. It's okay princess. We'll find you something. Doesn't Millie have clothes that she keeps here for you?" I ask G.G. but I really direct my question to Dagen.

We're far from home but her mom and dad always have a closet full of clothes and toys waiting for the kids when we visit.

"Well," Dagen starts. "Since little Miss Dare only likes to play in the dirt and in the creek, Millie has a load of jeans and shorts that are perfect for getting dirty. I don't think she has any sort of dress that would be good for a flower girl in her uncles wedding."

Danté, the man who swore he'd never settle down with just one woman, is settling down with one woman. But in all honesty, Marcie's the only one who could ever match Danté. That woman is his equal in feminine form. Kind of feminine.

Which is why I don't think she'll be too upset with the new development.

"Was someone talking about the greatest, most handsome uncle in the world? Well don't worry. I'm here." Danté comes swaggering into he barn, his usual devilish look on his face.

"Uncle D!" G.G. shouts and jumps from my arms.

She runs straight to him and leaps into his arms, hugging him tight. I witness the mud smear all over his clothes, and I'm thankful that he has yet to get his suit on. That black on black on black would be a horrible mess.

"I'm sorry," she hiccups. "I was just playin' and got dirty. Please tell Auntie Marcie not to be mad."

A tattooed hand rubs her back and Danté kisses her head. "Aw, giggles. It's okay. She won't be mad."

G.G. lifts her head, smiling through her tear soaked face at the nickname her uncle gave her, and asks, "Promise?"

"Promise. C'mon. We'll get this taken care of. Let's go find your Millie and then we can explain to her." D squeezes G.G. tight to him and winks at us before turning and walking out of the barn.

I never thought I'd see the day that Danté not only fell for a woman, but fell hard for a little girl he can't live without.

Mal, yes. He's probably going to hop on Sunny every chance he gets, making as many babies as he can convince her to. I have a feeling Calix is just one of many.

"Hendrix." Dagen turns her attention on me and I gulp.

I step closer to her and place my hands on her shapely hips. Having babies has only made this woman sexier. I didn't think it was possible, but just like as she always does, Dagen proved me wrong.

"You look delicious, little mouse." I lean in to kiss her, maneuvering around Olive as she sleeps in her carrier.

Gemma favors me in looks —and obviously attitude— with her dark blonde hair and blue green eyes. But Olive, she's all Dagen. Brown hair, soft and shiny, green eyes, and a smile that lights up my world.

A hand smooshes in my face, and I'm stopped dead in my tracks.

"No way, mister. I am mad at you. You couldn't tell her no just once, could you? I swear, you give into that girl every time."

I remove my face from her palm and pull out my best Mr. Wolf face and voice.

"Oh, little mouse. It's so cute how you try to act tough." I let my fingers dig into her waist and watch her shiver. "How about we let Olive have some special time with Auntie Sunny and Uncle Mal, and you and I can have our own special time."

She tries very hard to look fierce, but I don't miss that saucy smirk that comes through.

"You're bad, you know that." She scratches her fingers through my stubble and it's all the indication I need to know I better find Malik...*now*.

"They don't call me the Big Bad Wolf for nothing." I turn my head and snap my teeth at her fingers.

"Who the fuck is *they*? Show me who she is so I can kick her teeth in."

My face lights up with joy seeing how much of my darkness has infiltrated my ray of sunshine. And in turn, her light now runs through my veins.

"It's only you, little mouse. Now," I reach around and smack her ass. "Give me Olive so I can pass her off. You...*run run run, little mouse.*"

I growl, my predator smile wide and menacing, and it only takes a minute for her to pull Olive from her little sling and practically toss her at me.

I take my chunky nugget and watch as my wife spins on her heels and begins to run out of the barn. She looks over her shoulder with a smile and a wink, and I bolt in search of Mal.

As the years have gone by, our little games only get more adventurous and more primal. And my little mouse craves the chase and the pain.

This time I had to be sure to leave my mark where people wouldn't see it when she walked down the aisle in her bridesmaids dress. Her still flushed cheeks and erect nipples told me she was replaying the way I made her scream. Not even the fact that Gemma walked down the aisle in purple DARE Inc. riding pants and white DARE shirt could make her mad. I do give my G.G. credit for wearing her fancy shoes and a bow in her hair.

And she should thank me for giving her mama something else to think about besides the muddy mess she was just hours ago.

If anyone would have told me years ago that this would be my life, I would've called them a fucking liar. Who knew a silly dare and game of darts would lead to a happiness I never knew was possible. Nothing can ever take that away.

I fucking dare them to try.

ACKNOWLEDGMENTS
A FINAL WORD...

I'm a bit long winded when it comes to acknowledgements and thank you's, but the support that surrounds me with each book I write continues to grow and I just can't say thank you enough.

So with every book, I always say it was my favorite. But this time, I mean it. Hendrix and Dagen are my absolute dream couple, and I fell in love with them every time they showed me another facet of their character. Who knew there was a bad boy hiding inside of me?

I really tried to give Hendrix the perfect mix of primal and bad boy with a dash of swoon that all you book girlies want. He's a character that has existed in my mind for quite a long time, and I'm happy to finally be able to share him with you.

And for those of you who have already "visited" Mag Creek, I hope you enjoyed catching up with the crew again. I know many of you messaged me, begging for Dagen's story, and my fingers are crossed that I delivered just what you were wanting.

Baby Bird is all grown up and Daddy Vaughan sure did show a different side of himself. But be honest, you still liked it. He can do no wrong.

I am not a bike expert by any means, despite the hours of research I did. And as much as I would like to be flying down the highway on my own Duc, I am firmly a four wheel girl. I owe a huge thank you to Whispe.r6 and the missus for helping me out with all my "is this right?" and "is that possible?" questions, and for not turning me away when my unknown ass popped into your DM's. Maybe one day I'll make it up to DFW and you can take me for a nice, quiet and calm ride. (I'm sure that is as likely as a spaceship landing on your front porch.)

This year was nothing short of crazy and through it all I had my hoochie right there by my side. Cami, you know I got you, and having you at my back is the best feeling in the world. Thank you for always being my hype queen, for giving me a kick in the ass when I need it, and for never letting me give up. Love you.

Alyx! My bestest gal. Thank you for keeping me on track and keeping me laughing. Nothing is a better motivator than the little cursor, blinking right on my heels with each word. You're the other half of my brain and I still can't believe you won't just sell the farm and move to Texas and buy a compound with me. I'm so grateful I found you and will chase you down, tie you up, and lock you in my basement if you ever try to leave me. Yeah? Why are we like this?

J to the Hutch. The one person who understands the insane ups and downs on this crazy ride in the life of an author. We all need that one person who just gets us, and I'm thankful you get my brand of crazy. I hope to continue to travel this wild journey with you by my side.

Mindy Babe. My beta babe turned editor extraordinaire and friend to the end. I love you to bits and will work my very hardest to shower you with thank you's for all that you do. To think that it was a snake that brought us together. Maybe I should send a thank you letter.

To the real life Kins, the namesake of everyone's new favorite side kick. My cornbread sister. The love and support you show me is abundant. I can't wait to squeeze the living tar out of you, sister.

Jolly Berry, my favorite Brit. Thank you for not tossing your phone out the window every time I completely missed a word mid sentence because my fingers are faster than my brain. The minute this author gig pays off, I'm hopping on the next flight out to see you. Hope you have room!

As always, my biggest thank you goes out to all of the readers who continue to support me by reading my words and falling in love with my stories. So many times I have wanted to throw in the towel, but you all showered me with more love than I ever knew existed. I promise to always work hard and never let you down.

Thank you all my lovelies and until next time.

Ryan

ALSO BY RYAN MARIE

Magnolia Creek Series

The Pieces Left Behind

West Bound

Trust Bound

Without Bound

The Men of Havoc

Big Pucking Deal

Body Checking

Through the Fire

A marriage on the rocks novella

ABOUT THE AUTHOR

Ryan Marie is a big city girl living in a small town literary world. An avid reader, Ryan loves cuddling up with a steamy, slightly unhinged book. She loves building your next book boyfriend and delivering those Happily Ever Afters, but not before making you cry those big tears. When she isn't working on this author gig, you can find her yelling at the tv as she cheers for her San Francisco 49ers and Houston Astros.

Ryan lives in a Houston suburb and is married to her high school sweetheart (a man with the patience of a saint) and their two kids, along with their two giant dogs and a little cat named after a superb Tight End (hi Georgie Kibble).

Catch up on all things Ryan Marie at www.authorryanmarie.com

Printed in Dunstable, United Kingdom

69093139R00251